PRAISE FOR CURSED IN LOVE

If spreadsheet sex is wrong, I don't want to be right… Smokin' hot and laugh-out-loud funny.

—CHRISTY SWIFT, AUTHOR OF *CELEBRITY CRUSH*

The perfect blend of mysterious small town and sassy modern heroine, with a hero to swoon for.

—KATE JOHNSON, AUTHOR OF *HEX APPEAL*

Witty, steamy, and impossible to put down—*Cursed in Love* has all the best parts of a paranormal romance.

—LAUREN EVANS, AUTHOR OF *CASKET CASE*

Readers will love their time in Sapphire Springs—and will no doubt be clamoring for more!

—HAZEL BECK, AUTHOR OF *SMALL TOWN, BIG MAGIC*

PRAISE FOR FATE AND FURY

This romantasy is going to take readers by storm.

—@READINGWITHSAMMY

A thrilling and darkly seductive entry into the world of Slavic-inspired romantasy.

—@BOOKCANDLELIGHT

I am destroyed! I am not okay! I LOVED this book! … An excellent blend of romance and plot with conflict brewing all over the place…a really sexy, haunting, forbidden romance.

—@SARAHS_READING_BOOKS

One of my BEST reads of the year! Fast-paced with incredible world-building and storytelling, this book is a fantasy lover's dream. 10/10. A masterpiece. Highly recommend to everyone—don't sleep on this one!

—@CHAPTERSANDCOMFORT

This book is an absolute masterpiece of dark fantasy and forbidden romance, and it's one of those rare stories that grabs hold of your heart and refuses to let go… I am OBSESSED.

—REBECCA, GOODREADS REVIEWER

PRAISE FOR THE SEVEN SINS SERIES

WINNER, 2022 Gold Moonbeam Award for Best Book Series * 2022 Silver IPPY Award for Young Adult Fiction * 2021 North Carolina Indie Author Award in YA Fiction **FINALIST**, 2021 & 2022 Foreword INDIES Award in YA Fiction **SHORTLISTED**, Manly Wade Wellman Award for Science Fiction and Fantasy

This book is absolutely unputdownable.

—MICHELLE HAZEN, AUTHOR OF *BREATHE THE SKY*

A beautifully crafted story with so many intense moments I couldn't stop reading. This is the best book I've read in a long time.

—YA BOOKS CENTRAL

A romantic dystopian with a fantastic—and unexpected—twist... *Seven Sins* is powerful, sexy, hopeful, and unsettling.

—HEIDI AYARBE, AUTHOR OF *FREEZE FRAME*

An absolutely mind-blowing, spine-tingling, action-packed extravaganza…an electrifying, imaginative, phenomenally well written book. The tension, banter and angst blazes.

—EMERALD BOOK REVIEWS

A series everyone should know about.

—M. LYNN, *USA TODAY* BESTSELLING AUTHOR OF *THE QUEENS OF THE FAE* SERIES

PRAISE FOR THE DREAM KEEPER'S DAUGHTER

A splendid mix of time travel, romantic yearning, and moving on after grief.

—*PUBLISHERS WEEKLY*

*To anyone who's ever made me do an
icebreaker exercise.
I'm going to assume you were under a curse,
and forgive you despite your transgressions.*

*Donovan, on the other hand, may be less
understanding.*

CURSED IN Love

EMILY COLIN

ISBN (Pbk.) 978-1-961469-12-9
(Ebook) 978-1-961469-11-2

Published by Black Orchid Books
Wilmington, NC
Cover Design by We Got You Covered

Author's Note

Cursed in Love began its existence as serialized fiction, which was a fabulous adventure! I'm thrilled to bring you Rune and Donovan's story in book form. Before you start reading, though, I just wanted to share a quick content warning.

Much like me, Rune deals with traumatic situations by using dark humor—and she's had a lot of trauma to cope with! *Cursed* includes violence, references to childhood abuse, arson, and foster care placement, mentions of suicide, and parental death (before the story begins).

But it's also really funny. I promise. Just ask Rune, if you don't believe me.

CHAPTER
One

I DIDN'T WAKE up this morning with the intention of saving a man's life. And a good thing, too, since there's absolutely zero chance that he'll listen to me when I try.

I don't know who the man is. Never seen him before in my life. But I'd lay better than even odds that if I keep walking down Alistair Street, putting one of my purple-flowered Doc Martens in front of the other, soon enough he'll show up. Brown hair, past due for a haircut. Lame graphic tee. Mack Weldon sweatpants, which cost more than I can afford to spend on groceries in a week. Fancy watch advertising that he's slumming it in this outfit, for sure.

I don't know his name. Where he lives. Where he's coming from or where he intends to go. But I know one thing for sure: If I don't manage to intercept him somehow, there's no way in hell he's getting there.

My phone buzzes, and I dig it out of the back pocket of my jeans. It's Charlotte, of course. Who else would it be?

CHARLOTTE

Where are you?

CHARLOTTE

I've been sitting here for ten minutes. I grabbed
the best table and now the dude with the
Mohawk and the aggro twins are giving me
the eye.

CHARLOTTE

Are you alive, Rune? Should I drink your chai
latte myself? Pour it in a potted plant? Call the
police?

I could pause in pursuit of my quarry to answer her. But what if that makes the difference between the man's life and his death?

He's a stranger with bad fashion sense. I shouldn't care whether he lives or dies. All I know is that I *do.*

I was having such a *nice* morning. My favorite skinny jeans, the ones which even I can admit make my butt look good, were actually clean. My frizzy hair, for once, was behaving. The zit on my chin had disappeared. And I was on time to meet Charlotte at our favorite coffee shop, not running behind like usual. But three steps out the door, and I knew the man was going to die if I didn't stop it. Now here I am, on the 8:00 a.m. train to Doomsville.

I shove my phone back into my pocket with difficulty and resign myself to dealing with Charlotte later. Maybe she was kidding about the potted plant. Although Charlotte is a lawyer. She doesn't make careless threats.

What a horrible waste of my much-needed caffeine.

A moment later, I forget all about my chai latte. Because here I am, at the intersection of Alistair and Caneel. The familiar feeling of inevitability is bearing down on me. I wish this time they would hear me. That they would listen.

They never do.

The light is about to change. I know it like I know my own

name. I don't see him, but he has to be here somehow. He must be.

They always are.

Twenty-one seconds to impact.

"Stop!" I shriek at the top of my lungs. "The—the bus…it's going to lose control…stop!"

Ten heads swivel toward me. Ten people look at me like I'm crazy. A dude pushing a stroller gives me a disgusted glance and steers out of my way, giving me a wide berth. A grandma carrying a bag of apples clutches it to her chest, as if I might lunge at her like a rabid raccoon and snatch it away.

In my mind's eye, I see it: the bag of apples breaking open, scattering all over the sidewalk. The dude with the stroller pausing to help. The grandma stepping into the street to retrieve the fallen fruit, right in the path of the bus. The driver's pale face and wide eyes as he swerves to avoid her, right into the path of—

Seventeen seconds to impact.

I have to save him. I have to stop it. Otherwise I will dream and dream and dream—

I'm running now, pushing my way through the crowd, my breath rasping in my lungs. And here comes the bus, its air brakes squealing as it slows for the still-red light. My head turns left and right, looking for the guy, but he's not here. He's nowhere.

What the actual fuck.

In desperation, I double back toward Grandma and grab for the bag of apples. If I can stop them from falling, from rolling into the road, then maybe I can save him.

But when my fingers close around the bag, she resists. Not that I blame her. "Get off me!" she shrieks. "Let go!"

"I'm trying to *help* you," I hiss, yanking the apples free. I know good and well that if I don't get there in time, if I don't stop this, she'll blame herself. She'll work herself into a guilt-induced heart attack, right around the corner in Senior Hot Yoga two days from now.

But Hot Yoga Grandma isn't listening. She's howling. And *here* comes the doomed try-hard in his lame AF tee and overpriced sweatpants. His $200 sneakers pound the pavement as he races toward me in an effort to wrest Grandma—or, more accurately, Grandma's apples—from my clutches. Way to show up, dude. Douchecanoe to the rescue.

Thirteen seconds.

The guy's yelling at me now, something about *assault* and *thief* and *what the hell is your problem*. But I'm not listening because here goes the light, changing from red to green. *Fight me for the apples, dude,* I think as I watch the bus begin to turn the corner. *Call me all the names you want. At least that way, you're not dead.*

I tug at the bag of Granny Smiths. The guy tugs back. For a moment, I actually think I might have thwarted fate.

But no. Because the bag rips straight down the middle and there go the apples, bursting free and tumbling onto the sidewalk.

I *hate* times like these, when I show up to save the day and wind up causing the damn problem myself. Am I the chicken? Am I the egg? Where is the beginning and the end in the Ouroboros of the curse that is Rune Whitlock's life?

I don't have time to contemplate this, though, because...

Ten seconds.

Here goes Hot Yoga Grandma, chasing after her apples, right into the road. Seriously, what pie could be worth risking your life? Does she not see the bus? How could anyone miss it?

Everyone is screaming now, a chorus of *No* and *Watch out* and *The bus the bus the bus.* Where were these people eleven seconds ago?

With a doomed sense of déjà vu, I look up and see the bus driver's terrified, pallid face. He's screaming, too, though I can't hear him. He's convinced he's going to hit Grandma, which he isn't. Who he's going to hit is—

I turn, my body moving as if through molasses, to grab for the dude who brought me here to begin with. To stop him. But he's not there. He's freaking gone.

Seven seconds.

I scan the crowd, searching desperately for him. People are stepping on the stupid apples. The air smells like cider and my mouth tastes like metal and my heart is threatening to burst through my chest—

There he is. Striding into the road, putting himself between Grandma and the bus, one hand up like a crossing guard. Like he can stop the bus with sheer force of will, as if he's Magneto or something. Or like he's an overprivileged dude who's gotten everything he's ever wanted, just by showing up.

Like he's about to die.

God*damn* it. I really liked these jeans.

With three seconds to go, I shove through the crowd, get a running start, and launch myself through the air into the street, right at Overpriced Sweatpants. I body-slam him in a move worthy of WWE, knocking him out of the path of the bus with inches to spare.

Two seconds.

The world whirls. The guy swears at me. The bus squeaks by, so close I get a faceful of exhaust and start to choke.

One.

We land hard, with me somehow on the bottom, taking the brunt of the impact. My jeans are *ruined*, torn at the butt and both knees. From the way it feels, I'm pretty sure I'm lying in a puddle of fresh-squeezed apple juice. Overpriced Sweatpants is stretched full-length on top of me, crushing me into the asphalt. I can smell his expensive, citrusy cologne.

If we were in a rom-com, this would be the moment that I looked up into his panicked, crystalline blue eyes and realized I'd just met the love of my life. Time would stop as we gazed at each other. Cue awkward dialogue, hot sex, misunderstandings, and, of course, my happily ever after.

But this isn't *The Wedding Planner*, I'm not a female version of Matthew McConaughey, and he's sure as hell not J-Lo. Not with this fashion sense.

Overpriced Sweatpants glares down at me, clearly furious.

There's a red scrape on his cheek and not a hint of my happy ending in his infuriated eyes. I wait for him to thank me for saving him, or at least to apologize for ruining my jeans. I entertain the notion that perhaps he'll even offer to buy me a new pair.

"What's your name?" he says instead, his chest heaving against mine.

"Rune," I offer, equally out of breath. "Rune Whitlock."

The dude whose life I just saved bares his teeth at me, like he's preparing to take a bite. "Well, Rune Whitlock," he says, "you're under arrest."

CHAPTER
Two

"TELL ME AGAIN," Charlotte says as she drives me home from the police station, having somehow convinced the cop to not press charges. We both know it's a good thing my juvenile records are sealed; otherwise, she might not have been so lucky.

I heave a sigh. "I was trying to save his life," I say, for the eightieth time. "I know how it looks. I know you don't believe me."

My best friend rolls her eyes. "It doesn't matter what I believe. I'm your lawyer, and you sure as hell needed one. But damn, girl, it's not even 8:00 a.m. Did you really have to throw a hot undercover cop in the path of a bus before I finished my coffee?"

There's no point in trying to explain myself to Charlotte. That's the nature of my curse: to see the future at unpredictable times and never, ever be believed. Me in a Nutshell: Rune Whitlock, Unreliable Seer, Graphic Designer, and now, Professional Cop-Tackler.

So instead I just thank her for springing me, then run inside to change and grab my laptop for the meeting that I have exactly twenty-nine minutes to get to. I work from home for a reason. Exhibit A: this morning's incident. But my boss insisted that I come into the office today, to discuss some new project. And if there's one thing Ethan hates, it's tardiness. His email signature is a line from *The Merry Wives of Windsor* that reads, "Better three hours too soon than a minute too late." Rumor has it he fired his last secretary for showing up to work at 9:02.

I can't be late. I need this job.

I scrub the blood from my knees, yank my leggings over the plum-sized bruise on my butt, find my one business-casual black skirt in the back of my closet, and button my favorite lavender blouse. I do the fastest makeup job ever. Then I snatch my purse and laptop bag from the dining room table and race out the door.

I have a full gas tank. I am careful not to speed, lest I tempt fate.

But my car dies anyway, smack in the middle of Sapphire Springs' busiest intersection (ha!), half a mile from my destination.

Somehow, I manage to coast to the side of the road. Leaping out of my crappy Subaru and grabbing my purse and laptop bag, I check the time, gulp, and start to run, as fast as I can go in my high heels. Which, for the record, is not that fast. My laptop bag bangs against my side, doubtless giving me another bruise. My purse threatens to spill its contents onto the ground. And my heels keep getting stuck—in the grass, in the cracks in the sidewalk. With my luck, I'll sprain my ankle soon.

Eff this. I yank off my heels and, with them dangling from my hand, limp-sprint past Brew Box, where Charlotte and I would've had coffee this morning if I hadn't been busy getting tossed into the clink. Past The Bookaholic, where I spend my Sundays browsing. Across the street, darting between cars that honk and swerve to avoid me. And finally, through the double doors of downtown Sapphire Springs' tallest building, a stone-and-glass monstrosity that the historical society must've been paid off to allow through zoning.

"Rune Whitlock," I pant to the grizzled guy at the security desk. "I have a meeting with Ethan Godfrey. Smashbox Analytics."

The guy peers at me over his glasses, as energetic as the sloth in *Zootopia*. "...Rune..." he says, running his finger down a list at the speed of slow-drip molasses. I shift from foot to foot, shifting the straps of my laptop bag and purse, desperately eyeing the elevator. Sweat plasters my hair to my face.

I cannot lose this job. It's not like I have a safety net. Or a family to catch me if I fall.

I glance at the security guard again, then back at the elevator. There's a man standing in front of it now, his back to me, holding a coffee from Brew Box. His dark jeans are pressed. His hair is perfectly combed. He is the opposite of me in every way: not sweaty, not disheveled, not held hostage by Sloth Security. Also, caffeinated. I hate him, right down to the depths of my cursed, cop-tackling soul.

"...Whitlock..." the guard mumbles. I'm tempted to launch myself over the desk and strangle him. But I don't need to be able to predict the future to know that wouldn't end well.

"Ah, here you are. You can go right ahead. Just sign your name...and you'll need a badge..."

The elevator pings, announcing its imminent arrival. The doors open, and Mr. I-Iron-My-Jeans steps through.

I snatch the pen from the security guard's hand, scribble something illegible on his clipboard, slap the badge he hands me onto my shirt, and charge for the elevator just as the doors begin to slide shut.

The man inside sees me coming. I know he sees me, because his eyes fix on mine and widen with something akin to horror. But does he hold the elevator? He does not.

Bastard.

I skid to a stop in front of the doors and shove my arm

through the opening. I swear to God, if they close on me like monster jaws and drag me down into the elevator shaft to die a horrible death, I am coming back to haunt this guy's ass.

Luckily for me—and him—the doors slide open. I hurtle inside and slump against the mirrored wall, my chest heaving. The doors slide shut again. And then it's just me and Ironed Jeans, standing there in silence as the car begins to rise.

He takes me in—curly brown hair spilling out of its bun, heels looped over my finger, face flushed from running—and his eyes widen even further. They're the darkest blue I've ever seen, so dark that if I wasn't seeing them up close, I might mistake them for black.

"What floor?" His voice is low and scratchy, like he's not used to speaking. It's an undeniably sexy voice, which is *not* what I should be thinking about right now. Especially not about a guy with the people skills of an ice floe.

"Five," I huff out, but he doesn't move. And that's when I notice that the button for the fifth floor is already lit up.

We are going to the same place. Freaking perfect.

Well, Smashbox is a big company. With luck, we'll never need to see each other again.

The elevator rises in silence. It isn't a huge elevator, and Ice Man and I are standing too close to each other for comfort. He smells like cedar and vanilla, which has the unfortunate effect of making me either want to burn him or bite him. Instead, I busy myself with sliding my heels on, twisting my hair back up into its bun, and tugging my blouse and skirt into place. Mission accomplished, I glance at the wrap-around mirrored wall to make sure I'm presentable. Shoes, check. Skirt and blouse straight, check. Mascara not smudged, ch—

Holy bananas.

Ice Man is staring at me in the mirror, those impossibly dark blue eyes fixed on mine. When he realizes I've caught him in the act, he drops his gaze to the floor and scuttles backward. If he could press himself through the opposite wall of the elevator and come out the other side, he probably would.

Sweet Jesus. I know I'm sweaty, but I can't smell *that* bad.

A strange tension hovers in the air between us. Or maybe it's not that strange. Maybe he's not just rude, but a stalker, too. Or maybe I should invest in higher-quality antiperspirant.

I cannot with this day.

The elevator car jerks to a stop and the doors open. My reluctant companion launches himself through them like he's jet-propelled, as if he can't get away from me fast enough. *Don't worry,* I think, following in his cedar-and-vanilla-scented wake. *The feeling is definitely mutual.*

Smashbox's lobby looks exactly like it did every time I've seen it: ocean-themed art that probably cost more than my worthless car, fish tank filled with exotics, white couch with patterned pillows in aquamarine, cerulean, cobalt, cornflower, and turquoise. Fifty Shades of Blue.

It's probably meant to be soothing. But I am late. I am not soothed. And I can't turn off the designer part of my asshat brain, which is occupying itself with trying to pinpoint the exact shade of Ice Man's eyes.

Ice Man, who is all but sprinting down the hallway that leads to—

"Rune!" Ethan's too-hearty voice fills the air. I turn and there he is, neatly trimmed beard and short dark hair, coming out of his glassed-in, ultramodern office. "There you are."

"I'm so sorry I'm late," I blurt. *Please, God, don't fire me.* "My car died on Orchard Street—and then I ran, but the security guard—"

"Not a problem. You're here now." He's honest-to-God grinning, like he doesn't care that I'm late at all. Maybe he's had a personality transplant. Or maybe I whacked my head when I tackled that cop and I'm unconscious in an emergency room somewhere.

Ethan looks in the direction of Ice Man, who, true to his name, has frozen and is staring at the two of us. "Donovan? What are you doing over there?"

Looking like he wishes he were somewhere, anywhere else, Ice Man sets his shoulders and strides back toward us. He looks down his nose at me, and I fight the urge not to shrink.

"Rune," Ethan says, "this is Donovan Frost. That new project I was telling you about? He's the other half of your team."

Unbelievable.

I'm not just cursed. I'm screwed, too.

CHAPTER
Three

I MAY NOT WORK in the office at Smashbox, but I do interact with other employees. And I've heard a lot about the company's premier data engineer and developer, Donovan Frost. *Sexy as sin but cold as ice*, from Jill in accounting. *Has to have everything his way*, from Georgia in marketing. *Never talks to anyone, prefers coding to conversation, brusque, brilliant but demanding, probably has sex according to a color-coded spreadsheet, wouldn't be surprised if he starches his underwear.*

Well, now I've met him, and I can imagine his reputation is well-earned. Except for the brilliant part. I suppose that remains to be seen.

"We're going to be working together?" I say, pasting on what has to be the world's sickliest smile, just as Donovan blurts out, "Just the two of us?"

You don't have to sound so horrified, I think, shooting him a disgusted look. He ignores it, his gaze fixed somewhere over my shoulder.

"Well, there will be other people involved, of course. A team of app developers, for example," Ethan says, frowning as he glances between me and the aptly named Mr. Frost. Talk about growing into your name. "Is there a problem here?"

I need this job. I need this job, I repeat to myself, trying to ignore the prospect of working every day alongside a man who can't be bothered to hold the elevator for me, hides in the corner of the car, and then flees from me as soon as the doors open, like my very existence is poison. "Not at all," I say, resurrecting the sickly smile.

Donovan's eyes fall on my face, and he grimaces at the sight of the smile—or maybe, just at the sight of *me.* "Of course not," he says, each syllable ice-tipped.

God, what is his *problem?* "So," I say, forcing cheer into my voice, "what's this project all about?"

Ethan grins. "Why don't we talk about it in my office?"

Donovan and I trail after him to the office at the end of the hall. I haven't been in here in quite a while, but it hasn't changed much either, other than the addition of a new baby to the family picture on his desk and an expansion of his inexplicable Marvel bobblehead collection to include Doctor Strange. Same floor-to-ceiling windows comprising one entire wall, fake plants trying too hard to look real, bookshelves displaying Smashbox's awards and accolades, walls displaying Ethan's degrees. This high up, we have an excellent view of the mountains that surround Sapphire Springs. The sky over them is darkening, portending a storm.

Ethan gestures for us to sit. We slide into the leather armchairs across from his desk, Donovan clutching his Brew Box cup like a lifeline, me feeling like I've been called to the principal's office. And then we wait while Ethan fiddles with his keyboard, looking anywhere but at each other.

"So," Ethan says at last, "let me properly introduce you. Rune Whitlock, creative genius, meet Donovan Frost, Smashbox's gifted senior developer and data engineer."

"Nice to meet you," I say, even though so far, it's been anything but.

Donovan gives me a stiff nod in return. He doesn't offer to shake my hand.

"Rune normally works from home," Ethan says, unfazed by

what must be Donovan's usual attitude. "She isn't typically here at Smashbox. But you've seen her work, Donovan. She updated our logo, redid our website, handled all the collateral for the Ciderology campaign, which as you might remember, won a Green Dot Design Award..." He goes on, listing my accomplishments like I've hired him to do my PR. The Ice Man sips his coffee, showing no indication of thawing, listening like maybe there's going to be a quiz on it later.

"And Donovan," Ethan says when he's run out of things to say about me, "designed the Titan security app, which has made our company a *lot* of money. You would know, Rune; you worked on their marketing campaign. He's an unparalleled data engineer and an app developer in one, which is somewhat of an unusual combination. He's an analytics guru; you're the expert at making things look good. The two of you have vastly different skill sets. Which is why you're perfect to collaborate on this project."

"Let me get this straight," I say when I'm sure he's done. "We're the perfect collaborators because we're...opposites?"

"Exactly." Ethan looks pleased. "And your skills complement each other nicely. That's what we need here—out-of-the-box thinkers who can design a gorgeous product that will function smoothly behind the scenes and on the front end, with the graphic user interface. I know you don't normally come into the office, Rune, but this is different. To get the creative synergy you need, the two of you will be collaborating in person, every day."

He's speaking English, but somehow, I must have misunderstood. "I can't...work from home?"

Ethan shakes his head. "Not on this one. Sorry. I want the two of you together, in the same space. Bouncing ideas off each other. Able to spin your chairs around when you come to a brilliant conclusion and brainstorm face-to-face."

"You want me to share my *office*?" Donovan's jaw tightens, as if Ethan's told him we need to share a bedroom, instead.

"Is that a problem?" Ethan says, eyebrows knitting. "Because if so—"

"No." The fingers of Donovan's free hand beat a tattoo on his knee. "Not at all."

But, of course, it's all too clear that it *is*.

I have to fight the feeling that settles over me, the familiar voice that rears its ugly head: *not wanted, not good enough, wrong wrong wrong*. A lifetime of growing up in foster care—never the right kid to keep, shunted from house to house for being too strange, knowing things that families would rather keep secret—gave that voice years of fodder. Even the kids at school wanted nothing to do with me. *The weird girl. The girl with no parents. The girl who talks to herself, the girl who stares into space, the girl who thinks she can see the future, the freak.* Only Charlotte stuck by me, and because her mother was the mayor of Sapphire Springs, that helped a little. But her mother never liked me much, either.

I tend to make people uncomfortable, if they spend enough time with me. Even though I'm cursed to never have them believe my predictions, they still sense I'm different somehow. The only place I've ever felt like I fit in, other than at home with my cat, Valentine, is with Charlotte's family, and that's mainly because her daughters are too young to know any better. But I've worked hard at putting on an act, smiling and asking the right questions and working hard to make sure people feel at ease. Donovan never even had a chance to get to know me before he decided he couldn't stand me. That shouldn't hurt, but somehow it does.

"I won't go through your files," I say, too loudly. "Or...or touch your computer screen. Or steal your passwords. Or whatever it is you think I'm going to do."

Donovan's nostrils flare. "You couldn't steal my passwords if you tried."

As if to punctuate his statement, thunder booms, so close I swear Ethan's windows tremble. A moment later, the sky opens up and rain pours down, streaking the glass. Hello, terrible omen.

Ethan is undeterred. "Donovan is very particular. It's what makes him such a good engineer. You'll loosen him up a little,

Rune. It'll be good for him," he says, like Donovan isn't in the room at all.

Donovan chugs his coffee as if he wishes it were something stronger. He doesn't say a word.

"Um," I venture, watching lightning flash over the mountains, "you haven't said what the project is. Or the timeline. Or the deliverables. Or, come to think of it, the client."

"Haven't I?" Ethan frowns at an email that's just popped up on his computer screen, then glances back at me. "The timeline is six months, starting now. I hate to be cloak-and-dagger about it, but our client has asked to remain anonymous. I suggested an NDA as an alternative, but…" He shrugs. "All I can say right now is that the project involves creating a package to compete with genealogy software like 23andMe and Ancestry. We'll be revealing more information to both of you on a need-to-know basis."

"Six months?" For the first time, I hear a crack in Donovan's impassive façade. "You expect me to do this by myself…in six months…alongside my other responsibilities?"

"Of course not. This will be your only project. And you're spearheading it, not lone wolf-ing it, obviously. As I said earlier, you'll pull in teams as you need them, based on my approval. App developers, UX designers…"

"But—but—" Donovan runs his hand through his hair. "I'm in the middle of the Nebula project. You've got me crunching data for at least two other clients. What am I supposed to do about them?"

"Hand them off," Ethan says, rising to his feet. "You've got a competent team. Take advantage of them."

"But—" Donovan says again.

"I'm sorry. I know you like to finish what you start, but this is too good an opportunity to pass up. It could do wonders for the company. Get your name on this, Donovan, and people will be lining up at your door. Yours, too, Rune."

I want to tell him that I have no desire to have anyone lining up at my door. That I'm happy with my life as it is—or, if not happy, at least able to maintain it. I may not have a family, someone to love, or answers about where the hell I came from, but at least I'm stable, which is more than I'd ever hoped for. My experience with change—and I have a lot of it—has rarely been good.

But you don't tell your boss that, not when you need the financial security your job provides. Not when he pays for your health insurance and your mortgage on your little cottage and your chai lattes. So I just say, "I'll do my best."

"That's what I like to hear. Now, sorry to run you both off, but something urgent's come up." He shifts his gaze to the windows, where rain is sheeting down. "You said you had car problems, Rune. Do you need a ride?"

Right. My Subaru, abandoned half a mile away. "I can take an Uber."

As soon as I say it, I realize the error of my ways. Sapphire Springs has two Uber drivers (not an exaggeration), and in this weather, they're both likely in high demand. I'll be waiting forever.

Ethan must come to the same conclusion, because he says, "Don't be silly. Donovan will drive you."

Donovan will what? "That's not necessary," I protest, just as Donovan says stiffly, "I really don't think—"

"Nonsense!" Ethan says, clapping his hands. "The two of you need to learn to work together. And right now, you can barely hold a conversation. A little drive would be good for you. Get to know each other a bit." He grins, as if he's just announced that he's giving us both huge raises. I've never seen him look so happy.

If I didn't know better, I'd suspect Ethan Godfrey had a little matchmaking in mind.

But honestly? The only thing he's setting us up for is failure.

Four

DONOVAN and I ride down to the lobby without speaking, which is probably for the best. The smell of cedar and vanilla permeates the space between us again, and I'm still evenly split between sinking my teeth into him and lighting him on fire.

There are 150 employees at Smashbox. Of all of them, why is *he* the one Ethan stuck me with? And how am I going to collaborate creatively with someone who can't make eye contact with me or unhinge his jaw long enough to utter multisyllabic words in my general direction?

Also, how am I going to handle coming into the office every day? There is a reason I work from home. My life is carefully engineered to accommodate my…ability.

It's just temporary, I assure myself as the elevator door opens and, with his customary excellent manners, Donovan strides out in front of me. *We'll work on it, we'll get it done, and I'll be free of Mr. Personality. Then, everything will go back to normal.*

The security guard at the front desk gives us a cheerful wave as we walk by. Donovan, predictably, is oblivious. I wave back, trying not to look as discouraged as I feel. It's not Sloth Security's fault this day has turned out to be a shitshow.

Rain pelts the street outside, hammering the building so hard I can hear it. The few cars braving the weather are kicking up waves of water in their wake. Donovan yanks the door open, I step through, and together we stand beneath the awning. It's even worse close up: the rain is falling in great slanting sheets, the wind whipping it sideways. Lightning strikes the mountains again. On its heels, thunder booms, and I flinch.

Donovan opens the umbrella he brought downstairs. Immediately, the wind threatens to rip it from his grip. "My car's about two minutes away," he says, holding on tight. "Can you walk in those, or…?"

He points at my feet, doubtless remembering the condition in which I arrived at Smashbox. Maybe he's trying to be nice, but his judgmental expression tells me otherwise.

Then again, maybe that's just his face.

"I can walk," I say, giving him the look the question deserves and shoving my purse into my laptop bag to protect it.

Donovan sighs. "Come on, then." He stalks out from underneath the awning, and I trot after him, doing my best to keep up with his far longer legs.

He walks quickly, not that I can blame him. I don't want to be out here, either. But no matter what I told Donovan, my heels aren't made for jogging in regular weather, far less in a freaking monsoon. More than once, I almost lose my balance, but I grit my teeth and persist. Rain sloshes over every inch of me as I scuttle along, threatening to soak my lavender shirt. I clutch my bag close, determined not to flash Donovan on top of everything else.

When I steal a glance at him, I can't help but notice that he's unaccountably, impossibly dry. Something about the angle of the umbrella, combined with his height, is protecting him, whereas I have begun to resemble a proverbial drowned rat. My hair is straggling out of its bun again, I'm pretty sure my mascara is running, and there's something wrong with one of my shoes. It's…wobbly, in a way that can't bode any good.

The next time I slip, Donovan actually notices. "Are you sure you're okay?" he says, peering down at me. "You're not exactly dressed for this."

I should tell him that *okay* is the very last thing I am. That my knees hurt, my butt aches, I'm pretty sure the seam of my skirt is ripping, and if he could just slow down rather than zipping down the street like the lead car in the Indianapolis 500, maybe I wouldn't have to sprint in these damn shoes to keep up. But my pride is all I have left, so I say, "I'm fine. Let's just get there."

He takes my word for it, heading straight for a puddle that he can easily step over. I, on the other hand, have three choices: go around and abandon the umbrella, jump, or wade through.

"Would you wait—" I begin, pitching my voice to be heard above the pounding rain. When he doesn't respond, I jog after him…and then the heel of my shoe catches in a crack in the side-walk and snaps straight off. I lose my balance again, and this time, there's no getting it back.

For an instant, I entertain the bizarre notion that Donovan will catch me. But he just stares at me, mouth stretched wide like he's got the starring role in a Munch painting, as I teeter, wheel my arms frantically for balance, and capsize into the puddle—fancy skirt, laptop bag, and all.

It says a lot about my priorities that my first instinct is to protect my laptop rather than, say, my face. But my Mac is my livelihood, after all. And it's not like I can afford another one.

I wind up on my bruised butt in the puddle, my legs splayed, my laptop bag crushed against my chest and the rain beating down on me. The seam of my skirt is definitely toast now. There are *things* floating in here: dirt and fast food wrappers and even a hair tie. I half expect to see the paper boat from *It.* This has been a Pennywise kind of day.

"Are you all right?" Donovan looms over me, still holding the umbrella. And, I realize, the heel of my shoe, which he's somehow retrieved. He looks like he's struggling not to laugh.

"If you say *I told you so*," I snap at him, struggling to get to my feet, "I will kill you."

His teeth sink into his lower lip, as if it's a physical effort to restrain himself, but somehow he manages. Instead, he reaches out to me with his free hand. "Anything broken?"

Muddy water sluices from my ruined skirt as I let him pull me to my feet. His hand is warm and dry and I *hate* him. "Just my dignity."

"At the risk of wounding it further," he says, sounding a little choked, "I guess I shouldn't mention that people are staring."

Balancing on one leg, I look around to see what he means. I was unlucky enough to take a spill in front of the yoga studio, which has a glass storefront, and I can count at least four familiar faces plastered against it: Jenny, a former beauty queen who operates Sapphire Springs' animal shelter; Bea, who owns the studio and whose logo I designed; Hot Yoga Grandma, whose apples I liberated this morning (because of course); and D'Andre, the local gossip.

Bea is snickering. Traitor. And Jenny is…waving at Donovan, who waves back at her, smiling like an actual person rather than a human version of Oscar the Grouch.

Great. Maybe it's only me he can't stand. And the entire staff of Smashbox.

In about five minutes, this scene will be all over Sapphire Springs. D'Andre has already pulled out his phone. I can see the rumor mill churning now. Combined with this morning's arrest, I'll never live it down.

As if my reputation weren't bad enough already.

I yank off my broken shoe, then my good one, tears prickling behind my eyes. "If you'll stop flirting with Jenny," I snap, "then maybe we can get out of the rain? Not that it'll make much difference to me at this point, but still."

Donovan jerks his gaze away from the yoga studio. "I wasn't —oh, never mind. Yes. Of course. Let's go. If you…can you…"

His eyes flicker over my feet, then the rest of me, growing more horrified by the moment. I can practically see the wheels turning in his mind: *There are sharp objects on the ground. She could cut her feet. Maybe I should offer to carry her. But no, she's wet and dirty. If I carry her, then I will be wet and dirty, too. And then… and then…* Cue system shutdown.

I try not to think about how it would feel to be held against that broad chest. To inhale that cedar-and-vanilla scent and be close enough to determine the precise shade of blue of his eyes. It's a horrible joke that he is so attractive and so awful, all at the same time. I have absolutely no business fantasizing about shutting his obnoxious mouth by pressing a kiss to those stern lips and—

No. No no no. Crime scene, Rune. Do not cross.

Donovan is still staring at me like I'm a puzzle he doesn't know how to solve. Irritated with us both, I stomp away from him. A moment later, he catches up, lips quirked. "Where are you going?"

"To your car."

"But you don't know where it is," he points out. "And I have the umbrella."

"So what? It's not like I can get any wetter."

"Your laptop can." His eyes fall to the bag, which I'm holding in a death grip against my chest. Then they skitter away, and I could swear the implacable Donovan Frost is *blushing*.

I glance down at myself. Sure enough, my shirt has given up the ghost and unbuttoned itself, revealing an impressive amount of cleavage.

Oh dear God. "Fine," I say, feeling my own cheeks heat. "Lead the way."

He does, walking a little slower this time. But the damage has already been done. Now all I can do is mitigate the fallout.

CHAPTER
Five

DONOVAN'S PRIUS, just like the rest of him, is spotless. I'm tempted to ask him if he irons it, too. But I'm too busy trying not to get filth all over it. I stand, clutching the handle of the open door, biting my lip.

Without a word, he reaches into his back seat and grabs a towel. I assume he's going to offer it to me, to dry myself off. But instead, he unfolds it and drapes it over the passenger seat, so I won't sully his precious upholstery. Whatever little *moment* passed between us when he helped me out of the puddle and then blushed is long since gone.

Bastard, I think, loud enough that I'm surprised he doesn't hear it. But telepathy isn't one of my gifts, more's the pity. Instead, I slide into the car, snatch the towel off the seat, and make a show of drying myself with it before spreading it out on the seat once again. I'm pretty sure I hear a horrified gasp from Donovan's side of the vehicle, but I don't bother looking at him to make sure.

No one so attractive should be such an unmitigated, narcissistic ass. If I have to look at his relatively dry, unruffled self right now, I might punch him. And I don't need a second arrest today.

"Where are you parked?" Donovan asks as he starts the car. Unlike my Subaru, it doesn't clank or rattle. I try not to be jealous of this, too, as I dump my laptop bag and heels onto the floorboard.

"Orchard and Dearborn." I resign myself to glancing in his direction. "That's where it died on the way to the meeting this morning. I'm going to call AAA, get it jumped or whatever."

He looks troubled by this, one dark eyebrow rising. "And you're just going to wait for them in the rain?"

Don't tell me Ice Man cares about my well-being. "No. I'm going to wait in the *car.* It works perfectly fine as a shelter. Just not, you know, as a mode of transportation."

Donovan doesn't laugh at my feeble joke. "Oh, okay," he says, drumming his fingers on the wheel. "Because I can't wait with you. I have somewhere I have to be."

I knew his question didn't stem from concern about a fellow human being. He just didn't want to be *inconvenienced.* "No need," I say, my voice as cold as his. And then we fall into silence as he pulls away from the curb.

I fight the desire to turn on the radio. To roll the window down, despite the rain, just to let some life into this car. To start babbling about something, anything, to break the quiet. I actually sit on my hands to stop myself from reaching for the volume knob on his fancy stereo. Outside the rain-streaked window, the shops of Sapphire Springs' quaint downtown slide by: The Music Bar, locked up tight at this early hour; Brew Box, which I eye longingly; The Bookaholic, which is the perfect place to be spending a rainy morning like this one. I could ask him to drop me off right here, then set up with my laptop in the back and work until the rain subsides.

But then I wouldn't be getting to know my new co-worker, like Ethan wants. Plus afterward, I'd either have to call an unavailable Uber with money I don't have or limp the rest of the way back to my messed-up car in my bare feet.

There's no way around it: I need to stay in this car with Donovan Frost, for the ten minutes it'll take for us to reach our destination. But I can't do it in silence so heavy, it feels like an oppressive weight that's crushing me back against my seat: the G-force of mutual enmity.

"Okay," I say finally. "Can we talk about this?"

Those unfairly gorgeous eyes of his shift sideways, toward me. "Talk about what?"

Is he really going to make me say it? "You know what. The way you're…being."

That earns me a snort, potentially the most emotion I've seen from him in our short acquaintance—unless you count disgust-slash-horror. "No, I don't think I do. How am I being, exactly?"

"Like…that!" I gesture toward him, encompassing his ramrod-straight back, curled lip, and refusal to acknowledge the fact that his attitude is somewhere between oblivious and obnoxious.

"You just gestured at all of me." His lips twitch. I can't tell if he's repressing the desire to laugh or eject me from his vehicle, right into the thunderstorm.

"Exactly! All of you is…impossible. You obviously can't stand me, and I have no idea why, since we've just met. But we have to work together, so can you please get over whatever crawled up your butt? Because otherwise, this is going to be a long six months for both of us." There, that was mature. Sort of.

From what I can tell, given that all I can see is Donovan's profile, he looks bemused. "Why do you think I can't stand you?"

Oh dear God. "Is this some kind of Socratic questioning technique? I have eyes! You've been nothing but rude and dismissive since the moment we met."

"I'm driving you to your car," he points out, his tone deadpan.

"Reluctantly," I retort. "Ethan practically had to bribe you."

"Because I have a deadline! It has nothing to do with you!"

Now it's my turn to snort. We sink back into oppressive silence, and this time I do nothing to break it. Nor does Donovan, who's intently focused on the road, as if he's navigating a tricky mountain pass rather than the near-empty, if soggy, streets of downtown Sapphire Springs. I fold my arms across my chest, sinking down low in my seat, counting the minutes until I can get back to my car and call AAA. Then I can go home, super-glue my broken heel, heat up last night's enchiladas, and binge a romance novel. A humble plan, but mine own.

But you know what they say about plans. Because right as this one occurs to me, a familiar tingling sensation begins in my palms. It climbs up my arms, electrifying my body as it goes, like I've been plugged into a low-grade electric current.

Oh, no. Not now. Not here. Not again.

I clench my fists, trying to ground it, to contain it before it spreads. But that has never, ever worked before. It doesn't work now.

The tingling climbs higher, up my neck and cheeks, until my entire head buzzes with it. It intensifies, until it's less of a tingle and more of a full-on blaze. The car and the street outside start to blur. And in my mind's eye, somewhere between this world and the next, a door cracks open, red-tinged light seeping through.

It's been a long time since I've had two premonitions in twenty-four hours. Not since a day I really don't want to think about, many years ago. But that's exactly what's happening now.

Maybe, I think in desperation, *I can just decide not to walk through that door.* But it's luring me onward, a siren song I can't resist.

I open my eyes wide, trying to focus on the details of the world around me. Trying to stay. Because if not, in about two seconds, Donovan is going to be sitting next to Zombie Girl. But no matter how hard I try, the light grows brighter and brighter, the door cracking wider.

I'm still *here* enough to see Donovan steal a glance at me, then shift his weight uneasily. "Um…you look really upset. I know I can be—that is, I didn't mean—will you please say something?"

I want to. I really do. But I'm frozen, the way I always am when a premonition sets in. Like my body, caught between *here* and *there,* is incapable of movement in either place. Maybe it's like what happens to people during REM sleep, so they can't act out their dreams. Who knows? I've never met anyone else like me. I never knew my biological family. In this, as with so much else in my life, I am alone.

Donovan huffs. "Oh, *now* you don't want to talk?"

Asshole, I think. But I can't speak.

He runs a hand through his hair. "That came out wrong. What I mean is, maybe we should start over. But we can't if you ignore me."

I try to answer him. To tell him I'm not doing this on purpose. But I can't resist the compulsion to step through the door and into that red-tinged light.

I just hope I can endure whatever's on the other side.

CHAPTER
Six

THE DOOR DOESN'T SHUT behind me. It never does. That's one of my greatest fears: getting trapped in the world of my visions, unable to find my way back. As long as the door stays open, even if I can't exit of my own accord, at least I'm not marooned. It's a small comfort, but better than nothing.

Though his voice comes from far away, echoing as if down a long tunnel, I can hear Donovan talking to me, asking if I'm all right. But I can't answer him. Until the premonition releases me from its grasp, I'm at its mercy. I wait for it to come, there in the red-tinged light on the wrong side of a door to nowhere.

I don't have to wait long. A wave of crimson washes over me, obscuring everything. Then it recedes, leaving only the vision behind.

I am Donovan, my hands gripping the leather steering wheel, peering through the rain that lashes the windshield. I see through his wide blue eyes as a red Camaro crosses the double yellow line and swerves toward him, feel his heart pound with terror. He turns, and now I see my own face, wild-haired and wild-eyed and white with panic. A strange brew of emotions swirls through him at the sight: protectiveness, exasperation, disbelief, and a more complicated feeling I don't have time to name. Tires shriek, and he jerks his head back around. Something is burning, the stench of it filling his lungs, stinging his eyes. The Camaro is getting closer and the squeal of tires is getting louder and although Donovan mashes the brake pedal as hard as he can, there's no way he's going to be able to stop in time—

I brace for impact. But it doesn't come. As if a giant hand has grabbed hold of me, I'm snatched out of the premonition, sucked through the door, and dumped back into reality: wet clothes, pouring rain, obnoxious companion. I rest my face against the passenger-side window, relishing the sensation of the cool glass against my skin as the world settles. My head swims with dizziness, and my whole body trembles from the massive adrenaline dump.

My premonitions take a lot out of me, and I never even had breakfast this morning. Dear God, I could use something with a bunch of sugar in it right now. I doubt that Mr. Uptight has anything like that in his car, though. Knowing him, there's probably a box of high-fiber bars stashed in his glovebox, which—

Why am I thinking about Donovan's fiber consumption? We're going to wreck!

I jerk upright, my surroundings blurry, my eyes focused somewhere between the world in my premonition and this one. Donovan is still talking, but his voice is barely audible, like a radio that's turned down too low. I concentrate and tune him in, then wish I hadn't. "What's the matter with you?" he's saying. From the irritation in his voice, he's been saying it for some time. Talk about a shitty bedside manner.

I need to pull myself together. This is bad. So very, very bad. But instead, I mutter, sounding as annoyed as I feel, "The Ice Man Cometh."

"What? Do you need to go to the hospital? Should I call 911?"

I can't tell if he's actually concerned or if he's just pissed off. "Not yet." My vision has finally cleared, and I scan the road in front of us for any evidence of the oncoming red Camaro. Two premonitions in one day is draining, all right. But they are never, ever wrong.

Rain slicks the pavement. Donovan's windshield wipers squeak. I crack the window and crane my head outside, boosting myself up to see as much as possible. No Camaro, but the car fills with the doughy, sugary scent of fresh beignets from Charlotte's sister's bakery, just around the corner. My mouth waters, and my stomach growls.

"What are you *doing*?" Donovan demands. "Sit down. That's not safe. And you're getting soaked."

At this, I start laughing and can't stop. He sounds like a scolding mother hen. "I'm already soaked. And you wouldn't believe me if I told you."

"Sit down," he says again, cranking up the heat and taking his eyes off the road to glare at me. It's a good, solid glare, with the full force of his unpleasant personality behind it, and I oblige. In fact, I lean back against the seat and close my eyes, rehashing the vision in all of its complexity. Somewhere in it is a detail that could save us. Or at least allow me to hurl myself out of the car prior to impact.

But that would only mean saving myself. And as much as I can't stand Donovan, I couldn't live with myself if I did that to him.

Not to mention, we were both in the vision. I know from experience that if I try to subvert it somehow by taking myself out of the equation, something will go wrong: my seatbelt will jam, the car door won't unlock. No, for better or worse, we're in this together.

"Are you sleeping? Meditating? What?" Donovan demands.

I concentrate, seeing the rain-streaked street from my vision. The traffic lights buffeted by the wind. The limbs of the live oaks bending low, just like they do in the stretch of Orchard Street before it exits Sapphire Springs' quaint downtown and becomes a commercial thoroughfare—

My eyes snap open. "Pull over!" I scream.

He shoots me a startled look. "What?"

At this, I finally lose my temper. "Why do you keep saying

'what'? Are you a parrot? Is your vocabulary as limited as your social skills? Pull the car over!"

"I absolutely will not! And did you just say—did you just call me—"

He sounds so indignant, it might actually be cute, if a) he wasn't him, and b) we weren't about to die in a fiery wreck. "Will you just *listen to me*? Pull the damned car over!"

I harbor a faint hope that, since I didn't couch the demand in the context of a premonition, he'll actually comply. But instead, he white-knuckles the wheel as if he thinks I'm going to lunge across the space between us and wrest it from his grasp. He opens his mouth, then closes it again, like the world's most attractive—and infuriating—guppy.

"I don't know what's going on with you," he says finally, in a low, measured voice, "but if you take meds and you've gone off them or something..."

I narrow my eyes, prepared for him to say the most offensive thing possible. After all, it would be on-brand. But what comes out of his mouth instead surprises me. "I could pick them up for you," he says. "If it's an issue of money... I know medication is expensive. And the health care system in this country is terrible. I could take you to get them, and I could pay—"

A hysterical giggle escapes me. Who would've ever thought that Donovan Frost, non-holder of elevator doors, insulter of well-planned outfits, and generally appalling human being, would turn out to be a prescription drug Samaritan?

Of course, that's what he thinks, though. That the chemistry in my brain's gone haywire, and poor little freelance graphic designer me can't afford my medication. Hell, I can't even afford a working car or shoes whose heels don't snap off mid-stride. I don't know whether to be offended at his assumption, impressed he's offered to help, or pissed off that he's *still not listening to me*. I'm busy trying to save our lives, and here he is, babbling about my imaginary meds. Meanwhile, we somehow need to find a way to collaborate on a project whose failure could cost me my job...if we survive this crash. The more I think about it, the harder I laugh. It's either that, or start sobbing.

Donovan's jaw tightens as we pull up to a stoplight, until I'm afraid he might crack a tooth. "It was just a thought," he says. "I'm sorry if I overstepped."

I squint, peering through the windshield for any hint of the Camaro, and wrack my brain for an excuse he'll believe. "Thanks for the offer, but I'm not on any meds. It's just that it's pouring so much," I say, trying to sound pathetic. It's not hard. "I really don't like driving in storms. And I didn't have breakfast today, because…well, this morning didn't exactly go as planned. Could we maybe go get a bite to eat, just until the rain calms down? Peach Tree Grille's right across the street, and they have the best milkshakes in Sapphire Springs."

"Milkshakes for breakfast, huh?" His lips twitch.

"What's wrong with milkshakes? They're delicious." And filled with sugar. "There's a caramel-chocolate one that will change your life, I promise. I'll even buy."

His brows knit, as if I've proposed the unthinkable. And then the rock-hard line of his jaw softens, and I know I have him. "Sure," he says, sounding nicer than he's been all day. "You should've said you were hungry. I've probably got a protein bar in here somewhere, to tide you over."

Of course he does. I repress another giggle as he reaches across me to open the glovebox—half at his predictability, half out of relief. Maybe we won't die today, after all.

But then my laugh dies in my throat.

The light changes, and the red Camaro pulls out from the Peach Tree Grille parking lot. Donovan hands me a Clif bar and pulls into the intersection, babbling something about the significance of good nutrition and how breakfast is the most important meal of the day.

And then, three horrible things happen in quick succession.

Lightning strikes the oak tree directly across the street, which bursts into flame.

I scream, and Donovan takes his eyes off the road, grabbing my hand in instinctive horrified solidarity. Or maybe he's just trying to shut me up by crushing my fingers.

And the Camaro swerves to avoid the oak's splintered, smoking limbs, careening across the double yellow line and heading right for us.

Donovan lets go of my hand and hauls on the wheel, muttering a steady stream of obscenities. But the asphalt is wet and the car hydroplanes, going into a skid. He tries to turn into it, then tries to fight it, but across the road we go, snapshots looming up and then disappearing again: oak on fire, Peach Tree Grille's cheerful coffee-cup sign, red Camaro, oak aflame again. I dig my nails into my palms so hard I'm sure I'm drawing blood as Donovan chants *shitfuckchristonagoddamnpony* with such intensity, it sounds like a prayer.

The last thing I see before the red Camaro consumes my field of vision is the horrified face of the police officer who arrested me this morning behind the wheel.

There is a bone-rattling impact and the thud of metal on metal.

And then, nothing.

CHAPTER
Seven

"RUNE. RUNE! WAKE UP."

Two very strong, very insistent hands dig into my shoulders, gripping hard enough to let me know they mean business. I don't like them at all. They remind me of another set of hands, belonging to a man I've tried very hard to forget. Of the night I set his world on fire, then stood and watched it burn.

I *smell* fire now, just as I did that night. It curls into my nose and sears my lungs, making me cough. Am I back there, with *him*, somehow? Has he finally sought his revenge?

I swore I would never let him touch me again, or Julia, either. That I would protect her with my life. I paid for what I did, but it was worth it. To my dying day, I won't change my mind.

In the darkness behind my closed eyelids, I twist, trying to get away from the hands that have me in their grip, but no dice. Fear trembles through me, and *his* voice echoes, bubbling up from the deep well where I spent years stuffing it away: *I will find you, girl. You think you've won, but you're fooling yourself. I will get to you, and we'll see what goes up in flames then.*

"No," I whimper. "Let me go, get off me, no!" Cold sweat trickles down my spine, and my heart takes up an alarming rhythm. My chest heaves, struggling for air.

The last thing he said to me that night surfaces, an intimate whisper, like he's right next to me. *You may have nothing now, girl, but it won't always be that way. No one will ever love a freak like you. But you will love someone. And when you do, you'll see my face. It'll be the last thing you ever see before I take what you love most away for good.*

"Valentine," I whimper. She's small, defenseless. She never hurt anyone. And I won't—I won't let him—

Another voice penetrates the darkness. Gone is the icy reserve I associate with it. Instead, it's tight with anger. "She doesn't like you touching her. Back off, man."

"You back off, Frost," says the first voice. "Let me do my job."

"Your *job* is harassing innocent women who use the words *get off me*?" the owner of the second voice snarls. "Is your body cam on right now, Cooper? Because I happen to have a very good lawyer, and I'm sure she'd have a field day with whatever the hell is going on here."

"You're not the only one who has a good lawyer." It comes out as a growl.

Maybe their argument should unnerve me. But it has the opposite effect: The more they bicker, the more the here-and-now world settles into place, and the more that awful memory retreats. The cold sweat crawling down my spine evaporates, as does the weight on my chest. I blink, and the darkness falls away to reveal two sets of blue eyes fixed on me: one crystalline as a Norwegian fjord, the other dark as a smudge of rich cobalt on canvas.

Oh, right. The wreck. Did I…pass out?

I must've, because *his* voice is gone. I still smell fire, but now I can see the source: the oak tree across the street, sizzling from the lightning strike. There are hands on my shoulders, all right, but they don't belong to *him.*

I'm not in front of a ramshackle house, holding a match in my hand and facing down a monster. Instead, I'm sitting in a car in the middle of Orchard Street, soaked to the bone. Two very pissed-off-looking men—Donovan Frost and Hot Cop

Summer, now in uniform—stare down at me. It's discomfiting, like being the subject of an experiment I didn't agree to participate in, and I avert my eyes, looking somewhere, anywhere, but at them.

The rain has, mercifully, slowed to a trickle. From my perch in the passenger seat, I can make out the crumpled front end of Donovan's Prius. The Camaro isn't looking so great, either, though Officer Asshat has moved it to the side of the road.

His hands still grip my shoulders, and Donovan gives them a pointed glare.

"She's awake," he snaps. "So now you can let go."

Holy bananas. Donovan Frost, of all people, is *defending* me.

Maybe he's not a total bastard, after all.

Hot Cop Summer relinquishes my shoulders. But he's still glaring, like it's somehow my fault he lost control of his souped-up muscle car and slammed into us.

I want to call him on his attitude, but I force myself to be polite. The last thing I need is to get dragged down to the station twice in one day. "Nice to see you again, Officer," I say, blinking up at him. "At least you're not on top of me this time."

Oooookay, that came out wrong.

Two sets of blue eyes narrow dangerously. "You two know each other?" Donovan says, just as Cooper bites out, "You threw yourself at me!"

Okay, so that didn't come out so well, either.

I rub my forehead, trying to figure out a way to explain that doesn't paint me in the worst light imaginable to my new co-worker. But because God hates me, before I can say a word, D'Andre pedals up to us on the bright-blue bike he rides everywhere, *sans* helmet. "Everyone all right?" he says, sounding gleeful at the chance to be first on the scene.

"We're fine," Cooper says, clenching his jaw. "Looks worse than it is. Just a fender bender. Keep going, before you cause another one."

"You and Rune aren't having the best day." D'Andre's hand

dips into his pocket, doubtless going for his phone in an effort to surreptitiously record the whole thing.

"Yes, I know," Cooper says, at the same time Donovan mutters, "No shit."

Cooper rolls his eyes skyward. "Get your hand out of your pocket and go home, please, D'Andre. Or wherever you were going to begin with."

"To get a green smoothie," D'Andre supplies, pedaling closer and peering between the three of us, as if for clues. "I always get one after yoga. I could bring you one, if you—"

Cooper takes a deep breath in, then lets it out. He looks like he's counting to ten. "I. Do. Not. Need. A Smoothie."

"Too bad," D'Andre says, shrugging. "The choco-strawberry-boonana might sweeten you up a bit." And off he pedals, down the rain-spattered street, giving me and Donovan a cheerful wave over his shoulder as he goes.

"Put on a damn helmet!" Cooper yells at his back. Predictably, D'Andre ignores him.

Great. Recording or no, this little incident is going to be all over the Sapphire Springs gossip network by nightfall. I'd bet my next premonition on it.

Officer Cooper runs a beleaguered hand through his hair and mutters something like *choco-strawberry-boonana my ass.* Then he fixes his gaze on me again. "*Are* you all right?"

At the thought of having to run interference about all of the absurd events that have befallen me today, my tact evaporates, along with my patience. "No. No, I'm not! My butt hurts, if you must know. So do my knees. And my face. Also, if we're being blunt here, I could have done without running into you again."

"Strictly speaking, *I* ran into *you* this time. For which I apologize." He clears his throat. "And what's wrong with your, um, butt?"

"She fell in a puddle," Donovan says gruffly. "I need your insurance information, Cooper. And to get my car out of the goddamned road. Are we done here?"

"Ms. Whitlock was unconscious," Officer Obvious points out. "Do you want me to radio EMS?"

"No," I say, shaking my head vigorously, which turns out to be a mistake. God, I need some Advil. "No ambulance. I just...I want..."

What the hell do I want, other than to forget this day ever happened? My eyes flit across the street, falling on the lit coffee cup logo of the Peach Tree Grille. "A milkshake," I say triumphantly. Maybe D'Andre had the right idea.

"A *milkshake?* Are you delirious?" Cooper's staring at me again. Between him and the glowering yet gorgeous Donovan, I'm half-tempted to make a crack about how my milkshakes bring all the boys to the yard. Somehow, I restrain myself.

"Yes," I say with what dignity I can manage.

"We were about to have one, before you lost control of your vehicle and careened across two lanes of traffic." Donovan sounds every bit as icy as he did back in Ethan's office. He *really* doesn't like Officer Cooper, which...not that I do, either, but what the hell is *his* problem with the guy?

"I didn't *lose control.* There was a—oh, forget it, Frost. You"— Cooper points an accusatory finger at me—"sit tight. Let me know if you feel dizzy and if you change your mind about the ambulance. And you"—he points the finger at Donovan—"move your car while I get my registration." Turning his back on both of us, he stalks off toward the Camaro, leaving me and Donovan alone together.

But Donovan doesn't round the car to the driver's side. Instead, he peers down at me, and when he speaks again, his voice is unexpectedly soft. "Are you really all right?"

His solicitousness gets under my skin. Where does he get off, pretending to care about me after the way he behaved at Smashbox? "Other than my butt, my knees, and my face, I'm fine," I say, trying to match his haughty tone.

His lips twitch, the way I remember them doing before the

crash. "I thought maybe you didn't want to say anything in front of Cooper. You two obviously have a history."

At this, I crack a smile. It hurts my cheek. "Oh, we do. It dates back to this morning."

"But you called him 'valentine.'" Donovan looks so confused.

I can't help myself; I start to laugh. I double over, ignoring my bruised everything, and giggle until tears run down my cheeks. And then I'm full-on sobbing without warning, so hard I can't catch my breath.

"Rune? What's wrong?" Donovan's voice is cautious, like he's trying to figure out how to disarm a bomb and doesn't want to trigger it by mistake. But it's too late: this particular bomb has already exploded.

His face blurs through my tears as I wrap my arms around myself, wracked with shivers. "What if my laptop's broken? I can't afford a new one. Plus I'm w-wet," I wail, unable to contain myself, "and I'm hungry, and I hurt, and my sh-shoes..."

Donovan's brows lower, and he backs up, looking horrified. I hear him rummaging in his trunk—maybe for an emergency flare to rescue him from the dire meltdown in his front seat. But a moment later, he reappears, inexplicably clutching a handful of fabric. "Here," he mumbles, thrusting it at me.

Sniffling, I unfold it, and my eyes go wide.

Donovan Frost, Ice Man Incarnate, has handed me a hoodie with a caricature of my cat printed on the front.

Eight

IF YOU'D TOLD me when I woke up this morning that I'd be sitting opposite a gorgeous, taciturn man in one of the Peach Tree Grille's red vinyl booths, barefoot and wearing his hoodie, I would've said you were crazy. But here I am, swallowed up by Donovan Frost's vanilla-and-cedar-smelling sweatshirt, perched crisscross-applesauce on my seat. Donovan himself is cautiously sipping the chocolate-caramel milkshake I insisted he order. It's vegan, made with coconut milk, because apparently the Ice Man is lactose intolerant.

In a day of strange developments, this little rendezvous might be the weirdest one yet.

"Well?" I ask, hands wrapped around my own milkshake—mint chocolate chip, because even though the chocolate-caramel one is clearly the best, I make it a rule to never get two of the same flavor. Otherwise, how are you going to share?

Not that I usually have anyone to share with, other than Charlotte and her girls, but it's the principle that counts.

Donovan spent the time while we waited for our milkshakes to arrive aligning the salt and pepper shakers perfectly with the ketchup bottle, then sorting the little jam packets by flavor, presumably to avoid making conversation with me. Now he leans back in his seat, stretching out his long legs. "Well, what?" he says, the two syllables clipped.

"Is your milkshake good?"

He eyes me, looking incredulous. Gone is the sympathetic guy who asked me if I was all right and then handed me his sweatshirt when I sobbed that I was cold. "*That's* what you want to talk about?" he says, arching a dark brow. "Not whatever the hell was going on with you before we crashed, or the crash itself, or why Cooper was *on top of you*, yet the two of you seem to hate each other's guts?"

Talk about the pot and the kettle. "My blood sugar's not high enough to deal with any of those things." It's an evasion, sure, but it's also the truth. "So…"

Those eyes—sapphire, maybe?—narrow at me in what I'm fast realizing is his signature look. "The milkshake is fine."

"Just fine?"

"Delicious. Delectable. Hyperglycemia-inducing." He waves an impatient hand at me. "Drink up, though why you wanted something cold when you're apparently freezing is beyond me. Then talk."

"Has anyone ever told you that your manners are deplorable?" I mutter, closing my lips around my straw and taking a long pull of my milkshake nonetheless. The bite of the mint and the smooth sweetness of the chocolate are intoxicating, and I let out a moan of happiness.

Donovan's gaze falls to my mouth, and he shifts in his seat. When he looks up, his expression is appalled. "Seriously? Do you have to make those…noises?"

"Oh, knock it off. It's not like I'm going for the full *When Harry Met Sally* reenactment. Also, this place is empty." I take another drag of my milkshake, giving a pointed glance around. Other than Mrs. Grant behind the counter, who's worked here as long as I can remember and is half-deaf, we're the only people here. "If you're so insistent that I drink my milkshake, then *you* answer a question for *me*. Why does your sweatshirt have a picture of my cat on the front?"

"Your…?" For the second time today, Donovan Frost is staring at my chest. The weight of those jewel-blue eyes of his, regarding me with singular, intense focus, is unnerving.

I refuse to give him the satisfaction of letting him know he's gotten to me. "My cat. Valentine," I clarify. "That's who I was talking about, by the way. Not Officer Asshat."

He sputters, spraying vegan ice cream across the table. "*What did you call him?*"

"If the shoe fits…" I push my spare napkin in his direction. "Anyway, that's Valentine on the front of your hoodie, for sure. She's got that little white heart on her forehead and the white ace of spades on her chest. Did you hack into my phone and steal a photo of her, or what?"

His jaw drops. "Excuse me?"

"I'm joking. Sort of." My gaze drifts away from him, toward Mrs. Grant. She's typing away on the iPhone her granddaughter got her for her birthday, lips pursed. As I watch, she glances toward me and Donovan, who's fastidiously dabbing the table clean, then types faster.

"It's from the *animal rescue* shelter," he says, folding his damp napkin into…is that a parallelogram? "A fundraising item that didn't work out. Why would you insinuate that I hacked into your phone? Do you think that's what I do with my spare time? Besides, we just met today!"

My brow knits in puzzlement. Valentine was rescued from the shelter, true, but… "Who knows what you do when you're not trying to reprogram the world. Break into people's houses and organize their things? Neglect to hold elevator doors for desperate women? Anyway, explain why you have—"

Donovan unfolds another napkin to use as a coaster for his milkshake. The dude has some serious issues. "I answered your question. Your turn to answer mine."

There's no way I'm getting into the whole premonition thing with *him*, of all people. It's not like he'd believe me. "I told you. I hadn't eaten. It makes me weird. As for the crash, it sucked, end of story. A perfect fit with the rest of my day."

"And Cooper?" He crumples napkin #3 into a ball. "Did he do something to you? Is that why you got so freaked out when he tried to wake you up? How do you know him, anyhow?"

I sigh, looking at Mrs. Grant. She's shifted so I can see her screen, which clearly displays our town's Facebook group, Sapphire Springs Shenanigans. On it is a photo of yours truly, splayed in the puddle, with Donovan looming over me. She scrolls again, and it's a blurry image of me, Donovan, and Officer Asshat. D'Andre must've taken it when he was biking away. Again, and it's a video of me and Cooper tussling on the asphalt, the bus half-visible in the frame.

"Are you going to answer me?" Donovan demands.

I throw my hands up. That damn cedar-and-vanilla smell wafts everywhere, and I hate myself for liking it so much. "I don't know why you care so much about me and Officer You-Know-What. But you want an answer? Look right there." I point at Mrs. Grant and her three-models-newer-than-mine phone.

His gaze tracks, following my finger. His eyes widen. And then he runs a hand through his hair, so roughly the dark strands stand on end. "What the— Why are the two of you rolling around in the street?"

My head sinks onto my folded arms. "I was trying to save him from being hit by a bus," I mutter to the Formica. "So naturally, he arrested me. This morning. Are you happy now?"

There's a long, weighted pause, during which I don't bother to look up. I'm too exhausted to move, let alone to deal with whatever insult he lobs my way. "Go ahead, Frost. Gloat."

Silence. And then a peculiar sound emanates from the other side of the table. It's low and throaty, and also a little rusty, like whoever's making it is out of practice.

I lift my head and peer at him, just to make sure. But, yup. The imperturbable Donovan Frost is *laughing*.

"Knock it off!" I snatch up his napkin parallelogram and hurl it at him, but he dodges and it lands on the table behind him. Mrs. Grant gives me a disapproving glare, right before she types something else. I swear to sweet purple ponies, if she takes a picture of us and posts it on Sapphire Springs Shenanigans, I'm going to lose it.

"You…you tackled him?" Donovan chokes out. "And he actually arrested you? Why aren't you in jail right now?"

"Like he said, I have a good lawyer."

Donovan sobers, as if it's just dawned on him that I heard everything he and Cooper said when I was out of it. Leave it to him to be pissed off about being caught acting decent. "You invite chaos wherever you go," he says, realigning the salt and pepper shakers like he's trying to cleanse himself of my bad influence. "And I don't do chaos, Rune."

After the day I've had, this final indignity is too much. "I'm not suggesting that you *do* me!" I snap. "We just need to work together, to make Ethan happy. That's it. Get over yourself!"

Too late, I wish I could take the words back. Donovan blushes fire-engine red, the color of the booth we're sitting in. If Mrs. Grant were a dog, her ears would be pricked—no pun intended. She's definitely put *something* on the Facebook page, because through the plate-glass window behind Donovan, I see the members of her seniors' book club, the Sinning Spinsters (otherwise known as the Sinsters), traipsing down the street, straight for the Grille. And every single one of them is holding their phone.

Damn, damn, damn.

"I—" Donovan stutters, staring at the table. "I didn't mean—I wasn't implying—"

I need to smooth this over, and fast. The very last thing I need is for it to get back to Ethan that his senior data engineer and the graphic designer who's supposed to be collaborating with him on Smashbox's prize project are in the midst of a sexual harassment debacle in the middle of the Peach Tree Grille. "Forget it." I drain my milkshake, preparing to make a quick getaway. "Let's just go."

He shakes his head, gaze still fixed on the Formica. "I'm

terrible at…people. Obviously. I shouldn't have said what I did. I mean, yeah, you did knock a cop into the street, get arrested, have your car break down, fall in a puddle in front of the biggest gossips in town, and then get in a car wreck all in one day, but—"

"Not. Helping." The Sinsters are getting closer by the moment. I consider faking my death, but that would probably just get plastered all over the Facebook page too.

"Sorry! It's no excuse, but Cooper gets under my skin. Brings out the worst in me."

"I see that." All hope of escape is gone; the Sinsters are assembling outside the door. Might as well ask what I want to know. "Why do you have such a problem with him, anyhow?"

"Because," he says, dragging his gaze away from the table and meeting my eyes at last. "Officer Asshat is my brother."

CHAPTER

Nine

"I'M SORRY. COME AGAIN?"

Donovan's jaw sets. "Same mom, different dads. I'm not a fan."

"Of Cooper? Or his dad?"

"Both." He scrubs a hand through his hair again. "Either."

Sapphire Springs is *small*. While I was born and raised here, Donovan is a recent arrival, courtesy of the job at Smashbox. He probably would never have moved here otherwise. I've never run into him at the Halloween Howl or the Spring Fling or even the damn grocery store. And I can't imagine he's out there championing the town's virtues to the brother he despises...who I've also never run into anywhere in town. This makes no sense.

The questions come boiling out before I can stop them. "Did he just move here? Why is he here, anyway? And how come you can't stand him?"

"Six weeks ago," Donovan says, ticking off the answers on his fingers. "Damned if I know. And let's just say Cooper and I are... incompatible."

I blink at him, realization breaking over me. "You call your brother by his last name?"

"He's lucky," Donovan forces out between clenched teeth, "that I call him anything at all."

There has to be more to this story. I'm dying to know what it is, especially because Cooper was the subject of my premonition this morning and then fate stuck me in a car with Donovan, whereupon I promptly had *another* premonition that brought his brother back into my life a second time. Hearing the monster's voice in my head when Cooper was touching me, then thinking about Julia…what if it's all connected?

I have nothing but questions. But by the way Donovan's jaw is locked down tighter than Fort Knox, I doubt I'm going to get answers anytime soon.

I try anyway, leaning forward to ask what happened between them that was so horrible, when the door opens and the Sinsters come barreling in, Hot Yoga Grandma among them. Their eyes lock on me and Donovan like rifle sights. And then, in unison, they chorus, "Hi, Rune."

I shrink down in my seat, wishing I could disappear. "Hi."

"We're just here to discuss our book of the month. Right, Betty?" Louise Fontaine, who's been Sapphire Springs' head librarian since I was little, winks at Mrs. Grant over her bifocals.

"Right," Mrs. Grant says, looking utterly unconvincing as she scoops a copy of Lucy Score's *By a Thread* up from behind the counter. "Down-on-her-luck heroine meets rich but grumpy hero for some spicy workplace sex. Have you read it, Rune?"

Real subtle. I have, in point of fact, read *By a Thread*, but I'm not about to discuss it with a bunch of septuagenarians…especially when they seem to intend for me to use it as a how-to manual. How does this *happen* to me? "Nope. Sorry," I say, hoping my brusqueness will put an end to this nightmare. But no.

"That's too bad," Mrs. Fontaine says. "Oh, well. You can listen in to our discussion. You might learn something." And then, to my horror, she winks at Donovan, too.

The Sinsters settle down in the corner booth, and Mrs. Grant bustles around, getting everybody coffee and pie. Then she sits down, and all of them whip out copies of *By a Thread*, whereupon they promptly begin critiquing a certain salacious workplace bathroom scene, starring the book's brooding hero, Dominic Russo.

When I turn my attention back to Donovan, he looks stricken. "What fresh hell is this?" he hisses.

"The Sinster Romance Book Club." I shrug. It speaks for itself, especially right now, when he's got a front-row seat.

"The *what*?"

"They get together every month and read the smuttiest books they can find. Sort of an up-yours to the stereotype of prim and proper, older women. Since Mrs. Grant started it, they meet here. Although to be honest, I don't think they're supposed to get together until next week. I guess you could consider this a special session."

I didn't think it was possible for Donovan to look more horrified, but he manages it. "There is something very wrong with this town."

"You're telling me." I slurp up the remains of my milkshake. "It could be worse. You should've been here the time they read an erotic romance and decided to demo all of the sex toys right on the counter. Now *that* was an eyeful."

Donovan's eyes dart from Mrs. Grant to Mrs. Fontaine to Hot Yoga Grandma, who's pulled out her knitting. Her needles click, a hat for her newest grandson taking shape while she enthusiastically offers her opinion on the size of Dominic Russo's equipment and his skill at wielding it. "You're joking."

"I mean…"

His eyes scan my face, disbelief clear in their depths. "Wait, you *are* joking, right? Tell me they didn't really—"

"You want the truth, Frost?" I give him a wicked grin. It's nice to see someone else suffering for a change. "Or do you just want me to say something that'll make you feel better?"

Donovan buries his head in his hands, as Mrs. Grant utters a stage whisper in which the words *thong* and *I'd drop to my knees for him if I didn't have arthritis* are undeniably audible. "Christ Jesus," he says to the Formica. "So in this little bathroom scenario that I can't help but hear them describing, am I—"

"Dominic Russo? Yes, unfortunately."

"Oh my God. This is not—I—" At a loss for words, he rummages in his pocket and comes up with his wallet, dropping a handful of bills onto the table.

"We haven't even gotten the check yet! Plus, I can buy my own milkshake."

"You were the one who wanted to leave," he growls at me. "Besides, we were in a wreck. With me driving. I'll buy your damn milkshake. And…crap, I've only got hundreds."

Now it's my turn to gape at him. Sure enough, he's rained Benjamin Franklins all over the Formica. "Why do you—ugh, never mind."

He grunts, scooping up the bills and ferreting through his wallet with a desperation I haven't seen since Charlotte ate a bad corn dog at the fair last year and had to make a mad dash for the Porta Potty. Mrs. Grant, who, it occurs to me, has probably not brought the check in an effort to prolong our agony, leans out of the booth and mouths at me, "Sugar daddy, yes!"

I want to die.

Triumphantly, Donovan locates a twenty and plunks it in the middle of the table just as my phone dings with a text.

CHARLOTTE

Are you okay, Rune? What the hell is happening?

ME

I wish I knew.

CHARLOTTE

You're having milkshakes with…spreadsheet sex guy? Whose car you were in when it wrecked?

My face heats, and I glance over at Donovan, to make sure he hasn't seen. Luckily for me, he's poking around in his wallet, organizing the bills by denomination.

ME

How did you know any of that?

CHARLOTTE

Have you seen the Shenanigans page today?

ME

Yes. Lots of unflattering pics of me. Why?

CHARLOTTE

...

...

Oh, sweet summer child.

With a feeling of impending doom, I open Facebook. There, at the top of the Shenanigans feed, is a picture of me and Donovan, sitting across from each other at this very table. The Sinsters must have snapped it when they first came in, in the wake of Donovan's confession about Officer Asshat. His expression is...intense. I'm transfixed, hanging on his every word. Above it is the caption: *Sinsters sighting! Rune Whitlock and 'friend' recovering from car crash at the Grille. #sweettreats #fatedmates #goals #firstdatemagic*

I let out an undignified squeak. Startled, Donovan looks up. "What's the matter?"

"Here," I say, shoving my phone at him. He takes it, brows knitting as he reads. His mouth forms the words 'first date magic,' but he doesn't make a sound. Maybe he's been rendered incapable of speech.

I glare at the table around which the Sinsters cluster, clutching their copies of *By a Thread*. Like little kids hiding comics inside their textbooks so the teacher won't see, each of them has their cell phones sandwiched between the pages of their open novels. And every single screen I can see is showing that damned post.

Mrs. Hernandez, the high school's retired robotics team coach, is typing furiously. A moment later, I hear the telltale 'bing' as a comment pops up on all of the Sinsters' phones.

Donovan's eyes widen, and I lean over the table, trying to see. "What did she write?"

Expression unreadable, he tosses the phone in my direction. It skitters across the Formica, coming to a stop just north of a spatter of milkshake.

Update: Trouble in paradise? #firstdatemagic turns #firstdateminus when Rune and 'friend' argue over splitting the bill. Fate brought them together, but will finances tear them apart? #staytuned #eyesontheprize #sinstersforthewin

Sweet purple ponies on ice skates. "I'm gonna kill them," I mumble. "I'm gonna confiscate their phones, make you hack into every single one, and remove the Facebook app permanently. I'm gonna film their next Sinster sex party and stream it at all of their family holidays from here to eternity."

I glance at Donovan for support, but he just sits there, looking like a carp that someone smacked over the head with a mallet, if said carp had a jawline that could slice diamonds, unfairly sexy hair, and a semi-permanent pout.

"Don't you have *anything* to say?" I demand.

His jaw works, once, twice. And then he pushes to his feet. "Yeah, I do. One, as I keep telling you, I'm not a hacker. And two? Let's get the hell out of here."

CHAPTER

Ten

DONOVAN and I don't speak on the way back to his Prius. I'm sure I look ridiculous, barefoot and wearing a cat hoodie that reaches my knees. He, on the other hand, looks like the poster child for tall, dark, and brooding. And after that Facebook post, I don't blame him.

We reach the car, and he walks around it, re-inspecting the damage. A furrow appears between his brows. If anything, he looks broodi-er.

I can't take the silence anymore. "Maybe *you* should call AAA."

"Nah. It's cosmetic. Totally driveable. Just need a body shop." The words emerge in a low, disgusted rumble. "Fucking Cooper." He slides his blue gaze my way. "I mean, *freaking. Freaking* Cooper. Sorry."

This makes me snicker. "You can curse around me, Donovan. I won't melt."

Donovan makes an indecipherable noise and stalks to the driver's side. "I'll look at your laptop if you want," he offers, unlocking the doors and sliding behind the wheel. "Just to make sure nothing happened to it in the crash. I can't today, but bring it to the office and I will."

"Um, thanks. That would be great." My surprise must show in my voice, because he cuts his eyes at me.

"It's not, like, a personal favor. We have to work together. How are we going to do that if your Mac's bricked?"

Right. Of course he's only doing it out of his own self-interest, not to help a fellow human being. I give him a curt nod, and we ride the rest of the way to my car in silence, broken only when I give him directions.

After an eternity, we pull up next to my battered Subaru. Eager to put this catastrophe of a day behind me, I busy myself with gathering my belongings—laptop bag, purse, shoes. I'm about to get out of the car when I realize I'm still wearing Donovan's sweatshirt.

"Let me give you back your hoodie." I set my stuff on the floorboards and start to wrestle it over my head.

"No need. It's got your cat on the front, right? So you've got borrowing rights. Just bring it with you the next time you come in to Smashbox."

Did Donovan Frost just make a joke? "Oh…okay. If you're sure."

"It's no problem."

Awkward silence falls between us again.

"So…bye, I guess," I tell him. "Thanks for the ride. Sorry about the crash. And the social media debacle. I'll see you in the office tomorrow. With, um, your sweatshirt."

I'm about to open the door and flee when he clears his throat. "Are you going to be okay? Do you have anyone you can call? Because I can wait for AAA with you, if you're not comfortable here on the side of the road."

It's a thoughtful offer, with no obvious upside for him, and so unexpected, it catches me off-guard. "Don't you need to get back to work?"

"I make my own hours," he says, shrugging. "As long as the job gets done, Ethan doesn't give a shit. So, if you need someone…"

"What about your deadline?"

He cocks his head. "My what?"

"Your *deadline*. You know, the one you told me you had, earlier. The reason you said you didn't want to drive me to my car."

Donovan doesn't say anything for one beat, two. His hands clench on the wheel, like the question pisses him off—because honestly, what doesn't? But just when I think he's ignoring me completely, he turns, looks straight at me, and says, "Some things are more important than deadlines, Rune."

This is only the second time he's used my name. The first time, it purely pissed me off. But this time, delivered in that sincere baritone, with his drowning-deep blue eyes fixed on mine—

Yeah, it's enough to make a lesser woman drop her panties, but that's not what gets me.

Donovan's looking at me…as if he actually cares.

For a moment, I let myself believe it's true. That the Ice Man façade is just an act, that he stood up for me with Cooper because he gave a crap that I was knocked unconscious, not just to get in a dig at the brother he hates.

It *would* be nice not to have to do everything on my own for once. To have someone to talk to, someone to drive me home if my car needs to be towed. And I could do worse than having that someone be a guy who's seriously not hard on the eyes. Yeah, his anal-retentive nature's annoying, but maybe there's a flip side. What would it be like to have all of that attention to detail focused on my body? On making me feel good?

"Rune?" Donovan prompts me. "Are you spacing out again?"

I open my mouth to break my golden rule: *Thou shalt not depend on anyone other than yourself, unless you abso-freaking-lutely cannot help it.* And that's when Jenny drives by, in the beat-up Jeep she uses to transport animals in need.

"Donovan? Rune?" She slows and pulls up right next to us, rolling down her window. "Are you all right? I heard you were in quite the fender-bender. And God, look at your Prius."

There's a reason Jenny's won every beauty pageant in a five-county radius. She's beautiful—all glowy dark skin and willowy limbs and perfectly styled locs. She's nice, too. She's always been that way, ever since kindergarten, when she told Connor Lawson to *please quit bullying Rune*, and then invited me to sit at her lunch table with the popular girls. Used to defending myself, I didn't wait to see if her admonition would be effective. Instead, I stood up and cracked Connor over the head with my tray so hard he got a concussion. Forget sitting at Jenny's table; I spent every lunch hour after that one in the principal's office.

The point is, I *like* Jenny. And it's clear to me that, for reasons unknown, she likes Donovan too. She waved at him from inside the yoga studio. She's pulled over to check on him now. And Donovan himself is *smiling* at her—a genuine, open grin that I've never seen on his face in our short acquaintance. Not even when he was laughing about me tackling Cooper.

"We're fine, Jen," he says, his voice surprisingly warm. "I'll still be there tonight. Just have some things to finish up at the office first."

I look down at myself, wearing the sweatshirt with Valentine's face on the front. The one he said came from an animal shelter fundraiser. And suddenly everything makes sense.

He's dating Jenny. Of course he is; she's a smart beauty queen with a huge heart. What she sees in *him,* beyond his holy-hotness-Batman exterior, is a mystery. Maybe his color-coded sex spreadsheets are just that damn good.

I was an idiot to think he'd ever be into me.

"Rune, you're okay, too?" Jenny shades her eyes, peering further into the car. "Poor you. First that incident this morning. Then the puddle. And then the wreck. Maybe you need to go get a hex removed, or something."

If she only knew. "Maybe," I say, giving her a tight-lipped smile. Why is it that everyone I encounter feels the need to recite a list of my humiliations?

It's not Jenny's fault, I remind myself sternly. She means well. And she's not responsible for the fact that I'm sitting here, wearing her boyfriend's sweatshirt, fantasizing about what his lips taste like and the way his hands would feel on my body.

I am such a mess.

Jenny glances between us. "I didn't know you two knew each other." Is it my imagination, or is there a slight edge to her tone?

"We don't. Not really." Donovan waves in my general direction, like I just happened to fall from the sky and land in his passenger seat. "We got assigned to work on a project together at Smashbox. Her car broke down"—he gestures at it, sitting forlornly at the curb—"so Ethan volunteered me to drive her back from the office. But Cooper crashed into us, and, well, you must know the rest. Seems like all of Sapphire Springs knows by now."

I can't blame Donovan for making it abundantly clear that he and I don't have any kind of personal relationship. That he in no way *chose* to spend time with me. I'd do the same thing, if my girlfriend found me on the side of the road with another woman, after the Sinsters captured us on video sharing milkshakes and labeled us with cute hashtags. But it still stings.

"I was just leaving," I say, yanking the car door open. "Again, thanks for the ride."

Donovan's eyes follow me as I cross to my Subaru. Probably to make sure I don't step on broken glass and need a trip to the ER, thereby further compromising his afternoon. I can still feel his gaze as I unlock my door and settle into the driver's seat. If he doesn't trust me to walk three feet, how are we possibly supposed to spearhead a project together?

I'm still fuming when Jenny calls, "Bye, Rune! See you tonight, Donovan!" She waves and pulls away, heading in the direction of the shelter. A second later, he gives me one last unreadable glance and pulls away too, leaving me on my own.

Drawing a steadying breath, I pull out my AAA card, put in an online request for assistance, and lean my head back against the seat. "Your battery will start," I say aloud, leaning into the positive affirmations that Charlotte always tells me to do. "You'll drive home, have the world's biggest glass of wine, and forget today ever happened." Great plan. Except I'll have to work with the Ice Man every damn day for the next six months, and I'm pretty sure the Sapphire Springs gossip network will never let me live today's events down.

I tell myself I'm going to have an ordinary night. That the worst has already happened.

But for someone with a gift for predicting the future, I'm sure as heck wrong.

CHAPTER
Eleven

IT TAKES A WHILE, but the AAA guy finally comes. After a jump, my car starts right up. I drive home, winding through Sapphire Springs' shaded streets until I arrive at the little cottage where I've lived for the past five years. As always, as soon as it comes into view, pride fills me.

The way I grew up—always in trouble for sassing or fighting, bouncing from one foster home to another, then my stint in juvie —I don't think anyone anticipated I'd wind up owning a place like this. Least of all, me. But in the juvenile detention center, there was an art teacher who noticed the doodles in the notebook I always carried, wheedled me into showing them to her, and then convinced me they were actually good. I earned my GED, then went to community college for a degree in graphic design. Two years later, I had my bachelor's courtesy of an online program. And then, to my shock, people started *hiring* me.

I went from Rune Whitlock, ostracized delinquent, to on-demand graphic designer. I never intended to stay in Sapphire Springs. But after Ethan offered me a full-time gig at Smashbox, the money was too good to pass up. Now, at thirty-two, I have a home of my own, someplace where I finally belong. Where no one can kick me out.

My cottage is cozy, with white split-shake siding. It has a wide porch with a swing and rocking chairs, the ceiling painted sky-blue and ivy twining around the white brick columns. Asters, mums, and lantana bloom in the tiny front yard, ushering in the arrival of fall, and a statue of Cassandra, the patron saint of disbelieved prophets, has pride of place at the center of a burbling fountain. It's my sanctuary, and as I swing into my driveway, I want nothing more than to shut the door behind me, change into yoga pants, and nurse my wounds over the promised glass of wine.

But as I limp up my walkway, shoes looped over one finger, lugging my purse and laptop bag, I freeze. Because perched in one of my rocking chairs, wearing an outfit that looks like it costs more than I make in a year, her sky-blue Ferragamo bag crouched by her feet like an obedient dog, is someone I never thought I'd see again.

Julia.

"I always wanted to ask you," my former foster sister says, fidgeting on the edge of my couch, where she waited while I changed out of the ridiculous sweatshirt and my ruined outfit. Valentine curls around her ankles, happy to have a visitor. "How did you know what was going to happen to me? What he was going to try to do?"

The real answer—that I saw the monster hurting her in a vision; that I knew I would do anything at all to stop him—is one she won't believe. I give it to her anyhow. "I had a premonition."

Julia gives me the small, shy smile I remember from the eight months we spent living in the monster's home. I was fifteen and she was twelve. We were opposites in every way: I was outspoken and brash, where she curled into herself, as if trying to make herself invisible; I spent my time in detention and she spent it on the middle school honor roll; I was curvy, with brown hair that had a mind of its own and gray eyes too big for my face, like one of those velvet painting waifs, whereas Julia was a redhead and everything about her was angular, like a fox.

She was sneaky like a fox, too, and quiet. But he saw her, anyway.

"You don't have to tell me. I just..." She twists her straight, auburn hair around her fingers, a nervous habit I remember from all those years ago. "I never thanked you. And I should've. I owe you everything."

I get to my feet, pacing my living room. All of the familiar, meaningful objects—a jar of sea glass collected over a multitude of trips to Ocracoke Island, a painting of this very cottage hanging over the fireplace—seem suddenly empty, like the set of a play. "You don't owe me jack," I tell her. "And I didn't do it for thanks."

Julia lets go of her hair and wrings her hands, her eyes filling with tears behind her horn-rimmed glasses. "They put you in that terrible place. And I never once went to see you. Even though I got moved out of Sapphire Springs after that night, I could've asked my foster family to take me. They were good people; they would've done it. At the very least, I could've written. But I didn't, because I didn't want to think about what happened. And I—" She hiccups, then meets my eyes. "I am so ashamed."

She looks so miserable, it tears at my heart. I come to a halt in front of her and sit cross-legged on the floor. Valentine crawls into my lap, and I stroke her soft fur.

"We weren't exactly friends, Julia. If you'd come to visit, what would we have talked about? The fortieth A you'd gotten that semester, or my fiftieth detention?"

It's meant to make her laugh, and her mouth does quirk up in a smile. But then it falls into a frown again. "I was so *mean* to you, Rune. I thought I was better than you, because you were always messing around and failing your classes. Everyone said you were a freak." Her eyes flash to my face, anxious, but I just shrug. This is hardly news to me.

"I was scared that if they thought we were the same, they wouldn't want me anymore. That they would send me away. But in the end, they turned out to be the worst kind of people. And you…the one I said awful things about…you s-saved me. You went to juvie for it. And what did I do? I n-never spoke to you again."

She's full-out sobbing now, tears pouring from her brown eyes and dripping onto what I'm pretty sure are Brunello Cucinelli jeans. Perusing fashion magazines is one of my guilty pleasures, even if I can't afford half the stuff on their pages. Heaving a sigh, I get to my feet and rummage in my purse for tissues. "Here," I say, pushing them into her French-manicured hand.

Julia wipes her eyes and sniffles some more. "You're being so n-nice," she whimpers.

"Why wouldn't I be? You were a *kid*, Julia. You think I'd honestly be mad that you didn't thank me for putting an end to something that never should've happened in the first place?"

My voice comes out harsher than I mean it to, and she sits up straight, those brown eyes scanning my face with the acuity I remember from when she used to make me quiz her for math tests. "He hurt you, too," she says, tears still clogging her voice.

It isn't a question, and so I don't treat it that way. Instead, I just shrug.

That clear brown gaze travels over me from head to toe, lingering on the bruises on my elbows and the scratches on my arms. "You're hurt right now! I was so upset, I didn't notice. Why didn't you say? What *happened* to you, Rune?"

"I was in a car wreck." It's easier than getting into the rest. "But I'm fine. What are you doing here, anyway? How did you find me?"

Julia hadn't come back to Sapphire Springs after the night I piled the monster's belongings in his yard, set them aflame, and then threatened to torch him and his house unless he backed off.

When he refused, I made good on my promises. He got what he deserved, both from me and from the court system. I didn't regret it.

"You're easy to find," Julia says, giving me a watery smile. "I just went to the Peach Tree Grille—God, I can't believe that place is still there!—and asked Mrs. Grant. She remembered me, gave me a free milkshake, even. There was a weird group of women sitting around a table, talking about"—she lowered her voice—"lap dances and sex toys. They were, like, seventy. But anyway, they all seemed to know *you*. And Mrs. Grant was super happy to tell me where you lived."

"That's the Sinsters." I roll my eyes. "Don't even ask. And yeah, I just bet she was."

"You've done well for yourself," Julia ventures. "This place is totally adorable."

I snort, dislodging Valentine and sitting down beside her on the couch. "By which you mean, what a shock it is that I'm not living out of the back of a broken-down camper van."

"No! Not at all," she says, blushing. "I just...it's beautiful, Rune. Really. And I'm happy for you. It looks like you've finally found some peace."

"So have you, apparently. Looks like all those honors classes paid off."

Julia blushes harder. "I do okay for myself."

"Heard you went to Harvard," I say, unable to resist needling her, the way I used to.

"I—um, yes, I did. And then Wharton, to get my MBA. I work in emerging markets now, empowering microbusinesses. My specialty is helping underserved women. Especially women who've been abused."

Her eyes meet mine, and I see the resolve in them. "That's your way of giving back, then," I tell her. "It's all the thank-you I need. But it still doesn't explain why you're here."

She looks away from me, smoothing the unused tissue out on her lap. "I—um, well. I came to warn you."

Every hair on my body stands up. "About what?"

"Him." Her voice falls to a whisper. "I...I keep tabs on him, Rune. He's gotten early parole, for good behavior. They're letting him out."

My mouth goes dry. I try to swallow, but my throat makes a strange clicking sound.

"Rune?" She squeezes my hand. "I'm sorry. I wanted to tell you in person. I hope he won't do...you know, any of the things he was threatening that night. But you deserve to know."

"Thank you." I force the words out through the pinhole of my throat. No wonder I felt *his* hands on my shoulders today, rather than Cooper's. Some part of me must have known.

"Don't thank me." Her voice is stiff. "Everything good in my life—the family I have now, my degrees, my career—I owe to you. This is the least I can do."

She drops my hand and stands, snatching up her bag. "I have to leave. I have a flight to catch. But I just found out, and I wanted to make sure to tell you before I go."

I walk her out, to my front porch. She wraps her arms around me, and I let her, even though I don't ever remember us hugging before. It's the tight, life-affirming hug shared by survivors who stand in the wreckage of an earthquake, afraid that the ground may begin to shake again. Standing on my beautiful, perfect porch, I watch her drive away.

And then the red haze of my third premonition in one day descends on me again.

CHAPTER
Twelve

THE DOOR CRACKS OPEN, and the red light gleams from within. I take one inexorable step toward it, then another. Something about this time feels different, more ominous. I don't want to go. But I can't stop myself.

In the distance, brakes squeal. Through the veil that's descended over *here*, I see a car pull to the curb. Julia, maybe, coming back to check on me?

For a moment, I entertain the hope that it's her. That she hasn't left me alone to deal with the enormity of the revelation that the monster who attacked us both will soon go free.

But no—whoever's moving toward me is bigger than Julia. The strange double vision that always accompanies my premonitions has taken over, but I can tell that much. Is it *him*? Is he out already? Did he follow her somehow, straight to my door?

Nausea rocks me at the thought of *him* finding me like this, at his mercy and under the sway of a premonition, unable to fight back. I double over with the force of it, clutching myself. My pulse pounds in my ears, my throat, my chest.

Dimly, I hear a male voice calling my name, asking if I'm all right. Relief sweeps me: It isn't *him*, I can tell that much. But the roaring in my ears prevents me from deciphering anything more.

Still, I try to fight free of the magnetic pull of that doorway, of whatever lies on the other side. What if it's the monster, not *here* but *there*, come to make good on his promises? What if this time I see my own undoing, and am helpless to change it?

"Help," I murmur, although I'm not sure if I've said it aloud or just in my own head.

"Rune!" The voice is closer now. I blink, trying to see who it belongs to, but all I can make out is a shadow moving toward me in the real world, even as I retreat further and further in the direction of the doorway. If this new arrival means me harm, I am so screwed.

Then again, maybe I'm screwed anyway. Because the door is open wide, and something is sucking at me, pulling me in. I glance down and see tiny, red waves lapping at my feet.

It's an undertow, somehow reaching from *that* world into *this* one. And it's strong.

It knocks me off my feet, sweeping me through the doorway. I cling to the frame as I pass through, fighting to hang on, but it's no good. The current rips the wood from my fingers, and then I'm washed through into the room beyond. Only this time, it's not empty.

This time, it's filled with an ocean of blood.

I shriek, a sound that rings in my ears and reverberates off the walls, and try to flee. But the blood's rising higher and higher, and the current is powerful. There's no getting away. I strain against it, struggling to make it back to the doorway, but it pulls me back, so hard I fall on my bruised butt *again*. This time, though, I barely notice the pain. I'm too busy scrambling to my feet, drenched in crimson and smelling like a butcher's back room.

Oh god oh god oh god.

And then, from somewhere inside this nightmare place, a man speaks.

"Our day will come, Rune."

It's not the voice of the monster, but it might as well be. It reverberates with power and intention and *evil*. I recognize it, but how? The lapping of the water and the pound of my own heart-beat in my ears makes it impossible to distinguish who the voice belongs to. All I know is, it means me no good.

I spin in a circle, trying to pinpoint the source of the voice, but I'm alone. Just me and a room filled with a rapidly rising sea of blood and an invisible Wizard of Oz-style announcer. The room is small; there's nowhere for him to hide. Except the walls are retreating, fading back and back and back, and the blood is up to my waist now and *oh God*—

In all the years I've had premonitions—which is as long as I can remember—I've never experienced anything like this, where someone talks to me directly. Someone I can't see. It's always like watching a scene play out, like a snippet from a movie. This time, though, it's like *I'm* the one being watched. Like I'm a pawn in someone else's game.

Horrified by the thought, I struggle to keep my feet as the blood creeps upward, past my chest, my neck, my chin. Whose is it? How many people would have to die to yield so much?

I don't want to know. But, like it or not, I'm going to have to find out.

If I can't figure it out, I can't stop it. And if I can't stop it, wher-ever I go, whatever I do, this man's voice will whisper in my ear.

I'll lose what's left of my mind.

The walls of the room have vanished; I'm adrift in a grisly sea, the waves breaking on the horizon. I tilt my head back, struggling to keep my head above the surface, searching for a face to go with the disembodied voice. "Who are you? *Where* are you? What do you want?"

The voice doesn't answer. Instead, it devolves into an echoing, reverberating laugh. And in the distance, I see a wave rising, higher than all the rest, a wall of red bearing down on me. I try to paddle, to swim away, but it's no use.

The rust-and-salt scent of blood fills my lungs as the wave sweeps over me. I go under, choking and sputtering, clawing for the surface. I'm going to drown here, in an ocean of blood. I'll die on the other side of this door, and my body will be left behind, an empty shell—

"Rune!"

It's not the voice from the premonition, but the other one, the one from the real world. It's full of worry, but also laced with demand: a voice that isn't used to being ignored.

It's a lifeline.

I grab for it, this thin thread connecting me to reality like a rope thrown to a swimmer cast overboard. It feels solid in my grip as I haul myself up, hand over hand, my lungs straining for oxygen. My head breaks the surface, and I suck in a deep breath of precious air. My arms and legs churn frantically, desperate to stay afloat.

"Rune! Damn it—"

But I don't get to hear the rest of what my savior has to say. Because another wave comes, washing me clear through the doorway and out into the real world. The door clicks shut behind me, and just like that, I'm back on my stoop again.

I blink once, twice, clearing the red haze from my eyes. There's no blood. No monster, either. Just my garden in the fading light, asters and mums nodding drowsily, my fountain of Cassandra burbling away. And my unlikely companion.

He's crouching in front of me, his big hands dangling between his knees, as if he's afraid to touch me. His eyes are fixed on my face, and his hair is an unholy mess, like he's been running his fingers through it, the way he did earlier today.

I try to tell him I'm fine. That he should leave. That none of this is his problem.

But the world blurs, and for the second time that day, I black out. This time, I fall.

Straight into Donovan's arms.

CHAPTER
Thirteen

MY HEAD IS cold and wet, but the rest of me is overheating. Gentle, reassuring fingers stroke my hair back from my face. I can hear Valentine purring, a low, steady thrum, but I can't see her. In point of fact, I can't see anything; the world has dissolved into fuzzy darkness.

"Rune?" The fingers brush my cheek, their touch warm against my skin. I want to nuzzle into them. "Can you hear me?"

Bewildered, I blink—and find myself staring into the chiseled face of Donovan Frost, creased with an uncharacteristic expression of concern. It's *his* fingers on my face, *his* touch that's made me feel safe.

What in the actual…

"Ahhh!" I jerk upright, dislodging the package of frozen peas draped over my forehead. It drops into my lap, right on top of the plush blanket that was pulled up to my chin. No wonder I was freezing and smothering at the same time. "What are you *doing*?"

Donovan takes a startled step backward, nearly tripping over Valentine in his rush to get away from me. "I'm sorry! I was just trying to help!"

"By hovering over me Edward Cullen-style while I'm unconscious?" I pick up the bag of frozen peas and drop it on the coffee table, where it lands with a clink. "How did I get inside? Did—did you carry me?"

He glares at me, the knight-in-shining-armor act replaced by a crochety dude doing his best impression of Get Off My Lawn. "What was I supposed to do? Leave you lying on your porch? Step over you on my way inside to fetch some smelling salts?"

I glare right back. "Since we're playing Twenty Questions, what were you doing in front of my house anyway? Do you make a habit of stalking damsels in distress?"

Donovan folds his arms across his chest, those penetrating blue eyes of his boring into me. Valentine winds around his ankles, still purring, the traitor. "Do you make a habit of collapsing? Also, most people would just say thank you."

"Thank you," I mutter to the folds of the unnecessary blanket, now puddled in my lap.

"You're welcome. At the risk of invading your privacy, what the hell happened? That's twice today. Are you…sick?"

I shake my head, trying to figure out what version of the truth to give him. My filter must be broken, because I go with the plain, unvarnished version. "I have premonitions, okay? The rough ones sometimes make me pass out."

Now Donovan looks more pissed off than ever. His dark brows lower, and he makes a deep noise that can only be interpreted as a growl. "You don't have to tell me, Whitlock. There's no need to make up a crap story. *It's private* would suffice."

I should drop this subject. Pursuing it has never done me any good. But I've had a truly terrible day, and I can't let it rest. "What, you don't believe psychic powers exist?"

He snorts. "I believe in data. Evidence. Not some crackpot excuse for tricking gullible and vulnerable people out of their money. 1-900-give-me-all-your-life-savings."

Right. So, not only does he not believe me because of my curse, he doesn't believe people like me exist, on principle. We're a freaking match made in hell.

Donovan tilts his head, amusement quirking his lips. "Wait. Don't tell me you *do*?"

"I believe," I say, choosing my words carefully, "that there's more to the world than what we can see, touch, or hear. That there are forces out there we don't understand. And just because we can't measure or exploit them, that's no reason to dismiss the idea they might exist."

God only knows why I've chosen this moment to fight and die on the hill of my weird abilities. Maybe it's because those abilities saved Julia, and after seventeen years, she showed up with the proof that what I did that night made a difference. If I hadn't intervened, maybe the monster and hundreds more like him would have won.

"Agree to disagree," Donovan says, setting his jaw mulishly. "Are you going to tell me why you keeled over, or not?"

I sit up straight, occupying myself with folding the blanket. "I got some bad news, okay? From someone I hadn't seen in a long time. Plus, I haven't had dinner, which, as we've already established, makes me woozy. Satisfied?"

The Ice Man's features soften. "Why didn't you just say that in the first place?"

"Because. Like you said, it's private." I clear my throat, trying to reclaim a modicum of dignity—which isn't easy, given the circumstances. "Anyway, I'm lucky your date ended early. Otherwise, Mrs. Grant might've found me face-down on the porch steps and jabbed me with one of her fancy vibrators to get me to wake up."

"Her…" He gapes at me, then scrubs a beleaguered hand over his face. "Oh, God, why would you say that? Is this revenge for carrying you inside?"

"Maybe," I say, grinning. But my smile fades as it occurs to me that his act of gallantry might have had unexpected consequences. Mrs. Grant lives two doors down from me. And as already established, she's got a phone and she's not afraid to use it. "Did anyone see you?"

"I don't know! I was trying to make sure you weren't *dead*. Why? You don't think that damned Facebook group…" His voice trails off.

On cue, my phone buzzes. I ignore it.

"I hate this town," Donovan mumbles. "Everyone's in everyone else's business. You can't fucking sneeze without someone making a documentary about it."

For once, we're in perfect accord. Sapphire Springs is my home, but sometimes I hate it, too.

I pace to the window that overlooks my front porch, suddenly convinced I'll find the monster lurking there. If Julia tracked me down so easily, then so can he. I'll need a better security system. Maybe a dog. Or maybe I should move, go somewhere he can never find me.

No, I'm not leaving my home. I refuse to let him take anything else from me. I bested him once; I can do it again. This time, within the confines of the law.

My phone buzzes again, but I don't reach for it. I have no desire to see footage of myself limp in Donovan's arms as he carries me across the threshold, like a bride who overindulged on her wedding night. Today's been bad enough already.

"What's the matter now?" Donovan's tone is gruff, but when I turn to look at him, he's wearing the same concerned expression he had when I woke up—like he actually cares what happens to me. His attitude is giving me whiplash.

"Nothing." The last thing I want is to drag him into my problems. "Just checking for wayward Sinsters."

Those laser-sharp eyes of his flick to my porch, then zero in on my face. "We have a project to do together, Rune," he says, each syllable clipped. "Dishonesty's not the best basis for a strong working relationship. Also, it's one of my pet peeves."

The nerve. "Well, God forbid I don't behave exactly the way you want me to!"

He draws a deep breath, looking like he wants to snap right back at me. But when he speaks, his voice is calm. "Look," he says, squaring his shoulders, "we've both had a shitty day. Sounds like yours was even worse than mine. I don't want to press, but you're acting pretty damn squirrely. Does this have something to do with the bad news you got?"

I shrug, hoping he'll let it go. But no such luck.

"I can't believe I'm saying this, but do you, um, want to…talk about it?" The words leave his lips so reluctantly, I almost laugh.

"Thanks, but no." I give him a tentative smile. "There's something else you could help me with, though, if you want. Because you're right, today sucked, and I don't really feel like being alone right now." Not with Julia's words ringing in my ears and that premonition still fresh on my mind.

I take a step toward him, and Donovan's eyes go wide. Then he retreats, as if he expects me to launch myself at him and defile him on the hearth rug. "I…uh, I really…" he stammers, pupils dilating with panic. "You were just… I don't think we should…"

"Please, get your mind out of the gutter." I heave a resigned sigh, reaching for my laptop bag next to the coffee table. "You said you'd take a look at this, to see if the crash did anything to it. Maybe you could do that now, instead of tomorrow at the office?"

A peculiar expression sweeps Donovan's face—relief, combined with something I can't quite decipher. "Sure," he says, blushing furiously as he takes the bag from me. "I'm sorry I jumped to the wrong concl—"

The doorbell rings, cutting off his apology, and my heart starts pounding.

"Aren't you going to get that?"

Damn it. I stride to the door, wishing it had a peephole, and crack it open to see Charlotte standing on the other side, a pint of ice cream clutched in one hand and a box from We Knead Pizza balanced on the other.

"Rune!" she says. "I came as soon as I could get away. I've been calling, but you didn't answer. I've been freaking out."

That's Charlotte, obsessing even though she talked to me after the accident, and saw embarrassing photographic evidence of me and Donovan at the Grille. She's the only person who's ever fussed over me this way. I pretend it drives me crazy, but it's actually one of the things I love about her. Right now, though, I need her to go away. If she comes in and finds Donovan here, she'll never let it go.

"As you can see, I'm fine," I tell her. "In one piece. And I already ate. Thank you, though! Let's talk tomorrow!"

I try to close the door, but she sticks her foot in the gap. "Why won't you let me in?" she says, at the same time as Donovan says from behind me, "No, you haven't. What's the matter with you? Do you have a pathological aversion to the truth?"

A grin tugs at the corners of Charlotte's lips. "Who is that?"

"No one. It's no one," I say, desperately trying to shut the door. "Honestly, Char, I just need some rest. We'll have coffee tomorrow, and—"

But I never get a chance to finish my sentence, because she shoves past me and stalks inside. Where she gets an eyeful of Donovan, standing in my living room with Valentine twining around his ankles, my laptop in his hands, and his trademark scowl on his face.

Charlotte's grin widens, lighting her eyes.

"Sex spreadsheet guy!" she says.

Fourteen

"EXCUSE ME?" Donovan says, his scowl deepening.

I. Want. To. Die.

In a desperate effort to make things right, I blurt, "She said 'text spreadsheets nigh!' She's in an, um, futuristic production of *A Midsummer Night's Dream.* It's very cutting-edge."

Oh, no. Where the hell did that come from?

Both of them are staring at me, Charlotte with knowing amusement, Donovan with horror. So, of course, I dig myself a deeper hole. "She plays, um, Thisbe. Right, Charlotte?" I glare at her, daring her to contradict me.

"Of course." Charlotte's tone is deadpan. "This is my favorite line: *My cherry lips have often kissed thy stones.*"

Forget wanting to die. Now I just want to kill her.

"Why…why would you ever text a spreadsheet?" Donovan clutches my laptop to his chest, his expression appalled. "And why would you show up at someone's door to ask them to send a text?"

Of course, that's the part that upsets him. Once an anal-retentive data engineer, always an anal-retentive data engineer, I suppose.

Charlotte snickers. "Why, indeed. You are just *adorable*. Rune, where are your manners? Introduce us, please!"

Right. Because my manners are the problematic ones here. "Charlotte," I say, resigning myself to my misery, "this is Donovan Frost. He and I are *working together* on a new project for Ethan." I emphasize the words, hoping she'll take a hint.

"You don't say." Charlotte pushes the pizza at me and extends a hand to Donovan. "Charlotte Reid, attorney and Rune's best friend. Lovely to meet you."

He takes it, sizing her up. "Donovan Frost, data engineer and laptop repairman. I assume you're the one who bailed Rune out this morning?"

"And you're the one who crashed a car with her in it."

I've had enough of this pissing contest. "Yes, yes, everyone here has had a stressful day, with me at its epicenter. Got it. Luckily, Charlotte has arrived with pizza and ice cream—which Donovan can't eat. Alas, poor Yorick, he must depart." And not a moment too freaking soon.

"That's from *Hamlet*, not *A Midsummer Night's Dream*," Donovan says, quirking a dark eyebrow. "And I still have to take a look at your laptop."

Oh, for the love. "Can you look at it tomorrow? Charlotte and I have to, um, debrief about the play. And we have to stress-eat." I wave the pizza box. "I'd ask you to stay, but, you know, lactose intolerant and all."

"So sweet of you to remember." The words come out in a low rumble that I really, really shouldn't find as sexy as I do.

"I'm *very sweet*," I tell him, and Donovan snorts.

"Sure you are." He sets my laptop down on the coffee table, a considering look on his handsome face. "You know what you're like, Rune?"

"No," I say, my tone wry. "Do tell."

"You," Donovan says, "are like a chocolate bar with cayenne pepper in it."

Without another word, he turns and walks out, closing the door behind him.

"What the hell?" Charlotte says as Donovan's Prius pulls away from the curb.

I sink down on my couch and grab a slice of pepperoni straight from the box. Three premonitions in one day have left me starving. "Don't ask me."

"He's not wrong, you know. But he really hasn't known you long enough to say something like that. What in the name of God did the two of you get up to today? The Facebook page is on freaking fire."

I take another bite of pizza, nearly moaning at how good it tastes. We Knead Pizza guards the secret recipe for their tomato sauce closely. They won't even tell Charlotte's mother, and she's the mayor. "Please say Mrs. Grant didn't see Donovan carrying me inside."

She strides back to the kitchen, grabbing a couple of wine glasses from the rack and a bottle of red from the pantry. Pouring us both glasses, she hands me one and settles on the couch with her own. "Of course she did. I swear, it's like she has a telephoto lens. And sex radar."

"Ugh," I moan, burying my face in my glass.

"Anyway, tell me everything. Because it definitely seems like tall, dark, and grumpy's got a thing for you."

I almost choke on my wine. "He doesn't! He's dating Jenny Abruzzo."

"Saint Jenny?" Charlotte muses. "Well, that's too bad. He was looking at you like you were his own personal spicy chocolate bar."

"He was just excited to work on my laptop. Technology gives him a boner," I say, but absently. I have bigger things on my mind.

I don't want to tell Charlotte about the monster. She doesn't know what happened that night; I've never talked about it to anyone, beyond what I had to say in court back then. I'd much rather eat pizza and drink wine than revisit the worst time in my life. But maybe Charlotte can find out more than Julia knew—like, exactly when he's getting out and if there's a way to keep the bastard away from both of us without getting me locked up a second time.

"Earth to Rune." Charlotte waves a hand in front of my face. "You okay?"

I blink, startled back to myself. "I'm all right. Today was just… a lot."

"Did you hit your head in the crash?" she says, channeling Worried Charlotte again. "Maybe you shouldn't be drinking wine. I could call Jess and tell her I need to stay here tonight—"

Part of me wants to beg her to do just that. But I don't want to be a burden to Charlotte or her wife, especially after what I'm getting ready to say. Who knows—when Charlotte's heard the truth, maybe she won't even want to speak to me again.

"No need," I say firmly.

"Really?" She narrows her eyes at me. "If you're not concussed, and you and DJ Blue Eyes aren't doing the nasty, then why was he carrying you?"

It's now or never. "Charlotte, do you remember when we were in high school, and I got, um, sent away?"

My voice shakes despite my effort to keep it steady. Sensing my anxiety, Valentine jumps into my lap, curling up. I stroke her fur as Charlotte says, "Yeah, of course. Our junior year. After the fire at your foster family's house. What does that have to do with anything?"

I draw a deep breath. "That fire? I set it."

Bracing myself, I tell her almost everything. How the monster would sneak into my room at night. How his wife never stopped him. How, when I threatened to report him, he left me alone but turned his sights on Julia. How, before he could get his filthy hands on her, I confronted his sorry ass with a lit match in my hand.

I don't tell her about the vision that consumed me, the premonition where I saw him doing to Julia what he did to me. About how I knew that interfering with the natural order of things would cost me, if I could manage it at all. I could stop the monster from hurting Julia, but I would pay for it with my freedom. Just like I saved Officer Asshat and wound up in jail. Not for long, but still.

In my experience, magic—if that's what you want to call my gift—always has a price.

But Charlotte wouldn't believe any of that, so I don't bother with it. Instead, I just tell her about how he refused to let Julia go, how I screamed for her to run. And then I dropped the lit match right on top of those stupid baseball cards he was obsessed with and watched them burn.

"He came for me after that," I say, seeing not my cozy living room but the house that always stank of dirty dishes and cigarettes. Hearing the monster's bellows of rage as he chased me through one smoke-filled room after another, out into the tiny dirt courtyard. "But Julia ran, like I told her. Straight to a neighbor's house. They called 911."

Charlotte's voice is softer than I've ever heard it. "And did he catch you, Rune?"

"He tried," I say, petting Valentine's soft fur. "But, spoiler alert. I had a lot of other matches."

"You lit him on fire and burned his house down. And for that, they sent you away."

I nod, not brave enough to look at her face. "But he went to prison. Julia and I testified, and she…well, you remember her back then. Pure as the driven snow. Turned out there were a lot of other foster kids he'd abused. A real saint, that one."

"God, Rune." Charlotte's voice catches, and when I steal a

glimpse at her, tears are pouring down her cheeks. "How could you keep this inside, all this time? I'm your best friend! You were going through so much, and— Why didn't you tell me?"

"I didn't want to think about it. It was separate from my life with you, you know? I didn't want it to contaminate what we had. I was afraid you'd look at me differently if you knew." I swallow hard, then force myself to hold her gaze. "Do...do you hate me, Charlotte? Now that you know what I'm capable of?"

She's still crying, but when she meets my eyes, the expression in hers is fierce. "Hell, no. You were so, so brave, Rune. You should've been awarded a goddamn medal for what you did, not gotten locked up. Personally, I wish you'd burned the son of a bitch to ashes."

She throws her arms around me, holding me close. Between us, Valentine chirrups, none too happy at being squashed, and Charlotte draws back with a tearful laugh.

"I'm glad you told me. But...why now? And what does this have to do with Donovan?"

"Julia came back tonight," I tell her. "She's doing so well. She went to *Harvard*, if you can believe it. She has this amazing career... But she told me the monster's getting out of prison early, for *good behavior* or some shit. And I—I guess it just got to me. I passed out, and Donovan happened to be driving by, and he caught me."

"That bastard's getting out?" Charlotte has her don't-fuck-with-me attorney face on now. "Oh, *hell* no."

"That night, he made so many threats..." I swallow hard. "I'm scared of what he'll do, Charlotte. I don't want him anywhere near me, or Julia either. She and I put him away for years. I'm afraid he's going to come after us. And I just wondered if maybe you could look into it. Find out when exactly he's going to be released, and the conditions..."

She takes my hands, gripping them tight. "Of course I will. That man will never touch either of you again, Rune. I've got your back."

I hear her. I know she means it. But no matter how hard I try, I can't forget the moment that the ocean of blood consumed me, the waves sweeping over my head, dragging me under. Or that implacable voice, ringing in my ears: *Our day will come.*

I hope neither one has anything to do with the monster.

But I'm terrified I'm wrong.

CHAPTER

Fifteen

I WAKE up the next morning, determined to have a good day if it kills me. Or at least, a better day than yesterday, which really shouldn't be hard.

Every inch of me aches as I drag myself into the shower, and small wonder. My knees are scraped, and though I can't see it, I'm pretty sure my butt's bruised. But after I pop an Advil and do half an hour of yoga, I feel marginally better. I heat up a frozen breakfast burrito, wriggle into my second-favorite pair of jeans and the white, drape-collar top Charlotte bought me for my birthday, do my makeup and tame my hair, and I'm ready to go. Grabbing Donovan's sweatshirt and my laptop bag, I head out the door.

Don't think about the monster, I tell myself, and mostly, I manage it, except for the part where I make sure my mace is clipped onto my keychain and there's no one lurking on the porch or the sidewalk.

Things look up from there. I'm worried my car won't start, but miracles of miracles, it does. I get a spot right in front of Smashbox, my favorite barista makes me a perfect chai, and Sloth Security recognizes me and lets me right up.

Score: Rune, 4. Fate, 0.

I know I need to find out what that horrible premonition

means. I need to call an alarm company and wait to hear what Charlotte discovers. Right now, though, I just want to go to work, like a normal human being.

But 'normal' goes out the window when I walk into the office that Donovan and I are supposed to share.

The first thing I notice is that the place is spotless. The desk that must be Donovan's has a closed laptop, two curved monitors, and absolutely nothing else. No cup of cooling coffee or scattered papers. No framed images of the extraordinarily photogenic Jenny. It's the desk of a man with an obsessive need for order. Or maybe a control freak.

Shocking, I think as I place his sweatshirt in the middle of it, just to mess with him.

What *is* actually shocking is the desk on the other side of the room, set at an angle to give whoever sits at it the ideal view of the window that overlooks Orchard Street. On it is arranged, with perfect precision, a Smashbox to-go mug, a vase of asters, a granola bar, and, inexplicably, a small stuffed mouse toy, with a feathered tail.

I'm staring at this bizarre collection of objects when someone clears his throat behind me. I turn to see Donovan standing there, wearing dark-wash jeans that look like they were custom-made for him and a blue button-down that does altogether too good of a job at bringing out his eyes. "Um," he says. "Hi."

"Hi," I say back, feeling oddly self-conscious.

Both of us fall silent, and I heave an internal sigh. If this is going to be the scintillating level of our conversation, it's going to be a long six months.

"So," Donovan says, shoving his hands into his pockets, "what do you think?"

I tilt my head, confused by the question. "What do I think? I think that if Robert's Rules of Order were an object, it would be your desk."

His face falls, and too late, something occurs to me. Surely not, but—

I gesture at the vase of asters and its buddies. "Did you do all this? And if so, when?"

Donovan shrugs. "It wasn't a big deal. You needed a place to work. Facilities said it would be a couple weeks before you could requisition something, and I couldn't exactly have you sitting on my…" His voice trails off, his face heating like it did at the Grille, and I have to bite my lip to keep from laughing. Weirdly, his gaze tracks to my mouth and lingers. Maybe I have spinach from my breakfast burrito stuck in my teeth? I try to surreptitiously ferret out the offender while Donovan shifts his weight, like he's uncomfortable about something. And then I process the words that left his mouth.

"Hold on a hot minute. Did you buy me this desk? And everything on it?"

"I'll get reimbursed," Donovan says, his tone brusque. "Like I said, you needed to have your own workspace. Efficiency is important, and everything I read said designers need visual inspiration to be at their best. So, I faced the desk toward the window and got some of the same flowers you have in your front yard."

I don't know whether to be amused, touched, aggravated, or some combination thereof. "And the mug?"

"Hydration matters. And food," he says, jerking his chin at the granola bar. "Can't have you passing out. How will we meet our deadlines then?"

My lips twitch. "I see. And what about the toy? Is that to keep me entertained, so I don't talk too much and annoy you?"

"Don't be so egocentric." He prods at an invisible scuff on the hardwood with the toe of his black Oxford. "That's for Valentine."

I narrow my eyes at him, hands on my hips. "What is your obsession with my cat?"

It's his turn to heave a sigh. "I'm not *obsessed*."

"Tell that to your sweatshirt." I point at it, befouling the perfect symmetry of his desk, and I swear I can hear him start to decompensate as he strides over and scoops it up, tucking it into a messenger bag hung on a hook beside our office door.

"You can, um, hang your purse there, too, if you want. There are two hooks."

"Oh, are there really? Thank goodness."

He rolls his eyes so hard, it's a wonder they don't get stuck. "Just give me your laptop, Chaos. We've got a lot of work to do."

"I'm not sure how I feel about that nickname," I say, handing it over. "I might be tempted to return the favor."

Settling behind his pristine desk, he opens my laptop and grimaces. "Do your worst," he mutters, cleaning the screen with a tiny cloth he's produced from somewhere. "I can't wait."

After he proclaims my laptop fit for service, we get stuck in a meeting with Ethan, who, of course, heard about our wreck yesterday through Sapphire Springs' grapevine. As soon as we assure him that we have, indeed, survived in one piece, he launches into a spiel about how he has to deliver a presentation to our mysterious client tomorrow, and he needs us to start prepping materials for it immediately. We try to ask questions, but Ethan just emails us both links to a Dropbox file, hands me a folder filled with potential branding ideas and Donovan another one stuffed with God knows what, and hustles off down the hall to the lobby, yelling, "Sorry! I have a meeting!" over his shoulder.

Donovan stares after him, then looks at me, nonplussed. "A presentation. Tomorrow."

"That's what he said." I thumb through the papers in the folder, looking from one subpar logo concept to another.

"Without even talking to the client."

"Guess so."

"What," he says, gritting his teeth, "and I don't say this lightly —the fuck."

This is how we find ourselves alone at Smashbox nine hours

later, when everyone else has gone home for the day. My eyes are bleary from staring at my screen, trying one color combination after another, and based on the muttered obscenities emanating from Donovan's side of the room, I'm pretty sure he's not doing much better. I've long-since devoured the granola bar and am subsisting on bad break room coffee. Donovan, whose eating habits are as obnoxious as the rest of him, is sipping hot tea. He's scored an orange from somewhere, but he hasn't touched it. All he's done is poke at his keyboard and mutter.

"Won't Jenny worry about where you are?" I say at last, to break the silence that's sprung up between us.

He peers at me over the rim of his mug. "Jenny Abruzzo? What do you mean?"

"I mean," I say, annoyed at having to spell out the obvious, "since you two are dating and all, won't she be a little upset if you just, like, spend your whole night working at Smashbox with me?" Not that I'm any kind of competition, but still.

Donovan blinks at me owlishly, his dark lashes feathering over his cheekbones. "I'm not dating Jenny."

Now it's my turn to blink. "But, yesterday, when we ran into her, you told her you'd see her that night. And you have that sweatshirt with Valentine's face on it."

"Because I volunteer at the animal shelter." He says the words slowly, as if to be sure I understand. "I clean up after-hours, and help them with their website. The sweatshirt was from a fundraiser, like I told you. I got my clothes dirty one day, helping out, and they gave it to me." Setting his mug of tea down, he points at the stuffed mouse with the feathered tail, now edging perilously close to the edge of my desk. "I got a bunch of toys for the shelter's cats, and I had a few left over. So I brought one for Valentine. God knows, she's got her paws full, putting up with you, Chaos."

The last is said dryly, but I've spent enough time with him by now to know that the slight upward tug of his lips indicates amusement. "Very funny. So to recap, you're a good Samaritan who's really not dating Sapphire Springs' one claim to beauty pageantry glory."

Donovan picks up the orange and begins to peel it, setting the pieces of the rind in a neat pile: one, two, three, four. "I'm not dating anyone," he says. "To be perfectly clear."

"Oh," I say stupidly. "Why not?"

A fifth piece of the peel joins the rest. "I work a lot. How about you? Is there a Mr. Chaos who's going to be wondering about your whereabouts?"

"Why?" I counter. "Are you wondering whether such a mythical creature could possibly exist?"

"Just curious." He's succeeded in denuding the orange of its peel and is methodically separating it into sections. The entire office smells of it, tart and sweet.

"No Mr. Chaos. Mythical or otherwise."

"Hmmm," Donovan says, as if weighing this information.

My stomach growls, having apparently decided that a granola bar was an insufficient dinner, and his eyebrows rise. "Hungry?"

"I'm fine," I start to tell him, but he's already gotten up and is striding toward me, orange in hand.

"Open up," he says, to my surprise, and when I do, he slips the segment of orange into my mouth. The pad of his thumb grazes my lip, sending an involuntary shiver through me.

"Can I ask you one more question?" he says, studying my face. "Why did Charlotte call me Sex Spreadsheet Guy?"

I almost choke on my orange. "You heard that?"

"Yep." He grins at me.

"You are such an...an....ugh!" I shove his shoulder, which is pretty damn muscular for a guy who spends so much time in front of a computer. "And you just let me go on and on with that *text spreadsheets nigh* bit? What is wrong with you?"

"Me? I don't think I'm the problem here." He offers me another piece of orange. "Focus, Chaos. Sex Spreadsheet Guy. Discuss."

Maybe I never woke up after I passed out last night. Maybe

this is a hallucination. I decide to go with that theory, which is my only excuse for what happens next. "Blame Georgia in Marketing," I say, violating the #1 rule of the sisterhood: Never throw another woman under the bus. "She thinks you have sex according to a color-coded spreadsheet. She's pretty convinced of it, actually. Because you're so, you know, organized." *And hot,* I think, but mercifully manage to keep to myself.

Donovan blanches. "Holy shit. She…what? Is she friends with Mrs. Grant? Are they part of a cult?"

Despite myself, I snicker. "No cult. Just a lot of free time."

"Hmmm." He regards me, his gaze lingering on my mouth again. "How did Georgia come to this conclusion? Did she take a poll?" His eyebrows knit. "Did you vote in it?"

"There you go again," I sigh. "Always obsessed with the data."

For the second time since we met, I startle Donovan Frost into an honest-to-God laugh. "Rune," he says when he winds down. "This might be inappropriate, in which case please tell me so, but I, um, I really…"

There are so many ways he could finish that sentence: *I really think you're weird. I really dig oranges.* Or something else entirely, which, even though this man drives me insane, I would 100 percent be here for. Whether I was willing to admit it to myself or not, ever since I woke up to the sensation of his fingers stroking my cheek, I've wanted to feel it again. And the way he's looking at me right now, I could swear he's on the same page.

I hold my breath. And naturally, at this inopportune moment, my cell phone rings.

Slipping it out of my jeans pocket, I glance down to see Charlotte's name on the screen. I've managed to keep my worries about the monster at bay, but now they come roaring back with a vengeance. "I have to take this," I say, slipping past Donovan and out into the hallway. Whatever information Charlotte might've gleaned, I don't want an audience when I hear it.

"Hey," I tell her. "Hold on."

When I've gone far enough down the hallway to ensure privacy, I lean against the wall, across from a framed photo of a Tuscan villa. My heart's beating so hard, I can feel it pounding everywhere, in my wrists and throat and chest. "Okay," I say, though it's anything but. "Tell me."

Charlotte clears her throat. "There's no easy way to say this, Rune. Your monster died in his cell last night."

CHAPTER
Sixteen

"WHAT?" I say in disbelief.

"He's dead," she repeats. "The guard found him this morning. He took his own life."

"But…" My mind stutters to a stop. "Why now? He's been locked up since I was sixteen. He's about to get out. Why would he suddenly do this? It doesn't make any sense."

"Who the hell knows, Rune? The good news is, you and Julia are free. There's nothing for you to worry about. He's gone."

"Oh my God." My knees give way, and I slide down the wall until I'm sitting on the floor. "Thank you, Charlotte. Oh my God, thank you so much."

"I didn't do anything. But Rune, please don't ever keep something this important from me again. I just…when I think of you dealing with this all alone, it breaks my heart." She sniffs, like she's trying to hold back tears. "You can tell me anything, okay? Jess and I are here for you. Always. We and the girls are your family. You know that, right?"

"I know," I tell her. And I do. Charlotte wrote me letters the whole time I was in juvie. She never asked me what I'd done to get in trouble, just accepted me when I got out, as if I'd never been gone at all. I don't know what I've done to deserve having her in my life, but whatever it is, I'm grateful for it.

"Good," she says, in her usual brisk voice. "I've got to get back to the girls. They need dinner. But this weekend, we should celebrate. Emma and Sophie have been bugging me like crazy for another painting day with Auntie Rune. Come over and we'll make those chocolate-peanut butter cupcakes you love, okay?"

I tell her I will, and we hang up. For a moment, I just sit, staring up at the terracotta walls and the rolling hills of the Tuscan villa, in shock.

I'm glad he's dead. If that makes me a bad person, then so be it. I need to call Julia and tell her. But first, there's something else I need to do, while I have the courage. Something that will confirm the truth: I'm alive, and the monster isn't. After everything, I have survived.

In our shared office, I find Donovan studying one of his monitors, the folder Ethan gave him open on his desk. When he sees me, he pushes his chair back and gets to his feet. "Is everything okay?"

"More than okay," I tell him. "Everything's great." And before I can lose my nerve, I round his desk, go to my tiptoes, and press my lips to his.

Donovan doesn't move. He just stands there, doing his best impression of a statue, and I worry that I've made a terrible mistake. That I misinterpreted the tension between us earlier, and now I've done something I can never, ever erase. But before I can pull away, Donovan unfreezes. One of his hands rises, cupping my face, holding me still. And then he kisses me back.

His mouth is warm against mine, his lips unexpectedly soft. The kiss is gentle, but his free hand twines roughly in my hair, the low rumble that rises from his chest sending electricity shooting through me. I gasp as he licks along the seam of my lips, and he takes advantage of it, delving inside. His tongue strokes mine as the hand in my hair loosens, trailing down my spine. He tastes like tea and oranges and something deeper, a taste that's somehow just *him*.

Gone is the Ice Man. In his place is this guy, who seems to know exactly what to do with his tongue and his hands and oh, God, his *teeth*, which are currently nipping at my collarbone. His lips ghost along my skin as he kisses away the sting, and I give in to the impulse I've had since I met him, running my fingers through the dark strands of his hair. It's every bit as silky as I imagined, and I can't resist tugging a little, just to see what he'll do.

His head comes up, those blue eyes of his fixed on mine with unnerving intensity. God, they're even more gorgeous up close: sapphire and navy and aquamarine, all swirled together, like the sea on the verge of a storm. I skate my nails along the back of his neck, urging him to kiss me again. But instead, he stumbles backward, right into the corner of his desk, his hip catching the edge of the monitor he was staring at before. It almost pitches onto the floor, but for once he doesn't even seem to notice.

"Wait, Rune," he says, tugging at his collar as if it's too tight. "Just...wait."

Oh no. Humiliation City, here I come. "Did—did you not want me to do that? Because I thought that before, you—"

His eyes find mine again, and this time I'm the one struggling to catch my breath. His gaze radiates hunger, and he grips the desk behind him with both hands, so tightly his knuckles are white. "I wanted it," he grits out. "Obviously. I just... I need a minute."

"Okay," I say, because what else can I do?

We stand there, a foot apart, looking anywhere but at each other, the atmosphere between us thick with awkwardness. My mind races, trying to find something to say that will ease the tension in the air, but no words come.

"Look," I say finally, "maybe I should just—"

"Why did you do that?" Donovan blurts.

"Kiss you? Um, because I wanted to." I stare at him in bewilderment. "And I thought you might want me to, too. What other reason could I possibly have?"

His eyes fall to the floor. "You got that phone call," he says to the hardwood. "And then you came back and you…you…"

"Jumped you?" I can't help but smile. "Maybe you haven't noticed, since you've only known me for a couple of days, but I can be kind of impetuous sometimes."

"Oh, I noticed." He's still talking to the floor, like he can't stand to look at me, and the all-too-familiar irritation common to conversations with Donovan Frost sweeps over me again.

"Sorry I didn't schedule it in your calendar," I snap. "'One spontaneous kiss, to take place between the hours of 6:00 and 10:00 p.m.' Don't worry, it won't happen again."

His head comes up, and the expression on his face floors me. He's not angry, or cold. Instead, he looks…confused. "No…I didn't mean…that's not…"

I take pity on him. "Use your words, Donovan," I say, but nicely.

He sighs, loosening his death grip on his desk. "You wanted to know why I hate Cooper. I, um, never talk about this. But. Back in high school, I liked a girl. A lot. And I, um, thought she liked me too. She wrote me letters. Stuffed them in my locker. They were, um…" A hint of red tints his cheeks.

"Racy?" I offer.

"Sort of. But mostly they were very…sweet. She said she cared about me. I was, um, kind of nerdy back then. More nerdy," he says, intercepting my amused glance. "Braces. Bad skin. Worse hair. Kind of your plug-and-play coding geek. But she said she didn't mind any of that. She said I was nicer than the other guys at school, and smarter, and she knew I was shy but if I asked her out, she would definitely go." His fingers beat a tattoo on the surface of his desk. "So I…did."

I have a sinking feeling I know where this is heading. "Donovan," I say, "you don't have to tell me."

He barrels on, as if I haven't spoken. "She was popular, you know? When I went up to her after school, she was surrounded by a ton of people, including Cooper, who was your basic asshole jock. But I asked her, anyway. And she…she started laughing."

A wave of sympathy for him washes over me. "Oh, Donovan."

"She'd made a bet, you see. With Cooper. He bet I'd fall for it. She bet I wouldn't. If she won—well, who knows. But if he did, well, she had to go out with him." His jaw tightens. "I spent the rest of my senior year watching the girl I had a huge crush on date my brother, while both of them made fun of me every chance they got. Good times."

"What a colossal dickweed." Understatement of the year. "But I don't understand. What does this have to do with me kissing you?"

Donovan's gaze finds mine. "I like you, Rune. Maybe too much."

Now I've definitely fallen into an alternate universe. "You… like me? But you think I'm messy. And impulsive. And chaotic."

"You are all those things," he says impatiently. "But you're also beautiful. And talented. And smart. There's just something about you. I can't explain." He waves a hand, dismissing this. "But I don't get what the hell you see in me. I know I'm not exactly—fun. And that photo, with Cooper on top of you…the way he touched you after the car wreck…" His Adam's apple moves as he swallows. "It's stupid, I know. But I can't help wondering—"

The light dawns. "You think I'm pretending to hate Officer Asshat? You think I *made a bet* with him over making out with you?"

Donovan doesn't answer me, but the half-hopeful, half-resigned look on his face says it all.

Sweet purple ponies on rollerblades. Donovan Frost, Ice Man incarnate, is…shy. And anxious. Who could blame him, after what Cooper put him through?

"Let me clarify a few things." I raise a single finger. "I know you think I'm a compulsive liar, but I swear on Valentine's life that I find Officer Asshat too kind a term for your despicable ring-worm of a sibling. I have not now, nor at any other time, engaged in a bet with him."

Finger number two. "I understand very well what it's like to be bullied for being different, and I would never, ever treat someone else that way."

Finger number three. "As for what I see in you, I have no idea what you were like in high school, but now? You're hot as fire. You kiss like you should teach it for a living. And personally?" I gaze up at him through my lashes. "I happen to find smart, shy guys very, very sexy."

Donovan's jaw drops, and he shuts it with a snap. "Well, then," he says hoarsely, and reaches for me.

The energy around us feels charged as his hands close on my waist, pulling me against him. His mouth seals over mine, and his warmth seeps through me, setting my body ablaze. I breathe in his vanilla-and-cedar scent, craving more of it. More of *him*.

He lifts me onto his desk, heedless of the papers that scatter to the floor. When I wrap my legs around his hips, he makes the low growl that is fast becoming my favorite sound in the world. "I was wrong," he gasps. "You're not a chocolate bar with cayenne, Rune. You're a goddamn addiction."

And then, with truly diabolical timing, my fourth premonition in forty-eight hours hits.

CHAPTER
Seventeen

I WALK through the door into the red-tinged light and find myself not in the familiar white room, but outside, in a beautiful garden. It's a perfect fall day, rich with the scent of honeysuckle. I'm at the head of a grassy aisle strewn with rose petals, flanked on either side by folding chairs filled with people. For some reason, everyone's eyes are fixed on me.

Classical music drifts through the air, the plaintive call of a violin and the deeper, answering call of a cello. The sun streams down, dappling the garden, catching the sparkles in my dress: ivory lace with a champagne underlay, the train sweeping behind me like a wave as I walk. I'm barefoot, the grass soft beneath my feet.

At the end of my path is an arched arbor, the roof made of twisting limbs twined with white-flowered vines. Beneath it stands a man with his back to me, wearing a charcoal suit, impeccably pressed. His shoulders are broad, his hair dark as a crow's wing and gleaming in the golden light. I have the undeniable sense that he's waiting for me, and at the thought, happiness floods me. I feel insanely, incomparably lucky that this man will soon be mine.

This is my wedding day.

The musicians strike up a more soulful tune, and the man beneath the arbor turns. His piercing blue eyes meet mine, and his face lights with joy.

Holy hell. My groom is Donovan.

Shock reverberates through me as his lips form my name. But before I can take another step, a warm, viscous liquid washes over my feet. I glance down in horror to find red waves lapping at the hem of my dress. The rusty scent of blood fills the air, drowning out the perfume of the flowers, as the tide rises, buoying the chairs, flowing relentlessly down the aisle toward Donovan.

He screams my name, his face white with shock, and I fight the current, desperate to get to him. But it's no use. The train of my dress drags me down. I watch, helpless and desperate, as a wave sweeps over his head and the ocean of blood swallows him whole.

I'm sure the premonition lasts only a few seconds, but it feels like an eternity. When I open my eyes, I'm back in the office, sitting on the edge of Donovan's desk, still wrapped in his arms.

"Rune?" His voice is low, husky. "Are you okay?"

I shake all over, a fine tremor that runs through me from head to toe. Frowning, he takes me by the shoulders and peers into my face. "Did I hurt you?"

"N-no." I shudder, and he frees one of his hands, stroking my hair back from my face.

"Then what? Talk to me. Please."

"I c-can't." My teeth are chattering, so hard I almost bite my tongue, and Donovan's gaze darkens.

"If it wasn't me, then it was someone," he says. "You don't have to tell me. But God, Rune, I would never make you do anything you didn't want to. You know that, right?"

At the sincerity in his voice, tears stream down my cheeks. Wordless, I nod.

"Please don't cry." He wipes away my tears with the tips of his fingers, his touch so careful and deliberate. Just like everything else about him, until he lost all of his control in my arms. I want nothing more than to make him do it again. But at the thought of where that will lead—at what my premonition showed me—I cry harder.

This beautiful, infuriating man is meant to be my husband. And then, on our wedding day, our marriage will somehow cost him his life.

Donovan frowns, his teeth sinking into his lower lip. "You're scaring me, Rune. Did I—did I do something? I swear to Christ, I never meant—"

"It's not you." I pull away from him, trembling, and he lets me go, stepping away from the desk. As soon as my feet hit the floor, I back away from him, giving us both some distance. That doesn't help: now I can see him clearly, and he looks as ravaged as I feel. His chest is heaving, his lips swollen from our kisses. His hands open and close at his sides, like it's an effort not to reach for me. The pull between us is magnetic, as if we're two halves of a single entity that are trying desperately to find their way back to each other. To become whole.

I've never felt anything like it. Have never imagined I could.

But it's the one thing I can never, ever have.

"Donovan," I whisper, "I can't do this. *We* can't do this."

He peers at me, his features etched with confusion, pain shimmering in those unfairly gorgeous blue eyes. "What do you mean?"

It hurts to look at him. "I mean," I say, avoiding his gaze, "that this is wrong."

"Because we work together?" His eyebrows knit. "I know it has the potential for…awkwardness. But I'm not your supervisor, Rune. And there's nothing in the employee manual saying it's against regulations. So if that's the only reason…"

Despite the dire situation, I can't help snorting. "You looked it up?"

"I read the manual when Smashbox hired me!" He folds his arms across his chest, looking adorably indignant. "Didn't you?"

"Not in its entirety. And even if I had, I don't think I'd remember that little detail."

"I may have revisited it last night. Just out of curiosity."

My snort becomes a full-out laugh, only slightly impeded by my tears. "And here I thought dishonesty was one of your pet peeves, Donovan Frost."

"Yeah, well, until ten minutes ago, I thought *I* was one of yours." He takes a tentative step closer to me, and then, when I don't retreat, one more. "What just happened between us, Rune… I want you to know, I've never done anything like that before."

His eyes are wide, filled with wonder, lit with hope. I have to extinguish it. But I don't want to. All I want is to taste him again. It's intoxicating.

"What?" I tease, against my better judgment. "Almost have sex in your office? Disturb the order of your pristine desk? I'm afraid you'll have to be a bit more specific, Mr. Frost."

"All of that. Any of it. I've never *felt* anything like that." He prowls a step closer, his eyes on my face. "Tell me it's not just me, Rune. Tell me you felt it too."

I should tell him I didn't feel anything at all. That what happened between us was a mistake. That it meant nothing more to me than a meaningless, random hookup. It's the only way to save his life.

But God, the scorching look in his eyes, the memory of those big hands of his gripping my hips, his body moving against mine…

"Rune," he says again. My name is an incantation, a plea.

I can have this, just for tonight, can't I? It doesn't mean I have to marry the guy. I can just…not. What's he going to do, drag me to the altar by my hair?

I know better. But, as if driven by a force as inexorable as the one that powered my premonitions, I take one step toward him, then another. He meets me halfway, and I stand on my tiptoes, grabbing his shirt collar and tugging him down to me. The moment our lips touch, I'm done for.

My mouth opens under his, inviting, and his tongue traces my lips, then sweeps inside. One of his hands plunges into my hair, anchoring me to him. The other grips my hip, guiding us backward until he cages me against the door. He kisses the tears from my face, then trails hot kisses down my neck, his tongue flicking along my collarbone. "Tell me if you don't want this," he murmurs against my skin. "I'll stop, I promise."

I should tell him exactly that. But Donovan Frost is a man who hates liars. And just once, I want to tell him the truth and have him believe me.

"I don't want you to stop," I say, slipping my hands under his shirt. His skin is an inferno under my hands, like he has a fever. "I want—"

"What?" His hand leaves my hip, hitching my leg so it wraps around him. He presses against me and we both moan. "God, Rune, just tell me."

It's like I've drunk some kind of truth serum, because when I open my mouth, what falls out is something I'd hardly dared to voice, even to myself. I've been numb for so damn long. But now the monster is dead, and maybe, just maybe, I can let my armor fall.

"Donovan," I whisper, knotting my fingers in his dark hair. "I want you to make me feel."

He draws back at that, looking down at me. His pupils are blown wide, his irises only a rim of blue. "Jesus Christ. What are you doing to me?"

"I—"

"Whatever it is," he says roughly, "do it some more."

He lifts me then. I wrap my legs around his waist and we move together against the door, still, somehow, fully clothed. His mouth devours mine, his tongue licking at me and his teeth biting gently into my lower lip, nipping along my jaw. He presses against me, moving me how he wants me, and I dig my nails into his shoulders, gasping.

"Feel this," he whispers, one hand braced on the door above my head and the other supporting me, holding me up. "Feel *me*."

And, oh God, I do. I feel *everything*.

In that moment, I see our future, unrolling like a scroll in front of me. Nights spent twined around each other. Days spent trading banter and creating a life of our own design, my chaos and his obsessive organization somehow folding seamlessly together into a beautiful whole. We'll argue and we'll fight but we'll always come back together. Until one day he'll propose and I'll say yes and then…and then…

My premonitions always come true. And if Donovan and I give in to the attraction between us, it will only end one way.

In his death.

Seeing the future is my gift. And my curse.

I refuse to let it curse him, too.

Gathering every bit of my resolve, I flatten the palms of both hands against his chest and shove. Startled, he drops me to the floor and stumbles backward, his blue eyes dazed.

"Rune, what—"

"I don't want you to stop," I say again. "But we have to."

I yank the door open, snatch my purse from the hook beside it, and flee.

CHAPTER

Eighteen

IT'S JUST my bad luck that I run out of Donovan's office and straight into Ethan. Literally.

He's rounding the corner as I flee down the hallway, Donovan calling my name. My hair's in my face, the brown waves a mess from our ill-fated make-out session, so I don't see Ethan until I plow right into him with an impact that sends me stumbling backward…straight into Donovan, who's come after me.

Freaking perfect.

Donovan steadies me, his hands on my shoulders, then, just as quickly, lets me go. I step away from him, trying desperately to tame my hair and look like I wasn't just climbing Smashbox's data engineer's gorgeous body. What if Ethan can tell? Also, what is he doing here at ten o'clock at night?

"You two are working late," Ethan says. Is it my imagination, or are those five words laden with innuendo?

"I—well, we—" I begin, tugging at the hem of my shirt to straighten it. Surely it would be reasonable for him to assume that I look bedraggled because the two of us just collided. I was hurrying when he came around the corner. There's no way he got a really solid look at me.

Right?

"We were working on the new project. Like you asked us to," Donovan says, stepping smoothly into the breach. I spare him a glance, afraid even that will give away the fact that those full, sculpted lips of his just spent the past ten minutes glued to mine. To my annoyance, he looks cool and composed, the cuffs of his button-down perfectly aligned and his blue eyes as icy as ever. For an instant, I wonder if I've imagined the whole thing.

But no. My mouth still tingles from his kisses. And, much less romantically, my bruised butt hurts from its encounter with his desk. It's amazing what fails to make an impression when there's four thousand gallons of sexy, sexy hormones pumping through your body.

"Such dedicated employees," Ethan says, his teeth gleaming white through the neatly trimmed thicket of his beard. "I have to say, I'm impressed with your teamwork. The way things were going the first time the two of you were in my office, I thought I might have to send you to a cabin in the woods together, cut off from civilization, just to force you to learn how to get along. But here you are, collaborating into the wee hours. That car accident must've been quite the bonding experience."

I fight back the image of what it would be like to be snowed in somewhere with Donovan, in front of a roaring fire, a rom-com forced proximity trope come to life. He'd probably be stacking the kindling in size order or something equally control-freak-esque. Maybe shirtless, for maximum viewing pleasure. I'd sneak up and wrap my arms around him, scaring the hell out of him and disrupting his absurd organizational system. He'd be mad, of course, but I'd make it up to him by dropping to my knees right there and—

Oh. My. God. What the hell is wrong with me?

My face flames as I stammer, "Y-yes. Very bondage. I mean bonding." Jesus take the wheel. "Nothing says *get to know you better* like vehicular catastrophe," I barrel on, my mouth having apparently decided to carry on without my consent. "Unless it's an unprecedented deadline."

Great. Now I've managed to mention BDSM in relationship to my coworker and offend my boss in the space of four sentences. Maybe I should just strip and run naked down the hallway, for maximum humiliation.

Ethan, thank God, looks amused. His lips curl up, and he folds his arms across his chest. "You're right, Rune, the deadline was unprecedented. It surprised me as much as it did you. But you're two of my most trusted employees, and I knew if anyone was up to the task, you were. Exhibit A: you're still here, although it looks like I surprised you in the midst of a much-needed coffee run. Or maybe you were done and leaving for the night? In which case, I can't wait to see what you've come up with."

Instinctively, I fumble for my laptop, and realize I left it on my desk. My Mac is like an extension of my body; for me to be unnerved enough to abandon it is an indication of my messed-up state of mind. "I—I could show you," I say finally, fumbling for a hint of professionalism. "I can't speak for Donovan, but based on the details you shared with us, I have some preliminary mockups for a logo. I've also started putting together the basics of several potential branding packages. Without knowing more about the program's ultimate functionality, it's hard for me to tell if I'm spot-on, but you did give us a good sense of some complementary services that are already on the market, so hopefully I'm in the ballpark."

Ethan's face lights up. "Fantastic. When I saw the light was still on in your office, I hoped I'd get a glimpse behind the scenes. Shall we?"

He gestures in Donovan's direction, toward the half-open door through which I just escaped. With a sense of doom pervading every inch of my body, I trudge back the way I came, Donovan stalking beside me. He doesn't say a word, but his jaw is so tight, you could use it to crack walnuts. Luckily, this is so close to his usual Ice Man m.o., Ethan doesn't seem to notice.

Keep it together, Rune, I chant to myself as I walk over to my laptop and type in my password. But it's not easy.

God, what would we have done if Ethan had come around the corner two minutes earlier? He wouldn't even have been able to open the office door, because we were too busy devouring each other against it. I don't care what the employee manual says, that's about as unprofessional as it gets. And if I lose my job, I'll have to leave Sapphire Springs. This is a small town; unless I manage to score remote work, I won't be able to afford to stay here. I'll lose my little cottage, and Charlotte, Jess, and the girls, the closest thing I have to a family.

Now that the monster's dead, I don't have to worry that he'll come back here and find me. I can finally just…live. Sure, living means dealing with my premonitions, but that's the only life I've ever known. Sapphire Springs is my home.

I have to make this work.

"So," I say in my best here's-why-you-hired-me voice as Ethan comes to stand behind me, "in the materials you shared this morning, you said the client wants to project a classy image while simultaneously implying a sense of modernity and a cutting-edge sensibility. I've come up with three potential color palettes to use throughout the website and other branding materials, as well as the logo, although of course that needs to work just as well in black and white…"

Moving on autopilot, I take Ethan through the pitch deck I've put together. He asks questions and requests adjustments, all of which I address while doing my best to pretend that I can't sense Donovan's lurking presence. He's retreated behind his curved monitors again, but I can still feel him there, the air between us heavy with all we've left unsaid.

"Excellent!" Ethan says when I'm done. "I'm looking forward to showing this to the client tomorrow. Yes, it's Saturday, but they're eager to see what you've pulled together. In the meantime, I've scheduled a meeting for us to meet with the historical society on Monday at four. One of the backers behind this project serves on the board, and there are two professional genealogists who might prove to be an excellent source of inspiration for both of you."

This is one of my least favorite things about Ethan: he always assumes that you can make time for whatever he's got planned. But he pays well, and he's so much like a golden retriever—excited and joyful even while he's tramping mud all over your white carpet—that it's hard to be mad. "Monday at four," I say, pulling out my phone to add the meeting to my calendar. "Got it."

"Frost!" Ethan says cheerfully, turning to address the man behind the monitors. "Have you taken a look at this? Rune's come up with some stellar options here."

From Donovan's direction comes a noncommittal grunt. "Design's not really my thing. You hired me to code, so that's what I'm doing."

It's so blunt as to tip over into nastiness, but Ethan must be used to this—either that, or he doesn't care—because he ignores it. "Yes, but the two of you are supposed to be working together. Who knows, maybe Rune's work will inspire you. Get over here, would you?"

With another grunt, this one of annoyance, Donovan gets to his feet, in full-on Ice Man mode—either genuinely disinterested, aggravated with Ethan, or pissed that I fled without much of an explanation. Try as I might, I can't see a hint of the man who pinned me against the door. He comes to stand next to my desk, a good two feet away, and Ethan sighs. "How are you going to see from there? I know you don't care for humans, Frost, but Rune's not going to bite you."

My face flushes at the memory of Donovan's teeth nipping at my collarbone. The back of my neck feels like it's on fire as he edges closer, until he's close enough to touch. He's careful to keep a couple of inches between us, but I swear the tension's so thick, it's tough to breathe. "Nice," he mutters, eyes fixed on the screen.

"You don't even know what you're looking at! Rune, show him the iconography options you're proposing for the website.

One's more sleek, but the other's more intricate. I'd love to know your opinion."

"I'm not really qualified—" Donovan begins in a low rumble, just as the lights in the office flicker. And then, in spectacular fashion, they all go out, leaving us in inky darkness.

CHAPTER
Nineteen

"SHIT!" Donovan says, and I hear him fumble toward his desk, probably making sure his backup's backup's backup is functioning or whatever the technical term might be.

I ought to be concerned about my laptop—it's not plugged into a surge protector, and the pitch deck wasn't backed up to the cloud. If my Mac's fried, I'm screwed. But instead, the familiar red haze creeps over my vision again. And when it clears, seared into the air six inches from my face is a fiery symbol: a scroll, crossed with a dagger.

I stare at it, mouth agape. The symbol's huge, as wide across as my desk and blazing, with the scroll's edges curling and the dagger's blade razor-sharp. Flames dance around the edges, casting flickering shadows on my face. Heat radiates from it, scorching me.

In all my years of having premonitions, nothing like this has ever happened to me before. Could it be a trick of the light, somehow reflected from a wild party that I had no idea downtown Sapphire Springs was hosting? That must be it: they overloaded the power grid and somehow we're seeing their bizarre scroll-and-dagger bat-signal up here.

Even as I formulate the idea, I know it's absurd. For one thing, as evidenced by the Shenanigans disaster, everyone knows everyone else's business in Sapphire Springs. If there was some type of wacky, power-grid-overloading bacchanalia going on downtown, I'd know about it, whether or not I wanted to. For another, this is the tallest building in town. It makes no sense that a symbol projected from the ground would wind up in the middle of Donovan's fifth-floor office, much less emitting enough heat to rival a sauna. And for a third, if our power is out, then the hypothetical party-hoster's probably is, too.

Still, I can't help but give it a shot. "Does anyone else see…" I begin, hoping against hope that their answer will be *Yep, of course, super weird, right?*

But before I can finish my sentence, the lights flicker once again and the power comes back on.

There's no more red haze. And no symbol emblazoned on the air. Just Donovan poking at his keyboard, Ethan looking bemused, and me, trying not to panic.

"Are you okay, Rune?" Ethan says, peering at me. "You look like you've seen…well, I'd say a ghost, but that's rather clichéd, isn't it?" He chuckles. "Wish we had ghosts in this building, actually. We could probably monetize them around Halloween. You could make us some killer graphics." He grins at me. "Get it, Rune? Killer graphics? For a ghost tour?"

I give him a weak smile. "Yeah, I get it. Super funny. Um, no. No ghost. I, uh, don't like the dark, that's all." The moment the words leave my mouth, I wish I could take them back. *Don't like the dark?* What am I, five?

"Oh, I get that!" Ethan says. "Don't tell anyone, but I slept with the light on until I was fifteen. Drove my brother crazy." He winks at me. "You okay over there, Frost? Lose anything important?"

Donovan's head jerks up, as if he's just realized he's not alone in the room. "No," he says, sounding distracted. "I thought for a moment—but I'd made sure to put redundancies in place—we're fine. Fine," he says again, like he's trying to convince himself.

Surely if he or Ethan saw the symbol, they would have said something. But I have to ask, to be sure. "Um," I say tentatively, "did either of you see anything when the lights went out?"

"You mean, like with my unbelievably awesome night vision?" Ethan asks, just as Donovan mutters, "Only the last six months of my work going down the drain."

So much for that. Also, how the hell Ethan is so chipper at 10:00 p.m., after getting into the office at who-knows-what-o'clock this morning, is beyond me. Literally the only thing I've ever seen get under his skin is lateness. At the moment, for instance, he's chattering on about a legally blind astronomer who actually does have incredible night vision. Under other circumstances, I'd be intrigued, but right now, all I want to do is figure out what the heck just happened.

What does the symbol mean? Why would it appear now, and only to me? What's it trying to tell me? And if it's another kind of premonition, how am I supposed to act on it if I have no idea what it stands for?

A scroll. A dagger. And those flames. Could the symbol have something to do with the ocean of blood and the premonition of Donovan's death, and if so, what?

Exhaustion crashes down on me. Suddenly I feel every bruise and scrape from the past twenty-four hours, not to mention the emotional weight of seeing Julia again, discovering the monster's death, finding Donovan only to lose him, and all of my premonitions. I just want to go home and sleep for about a thousand years, except I can't. I need to reverse image search that stupid symbol, to see if I can dig up anything that will tell me what it is and what I'm meant to do about it. And to do that, I need to get out of here.

"I'm sharing the pitch deck with you now," I tell Ethan, leaning over my laptop. "And then I'm going to go home, if that's okay with you."

"Of course it's okay." He beams at me. "It's late on a Friday night. I should've brought the two of you pizza, or something. Besides, better get going before we have another surge. I'll stick around for a while, wrap up some loose ends, but you two should get out of here."

Donovan clears his throat, emerging from behind his monitors once more. "I just need to check on a few things, Rune, but if you wait a couple minutes, I'll be leaving too. Do you want me to walk you to your car?"

It's a kind offer, but the last thing I want is to be alone with him right now. The hell with investigating that stupid symbol; I don't trust myself not to drag Donovan into an alleyway and kiss him until neither of us can breathe. And downtown Sapphire Springs is full of all kinds of convenient nooks and crannies. Hell, it probably has video cameras that the Sinsters have set up, just to catch folks in exactly this kind of nefarious act. With my luck, they'd publish it in the online version of the Springs Sing, our local paper. And even if Ethan's somehow oblivious to the goings-on on the Shenanigans page, there's no way he'd miss *that*.

"No, I'm good," I say, trying to sound easy-breezy rather than how I feel: like every single one of my nerve endings is aflame with an unfortunate blend of anxiety and desire. I sling my laptop bag over my shoulder and grab my purse, unable to meet Donovan's eyes. "We're talking downtown Sapphire Springs, you know? The worst thing that could happen is that a black cat will cross my path, and honestly, I think I've used up my quota of bad luck for the day."

"If you're sure," Donovan says, looking from me to the window and back again.

Maybe I'm being naïve, but with the monster dead, I feel like nothing can touch me. Yeah, I need to figure out the deal with the symbol and my premonitions, but physically, I feel invincible tonight. Like I want to celebrate my body for being strong, for surviving, and for outliving the greatest threat it ever faced. Making out with Donovan again feels like an awesome way to commemorate this turn of events. It also feels like the first step on the road toward disaster.

But he's looking right at me now, his expression concerned

and almost…sweet, and all I can say is, thank God Ethan's in the room right now. Because otherwise, I'd be hard-pressed not to hop back on Donovan's desk and have my way with him, premonition or no premonition.

No, Rune, I tell myself. *Bad, bad, bad.*

"I took martial arts classes for years," I say, forcing a smile. It's the truth; if the monster ever came for me again, I wanted to be able to defend myself. "Plus, I have mace on my keychain." I hold it up so both he and Ethan can see. "I'm good, I promise."

Before Donovan can say another word, I wave goodbye and leave, breathing a sigh of relief as soon as the elevator's doors whoosh shut behind me. The lobby is deserted, and when I step onto the sidewalk, there's no one to be seen in either direction.

I should feel happy to finally be alone, to have the space to think through everything that's happened tonight. But instead, no matter what I told Donovan, I feel on edge, ill-at-ease. And the whole time I walk down Orchard Street, past The Bookaholic and Brew Box and the yoga studio, I can swear I feel the pressure of someone's eyes on my back.

Watching me.

Twenty

SO MUCH FOR making chocolate-peanut butter cupcakes. Instead, Charlotte and the girls drag me to Books, Bites, and Bedlam, Sapphire Springs' annual library fundraiser, put on by— you guessed it—the Sinsters. Jess begged off, claiming it was "too peoply." Which I get; just about everyone in Sapphire Springs turns out for this.

Normally, BBB is one of my favorite events of the year, the highlight of the beginning of fall. I love everything about it: the sweet aroma of caramel apples; the Ferris wheel, from the top of which there's a great view of the mountains that surround Sapphire Springs; the carousel, with its hand-painted horses and cheerful tunes; and the way the whole town comes out to support a good cause. As a kid, when things were really crappy, I'd come here and just wander around, absorbing the way everyone seemed so *happy*. It always felt like magic to me. But today, with the events of the past forty-eight hours hanging over my head, I'm having a tough time.

I Googled that symbol, but came up with absolutely nothing. Did I hallucinate it? I'm sure I didn't. But then what was it? And what could it possibly mean?

"Auntie Rune!" Emma tugs at my hand as we step beneath the

arbor that marks the entrance to High Valley Park. "Look, there's a petting zoo. They have *llamas*. I heard they spit. Is that true? Has a llama ever spit at you?"

I force a smile. It's not too hard, given that Emma and Sophie are my two favorite people in the world. "Nope," I say, stroking her silky black hair. While Emma's the mirror image of Noah Yoon, the girls' bio dad and one of Charlotte and Jess's good friends, Sophie looks like Charlotte: heart-shaped face, freckles, and brown eyes that can transform from sunny to stormy in an instant. That's where the similarities end, though. Where Sophie's content to go with the flow, Emma's a planner, like her mother. And right now, she's busy scheduling every moment of our day.

"So, first we're gonna get cotton candy," she says, ticking the list off on her fingers. "Then we can ride the carousel, right, Mama? You said. And then we'll be hungry, but since there are food trucks, we can all choose what we want." This comment is directed at Sophie, a notoriously picky eater. "*I'm* gonna have tacos, plus apple cider with real cinnamon sticks. Then we can go to the petting zoo. And then—hey! Where are you going?"

Sophie, who as per usual could give two figs about Emma's itinerary, has darted toward the lawn where all of the food vendors are set up. She's heading not for the cotton candy stand but for the Peach Tree Grille's setup, from which the delectable smell of chargrilled burgers emanates. A girl after my own heart.

"Come back!" Emma wails, chasing after her sister. "You didn't hear the best part!"

Charlotte chuckles as she watches Emma weave between the white tents and milling families, in desperate pursuit. Then her eyes narrow, fixing on my face. "Now that we're alone, I wanted to ask if you're okay, after…well, everything. I know what I told you was good news, but I'm sure it had to be shocking. And today —you don't seem like yourself."

"I'm fine," I say, pasting on what I hope is a sincere smile.

Charlotte snorts. "Have you forgotten what I do for a living? I can tell a liar a mile away. You don't *have* to be fine, Rune. I'm here for you."

I wish, more than anything, that I could tell her about my premonition about Donovan. About that horrible voice, saying *Our day will come*, and the bizarre symbol that flashed in the air right after the power died. But she would think I'd lost my mind. So instead I say, "It's just a lot to process. But I'm all right, I promise."

"Hmmm." We thread our way between the souvlaki tent and the gourmet ice cream sandwich truck, in the wake of the girls, before she speaks again. "This wouldn't have anything to do with the gorgeous laptop repairman who was at your house two nights ago, would it?"

I haven't told Charlotte that Donovan and I hooked up. That would open the door to a whole lot of questions I'm not willing to answer. But now, I'm in the uncomfortable situation of having to lie to my best friend. "What? No! Of course not," I mumble unconvincingly.

"Because," Charlotte says, coming to a halt a few feet from her sister's cupcake table, where Emma and Sophie are engaged in a heated argument, "you could do a lot worse."

"You don't even know him!"

"I know he's easy on the eyes," she says. "Which is a start. And he stayed with you after you passed out. He didn't have to do that. I saw the way he looked at you. Are you absolutely *sure* he's dating Jenny?"

Ugh to the ninety-eighth power. "He's not, all right? It turns out he just volunteers at the animal rescue shelter. I, um, misinterpreted."

Charlotte breaks into a huge smile. "I knew it! See, he's a good guy. Maybe you should give it a chance, see where things go."

Oh, I gave it a chance already, Charlotte. On his desk. Against the door. "Maybe," I say, in hopes that this will get her off my back.

But no dice. "I've always wondered why you don't really date anyone," she says, regarding me with her trademark penetrating gaze. "First, I thought you just weren't interested. But then I could see you *were,* and held yourself back." She squeezes my hand again. "I get it now. I know you've been afraid to let anyone in because of that monster. But he's gone, and it's time for you to be brave. You deserve love, Rune. You have such a big, beautiful heart."

Her sincerity makes my heart ache. "Charlotte, you and the girls are my family, and I love you all so much. Even when you argue over llamas and chocolate frosting." I gesture at the girls, who are in dire need of an intervention. Charlotte's sister, Roni, is trying to reason with them, or maybe bribe them with cupcakes. But if the rising tide of red in Emma's cheeks is any indication, she's failing miserably. "I appreciate the vote of confidence, really. But I don't know if I'm ready for anything more." Especially because my future husband is destined to bite the dust at the altar.

Roni is casting desperate looks in Charlotte's direction, but my best friend ignores them. "All I'm saying is, you never know when Mr. Tall, Dark, and Spreadsheet might sweep you off your feet. Just promise me you'll keep an open mind, okay?"

I laugh, despite the turmoil inside me. "All right, I promise. Now, we better do something about your children, before they take the cupcake stand down WWE-style."

We end up stopping at the mobile truck for Sapphire Springs' blood bank, and along with what seems like half the town, Charlotte and I do our annual good deed of donating. Then, one chocolate velvet cupcake (mine), one peach cobbler cupcake (Sophie's), one cotton candy (Emma's), and one United Nations-quality negotiating session (Charlotte's) later, we're on our way to what, as far as my best friend is concerned, is this event's star attraction: The Rolling Tome, Sapphire Springs' bookmobile. All the books are donated, and the sales go toward buying new ones for the library—which, in Charlotte's opinion, gives her carte blanche to buy as many as she wants. Charlotte's TBR is as tall as Emma, and most of it is stacked on her bedside table. Poor Jess, is all I can say.

By a miracle, we make it to the bookmobile without World War III breaking out or Sophie escaping again. Charlotte disappears inside and the kids follow, charmed by the giant teddy bears that form a barrier between the adult and children's section. I linger by the outdoor racks, checking out a display of Ilona Andrews novels to see if they've got the one I've been trying to find forever. Whereupon I'm promptly accosted by Mrs. Fontaine, her silver-streaked hair flowing to her shoulders and her blue eyes sparkling with glee.

"Rune, dear!" she says, holding up a copy of *Blood Heir*. "Looking for this?"

How the heck does she know? "It's like you're psychic," I mutter, taking it from her.

"Hardly, dear. Just a connoisseur of my patrons' interests. This one came in and I held it specially for you. Although"—she drops me a wink behind her horn-rimmed glasses—"maybe you won't be doing as much reading as usual, eh?"

"What do you mean?" I say, a sinking feeling in my stomach.

"Well, we saw you with Donovan at the Peach Tree." She gives me a Cheshire Cat's grin. "You two made quite the pair."

Oh, sweet purple ponies on steroids. "Yes, I know you saw us," I tell her. "I think all of Sapphire Springs knows. Hashtag fatedmates? Hashtag firstdatemagic? Really?"

"Just giving you a little help, dear. After all, who knows where things between the two of you might lead? I can see the headline in the Springs Sing now: *Whipped Into Love: From Milkshakes to Marriage*. Catchy, no?"

She's grinning diabolically, and too late, I remember how eager she was for me to read *By a Thread*. God, she'd probably submit a wedding announcement to the town's free paper just for shits and giggles. "We're not dating!" I say, much too loudly.

My exclamation brings Charlotte, Emma, and Sophie to the door of the bookmobile, just in time for Mrs. Fontaine's next suggestion: "Or, oooh, I know! *The Sweetest Proposal.* Do you like that better?"

"No one is marrying anyone!" I shriek, loud enough that a bluebird roosting atop the bookmobile gives me a judgmental glare and takes flight.

"Methinks the lady doth protest too much," Mrs. Fontaine says, wagging a finger at me. "But perhaps the Seer of Sapphire Springs can give you the answers you seek."

"The—what?"

"Right over there," she says, pointing. "A glimpse into your future."

I follow her index finger to its natural conclusion and see a tent draped with tapestries, closed on three sides. At the front is a beaded curtain hung to look like a door and a sign that reads, *Get Your Fortune Told! It's For the Books!*

Seeing more of the future is the very *last* thing I need. Not to mention, if there's a Seer of Sapphire Springs, she's standing right in front of them, not ensconced inside that tent. "Thanks so much, but I'll pass."

But Sophie and Emma's eyes have gone wide, and they start jumping up and down. "Please, Auntie Rune?" Sophie begs. "It'll be so much fun!"

Charlotte joins in, the traitor. "Come on, Rune. Open-minded, remember?"

I want to say no. Christ on a bike, do I want to. But Sophie's got her little hands clasped beneath her chin, and Emma's already listing all the ways we can adjust our itinerary to make time for it, and so, with a sigh, I give in.

"All right, fine. Let's see what the Seer of Sapphire Springs has to say."

I CANNOT BELIEVE I'm doing this.

Sophie, Emma, and Charlotte tried to come in with me, but Mrs. Fontaine insisted I go alone. "The magic won't work if you're accompanied by others," she said, with another wink.

As I walk across the lawn toward the seer's tent, my only consolation is that at least whatever money I have to shell out for this crap will go toward the library, which is where I used to hang out after school to avoid the monster. Small wonder Mrs. Fontaine knows me so well; she practically raised me between the hours of 3:00 and 7:00 p.m.

I pause for a moment outside the beaded curtain, bracing myself for whatever absurdity lies within. Then I square my shoulders and walk through, straight into a cliché.

The tent is dimly lit, thanks to the tapestries draped over it, the air heavy with incense. Mood music is playing in the background. And behind a small table adorned with a crystal ball and a deck of tarot cards sits…Hot Yoga Grandma.

Fuck me running.

"Hello, Rune," she says when she sees me, raising a perfectly drawn eyebrow. "We haven't formally met, but I feel as if I know you."

I just bet you do, I want to say. *You and every other member of the Sinsters, with your sneaky little iPhones.* But I restrain myself. I've already assaulted the woman. Adding rudeness to the mix isn't going to help my cause. "Nice to meet you. I'm, um, here for a reading."

"Welcome," she says, offering me a serene smile. "I'm Ella Campbell, the Seer of Sapphire Springs. I expected I'd be seeing you sooner or later."

"You wouldn't be much of a seer if you didn't," I blurt, then want to kick myself all over again. "Sorry," I mumble. "For saying that. And, um, for the apples."

"Oh, I know you are, dear." She gestures at the folding chair across the table from her. "Have a seat, why don't you?"

Resigned, I sink into the chair. We sit in uncomfortable silence for a moment, until I force myself to make conversation. "So, how'd you…become the seer?"

If she notices my sarcasm, she doesn't react. "I'm happy to use my talents to benefit the library. We borrow all the books for our little club, you know. Plus, I get to stay out of the sun in here. Keeps my skin youthful." She pats one unwrinkled cheek, then picks up a stack of cards from the table and begins shuffling them. "You'll just have to decide if my gifts are worthy."

I suppress a snarky comment. "Got it. So, hit me. What do the cards have in store?"

"Cross my palm with silver first," she says, extending her hand. "Or plastic, whatever works. Readings are $10."

While she runs my credit card, my stomach growls. How long does it take to have one's fortune read? As a reward for enduring this, I promise myself all the fair treats I want. The greasier, the better.

Hot Yoga Grandma—sorry, Ella—hands my card back to me. It smells faintly of lavender. "Thanks for your donation," she says. "Now, think about a question that you want this reading to address. Be as clear as you can, since that will help to guide us."

Several questions pop into my mind instantly, like they were just waiting to be asked: *How can I save Donovan? What the heck was that weird symbol? What does the creepy 'oceans of blood' premonition mean, and how is it connected to Donovan's death?* I try to narrow them down, then realize that it's a pointless endeavor, since none of this actually means anything.

She shuffles the deck again, has me cut it, and then starts laying the cards face-down on the table in some kind of pattern. "Remember, Rune, these are simply a tool to help guide you. It's up to you to interpret their meaning."

Great. Then why are you here? I almost say, but manage to keep to myself just in time.

"The first card represents your past." She flips one over, revealing an alarming image of a tall building struck by lightning. "The Tower signifies a sudden upheaval or change. Does that have any meaning to you?"

"It could," I say, keeping my face as expressionless as possible. That's the thing about psychic readings, horoscopes, and all that jazz. The statements are so general, people read into them whatever they want to hear. Real premonitions, on the other hand, are vivid and terrifying. I ought to know.

She turns over another card. "This one, the Two of Cups, represents your present. It signifies a deep connection or partnership, possibly romantic in nature."

"Hashtag first date magic," I mutter.

"What was that?"

"Nothing. Please continue." God, this is a waste of my time. I could be eating the world's sloppiest burger right now, fresh off the grill. I could be petting a llama. I could be—

"Hmmm. Normally, I would read the card that represents your future now. But I think..." Reaching for another card, she turns it over. "Ah yes, the Ten of Swords. This card represents betrayal and the end of a difficult situation." She closes her eyes, leaning back in her chair. The candleflame flickers, even though there's no wind in the tent. "I see...a monster?"

I sit up straight, my heart pounding so fast, I think I might throw up. "What?"

"He's faceless, but very powerful." Her fingers clutch the card, nearly bending it in half. "And then I see...ah, yes, you, Rune! I feel heat. A lot of it. Victory. But then...fear. So much fear. A sense of being trapped. And then death, but not for you. For you, freedom."

Bile rises in my throat as her eyes flutter open, the expression in them unfocused. "It was never your fault, you know," she says, her voice gentle as she sets the battered card down on the table. "Now, you can let it go."

I have a new question, now. Namely *what the actual fuck.* No one, other than Charlotte, knew what I called the monster. Even if Ella knew I set him on fire years ago, there's no way she could know he died last night. I lean forward, hands knotted on the table, stomach churning. "Go on."

"The next card is the Five of Cups. It represents loss and grief, but also the possibility of healing. I see...a blood tide. It's rising, taking you out with it." Her hand is on mine again, pressing so hard, she's cutting off my circulation. "You must swim against the current, Rune, do you understand? Swim *hard.* Or you will drown, and along with you, everyone you love."

"You...you..." I struggle to find the words. "Are you just making this stuff up?" Or is it possible I've found someone else, finally, someone like me, with a talent beyond the ordinary? Is it possible we could somehow be...related? We look nothing like each other, but—

"I can only tell you what the cards show me. Now, the third card. This one represents your future."

She turns it over, revealing a skeleton riding a white horse, black flag in hand. "The Death card," she says, pausing. "This card often signifies transformation or the end of a cycle, but it can also indicate a literal death."

Donovan. I suck in a breath, inhaling a lungful of incense, laced with undertones of popcorn, cotton candy, and the crispy batter of funnel cakes fried in oil. Intellectually, I know that outside that beaded curtain, the festivities are still going on, just as they were. Still, the sounds of laughter and music seem distant, as if we're in a separate world.

"I see darkness surrounding someone you work with," she says, her voice low and steady. "This person was involved in the deaths of your family. There's a connection between them and your past, but the details are unclear."

"The deaths of my…are you serious? Do you *know* something about my family?" I clench my hands, my nails digging into my palms. "If you're joking, this isn't funny."

"I would never joke about something like this." She sounds offended. "Be cautious around this person and trust your instincts. There's more to the story than you realize."

"More to the—what story? Who are you talking about?"

She hesitates, glancing down at the spread. "The cards show that this person has a hidden side, one that they may not even be aware of. You must be vigilant and watch for any signs of deception."

Normally, I'd blow this whole thing off. But what she said about the monster and the blood tide has me on edge. What if she actually knows something? Worse still, what if she's talking about Donovan? "How am I supposed to watch for deception if I have no idea who you're talking about?" I snap.

I half-expect her to stand and tell me this session is over. That I've paid my ten bucks and she's not here to be yelled at by the person who rammed into her and knocked a full bag of apples into the street. But instead she says, "Does this mean anything to you, Rune?" Scooping up a pen and paper from the table, she sketches something, then turns it to face me.

All the blood leaves my head so abruptly, I'm afraid I might faint. Because on Hot Yoga Grandma's little yellow legal pad, sketched in clear, solid lines, is an all-too-familiar scroll-and-dagger.

I snatch the pad from her, holding it tightly, like it might vanish if I let go. "How do you know this symbol? Have you seen it somewhere before?"

She shrugs, her eyes wide and guileless. "I wish I could tell you more. But it's like I said before. The cards reveal what they will. It's up to you to interpret their meaning."

Dear God. It's like talking to a Zen koan. "But what should I do?" I ask, abandoning all pretense that this reading means nothing to me. "How can I keep myself and the people I care about safe?"

She leans in, her eyes filled with concern. "You must confront the truth, no matter how painful it may be. Only then can you find the strength to face the darkness and protect those you love."

I start to ask her, *what truth?* But then I know.

My whole life, I've never had the courage to dig into how I wound up in foster care. I was afraid of what I'd discover—that my parents didn't want me, that they'd been living in Sapphire Springs the whole time, happy as clams, while I was shuttled from one abusive, neglectful home to another. But if what she just told me is true, my parents are dead, and their deaths weren't accidental. Just maybe, they were murdered. And if that's the case, I have to bring the killer to justice—especially because, from what it sounds like, I might be next.

Someone—or something—is behind my premonitions about the blood tide and Donovan's death. I need to face my fears and uncover the truth about my family and my curse, even if it means risking everything.

I EMERGE from the tent into bright sunlight, half-expecting to step into another world entirely. But no: the Ferris wheel's still revolving in the distance, the tinny music of the carousel's still tinkling, and across the lawn, Mrs. Fontaine's still puttering with the novels on the bookmobile's outdoor rack. Nothing has changed—except everything is different.

Clutching the sheet of paper I ripped off the legal pad, I take another funnel-cake-laced breath. But this one does nothing to settle me. The festive sounds of the fair fade into the background, replaced by the pounding of my heart.

You must confront the truth, no matter how painful it may be.

Let's say my curse has something to do with the way my parents died. How would I even go about searching for them, to figure out how everything went so horribly wrong? I guess I could try to find the social worker who initially placed me, or the one who handled my case for years. Maybe she would know? If I discovered who my parents were, then I could ask around, maybe try to find people who knew them way back when. I could look in the library's archives, at old newspapers. A couple being murdered, leaving an infant behind, was surely big news. But what if whoever did it covered it up? Or what if I wasn't born here, in Sapphire Springs?

The magnitude of everything that's happened since I tackled Officer Cooper descends on me all at once, so overwhelming that dizziness sweeps me. Wrapping my arms tight around myself, I make a mammoth effort to pull myself together. I'm at the fair with Charlotte's sweet daughters. I can't be preoccupied with this whole mess, not now. It'll show on my face, and Charlotte knows me way too well. I don't want to bring any part of this to her, not until I have a plan. Because how would I ever explain?

The Seer of Sapphire Springs is real, and she told me my parents didn't die a natural death. She said a person close to me had something to do with it. Even if by a miracle, Charlotte believed that part, my curse would prevent her from believing the rest. And if she didn't believe my premonitions were real, there'd be no reason for her to have faith that Hot Yoga Grandma had validated them. She'd dismiss the whole thing as quackery brought on by monster-associated trauma, and doubtless be so worried about me, she'd suggest I seek help. In her shoes, I'd probably do the same thing.

Maybe I could just tell her that now that the monster's dead, I want to find out more about where I came from. That it's my first step toward starting over. She'd support me, I know she would. I bet she could even help me find the best way to go about my search. But that's just one part of this disaster. What about the rest?

I see darkness surrounding someone you work with. Could sweet, shy, hot Donovan really have something to do with whatever happened to my parents? I don't know exactly how old he is, but he looks close to my own age, thirty-two. He would've been a baby when they died. Still, what if it's not him, but his family, that's responsible for the loss of my family and my curse? What if he's heir to a legacy of blood and death?

The idea that the man I kissed last night might have a direct connection to the most painful part of my past sends a shiver down my spine. As I make my way back toward the bookmobile,

I replay every conversation I've had with him, searching for any signs of darkness they might've concealed and coming up blank. Sure, he can be cold and reserved, even grumpy. But when I woke up to him stroking my hair back from my face, when he told me about Cooper, when he kissed me like he did—I could've sworn that was the real him. Vulnerable and tender and commanding, all at once. That his Ice Man persona is a protective mechanism for the awkward, caring guy beneath, who just doesn't want to get hurt again.

What if I'm wrong, though? What if he's playing me, and the Ice Man is who he really is, through and through? What if the way he thawed for me was just a calculated act, designed to make me open up to him and trust him? What if beneath his gorgeous surface lurks nothing but darkness—the same darkness that haunts my visions, the one behind the ocean of blood?

The cards show that this person has a hidden side, Ella said. *One that they might not even be aware of themselves.* Is it possible that Donovan has no idea he's doomed to ruin me—and in the process, bring about his own death?

I stuff the torn paper into my pocket and weave between families pushing strollers, barely paying attention to where I'm going. I'm so out of it, in fact, that I don't realize I've made it back to the bookmobile until I bump right into the rack of novels that Mrs. Fontaine's tidying, sending a chunk of the paranormal section spilling into the grass. Fitting.

Steadying the rack, Mrs. Fontaine gives me the evil eye. I feel like I'm fourteen all over again, caught drinking chai in the stacks. "I'm so sorry!" I blurt, and kneel to gather the books up: Kelley Armstrong, Faith Hunter, and Kim Harrison. Some of my favorites. Normally, I'd be excited to browse through them, but right now, I couldn't care less.

Perceptive as ever, Mrs. Fontaine cocks her head as she reshelves them, brushing them free of debris. "You seem a little distracted, Rune. Well, a little more than usual. Did you find the answers you were after?"

She's turned away, messing with the books, like my reply doesn't matter much to her. But after my conversation with Hot Yoga Grandma, I find myself wondering if anything—and anyone—is really what they seem. "I found…something," I say slowly, watching her profile for a response. But as best as I can tell, her expression doesn't change.

"Did you really?" She tucks a strand of silver hair behind her ear, her tone neutral. "Ella can be quite intuitive. I've always thought so."

She knows something, I'm sure of it. Otherwise, why would she send me to have my fortune read? I can't believe it's just coincidence. On a whim, I pull the piece of paper out of my pocket and hand it to her. "Does this symbol mean anything to you?"

She takes it from me and unfolds it, frowning. And then her eyes spring wide. "Where did you get this?"

I start to answer her, just as Sophie pokes her head out of the bookmobile. "There you are, Auntie Rune! We thought maybe the psychic ate you."

"No one thought that," echoes Emma's disgruntled voice from behind her. "You're just saying that now because you're hungry. Which you wouldn't be, if everyone had just paid attention to my list! It's very organized."

God, she reminds me of Charlotte. "Well, maybe your mom's almost done," I say, my eyes still trained on Mrs. Fontaine's face. She's always been hard to read, even when I was younger and trying to talk my way out of overdue fines. This is no exception: she's schooled her face back to its normal cordial expression as she presses the folded paper back into my hand.

I want to ask her what the symbol meant to her, because clearly it meant *something*. But this isn't the time, in front of the girls and Charlotte, who's emerged with her arms full of paperbacks, Emma trailing right behind her. "Just ten more minutes," she promises her daughters. "Then we'll do the carousel."

"You always say ten minutes," Emma protests. "But it's always forever, and then we won't have time to—Sophie! Not again! Mama and Mom both said we can't get a dog. You're 'lergic. Come back here!"

With a sinking feeling, I turn my head to see where Sophie's darted off to this time. Sure enough, between the caramel apple cart and the taco truck is the animal rescue shelter's tent, showcasing adorable puppies and kittens who need a new home. It's an excellent marketing strategy, if less than sanitary, but right now, all I can think is that it's also an endeavor fueled by volunteers. Which means that the person I'm least prepared to see right now might be staffing the very booth Sophie's making a beeline for.

"Oh no. Mrs. Fontaine, could you please hold these for me?" Charlotte thrusts her books into the librarian's hands and runs off after Sophie, Emma right behind her. Giving Mrs. Fontaine a we'll-talk-about-this-later look, I follow.

Beneath the shelter's tent is a bulldog with a head the size of a dinner plate, the most adorable Siamese kitten ever, an assortment of big-and-little mutts, and Jenny, who waves at me with one hand while wrangling a Rottweiler mix with the other. There's a bunch of teen volunteers who are probably racking up credits for Beta Club, too. But no Donovan.

It's for the best. I know it is, especially in light of recent revelations. But then, why am I so disappointed?

Later, I tell myself, the folded piece of paper warm in my palm. *For now, just be grateful he's not here. You'll have to deal with him soon enough.*

Sophie's thrown her arms around the bulldog's neck, refusing to let go, and Emma's stomping her foot with frustration. Pushing my worries to the back of my mind, I'm on the verge of heading over to help when a sardonic voice rumbles from behind me.

"In the market for Valentine's sibling?"

I turn. And find myself looking into the cobalt-blue, extremely pissed-off eyes of the man I never intend to marry.

Twenty~Three

"YOU RAN AWAY," Donovan says, before I have a chance to reply. "Twice."

Are we really going to do this here, in front of all of Sapphire Springs? "This isn't the time," I hiss at him, slipping the paper with the symbol into my purse. "I'm here with Charlotte and her daughters. And, you know, people have *cameras*." I gesture at Mrs. Fontaine, who's stopped shelving books and is staring at us, not even bothering to pretend otherwise. Across the lawn, Mrs. Grant's frozen mid-burger-flip.

"I don't care about the cameras. I care about what spooked you so badly that you ran out without a word after the hottest ten minutes of my life." He bites his lip. "Did I do something wrong, Rune? Was that why you ran away?"

The anxiety in his voice nearly undoes me. "Technically speaking, I said several words," I hedge, uncomfortably aware of the fact that we're drawing attention. Charlotte's stopped trying to untangle Sophie's arms from around the bulldog's neck, and Jenny's eyeing us with unmistakable disapproval—which, given that the two of them aren't dating, I just don't get.

"Ah, yes. *I don't want you to stop, but we have to.* What could be clearer than that?" His jaw is set, his tone icy. But even on short acquaintance, I know him well enough to recognize the hurt that runs beneath it. More than anything, I want to fix it. But I can't. For his own good—and mine—I have to push him away.

"Not everything is black and white, Donovan," I snap.

The blue of his eyes deepens. I swear, I could spend all day looking into them, watching how they shift color in the light. "No?" he says, taking a step closer. "Well then, enlighten me."

Part of me wants to retreat. The rest wants to drag him into the bushes and have my way with him. I settle for grabbing his hand and pulling him through the crowd, doing my best to ignore the warmth of his fingers as they twine with mine and the electricity that surges through me at his touch. He doesn't say a word or ask questions as I tug him along, over a small footbridge, guiding us at last into the gazebo that sits at the edge of the park's lake. Mercifully empty, accessible only by the footbridge and a narrow path, the gazebo's about as private as we're going to get, unless one of the Sinsters is using a telephoto lens.

Donovan stands there, hands shoved into his pockets. "Well?"

"You didn't do anything wrong." I sigh, toying with the hem of my shirt.

"Then what? I don't understand."

With him right next to me, radiating that delectable cedar-and-vanilla scent, I'm hard pressed to remember why being with him is so wrong, much less to believe that he could be the one behind Ella's predictions. "We work together, Donovan," I manage. "It's not professional."

"I told you, I read the manual," he says stubbornly. "I'm not your supervisor, and you're not mine. There's no power differential. It's not a problem."

"That's what it says on paper! But what if Ethan had checked in on us two minutes earlier?"

He quirks a dark brow at me. "Then we would've given him quite a show."

Heat rushes through me at the thought of what the two of us must have looked like, my legs wrapped around Donovan's hips and my hands knotted in his hair, his mouth devouring mine. "That isn't funny! We could have both lost our jobs."

"On what grounds? It was 10:00 p.m. We had every reason to believe we were alone in the building."

I fight the urge to strangle him. "Not everything is about the official rules, Donovan. Some things are about optics. If Ethan had seen…if we…"

My voice trails off, and Donovan's gaze heats, dropping to my mouth. "You're thinking about it too, I can tell."

"I'm not!"

"Sure you are. And I don't blame you. I haven't thought about anything else since last night. And believe me, I've tried." His voice lowers. "God, Rune, why do you think I'm standing here with my hands in my pockets? It's because I'm afraid if I take them out, I'll wind up laying you down right on the floor of this gazebo and begging you to let me make you mine."

My jaw falls open. "You—what?"

"You don't know me very well yet, but I don't say things like that, Rune. I don't *do* things like that, either. But there's just something about you…" He frees one hand and runs it through his hair in frustration. "Christ, tell me you feel it too."

I should tell him that I don't. That he's lost his mind. But the best I can do is to squeak out, "I think you've been reading way too many of the Sinsters' spicy novels. Also, Mr. Stickler-for-the-Rules, I'm pretty sure we'd get arrested for public indecency."

"Don't change the subject. You asked me to make you *feel*, and I could have sworn I did. That you were as into it as I was. Was I wrong?"

I can see the doubt in those beautiful blue eyes of his. All I want is to erase it. "No." Surely I can give him that much.

"Why, then? And don't give me crap about the employee manual."

What can I say that will convince him? "We're too different. It would never work."

"Have you never heard the phrase 'opposites attract'?" he

argues. "When I called you 'Chaos,' I didn't mean it as an insult. I know what I said before, at the Grille, but that was just me being…" He swallows hard. "Sometimes, when I'm pushed out of my comfort zone, I can react poorly, okay?"

Now it's my turn to snort. "You think?"

"I—I like your chaos, okay? You have this energy about you, this charisma… I don't know how to describe it. But from the moment I met you, all I could see was you."

"The moment you met me?" I narrow my eyes at him. "You mean when you let the elevator doors close in my face and then backed away as far as you could, like I was radiating poison?"

Donovan's jaw clenches. "Damn it, Rune. Because I wanted… Are you really going to make me say it?"

"I think," I say, regarding him in puzzlement, "that I am."

"Fine!" He glares at me. "Because from the moment I saw you, I wanted to plunge my hands into your messed-up hair and mess it up some more. I wanted to pin you to the mirrored wall of that damn elevator and push up that little skirt and ravage the hell out of you. To see you wrecked just for me. And I hadn't even said one goddamn word to you yet, other than *What floor.*" He's breathing hard, his chest heaving. "So forgive me if I kept my fucking distance."

Shocked silence falls between us. I open my mouth, shut it again.

"Say something." His voice is tight.

I try, I really do. But for once, I'm speechless.

"If you won't talk, then I will," Donovan says. "You were so… alive, is the only word I can think of. You called me black and white, before? Well, it was like you stepped right into my world and filled it with color. And yeah, you made a mess. Hell, two hours after I met you, we'd already been in a wreck courtesy of my asshole brother and gotten splashed all over social media. And four hours after *that*, you fell right into my fucking arms."

"Don't remind me," I mutter.

"You fit, though. Like you belonged there." He liberates one hand from the pocket of his jeans and strokes the hair back from my face, his touch gentle. "I don't understand why I'm so drawn to you, Rune. I just know that I am. If by some bizarre chance you feel the same, then please give this—give us—a chance."

His tone is pleading, and my chest aches at the sound. It seems impossible to me that this beautiful man, who's willing to be so honest and vulnerable with me, could possibly be connected to the death of my family. But I've worked with everyone else at Smashbox for years. If not him, then who?

"Rune?" he says again, tracing the line of my cheekbone as if he can't help but touch me. And God help me, I feel just as drawn to him. What the hell is going on here?

"I *can't*," I say, my voice cracking.

"Do you…not want me?" I can hear the effort it takes for him to keep his voice level. "If that's the case, just tell me. I'll leave you alone, I promise. I'll never bring it up again."

Lie to him, a voice whispers inside me. Probably my common sense. But I can't bear to. "I do want you, Donovan. The way you felt in the elevator—I felt the same. Except for the part where I thought you were a total dick. But the pinning and the ravaging, check and check."

He sucks in a sharp breath. "You're killing me. Then *why*?"

"Trust me on this one." I stumble backward from him, sinking down onto the gazebo's built-in bench. The wind gusts, bringing with it the scents of cotton candy and popcorn, but this time I don't feel nostalgic for the few good moments of my childhood. This time, all I smell is loss. "Believe me when I tell you you're better off without me, Donovan. Please."

"Shouldn't that be my choice?"

Gah. In desperation, I fumble in my purse and pull out the piece of paper with the symbol scrawled on it. Maybe if I show it to him and he reveals his true colors—assuming that there are any true colors to reveal—then all of this will get a hell of a lot easier. "Do you recognize this?" I say, holding it up.

He bends closer to take a look, his expression pure puzzlement. "No. Should I? What does this have to do with us?"

If there's one thing my upbringing instilled in me, it's the ability to tell when someone's lying. Donovan is telling the truth. Which doesn't mean he's not connected to my parents' deaths, but it does take one variable off the table. "Forget it," I say, stuffing it back into my purse.

"I'm not even going to ask." His stern mouth curves up at the corners in an unexpectedly fond smile. "Just—Rune, tell me the real reason you don't think we should be together. Because nothing you're saying so far makes any sense."

I throw up my hands. When in doubt, go with the truth. "Donovan, I'm cursed. Being close to me will only bring you pain, all right?"

He shakes his head in disbelief, just like I knew he would. "That's not true. You've had a bad couple of days, that's all."

"No," I say slowly, willing him to understand. "I'm *cursed*. I can see the future. You're right, we're meant to be together. But the only way our relationship ends is in your death."

Donovan gives a low, uneasy laugh. "What are you talking about?"

Better for him to think I'm unhinged than to keep going down this road. "I know you won't believe me. No one ever does—hence, the curse. But when I passed out in the car and on my porch, it was because I had a premonition. And in the office, on the desk, I had another one. We're destined to be married. And the day of our wedding, if we go through with it, you'll die."

"Jesus." His jaw works. "You could've just said you didn't want to be with me, Rune. There's no need to resort to…whatever this is."

"This," I tell him, my voice even but dangerous, "is the truth."

"Uh huh. And you expect me to believe that you're some kind of…of prophet?"

"No! I already told you, I expect the exact opposite. No one ever believes me. No one *can*. But you wanted to know why we need to stay away from each other, and that's the answer. Because loving me will freaking kill you. Okay?"

We stare at each other, neither of us willing to yield. And then, from the path behind the gazebo comes the worst possible voice at the worst possible time, saying the least possible thing.

"I believe you, Rune," Officer Asshat says.

WHAT?

Before I can react, Donovan spins, his hands clenched into fists. "What the hell do you want?"

"Now, is that any way to talk to your brother?" Officer Cooper strolls into view, in full uniform, his gaze darting between us. The last time I saw the two of them side-by-side, I'd just gotten knocked out in a car wreck. This time, I have no such excuse. Now that I know to look for it, the family resemblance is clear: same shape to their blue eyes, though Cooper's are lighter than Donovan's; same slash of their high cheekbones; something similar about the angle of their jaws. But Cooper's hair is a light, sun-streaked brown, and there's a cruel tilt to his smile that I've never seen on Donovan's face, even at his most annoyed with me.

"Half-brother," Donovan mutters. He glares at Cooper. "I repeat: What do you want? We were having a conversation. Nothing to police here."

"Tomato, tahmahto," Cooper retorts, his smile widening. "I happened to be walking by. I overheard your conversation. And I just wanted to tell Rune: I believe her."

Donovan turns the glare on me, and I swear I feel the blood in my veins turning to ice. "Of course you do," he snaps. "It figures the two of you are in on this together."

He sounds furious, but beneath the anger, I detect an unmistakable note of hurt. And why wouldn't he feel that way? Last night, he told me exactly what Cooper did to him years ago. If he thinks I'm colluding with his brother to mock him all over again, no wonder he's pissed off.

"We're not in anything together. There is no 'we,'" I tell him, turning to Cooper. "And what do you mean, you believe me?" Donovan's right, Cooper just fucks with people because he can. It must be his m.o. Because there's no way he, of all people, believes I'm telling the truth about my premonitions.

"I think it's a pretty simple concept, Rune." He sticks his hands in his blue uniform pants, scuffing his polished shoes on the grass. "You said you were cursed. And I'm inclined to think you're telling the truth."

"Oh, now you're just being an ass." Donovan takes one threatening step toward him, then another. Thank God the Sinsters can't see us here. They'd be having a field day. "She tackled you out of the way of what she thought was a bus that would've run you over. You fucking arrested her for it. And then you hit *her* with your car. Sounds like you're the one in the negative when it comes to karmic brownie points, *Coop*." He spits the nickname like it's a malediction, taking yet another stride in Officer Asshat's direction. Now, he's close enough to grab his brother by the collar and strangle him. I'm not entirely sure he won't.

I look between the two of them, unsure what to think. Is that all Cooper meant—that I'm some kind of bad-luck charm? Because the alternative—the alternative is—

"Oh, that bus probably would've killed me," Cooper drawls, indifferent to the six-foot-plus, two-hundred-pound data engineer bearing down on him like grim death. He actually looks amused; that cool smile has reached his eyes, and from the way Donovan's shoulders stiffen, I don't think he likes it one bit. "But, I mean, we can't have people assaulting officers of the law. What would happen to our reputation then?"

Wait, *what?* "Did you just say you knew the bus would've run you over?" I step from behind Donovan, adrenaline whipping through me.

"Don't think I stuttered." Cooper's tone is as obnoxious as ever, but the way he's looking at me—there's something else in his eyes. Something...conspiratorial. I can't read minds, but if I could, I'd bet money that he's trying to get me to ask Donovan to leave, so he and I can talk. But why would he want that? Unless... unless...

There's just no way. Not after thirty-two years of no one believing me. After humiliation and loneliness and desperation and—

The piece of paper Hot Yoga Grandma gave me feels like it's burning a hole straight through my purse. It can't be a coincidence, can it? Her seeing that symbol...the monster dying...the rising tide of blood...meeting Donovan...and now this. What if the universe is trying to tell me something?

"If you knew I was trying to save your life," I say, stomping toward him, "then why the heck would you drag me off to jail? And also, *how* did you know?"

He holds up a single finger. "Number one, you didn't say why you tackled me until after I'd already cuffed you, at which point I had no choice but to follow through. Optics, remember? And number two, you said so."

"I...said so?" My voice cracks. "And you believed me?"

"I'm getting tired of repeating myself," Cooper says. "Can you ask Data here to leave? We need to talk."

"Anything you want to say to me, you can say in front of Donovan," I tell him. God, this looks *so bad*. I want—no, I *need*—to hear what he has to say. If he actually believed me, then it's a freaking Christmas miracle, smack in the middle of September. But the absolute worst person for me to have this kind of inexplicable connection with is the man who betrayed Donovan and made him doubt himself. Who's *still* making him doubt himself today. Because by extension, then Donovan will doubt me too. And even though I know we can't be together, that following through on the white-hot attraction and undeniable lure I feel for him can't lead anywhere but to his doom, it breaks my heart for him to think last night was nothing but a dirty trick.

"Oh, I don't think he should stay, do you?" Cooper runs a finger along the smooth wood of one of the gazebo's supports. "I think it would just confuse him. And you've done quite enough of that, Rune Whitlock."

What the hell is going on here? "Who *are* you?" I hiss at him. "What do you want from me?"

"I'm a small-town cop who's just come upon a recently released criminal in a gazebo with his brother, having a highly suspect conversation. Who just heard said criminal threaten his brother's life, if I'm not mistaken. Do you want to continue this little chat down at the station? Because there's not a helluva lot going on at this fair of yours, and I don't think my services will be missed." His voice is mild, but there's no mistaking its ominous undertones.

I fold my arms across my chest and stare him down. "You wouldn't."

"Try me," he says, staring right back.

Donovan looks from me to Cooper and then back again. "How do you two actually know each other?" he says. "Because I don't believe for a second that you met for the first time when you"—he points an accusatory finger at me—"tackled him"—the finger stabs in Cooper's direction—"into the street. Whatever elaborate scheme you have in mind to humiliate me, great, you succeeded. You might as well come clean and give it up now."

Cooper and I speak at the same time, which doesn't really help our cause.

"Jesus. You're still fixated on some stupid shit that happened years ago. This has nothing to do with that, dumbass," Cooper says, just as I blurt, "Donovan, I swear this isn't what it looks like.

I'd never seen or heard of him before that morning. I don't know what he wants, but there's no elaborate scheme. No scheme of any kind. The last thing I want is to humiliate you. I'm trying to protect you!"

"Well, you're doing a shitty job of it." He huffs, a jagged puff of air. "You know what? The two of you deserve each other. Talk all you want. I'm out of here."

Oh, no. "Please don't leave," I say, catching at his shirtsleeve. "Not like this."

But he won't look at me. "I don't know why you give a crap, Rune. You didn't want to date me anyway. So, now you have what you want. You could've just been honest. You didn't have to make up this elaborate ruse about being a fucking prophet, or whatever. But if Cooper's the kind of person you want to hang out with"—he rips free of my grip and shoves past his brother, knocking Officer Asshat momentarily off balance—"honesty isn't a concept that means jack to you."

My heart feels like it's shattering into tiny, jagged bits. "Donovan, wait. Please!" I call after him, but it's too late. He's already storming away.

Fury surges through me as I turn to Cooper. He's standing at the foot of the gazebo, hands still in his pockets, looking smug as a cat who's raided the refrigerator for the last cupful of catnip-infused creamer. "All right, Officer Asshat," I tell him. "You've got some explaining to do."

Twenty~Five

OFFICER COOPER RAISES HIS HANDS, like he's the one who was just threatened with arrest...again. "Me? I'd say you're the one who needs to 'splain, Lucy." He's grinning at me again, that cocksure smile that I'd like to slap right off his face.

First that snide Data comment; now this, straight out of *I Love Lucy.* Just when I thought he couldn't get any more annoying, he surprises me. "Knock it off," I snap. "Also, I don't appreciate you implying that there's something between the two of us, given the history you and Donovan have. And what do you mean, you believe me?"

"I mean exactly what I say." The smile fades. "I know you were trying to save me from getting hit by that bus, Rune. And I know you never expected me to believe you when you told me the truth. I know you're cursed to have *no one* believe you. And before you tell me it's none of my business, if one of your premonitions foretold my brother's death, then I damn well need to know about it."

This is too much. My legs give way, and to my consternation, Cooper leaps up the steps and grabs me by the arm, lowering me onto the built-in bench that makes up three sides of the gazebo. He lets go as soon as my butt hits the bench, like maybe I've been dipped in poison. Or, I realize when I lift my eyes and catch a glimpse of his dilated pupils, like he's afraid of me.

He knows. He *knows*. But how?

It's everything I've ever wanted. Everything I've dreamed of, since the first time the door to that little room cracked open when I was five years old and I walked through, emerging with knowledge I had no right to possess. But then why am I so terrified?

My vision turns spotty, and I bend, putting my head between my knees. "Who *are* you?" I whisper again to the stained floorboards.

"I told you. A small-town cop."

"And?"

"What do you mean?" The bench shakes as he sinks onto it beside me, being careful to keep his distance.

I draw deep, even breaths, willing myself not to pass out. Man, what I'd give for a cold towel on the back of my neck right now. Or a shot of bourbon. "A small-town cop and…?"

There's a long, weighted pause. Finally he says, "That depends. Are you gonna pass out again? Because I'd rather not have to tell you this twice."

"I'm not going to pass out." I sit up slowly, hoping I'm not lying. When I blink, the gray static has retreated, replaced with the saturated colors of Sapphire Springs in early fall: the deep blue waters of the lake and the changing leaves of the oaks that overhang it, where Charlotte, the girls, and I picnic on my birthday every year. This is a plus: at least I'm not going to find myself prostrate at Officer Asshat's feet like a bad Victorian heroine.

Oh my God, *Charlotte*. What the heck is she going to think happened when Donovan reappears without me? Maybe she'll be too preoccupied with the girls to notice. Maybe she—

On cue, my phone buzzes with a text. I dig it out of my purse, and sure enough, it's my best friend.

CHARLOTTE

> Sex spreadsheet guy is back, and he looks
> pissed. Like, hell hath no fury. What did you say
> to him? I thought you were going to be open-
> minded!

Damn it.

ME

> I'll explain later, promise

I swallow hard, then type, aware of Officer Asshat's eyes
on me:

> It wasn't my fault. Not really.

Three little dots, then:

> As long as you're OK. Fair warning, though. The
> Sinsters have been activated.

Triple damn it.

ME

> Duly noted. Catch you by the funnel cakes in 10.

I stick my phone back into my purse and fix Cooper with a
gimlet eye. "Start talking."

He sighs, running his hands through his hair in a gesture that
reminds me of Donovan and makes my heart twinge. "I really am
a cop. But the reason I've come to Sapphire Springs—well, it
wasn't just for a job. Not this job, anyway."

"What are you talking about?"

"Now it's your turn not to think I'm crazy." His blue gaze
slides sideways, and for the first time, the expression in it is hesi-
tant. "Are you aware of the fact that there are ley lines beneath
Sapphire Springs?"

I stare at his face, inspecting it for any hint of humor. I see none. But I burst out laughing just the same. "Come on, Officer Cooper. You're going to have to do a little bit better than that."

"I'm not joking, Rune. This is no laughing matter." He sounds as frigid as Donovan. Maybe they get their cold shoulder-talent from their mom.

I'm torn between pure joy at finally being believed and my suspicion that this man can't be trusted. Donovan hates him for a reason, after all. And he could be lying about believing me, just to get whatever it is he wants from me…or his brother.

"Ley lines. Got it," I say, tossing my hair and giving him my most winning smile. "Is this what they teach you at cop school when you need to interrogate a hostile witness? Throw the most ridiculous shit you can think of at them, so they confess to something lesser? *Yes, Officer, I foretold your brother's death. But ley lines are a bridge too far.*"

He heaves another sigh, this one so massive that the force of it ruffles the petals of the petunias in the flower boxes, bolted to the outside of the gazebo. "I'm not being a cop right now, Rune. At least, not the way you think. And could you maybe stop calling me Officer Cooper? It's weird."

"It's your job title! Besides, what do you want me to call you? It's not like you've told me your name."

"Fair enough. My name is Andrew. But my friends and close associates"—he gives me another direct blue glance—"call me Coop."

"Uh huh. Well, we're not friends. But as far as associates go, we're closer than I ever intended for us to be. So, *Coop*…start talking."

He extends his arms, cracking his knuckles. "Well, for starters, do you know what ley lines actually are?"

I dig deep, coming up with vague knowledge sourced from fantasy novels and TV shows. "Some kind of…of lines of power, right? They're thought to give off energy that the right people can harness. Like, um, in the Sacred Valley in *Charmed*."

He stares at me blankly, and I stare right back. "It's a *show.*

Like, y'know, *Star Trek* and *I Love Lucy*. What, you're the only one who can watch TV? Was my definition not scientifically accurate enough for you?"

"Ley lines," he says, slowly and deliberately, "are lines drawn between well-known historic structures and important landmarks. It's thought that they're there for a reason. To indicate where the earth's energy is particularly close to the surface, so it can be harnessed, as you so crudely said."

I've had about enough of this. "Oh, yes, Sapphire Springs, home of so many vital historic structures and landmarks. Stands to reason there would be ley lines here."

Coop gives me the same, exasperated glance I remember from my third foster mom: as if he can't believe how uncooperative I'm being, and it's his misfortune and his duty to have to put up with it. "I don't know why they're here, either, Rune. No one does. That's not the point."

I'm beginning to wish Donovan had strangled him. "What is the point, then? I'm not interested in a pseudo-history lesson. You say you know something about me. All I know about you is that you hit Donovan's car, you were a total asshole to him, and now you've threatened to have me arrested *again* if I don't hear you out. Well, you've got my attention. So talk, and do it quickly, because every single second I spend sitting with you here is another second your brother labors under the misconception that you and I are conspiring to make his life a living hell."

"You care about him." It isn't a question.

"I've just met him," I counter.

"Doesn't matter. You give a crap about him, and I don't know if that makes what I'm about to say better or worse." He laces his hands behind his neck. "But here goes. There's more than one reason why I'm an excellent cop, Rune. Why I had the pick of the litter, when I wanted to join the force here in Sapphire Springs. Look at my record; you'll see it's stellar."

"So you're good at your job. Congratulations." My heart's pounding so hard I can taste it. "So what?"

"I could have worked anywhere." It's not braggadocio; it's a statement of fact. "But I chose Sapphire Springs, even though my brother and I can't stand each other. Aren't you the least bit curious why?"

"Not really," I lie. "I'm pretty sure the answer is, *because you're a giant dick.*"

No sooner do the words leave my lips than I realize I've set myself up perfectly for an unfortunate rejoinder. But Cooper doesn't take the bait. Instead, he leans forward, unknotting his hands and bracing them on his knees. "Potentially. But that's not why I came to this charming little town. I'm here because there's been a spike in power in the ley lines beneath Sapphire Springs. My gift is to sense power, to be able to follow its trail. It's how I've brought so many kingpins down."

My mouth is as dry as the Sahara. But somehow, I manage to force out the question I asked him one last time. "What—what are you?"

His eyes fix on mine, and this time, the expression in them is almost...kind. "I'm a witch, Rune. And you...you are a seer."

Twenty-Six

MAYBE I HIT my head in that car wreck and never woke up. It would sure as heck make a lot more sense than everything that's happened in the last seventy-two hours.

"What do you mean, you're a witch?" Even the word sounds ridiculous, like something out of a bad movie. Or *Charmed*. I tilt my head, peering into his face, trying to decipher if he's just messing with me or, if by some twist of the imagination, he can possibly mean this. "There's no such thing as witches, *Coop*, and I don't appreciate you making fun of me this way."

Sometimes, strong emotion can spur a premonition. And sure enough, as I speak, I feel the familiar red haze descend, threatening to cloud my vision. Oh, God, not *now*.

Cooper shifts on the bench, fidgeting, then brushes at his arms as if to shoo away troublesome insects. "I'm not mocking you, Rune. I'm trying to tell you something important. And would you please dial your power back? It's biting all over my skin."

"Dial my…" Is he referring to the red haze? My breath catches in my throat. "You can feel that? But—"

"I told you, I'm drawn to power, and you're leaking it all over the place." He shudders, brushing at his arms again. "Now that I'm sitting next to you, I'm not surprised I crashed my car into yours. You're like a…a freaking magnet for someone like me. Someone really needs to teach you how to control yourself."

"Oh, now the accident was my fault?" My voice rises, and as it does, the red haze deepens. The door cracks open, luring me in. "And who do you think you are, telling me I need to *control myself*? Donovan was right. You're a—"

I've got a whole litany of expletives on the tip of my tongue, ready to hurl them at him like steel-tipped arrows. But with every word I speak, I can feel the world around me retreating as the door to that red-tinged room opens wider. Soon, whatever lies within it will prove impossible to resist. *Not now, not now, not now,* I chant to myself. But it does no good.

Through the fog, I feel Cooper's hands close around mine, gripping hard. His fingers are warm and callused as they twine with my own. "Focus, Rune," he urges. "Deep breaths, all right? Breathe with me, now. Inhale to the count of four, hold to the count of four, then out."

I want to tell him that if deep breathing exercises could've made my premonitions go away, I would've figured that ages ago without his help, thank you very much. But the truth is, the grip of his hands on mine is grounding, an anchor. I find myself following his instructions, clinging to him as he says, his voice low, hypnotic, "Focus on the world, on what's around you. On my touch and my voice. That's it, Rune. You can do this."

As I breathe with him, matching my slow inhales and exhales to his, the red haze retreats, and the pull of the room beyond the door lessens. Until at last the door shuts completely, and when I blink, I find myself on the bench, still holding Cooper's hands.

"There," he says, looking satisfied as he leans back. "That's better."

I snatch my hands from his. "How did you do that?"

"You don't have to sound so pissed off. I did us both a favor." He wipes his palms on his uniform pants, like I've got psychic cooties. "I told you I could sense power. Well, I can also direct it, sometimes. And that's what I did, with you."

I have so many questions. They tumble out of my mouth, one on the heels of the next, too quick to keep track of. "What exactly is a witch? Are they all like you? Can they all do what you do?" Before he can answer, my mind leaps ahead, spewing more queries. "You said I'm a seer. Do you know more people like me, who can do what I do? Do you"—I suck in air, then go for it. "Do you know who my parents are—*were*?"

Cooper's expression shifts, guardedness warring with sympathy in his eyes. "That's a lot of questions. What do you want me to answer first?"

"My parents," I say, biting my lower lip. "Please."

He stands, pacing the boards of the gazebo. "I'm sorry, Rune. I don't know anything about you or where you came from. I didn't know you existed until the moment you tackled me in the street. Quite an introduction, by the way."

Disappointment coils deep in my stomach. "But you said you knew I was a seer."

"Based on what I overheard you saying to Donovan, and the power I can feel rolling off you. Each type of psychic gift has a... flavor, I guess you'd say." He licks his lips, an unconscious gesture. "You taste like a seer. I don't know how to explain it any better than that."

"Oh." My voice is small, and he comes to a stop in front of me, gazing down.

"Were you adopted?"

"Something like that." I'm not in the mood to get into my screwed-up upbringing. Whoever Cooper might be, I don't owe him that. Except— "You weren't, by chance, responsible for the death of a certain man in prison two nights ago?"

Cooper's brows lower. "What are you talking about?"

"There was a man," I say, trying to figure out how to phrase this without giving too much of my personal history away. "He... hurt me when I was younger. Me, and some others. He went to prison for it. He was supposed to get out soon, but instead he...he died. I just thought maybe—since you're kind of like me—that you knew…" My voice trails off. "Never mind. It's stupid. Forget I said anything."

His eyes darken, his jaw tightens in a manner that's reminiscent of his brother's, and suddenly I'm looking at Cop Cooper. "It's not stupid, Rune. I don't know anything about what you're telling me. But I do know one thing: I'm drawn to power, and anyone who would hurt a little girl is nothing but a weakling. So it's no wonder I have no idea who he is."

Looming above me, his shoulders blocking out the sun and his eyes filled with banked rage, Cooper looks…dangerous. But I'm not afraid of him. I may not be able to sense power, but I can tell that right now, he's no threat to me. If the monster were still alive, though—well, let's just say it looks like Cooper would be all too happy to kill him all over again.

Maybe that should frighten me, but it doesn't. It makes me like him more. Granted, that's not hard, given how low my opinion of him was before, but it's something.

He shakes himself all over, like a bird trying to settle its feathers. When he speaks again, the rough edge is gone from his voice. "I wasn't sent here for you, specifically, Rune. I'm here because of the spike in the ley lines' energy, like I told you. But now that I can feel how powerful you are, I'm wondering if that spike has something to do with you."

"That makes no sense. I've lived in Sapphire Springs all my life," I protest. "Assuming there really are…ley lines…beneath the town, where even are they? And why would you suddenly feel that spike now? I've been here all along. If it has something to do with me, wouldn't you have felt it years ago?"

"You ask a lot of questions," Cooper says, sounding as judgmental as Simon Cowell.

"Yeah, well, can you blame me? You're the first person I've met who believes me about my premonitions. Which—why *do* you believe me, by the way?"

"Why doesn't anyone else?" he counters.

I throw my hands up, frustrated beyond belief. "You said it yourself! I'm cursed."

"Well, I have no idea who cursed you. And I believe you because I can feel your power. The curse is like—like a block on it. Something dark…a mark I can almost see, but not quite." He shudders, as if sensing whatever it is has stained him. "But even blocked and hampered, your power is undeniable, which means I can feel you're telling the truth. It's as simple as that."

Yeah, real freaking simple. "Well, the fact remains that I've never met anyone else who has any abilities beyond normal ones. Except…" Wait just one minute.

"Except who?" Cooper prompts me, when I don't go on.

I'm tempted to tell him everything about my little encounter with the Seer of Sapphire Springs. But what if he's not on my side, after all? He hates Donovan. What if he's lying about not coming to Sapphire Springs because of me, about not knowing who my parents are? What if *he* is the darkness that Ella Campbell warned me about, and by telling him about the piece of paper in my purse, I inadvertently kick off a chain of events that dooms Donovan to death? *I see darkness surrounding someone you work with…* What if Cooper himself is that darkness? Donovan certainly seems to think so.

"You weren't sent here for me," I say slowly. "But you were sent here. Why? Who sent you?"

His Cop Face is back on again. "That's a long story. And one I'd rather not discuss in the gazebo at a small-town fair."

Riiiight. "Well, until you're honest with me, I see no reason for me to return the favor." I fold my arms across my chest and stare him down.

Cooper looks mulish. "I'm just doing my duty, Rune."

"I don't give two figs about your duty. I don't know you. Donovan doesn't trust you. For all I know, you're leveraging whatever advantages you have against both of us."

"That's ridiculous! I just *helped* you!" He leans closer. "Look me in the eye and tell me nothing's been different for you lately,

Rune. That you haven't sensed anything…seen anything out of the ordinary. Tell me that, and I'll back off, all right?"

Holding his gaze is harder than it ought to be. It's as if I can feel the weight of his own power behind it, compelling me to confess the truth. But I manage, just the same. "I don't owe you anything, *Coop*. Not until you tell me everything you know."

His jaw sets. "You don't understand what you're asking."

"Yeah? Well, inform me, then."

"There are *channels*, Rune. Protocols. I can't just—you're asking me to—" He shakes his head, as if he literally can't force the words past his lips. For all I know, maybe he can't.

"Riddle me this, then, Batman. Is Donovan…like you? Can he do what you do?"

Cooper shakes his head again. "Now, that I can answer. Donovan isn't one of us. He's pure, Rune. He's innocent. And I'll tell you one thing. If your premonitions told you to have nothing to do with Donovan—that getting involved with him means his death—then you need to stay the fuck away from my brother."

Thanks, Captain Obvious. "I'd love to. But I can't! We work together. I need this job. What am I supposed to tell my boss? *So sorry, please reassign me, I've had a psychic vision?*"

"Figure it out," Cooper growls. "Because if you're as powerful as you feel, then you can do a hell of a lot of damage, Rune. And if Donovan gets caught in the crossfire, my family and I will make you pay."

Shoulders set as if for battle, he stomps down the steps of the gazebo so hard the structure shakes and strides across the footbridge beyond.

CHAPTER

Twenty~Seven

I WAIT until Cooper is nowhere to be seen before I make my way back across the footbridge, toward the funnel cake truck where I promised Charlotte I'd meet her and the girls. My entire body is shaking, and unanswered questions buzz through my mind like bees in a hive: *Who sent Cooper here? Where are the ley lines he told me about? Why does he have a gift, and not Donovan? Does he mean me harm? What does it mean that he's a witch, and what is he capable of? Are all witches different? How can any of this be real?*

Maybe it's absurd to feel this way, given that my ability isn't exactly…ordinary. But it's been a part of me for so long, it feels as natural as breathing. Whereas the existence of ley lines and witches just seems bizarre and fantastical.

Why couldn't it have been Donovan who believed my premonitions were real? Why did it have to be his asshat brother?

I need to talk to Donovan. To explain, though God only knows how I'll manage it. But when I step off the footbridge and back into the hullabaloo of the fair, he's nowhere to be seen. I give the animal shelter's tent a surreptitious look: no furious, arctic-eyed data engineer in sight. Fantastic.

Cooper's visible enough, bending to pet Mrs. Grant's

groomed-to-within-an-inch-of-its-life poodle and chatting with a couple of little kids. But he doesn't so much as acknowledge me as I stride past him, and a good thing, too. I can just imagine the field day the Sinsters would have with that.

The food truck comes into view, with its distinctive rotating funnel cake on top. As I get closer, I can hear Emma chattering about how each funnel cake likely contains four times the recommended daily dose of sugar, Sophie protesting that they're yummy, and Charlotte telling them both that it's a special occasion, but for the love of everything holy, could they please use their napkins? The normalcy of it centers me, and I plaster what I hope is a 'everything's-just-fine!' smile on my face as I come within a few feet of them and wave.

"Auntie Rune!" Emma says through a mouthful of funnel cake. "Whyduyuluklikuswrledalmon?"

My brows knit. "Excuse me?"

She takes a big gulp, swallowing, and tries again. "I said, why do you look like you swallowed a lemon? Do you want some funnel cake? It can help! I read somewhere that sugar counteracts acidity—"

When I was eight, like Emma, I was probably reading *The Lightning Thief.* Knowing Emma, she's probably going to ask for a subscription to *Scientific American* for her next birthday. "I'm fine," I assure her. "But I won't say no to funnel cake, if you want to share."

This is a strategic move on my part, because from the way Charlotte's eyes are trained on me, she's about to unleash her inner prosecutor. And if Emma is any indication, it'll be a whole hell of a lot harder for her to understand my responses if I have a mouthful of fried dough.

Sure enough, no sooner do I accept Emma's offering than Charlotte grabs me by the arm, drags me a little bit away from the girls, and hisses, "Start talking," right into my ear.

I point to my mouth, currently full of funnel cake, but she isn't having any of it. "I saw you drag Sex Spreadsheet Guy off toward the gazebo, Rune. And then he came haring back here like his ass was on fire, muttered something to Jenny, and ran off. Ten minutes later, here comes the dude who freaking arrested you from the exact same direction, looking equally pissed. So you tell me. What the hell is going on?"

Crap, crap, crap. What can I tell her that won't have her hauling me off for a psychiatric evaluation? "Okay," I say, choking down my funnel cake. "Here's the skinny. Donovan and I may have, um, hooked up in his office. Then we had a fight. Disagreement. Whatever. We had some unfinished business, which is why I wanted to talk to him. But then Officer Asshat came along. Turns out he's Donovan's half-brother, and they hate each other. Mayhem ensued. The end."

My best friend's eyes are the size of a supersized funnel cake. "That most certainly isn't the end! I have questions, Rune. So many questions."

You and me both. "What about them?" I say hopefully, gesturing at her daughters in hopes of distracting her.

"*They* can wait. This is big-time drama, Rune. I can't believe you didn't tell me the two of you hooked up! I'm a boring married woman. Don't you know I need to live through you?"

She's eyeing me so expectantly, I know I have to say *something*. And so, in desperation, I blurt out what's been on my mind since my session with Hot Yoga Grandma. "I want to try to find my parents, Charlotte. I'm ready. Can you help me?"

Back at her house after the fair, Charlotte installs the sugar-drunk girls in front of *Encanto.* Then she and Jess, a high school guidance counselor, ply me with far too much Darjeeling and have me jot down everything I know about my origins. It's a pitifully short list.

I feel a little guilty for using Charlotte this way. I'd love to be able to tell her the truth about everything that's really going on, to get her level-headed opinion. But while I know I can't tell her about curses, premonitions, or powers, I can ask her for practical help. For years, Charlotte and Jess have been gently urging me to find out more about my biological parents. I've always said no, that I wasn't ready. But now, for so many reasons, things are different.

"So," Jess says, tucking her short brown hair behind her ears as we sit around the coffee table in their high-ceilinged living room, "let me see."

I hand over the list. *I don't have a copy of my birth certificate. I don't know my parents' names. I think I was born in Sapphire Springs, but I'm not sure. I entered foster care when I was a year old. I don't know if I have any living relatives. I don't know if Rune is the name my parents gave me. I don't know who gave me the last name 'Whitlock.'*

Jess's pert nose scrunches as she hands the paper to Charlotte. "So you don't know a lot," she says. "That's okay. You haven't even started looking yet. The first step will be to go to the Register of Deeds when it opens on Monday and request a copy of your birth certificate. Then, you'll need to reach out to the social worker who handled your case, assuming she's still working, and see what she'll share with you about your file..." She goes on, her voice soothing, and I dutifully open the Notes app on my phone and jot her suggestions down. But as I type, all I can think of is whether, instead of giving me up because they didn't want me, my parents' lives were snatched from them. I imagine my mother clinging to me, my father screaming, as that blood tide rose and swept them away.

I drop my phone onto the coffee table with a clatter, startling Charlotte, who glances up from the pathetic list, and Jess, who gazes at me, wide-eyed. "I'm sorry," I say, forcing a smile. "Too much tea, I guess. Bathroom. Be right back!"

The overly bright smile still glued to my face, I hustle down the hallway, lined on both sides with pictures of Charlotte, Jess, and the girls: skiing in Boulder, on the Ferris wheel at the fair, wrist-deep in cake on Sophie's first birthday. I love them dearly. They're my family. But right now, all the happy pictures of them burn my retinas like acid.

I lock myself inside the bathroom at the end of the hall and sit down on the toilet seat, head in my hands. With its pale blue walls, fluffy white rug, and ocean-scented candles, I've always found this tiny little room to be a peaceful place. But not today. Because as I sit here, struggling to calm my breathing, the red haze that threatened to consume my vision when I sat in the gazebo with Cooper descends again, and this time, there's nothing to drive it back. I try breathing deeply until I see freaking spots, but nope. Much as I hate to admit it, the touch of Donovan's asshat brother is the only thing that's ever been able to halt one of my premonitions in its tracks. Certainly, nothing's stopping this one.

I feel it coming, heavy on my chest, fogging my mind. I *see* the haze. But through it, I see the world, too, the way I always do: that same double vision, as if my two realities are overlaid on top of each other. And in the world that's *here,* the bathroom light winks out.

There's no window, so when the light goes, it plunges me into complete darkness. If the commotion I'm hearing on the other side of the bathroom door is any indication, I'm not the only one. Emma and Sophie are wailing that *Encanto*'s turned off, and Charlotte's swearing a blue streak as her feet thud down the hallway and up the stairs to their playroom. I catch the words *fucking power surge* and *not again* and *have to talk to my mother about the goddamn overloaded grid* before her footsteps crest the landing and creak above me. For someone who participated in Cotillion and was raised to have perfect etiquette, she's in dire need of a swear jar.

Eyes tight shut, I rock back and forth, thinking about what

Cooper told me: that he came to Sapphire Springs because of a spike in the ley lines' power. Could that be what's happening here? Could this somehow be my fault, like he insinuated?

I have to talk to him again. But first, I need to get out of this room.

The door that always accompanies my premonitions hasn't appeared, and I wonder if it's been scared right out of me. Gingerly, I open my eyes.

And let out a shriek.

That fiery scroll-and-dagger symbol is emblazoned everywhere. On the ceiling. On the wall. Inside the sink. Atop the fuzzy bathmat. On the back of the door. Heat radiates from every direction, and I'm burning, burning alive—

"Rune!" Jess shakes the doorknob. "Are you all right? I heard you scream. Are you okay?"

Hold on, Rune, I tell myself. *Keep it together.* "I'm all right," I manage, my chest heaving. "J-just stubbed my t-toe. Don't mind me."

"Uh huh. Open the door." She shakes the knob again, which is currently blazing with fire, along with the eight other symbols all over her guest bathroom.

She won't be able to see them, I remind myself. *And they're not real. Come on. Ovary up, Rune. Open the damn door.*

Gritting my teeth, I reach for the knob. It's as hot as I feared it would be, and I have to suppress a hiss as I wrench the door open, to find Jess standing so close on the other side, I almost run right into her.

"See?" I say, doing my best impression of Rebecca-of-Sunny-brook-Freaking-Farm. "All okay. Everything's great! I gotta go!"

"But—"

"Just realized I left my computer plugged into the wall! Gotta check on it!" I babble, my hand balled into a protective fist as I barrel past her. "Thanks for the advice. So helpful. I'll keep you posted!"

"Don't you want to say—" Jess begins, but she's talking to my back. I've snatched up my purse from the living room couch and fled. It's only when I've gone two houses down that I duck into an alleyway, lean against the brick wall, and unfold my fist.

I was sure it was my imagination. But no. There on my palm, branded deep into my flesh, is the scroll-and-dagger symbol.

Twenty~Eight

I STAND with my back against the alleyway wall, staring down at the scroll and dagger branded into my palm. One of my premonitions has never stayed with me in such a tangible way before, unless you count the piece of paper that Hot Yoga Grandma scribbled the symbol on. But there's no denying this. My hand is alive with pain, as if I pressed it against a hot burner.

What is happening to me?

I'm not usually a crier, I swear. But the past few days have proven me wrong. Tears well in my eyes and trickle down my cheeks. Since I'm staring down at my palm, they also splash onto the brand, which stings and makes me cry harder.

The monster is dead. I found a sweet, smart, sexy man who wants to be with me. Charlotte and Jess are willing to help me find my parents. And yet, everything is so incredibly, indelibly screwed up. Why can't I just have a normal life, with normal problems? Why *me*?

My pity party of one is interrupted by a soft voice. "Rune?"

I jerk my head up. Mrs. Fontaine is standing at the mouth of the alley, peering in at me, her blue eyes filled with concern. "I thought I heard somebody crying. Whatever is the matter, dear?"

I have no idea if Mrs. Fontaine can see the symbol on my hand, but I'm not inclined to find out. That would open the door to a whole bunch of questions that I have no idea how to answer. I don't even know how to answer the one she already asked me. "Oh, I'm f-fine," I say, dashing away my tears with the back of my unwounded hand. "Just too much funnel cake."

"Uh huh." She bustles down the alley toward me, clearly not buying it. "Was it that handsome man of yours, the one who's so fond of computers? Because you're one of us, Rune, and if he said something to hurt you…"

Despite the fact that she's about half a foot shorter than me, saying those last words seems to have blown her up to twice her size, like an enraged puffer fish. I can't help but smile through my tears. "Donovan didn't say anything. Or do anything, either. It's not him. I'm fine. Really."

"Sure you are." She has hold of my arm now and is towing me out of the alley, so determined that it doesn't occur to me to resist. "Was it Ella, then? Did she tell you something untoward? I'm always saying she needs to be more careful, that she can't just blurt out the first thing that comes to mind when she reads those cards. 'You can do real damage!' I always tell her. And now look." She tugs me down the street, then up the steps of a whitewashed Cape Cod. "This is all my fault, really. I told you to go see her. Oh, I feel just terrible."

"Mrs. Fontaine," I say, trying to reclaim my arm and the remnants of my dignity, "it's not her fault either. I just need to go home and um, have a nap." Or a margarita, heavy on the tequila.

"Nonsense," she says, opening the bright yellow door and pushing me through. She comes in after me and shuts the door behind her, locking it with a snick.

I blink into the gloom. The whole street must've lost power when Charlotte and Jess did, because there are no lights on in here. Objects take vague form in the dimness: what I'm guessing is a coat rack in the corner, the sinuous curve of a staircase off to the right, the gaping maw of a doorway. A savory, spicy scent fills the air—some kind of baked casserole, maybe. "Where am I?"

"My house, of course." Mrs. Fontaine chuckles. "What, did you think I kidnapped you and dragged you off to some dreadful lair? You always did love to read those fantasy books, Rune. Of course, I have to admit it looks a little odd in here, what with the power being off and all. Just come on through into the other room. We have candles, and Drusilla's made her famous enchilada casserole. It'll be just the thing to perk you up. Come, come."

She hooks her arm through mine again, like the world's most cheerful tugboat, and pulls me through the doorway into the room beyond. And there, seated on cushions on the floor around a circle of candles, are Mrs. Grant, Mrs. Hernandez, and the Seer of Sapphire Springs herself, Ella Campbell.

At the sight of us, Ella raises those perfectly drawn eyebrows. "Found a stray, Louise?"

"Oh, you." Mrs. Fontaine waves a dismissive hand in her direction, then gestures toward one of two empty cushions. "I told you I heard someone crying, Ella. And here she is. Do have a seat, Rune. I'll fetch you some of Dru's enchiladas; lucky they finished cooking before the power went out. Just the thing for what ails you. Ella, don't you say one word to that girl while I'm gone. You've done enough damage."

"I'm not—" I begin, but it's too late. She's already gone, leaving me alone at a Sinister Convention.

This day just keeps getting better and better.

"Um, hi," I say, waving at each of them with my non-branded hand. The other one's clenched tight into a fist, even though it hurts badly to do so. More than anything, I want to run the burn under cold water, plaster it with aloe, and hope it goes away. But that's not happening anytime soon. Not while I'm stuck in Mrs. Fontaine's house, victim of her superhuman hearing.

She means well. I know she does. But her timing couldn't be worse.

"Why, hello, Rune," Mrs. Hernandez says, her tone every bit as stern as when I mis-programmed my robot and made Sapphire Springs lose at Regionals. "Fancy seeing you here."

Oh, geez. "I'm sorry to interrupt whatever this is, really." I gesture at the cushions and the candles. "I didn't ask to come in, I promise. In fact, I really should be going—"

"Don't be silly. We're just having a Sinning Spinsters meeting, to pick our titles for the next six months," Mrs. Grant says. "It's our little ritual, after the BBB festival every year. Unfortunately, we're having some difficulty agreeing on our next pick. Dru here" —she points at Mrs. Hernandez—"wants *Lord of Scoundrels*, which the rest of us have already had the tremendous pleasure of reading several times over. I vote for the first book in the Bootleg Springs series. And Louise thinks we simply *must* read *Book Lovers*, but I think it's much too on the nose. There's some sex-in-a-lake scene that she just won't stop talking about. Won't you be a dear and cast the tie-breaking vote?"

She holds up a small item that's little more than a blur in the candlelit room. I step closer, and realize what it is: a cutout of Chris Pine's face, glued to a popsicle stick. In front of each of the cushions is another popsicle-stick-impaled hottie: Chris Evans, Idris Elba, Keanu Reeves, Antonio Banderas in his prime.

Oh. My. God. "I, well—I really don't..." She looks so hopeful, I hate to disappoint her. "I, um, mainly read urban fantasy. Mrs. Fontaine could tell you. So I don't think I'm the best judge." My palm throbs, reminding me that I need to get home and do some-thing about it. Here's hoping aloe works on supernatural burns. "Like I said, I really need to—"

"Sit." The command comes from Ella Campbell, commonly known as Hot Yoga Grandma. But she doesn't look remotely grandmotherly at the moment. In the light of the candles, her face looks angular, severe. Her eyes are dark hollows. "And open your hand."

Crap, crap, crap. "My...hand?"

"Don't play dumb with me, girl! After what I read in your cards today, we don't have the luxury. Your hand. Open it, right now!"

I could disobey her. But instead I find myself sinking down

onto the cushion Mrs. Fontaine indicated, cross-legged, my purse in my lap. In front of me, a candle flickers in the nonexistent breeze. Slowly, carefully, I unfold my hand from its fist and raise my palm.

Ella sucks in a breath, and the temperature in the room seems to drop a degree. "That symbol. It's the same one I saw before, the one I drew for you. How did it come to be burned onto your palm?"

Her eyes are fixed on mine, those dark hollows drawing me in. "I don't know," I tell her, trembling. "Right after the power went out, I...I saw it. In the air. On the walls and the door of the room I was in. When I tried to get out, it...it marked me."

"This is bad," Mrs. Hernandez says in a monotone. "They have risen."

What in the everlasting hell? "You recognize this symbol?" Ella and I say at the same time.

Mrs. Hernandez doesn't answer. Instead, she yells, "Louise!"

There's a scuffle in the other room, and then Mrs. Fontaine comes skidding into the room, enchiladas in hand. "Honestly, Dru," she scolds, "there's no need to yell. I almost tripped and spilled the whole plate. The whole *enchilada*, one might say. If you could just be patient—"

"Forget the enchiladas!" Mrs. Hernandez barks. "Look." She grabs my wrist, her grip an iron fetter, and yanks my palm toward the firelight. The brand of the scroll and dagger stands out, an angry red against my pale flesh.

The plate of enchiladas falls to the floor, sauce and filling splashing everywhere. Mrs. Fontaine falls to her knees beside me, peering so closely at my hand that her silver-streaked hair falls forward, brushing the burn. "It's happening," she whispers.

I pull my hand back, clutching it to my chest. "*What's* happening? Tell me what this symbol is! Why am I seeing it everywhere? Why is it on my hand? And how the hell can I get it off?"

Normally, I wouldn't dream of cursing in front of Mrs. Fontaine. She'd probably smack me over the head with a ruler.

But this time, she doesn't react. "It's the mark of the Blood Witch-es," she says. "It hasn't been seen in many a moon."

Many a moon? What are we, in the 1800s? "The mark of... excuse me? What is a...a blood witch?" My voice cracks. Is that what Cooper really is? Is he responsible for this? I knew I was right not to trust him.

"Yes," Ella says, glaring at Mrs. Fontaine. "What is a blood witch, Louise? And why is my body tingling all over? Don't you dare say it's because of your graphic description of that lake scene, or the next plate of enchiladas is going on your head."

Mrs. Fontaine straightens, regarding the wreckage with disgust, as if she's just realized what a mess she's made. "First, I'll clean this up," she says. "And then, Rune and Ella...we need to talk."

CHAPTER
Twenty~Nine

FIVE MINUTES LATER, the enchiladas have been scrubbed away, the lights *still* haven't come back on, and I'm sitting in a circle with the Sinsters as Mrs. Fontaine clears her throat. It feels like storytime at the library, except my hand is burning and Mrs. Hernandez is nursing a giant glass of bourbon.

"What do you know about this?" I say, digging the piece of paper that Ella scrawled the scroll on out of my purse and holding it up in my good hand. "The mark of the Blood Witches, you called it? Why is it popping up everywhere I turn? Why is it burned into my freaking *palm*?"

Mrs. Fontaine pales. "Who drew that? Was it you, Rune? Because that symbol is dangerous, and you can't just leave it lying aro—"

"I drew it." Ella leans forward, getting so close to the candle in front of her that I'm afraid her boobs might catch fire.

"What do you mean, you drew it?" Mrs. Grant's voice rockets upward, painfully close to a squeak. "Where did you see this?"

"In my *head*. When I read Rune's cards for the fair. Maybe if the three of you weren't busy hoarding secrets, I would've known better. But no, you didn't say a word, and now here we are." She glares at the other Sinsters. "Answer Rune's questions, if you please. And then I have some questions of my own."

Mrs. Grant fidgets nervously on her cushion. "Before we explain about the Blood Witches, there's something else you should know. We—Dru, Louise, and me—we're...well, we're a..."

"A coven," Mrs. Fontaine says, her voice clear and firm. "All right? Now you know."

Stunned silence falls over the room—or, at least the part of it that Ella and I inhabit. And then, despite everything, I start to giggle. "A...a coven? Are you saying you're witches, too?"

"This is no laughing matter, Rune." Mrs. Hernandez glares at me over the rim of her glass of bourbon.

I try to bring myself under control, but it's useless. The events of the past few days, starting with my premonition about Cooper and culminating in this absurd moment, are just too much. I laugh so hard tears run down my face and my stomach aches, so hard that all four of the Sinsters are a blur. Dimly, I hear Ella demanding to know what they mean, whether they're serious, how they could have kept this from her, but I can't make out their answers over my hysterical giggles. I only wind down when Mrs. Fontaine plops a cool, wet cloth on my forehead, shoves a glass of bourbon into my non-burned hand, and tells me in no uncertain terms to shut up.

"If you're quite finished," she says, when my laughter subsides into hiccups, "yes, we are witches. Our families have been in Sapphire Springs for over a century. We were drawn here because of the power of the—"

"Let me guess," I interrupt. "The ley lines."

"How do you know that?" Mrs. Grant doesn't sound anything like the adorable old lady who wins Sapphire Springs' Peach PiePalooza every year. In the flickering candlelight, the lines of her face are menacing, and her voice is...not creepy, exactly, but demanding. The kind of voice that takes no prisoners, rather than taking your milkshake order.

"Officer Cooper told me." I take a sip of bourbon. It burns

going down, settling warm in my stomach. "Apparently that's why he's here, too."

"Andrew Cooper? The handsome young policeman you tackled in the street?" Ella frowns harder. "What does he have to do with this?"

"I'd like to understand that myself," Mrs. Hernandez says. "If the High Priestess sent him, we're in deeper trouble than I care to consider."

"The—High Priestess?" I gape at her. "Who the hell is the High Priestess?"

"Language, Rune," Mrs. Fontaine tuts, clicking her tongue.

"We've never spoken to her directly." Mrs. Grant's voice is hushed. "But she's in charge of all the southern covens. We speak with the regional rep, who passes our concerns on." She turns to Mrs. Fontaine. "Really, Louise, you'd think Marilyn might have done us the courtesy—"

"Enough!" Ella pushes to her feet. Even in the dim light, I can tell her face is red with rage. "I've spent hours with the three of you since I moved to Sapphire Springs. Knitting sweaters for your grandson"—she gestures at Mrs. Grant—"participating in your fundraisers"—she points at Mrs. Fontaine—"staffing the bake sale table so your robotics students could make it to regionals!" Her accusing finger points at Mrs. Hernandez. "We've had enough dinners together to feed all of Sapphire Springs. Discussed enough dirty books to set Rune's ears on fire." Now the finger is leveled in my direction. "I told you all about my little gifts, worried you'd laugh at me. That you'd think I was a fraud. And all along, you've been keeping…this…a secret! You tricked me into trusting you, but did you trust me? Not one whit!"

"We—" Mrs. Fontaine begins, but Ella isn't done.

"All along, I thought you wanted to be my friends. I was so happy that you reached out to me when I moved here. *Can't believe my luck,* I told my daughter. *Met the nicest ladies.* But this whole time, you've been lying to me about who you are!" Her voice is so loud, the Hummel figurines in Mrs. Fontaine's curio cabinet begin to tremble. "Were you ever planning to tell me? Or was all of this a *test,* so you could decide whether you wanted to recruit me into your little club?"

"Now, Ella," Mrs. Grant begins in an attempt to smooth things over. But instead, it has the effect of dumping gasoline onto a raging fire.

"Don't you 'now, Ella' me! You've been lying to Rune here, too! Do you want to know what I saw in her cards today?" She glowers at each one of them in turn. "Well, do you?"

No one answers. At last, Mrs. Grant ventures carefully, "Is this a rhetorical question?"

Ella's eyes bulge so much, I'm afraid she's going to explode, Violet Beauregarde-style. "I don't care if you're the goddamn Witches of Eastwick," she snaps. "As far as I'm concerned, you're *liars,* first and foremost. Rune can stay and talk to you all night long if she wants. As for me, I'm going home." Turning on her heel, she storms from the room, slamming the front door so hard that the resulting gust of wind puts half the candles out.

A stunned silence follows her departure. Mrs. Hernandez breaks it. "Namaste, my ass," she says as she bends to light the candles again. Only, there's nothing in her hands. Tiny flames shoot from her fingertips, setting each of the wicks aglow.

"Holy shit," I mutter. This time, Mrs. Fontaine doesn't correct me. "Did you just—how did you—"

"We'll explain everything to you, Rune, I promise," Mrs. Grant says. "But now, with the Blood Witches' symbol on your hand, and Ella seeing it in your cards…there isn't time."

Mrs. Fontaine takes my good hand in hers. "For generations, our mothers and their mothers before them have watched over the ley lines, just as we do today. Our gifts are tied to their power. But they've been unpredictable lately, ebbing and flowing. These outages," she says, waving around at the darkened room with her free hand, "have nothing to do with the electric grid. They're shorts in the ley lines, blowouts. And Rune—I think they're tied to you. Why else would the scroll-and-dagger be in your cards? Why would it brand itself onto your hand?"

"Me?" My voice cracks. "But I've been here for years," I protest, the same thing I told Cooper. "Why now?"

"I don't know." She shakes her head, squeezing my good hand. "But we'll figure it out."

A shiver racks me, thinking of what Ella said when she read my cards. "I don't understand any of this. Who are the Blood Witches? What would they want with me?"

"They're an ancient, power-hungry clan," Mrs. Hernandez says. "And a dangerous one. As for what they'd want with you, Rune…there must be more to you than meets the eye."

Hope surges within me. Cooper believed me, after all. Maybe they will, too. "Here's the thing. I'm cur—" I begin. But before I can finish the word, an odd buzz rises in the room—the sound of electricity crackling through the air. The lights flicker and come on, along with all of the other appliances in the house. And then, just as quickly, everything goes silent and dim once more.

What the hell?

I try again. And again. But the same thing happens. Apparently it's not enough not to be believed; now, I can't speak the words at all.

Tears well in my eyes, and Mrs. Fontaine pats my hand. "That's all right, sweetheart. For now, tell us what the cards said when Ella read them. And about Andrew Cooper." She bites out his last name, as if it tastes bad.

I want to believe I can trust her—trust all of them. But how can I? An hour ago, I thought they were just a bunch of spicy-book aficionados. All my life, they've hidden their true identities from me. How do I know they're on the side of the angels?

They want information. Well, so do I. And there's no way I'm giving up what I know until I take my shot. They've been here forever. Maybe they have the answers I'm after.

"I'll tell you," I say, looking from one of them to the next. "But first—I'm trying to find my birth parents. Do any of you know who they are? Where I came from?"

One by one, the Sinsters shake their heads, and my heart sinks. But then Mrs. Grant speaks. "My gift is to see into the past," she says. "To see what was, but only through the eye of the beholder. I don't know anything about your parents, Rune. But if *you* know— if the truth is buried in your mind somewhere—then I can show you."

I have no idea how such a thing is possible. If trying it might cook my synapses like the deep-fried Snickers bars I saw at Books, Bites, and Bedlam today. But I know one thing: if there's the slightest possibility it'll work, then I'm in.

"Yes," I tell Mrs. Grant, my heart pounding so hard I can taste it. "Let's do it. Now."

CHAPTER

Thirty

THE FOUR OF us sit in a circle on the cushions. In the center, the candles flicker, their flames casting long shadows as Mrs. Grant takes my hands in hers, holding the branded one gingerly. "All right, Rune. Whatever Ella told you, we need to know. And if this is your condition, then a deal's a deal."

A fiery tendril sprouts from thin air, winding its way around our hands, binding them together. Gasping in shock, I try to jerk away, but the tendril winds itself faster, wrapping tight. It doesn't burn, like the brand did, but it won't let go, either.

"We look to the east," Mrs. Grant says, her voice low, intent. "To the place where the sun rises, giving birth to each day."

"To the east," Mrs. Fontaine and Mrs. Hernandez echo in unison.

She tilts her head back, glancing upward. "We look to the north. To the place from which the snows come, washing us clean."

"To the north," the other Sinsters chorus.

"We look to the south. To the place from which the fire comes, burning within us." Mrs. Grant glances downward, at our joined hands, twined together with that fiery cord.

"To the south."

"We look to the west. To the place where the sun sinks, that it may be renewed once more." Her head turns to the left, fixing on the doorway that leads to Mrs. Fontaine's kitchen. I could swear I see a shadow move within it, slinking from table to stove and back again.

"To the west," Mrs. Fontaine and Mrs. Hernandez repeat, and now their eyes are fixed on the doorway to the kitchen, too.

What the hell is in there? Was I crazy to agree to this? I try to yank my hands away again, but no dice.

"We call on the spirits, and give thanks for the powers they lend us. For we are but the vessels for their gifts." Mrs. Grant's face is only visible to me in profile, but I can still see the small smile that lifts her lips. "Those who have come before, be with us now. We humbly request your presence, and accept the responsibility of your summoning."

The shadow from the kitchen sweeps through the doorway, toward us. It settles over Mrs. Grant, *into* her. And then she turns her head, her eyes meet mine, and I shriek.

Her eyes have gone completely black, the whites and irises swallowed up by her pupils. What in the ever-loving—

Mrs. Grant's mouth opens, and a voice issues from it. It's deep and cracked and…not hers at all. "What would you have of me?" it says.

I want to leap to my feet. To flee. But instead I say, "My name is Rune Whitlock," summoning all of my courage. "I'm trying to find out what happened to my family. Mrs. Grant said if there was a memory buried in my subconscious…if I'd seen something…she could help me remember."

She tilts her head, regarding me with those peculiar eyes. "Well, then. Let's begin."

Her hands grip mine even more tightly. And then I feel the strangest sensation…as if someone's riffling through my mind, flipping the pages of my memory back and back, like I'm a book they're reading from last page to first. I see me, sitting in this room with my hands in Mrs. Grant's. The bathroom at Charlotte's.

The fair. Donovan's office. The further back in time the memories go, the faster the pages flip. I'm graduating from college. I'm in the juvenile detention center. I'm in the yard with the monster, watching everything burn.

"Interesting," her voice says from far away. "But not impossible."

I want to ask her what she means. But I can't speak. I'm caught in a whirlwind of memories, the images rippling faster and faster. I'm in middle school, with kids laughing at me. Kindergarten, my hair in a braid, clutching my lunchbox, hoping to make a friend. Four, clutching the yellow-trimmed blanket that I've had as long as I can remember. Three, trying to warn my babysitter that someone's going to steal her wallet, only she won't believe me can't believe me and I don't have the words. Two, sitting in a wood-paneled, windowless room, playing with some plastic toys while adults whisper behind me. One, and…

I'm standing in a light-drenched room, painted a cheery yellow, filled with plants. On the wall hangs an abstract art piece, splashed with bright, primary colors. And in a cozy rocking chair, piled with pillows, sits a beautiful woman. Her wavy, dark brown hair, so like my own, spills over her shoulders and down her back. Bars of sunlight spill across her face, highlighting a constellation of freckles that dot her cheeks. But it's her smile, open and happy and free, that sends a wave of longing rippling through me.

I know this woman, not with my conscious mind, but on a bone-deep, visceral level. I recognize her. Everything within me gravitates toward her, like a plant long-deprived of sun.

She cradles a bundle in her arms. As I watch, she ducks her head and begins to croon to it, her voice soft and gentle. "You are my sunshine, my only sunshine…"

At the sound of her voice, the longing within me intensifies. I edge closer, but the woman doesn't glance up, and as I pass through the bars of sunshine that stripe the floor, I leave no shadow. Finally I'm standing next to her, peering down. My heart flutters, then starts pounding, so hard I can barely catch my breath.

In her arms, wrapped in the yellow blanket that's all I have left of my childhood, is a baby who stares up at her with my too-wide, thick-lashed gray eyes.

Holy crap. I'm looking at *myself*. And the woman holding me…this lovely, sweet, kind woman…is my mother.

I've always wondered if my biological parents loved me. If they couldn't wait to give me away, because I was different and unlovable, *wrong*, from the moment I came into this world. But here, watching my mother rock the baby that I once was, seeing her stroke my cheek, I know the truth. The ache that's always simmered inside me subsides, replaced with a relief so profound, I fall to my knees next to the rocking chair. I want to savor this moment. To stay here with my mother, forever, as she sings to me about how I make her happy, even when skies are gray. Here, in this cocoon of a moment, I've found perfect, absolute peace.

And then it splinters.

The sky outside the windows darkens, the bars of sunlight fading. My mother's head turns, and her eyes go wide. She leaps to her feet with me clutched in her arms.

"David!" she screams. "David!"

A man comes thundering into the room. He's tall, bearded, built like a lumberjack. Deep within me, recognition thrums: This is my father.

"Run," he says, his voice urgent. "Go!" Then he faces the window, raising his hands. *"Hic sunt dragones,"* he chants, louder and louder. *"Hic abundant leones."*

As my mother sprints for the door, honest-to-God dragons and lions materialize in the room, forming a barrier between my father and the window. The glass shatters, and hooded figures climb through, one after the other. "Don't be a fool, David," one of them shouts. "Give us the child, and we'll let you and your wife live."

I know that voice. I've heard it before. But where?

"Fortius!" my father bellows, and one of the dragons opens its

mouth, unleashing a stream of flame at the man. He dodges it, but the curtain behind him catches fire, and the baby I once was shrieks in terror.

The man in the lead, the one who spoke, tsks at my father, as if scolding an errant child. He pulls a knife from his pocket and cuts his arm, then dips his fingers in the blood and flicks it at the beasts. *"Evanescere,"* he says, his voice echoing off the walls, the floors, the ceiling. I can feel the power of it, as if the word has actual weight. And one by one, as the blood hits them, my father's beasts wink out of existence.

Blood witches, I think. Is this who they are? What they do?

What do they want with us?

The heat in the room is rising, degree by degree. Sweat slicks my father's forehead as he looks from one figure to the other. "Get out—" he begins, just as my mother screams again.

He wheels. Between her and the door is another group of darkly hooded figures. One of them grabs for her, and she kicks them in the shin. But she's holding me, and she can only fight so hard. Still, she struggles against the figure who holds her—holds *us*—prisoner.

"Non ducor—" she begins, but the man claps a hand over her mouth.

"No you don't," he snarls. "You think we don't know what you are? What you can do?"

My mother tosses her head, biting at his hand. She thrashes and kicks, but it's no use. One of the other figures wrests the baby from her arms, and it shrieks—*I* shriek—even louder than before. The flames are raging now, gobbling up the curtains, racing along the walls. I want to put the fire out. To save my parents. But when I tear at the man who holds my mother prisoner, my hands pass right through him. Because of course, I'm not really here.

Three of the men who climbed through the window have my father pinned, holding him back as he screams for me, for my mother. The leader dips a finger in his own blood again, but this time he paints it across my father's lips, trailing a bloodied fingertip down his throat. My father's mouth opens, but no sound emerges. The veins in his neck bulge as he tries again and again, struggling vainly to break free.

"We ruled once," the leader says, his face invisible beneath the hood, his eyes dark pits. "We will rule again. Let this be a warning to those who stand in our way."

And oh God, I know where I've heard his voice before. In my premonitions, saying *Our day will come.*

He stalks closer to my father, until their faces are inches away. My father stares back at him, and in his eyes I see only defiance. Not fear.

"Goodbye, David," the man says, and cuts my father's throat.

I hurl myself at the man, screaming, trying to rake my nails down his face, to gouge out his eyes. But he feels nothing, hears nothing. I know it's too late, that all of this happened so long ago, that I'm helpless to stop it. But I press my hands against my father's throat all the same, trying to staunch the flow of blood as he crumples to his knees.

It does no good. His eyes dull. He falls, face-first, to the floor in a pool of his own blood.

Across the room, my mother howls from behind the hand that's clamped over her mouth. "It's time," the leader says to the man that holds her back.

Oh. God. No.

She doesn't go down easily. Instead she strains toward baby-me, trying desperately to get away, twisting and writhing. Tears pour down her face.

But he kills her anyway.

My mother and father lie on the floor of the once-peaceful, once-beautiful room, crumpled and bloodied. Baby-Rune wails, coughing and choking as her—*my*—lungs fill with smoke. She reaches out for her parents, but no one pays her any heed. Instead, one by one, heedless of the flames that rampage through the room, the black-hooded figures cut their arms.

"*Non sine sanguine gloria,*" the leader intones.

"No glory without blood," the others echo.

As one, they dip their fingers into their blood, then raise their hands high. And in the middle of the room, that familiar scroll-and-dagger symbol materializes, burnt into the very air.

Their job done, the hooded figures flee through the window once more, taking baby-Rune with them, still wrapped in the yellow blanket. The last thing I see before the memory fades to nothing is the rocking chair engulfed in flame, fire devouring the last place where I felt safe.

I LAND BACK in my body with a thump, my pulse pounding in my fingertips, my throat, my chest. The room isn't dark anymore. The lights have come back on, the candles have gone out, and Mrs. Grant is sitting opposite me, looking like her normal self again. For a moment, I wonder if I imagined all of it. But my palm still aches, and when I unfold my fingers and look down at it, I see the scroll and dagger branded there.

I don't even realize tears are streaming down my cheeks until Mrs. Fontaine presses a tissue into my hand. "Here, dear," she says, her voice filled with sympathy.

I take it, dabbing at my face. But I can't manage to form a word. All I can picture are the vivid details of that terrible memory. Rage at those hooded men blends with grief over what I've lost, so profound that my body feels too small to contain it. I wrap my arms around my knees, rocking back and forth.

Who were the men—and maybe women—beneath those hoods? Why would they commit an act so atrocious? Who are the blood witches, really, and what did they want with my family? Why did they spare my life? And are they the ones who cursed me?

I have so many questions. They bubble up inside me, one on

top of the next. I hardly know what to ask first, and my throat is so thick with sorrow, it's hard to swallow.

Mrs. Hernandez grips my shoulder, half-sympathetic, half-urgent. "What did you see, Rune?"

I don't want to talk about it. I'm not sure I *can* talk. But if I'm to have any hope of getting justice for my parents, of lifting my curse and maybe saving Donovan, I have to try.

Swiping the tissue beneath my eyes one last time, I sit up straight. Maybe I can't trust the Sinsters—but I have to trust *someone*. I'm in way over my head, and I'd rather confide in women I've known all my life than Officer Asshat. Sure, he helped me control my premonition, but that's not reason enough to believe he's on my side. For all I know, he's working for these Blood Witches, and was told to do whatever he needed to in order to gain my trust.

By contrast, the Sinsters have been looking out for me since I was small, obnoxious Facebook posts aside. Mrs. Grant has been feeding me milkshakes and burgers for years; if she wanted to poison me, she could have done it long ago. And thanks to her, as devastating as witnessing my parents' death was, I gained something no one can ever take away: the indelible reality of their love.

I draw a deep breath and tell the Sinsters everything I just witnessed. As I talk, their eyes grow wider and wider, but they don't interrupt. By the time I describe seeing my father crumple to the floor and watching my mother die, all three of them look glassy-eyed. Mrs. Grant pales, pressing a hand to her mouth. "Oh, Rune," she whispers. "Oh, you poor thing."

"The man who killed my father," I say, looking between the three of them. "His voice was so familiar. And what he chanted when they cast that symbol—*Non sine* something—"

"*Non sine sanguine gloria*," Mrs. Hernandez says, her nose wrinkling with contempt. "The motto of the Blood Witches, those despicable excuses for human beings."

"He was like some kind of cult leader." I sniff, wiping beneath my eyes with the sodden tissue. "I don't understand any of this.

How did my dad make those dragons and lions come out of nowhere? Is that a...thing people can do?" I sniff harder, but it doesn't help. The tears are flowing down my face now, splashing into my lap. "My parents seemed so...so nice. Why would anyone want to hurt them that way? And why save me?"

The three of them glance at each other, as if trying to come to a decision. Then Mrs. Fontaine nods, and they look back at me once more.

"Rune," Mrs. Grant says carefully, "what did you say your father's name was?"

"My mother called him David." I peer at her through my tears. "So did their leader. Why do you ask? Do you...do you know who my parents are? Who *I* am?"

"David. You said he was tall and bearded, right?" Mrs. Hernandez's hands are knotted in her lap. "And your mother had long brown hair?"

"Yes. Like mine." I lean forward eagerly. "Did you know them?"

Mrs. Grant doesn't answer me. Instead, she turns to the other two Sinsters. "Could it be? They did die in a fire, after all...and they had an infant daughter... But everyone said she was killed, too. The police found bones..."

I jump to my feet, adrenaline pumping through me. "Who died in a fire? Who are you talking about?"

"The bones could have been planted," Mrs. Fontaine says, ignoring me. "Stolen from some poor soul. As for the method of death, everyone said there was barely enough left of the Duvals to identify them..." Her eyes drift to me, and her voice trails off in horror.

I can't take the back-and-forth anymore. "Will someone please explain to me what's going on?"

Mrs. Hernandez clears her throat. "Rune," she says, squaring her shoulders, "thirty-one years ago, in a town not far from Sapphire Springs, two powerful witches who match the descriptions you've given us died when their house burned to the ground. Their names were David and Lorelai Duval. They had a young daughter, Iris, and everyone thought she perished in the fire, too. But if we're right, Iris Duval didn't die at all. If we're right"—her voice catches—"she's standing right in front of us."

My vision goes fuzzy, and I have to steady myself on the curio cabinet. Inside, the Hummels rattle and shift. "Iris Duval...is my birth name? And my mother's name was Lorelai?"

Next to me, Mrs. Grant is pacing. "This is a crime of unspeakable proportions. Two of our own murdered that way, with their precious daughter forced to watch—and then to steal the child..." She takes my chin in her hands, shifting my face left and right. "Your eyes are like Lorelai's, now that I think about it. But I never suspected... Who would? To have you growing up right under our noses—one of our own—"

She drops her hands, her eyes hardening with anger. "All those years, going from one foster home to the next. There are protocols for the orphaned children of witches. A system, so that when your powers begin to manifest, you're not alone. What happened to you is a travesty, Rune. And I'm sorrier than I can say."

Tears rise in my throat again, and I push them back. "But... why put me in the foster system, then? If the Blood Witches wanted me so much, why not raise me themselves?"

"It would have caused too much suspicion." Mrs. Hernandez is on her feet, too, shaking her head. "They operate in secret. Their identities are a mystery—you saw those hoods. They walk among us. They look like us. But they're not like us." She spits the last few words. "If one of them suddenly acquired a small, traumatized child, questions would be asked. And that's the very last thing they can afford."

Mrs. Grant comes to a stop in front of me. "What *are* your powers, Rune? You do have them, yes?"

"I—"

"You can tell us," Mrs. Fontaine coaxes. "We'll help you. Guide you. We should have been doing this all along, if only we'd known."

I try again to describe my curse. To explain. But once again, the electricity crackles in the air. Once again, the word catches in my throat, and I can't speak it.

Grimly, Mrs. Grant folds her arms across her chest. "We'll get to the bottom of this later. For now, tell us what you can." She points at my branded hand. "How did this happen? And what did Ella read in your cards?"

I can't explain about my hand, since that's connected to a premonition. But I tell them what Ella saw. "*I see darkness surrounding someone you work with* is what she said. And she drew this symbol." I dig the napkin out of my purse again. "She said the person was connected to my parents' deaths, which means they have to be a Blood Witch, or aligned with them, right?"

"Most likely." Mrs. Fontaine's expression is fierce.

I look from one of the Sinsters to the next. "I'm going to find out who they are," I vow. "And when I do, I'm going to bring them to justice."

The Sinsters link hands. And then they reach out and weave their fingers through mine.

"Damn right you are," Mrs. Hernandez says. "And I'll tell you one thing, Rune Whitlock. You won't be doing it alone."

CHAPTER
Thirty~Two

I SPEND a good chunk of Saturday night with the Sinsters, learning everything I possibly can about Blood Witches (spoiler alert: not much, given the whole secret identity situation). What I discover boils down to this: they're power-hungry, greedy individuals who will stop at nothing to get what they want. And what they want, at least the way the Sinsters explained it to me, is control over the use and regulation of magic. Given that I didn't know magic existed before yesterday, this doesn't tell me a hell of a lot.

I'm desperate for more information, especially about my parents. But apparently, Cooper wasn't bullshitting me when he said that the dispersal of information was regulated. Mrs. Fontaine sketches the hierarchy out for me on a napkin: There's a coven that oversees the international use and regulation of magic, and then beneath that, there are national covens. In the United States, that's further divided into regional covens, each of which has a High Priestess. Sapphire Springs is in the southern region, and since we're not in a major metropolitan area, we don't have what Mrs. Fontaine actually calls "a local coven rep." So, the Sinsters report directly to our regional High Priestess, but only when summoned or at what Mrs. Fontaine termed "our annual convention." It was all I could do to stop from asking her if the convention took place in Salem, during Halloween.

Honestly, I think I might be a little punch-drunk, or maybe even in shock. Because the last thing I should be doing—the *very* last thing—is laughing about any of this. But gallows humor has always been my drug of choice, and as I stare down at Mrs. Fontaine's napkin, covered with hasty scrawls about coven reps and arrows denoting magical hierarchies, a desperate giggle bubbles up.

Before it can escape, I tell the Sinsters I have to go. They wave me out the door, with admonitions to be careful and too-long hugs. When Mrs. Hernandez pulls away, she's crying.

"I knew your mother, Rune," she whispers, patting my hand. "You're a credit to her. We'll find out who did this to your parents. And whatever's going on with your magic, we'll make it right."

As I shut Mrs. Fontaine's door behind me and make my way down the porch steps, I half-expect to step into Narnia...or at least, into the room with the red-tinged light. It seems impossible to me that, after the revelations of the past few hours, the rest of Sapphire Springs remains unchanged. But no: here are the neatly swept sidewalks with their overhanging oaks, the cars pulled into their respective driveways, the old-fashioned streetlamps and the starlit sky with its pale quarter-moon. The power's back on, so lights shine from kitchens and upstairs windows. It's all very cozy and domestic...except for me. I'm the one who's changed.

I have so many pieces of the puzzle. My premonitions. My curse. Donovan. Cooper. The Sinsters. The scroll-and-dagger symbol. My recovered memory about my parents. Now I just need to find a way to put them together, before the Blood Witches have the chance to make good on their promise in my premonition: *Our day will come.*

I'm half-dreading, half-anticipating Monday morning. Part of me wants nothing more than to charge into Smashbox and interrogate every employee about their connection to the magical world. And part of me is terrified of seeing Donovan again, for fear of how awkward things will be.

But when I walk into the office we share, he doesn't so much as lift his head. I settle down at my desk to discover that Ethan's cc'ed us on an email about how the client loved our presentation. Despite that, he's still got a bulleted list of questions and suggestions for both of us. Donovan and I work for hours across the room from each other, and...not a word. Until finally, I can't take it anymore.

"There's nothing between me and Cooper!" I blurt. It's the first thing I've said to him all day, other than "Hi," which he responded to with a grunt.

Unsurprisingly, he doesn't reply.

"Did you hear me?" I stand up, so I can see him over the wall of monitors that blocks him from view.

He doesn't so much as take his eyes off the screen. "Yes, I heard you, Rune. I just don't see a reason to respond. Whatever game you're playing, I have no desire to be a part of it."

"I'm not playing a game."

"Right." His fingers beat a rapid-fire tattoo on his keyboard, hard enough that it sounds like he's punishing it for its transgressions. "I forgot. You're cursed, and if I date you, I'll die."

"It's the truth. I know you don't believe me, but it is." I walk closer, close enough that I can smell the cedar-and-vanilla scent that emanates from him. He glances up at me, and God, those blue eyes of his...even cold with fury, they're so gorgeous, they take my breath away.

"I told you what my brother did to me, Rune. What an asshole he is. I poured my fucking heart out to you. And the whole time, you had some bullshit scheme going on with him behind my back."

"It's not like that!" I say, hands on my hips. The brand on my palm has faded, and I'm not sure if Donovan can see it, anyway. Who knows how these things work? Still, I have no desire to have to explain myself, just in case. "I swear to you," I say, folding my wounded hand into a fist, "I never saw Cooper's face or heard his name before the morning that I tried to push him out of the way of that bus."

"Sure," Donovan scoffs. "Then what does he want with you? Why did he say he believed your ridiculous story?"

He has me there. What am I supposed to say? *Your brother's a witch, I'm a seer, and we both know I need to stay away from you. Oh, and there's a Blood Witch on the loose at Smashbox who's responsible for the death of my parents. Want to help me find them?*

At a loss, I don't say anything, and Donovan's lips flatten into a thin line. "That's what I thought," he says.

I should let him believe that he's right about Cooper. It would be the easiest way to close the door on this discussion, for good. But I can't bear to do it. Even if he can never be mine, I can't stand for him to think that I would hurt him this way. That he's misjudged me so badly. "He didn't want me to date you, it's true," I say, the closest to the truth that I can manage. "But not because he wants me, or because there's some kind of plot going on. Honestly, he can't stand me. He just thinks I'm not good enough for you."

Donovan pushes back from his desk, rolling his eyes. "Oh, that makes so much sense. Because my brother thinks so highly of me, and the woman who supposedly tried to save his life is a subpar human being. If you're going to lie, Rune, at least try to make it believable."

He's on his feet now, glaring down at me. Only his desk separates us. And God, I want so badly to lean across it and kiss him.

"Donovan, please," I say instead. "That night—it meant something to me. If I could be with you, I would be. Please believe me."

He lets out a bitter laugh. "Let me tell you what I believe, Rune. I believe that we have to work together, to get this damn project done. And as far as I'm concerned, it can't be done soon enough. So we will coexist in the same space, and we will interact as we need to for professional purposes, and other than that, we'll each pretend the other one doesn't exist. Okay?"

"No!" I tell him hotly. "Damn it, Donovan, I'm trying to save your—"

"Everything cool in here?" It's Ethan, poking his head around the door. "I thought I heard yelling."

Donovan and I take an automatic step back from each other, even though the desk is already between us. "Everything's great," I say. "Just, um, getting a little bit passionate about the project."

I glance over at my irate coworker to make sure he's backing me up on this, but no luck. His hands are shoved in his pockets, and he's glowering in my general direction. Great. What happened to *interacting as we need to for professional purposes*?

"I see." Ethan's brow wrinkles in concern. "I came to get you for our meeting with the historical society. Don't want to be late, you know. But I have to tell you, I'd hoped the two of you would've warmed up to each other a little more by now."

"We're fine," Donovan says stiffly.

"Oh, sure." His gaze shifts between the two of us. "I take back my question. It's not cool in here. It's the freaking Arctic. Frost, you're more than living up to your name."

Donovan transfers the glower to Ethan, who—as usual—is unaffected by anything other than his own priorities. He winks at Donovan, as if the glower is an inside joke between them. "Listen, I've been meaning to organize a little overnight retreat for Smashbox. Not the whole company, mind you. Just a small group of my most productive employees, to focus on teambuilding and trust, that kind of thing. And looking at what's going on in here, I don't think there could be a better time."

A smile spreads across his bearded face, as if he's just announced that he's giving out free hundred-dollar bills. But Donovan and I don't return it. We're both staring at him with matching expressions of horror.

"You want us to hang out at some corporate slumber party where we'll sit around doing icebreakers and trust falls?" Donovan says, just as I stutter, "Overnight? Us? That's really not necessary. We have a lot of work to do."

"Exactly," Ethan says, smiling more widely than ever. "And you're not getting it done here. You're just arguing. What you two need is a little getaway. I've got the perfect facilitator. It'll be just the thing. Now come on, we don't want to keep the historical society waiting."

He turns, strolling out the door. Donovan stalks after him, and I follow, two thoughts on loop in my head. First: I've landed an all-expenses-paid overnight trip with the unfairly hot guy I need to keep my distance from, on literal pain of death. And second: depending on who Ethan's including in this nightmarish little gathering, he may have just handed me the perfect opportunity to discover which Smashbox employee is linked to my parents' murder.

CHAPTER
Thirty~Three

DONOVAN DOESN'T SAY a word on our way down in the elevator. He doesn't so much as look at me on the five-minute walk to the historical society's headquarters, a few blocks down Orchard Street. Ethan's right: I can practically feel the chill radiating off him. It's so strong, I have to fight a shiver with every step.

Or maybe that's just the way being close to Donovan affects me. Because watching his shoulders shift beneath the pressed material of his button-down, seeing the sunlight glint off his blue-black hair…it makes me want to pin him up against the storefront of Brew Box and have my wicked way with him. Thank God Ethan is with us, because I don't trust myself.

What the hell am I going to do on a freaking overnight getaway with him, where the entire purpose is for us to get to know each other better and learn how to get along? Maybe I can arrange to be bitten by a bat or a rabid dog or something. Because this little venture is doomed to go down in flames.

But no. I need to go. What better chance will I have to figure out who killed my parents? If the murderer is one of the people Ethan's included in the retreat, then I'll have the chance to investigate them up close. Which sounds great and all, but how will I tell if they're guilty? It's not like they'll have a scroll-and-dagger tattooed on their forehead or a luggage tag that reads, "Blood Witches R Us. I'm the problem, it's me." And I can't rely on my premonitions to tell me anything reliable: they only show me things that are about to happen, so unless whoever it is plans to conduct a blood sacrifice on our corporate retreat, I'm shit out of luck.

Impervious to the turmoil raging within me and the wall of ice that Donovan's erected between us, Ethan chatters happily all the way down the street, all about how we're going to have such an excellent time at the retreat, the setting is absolutely gorgeous, it'll be exactly what we need. I make polite conversation, but I can't seem to focus on anything for more than two seconds. Which is probably why I trip over an uneven piece of concrete and go hurtling through the air, one arm outstretched in a futile attempt to regain my balance, in the world's worst impression of Wonder Woman.

There's an instant when I'm honest-to-God airborne. And then I collide with something warm and solid and, along with whatever it is, go hurtling to the ground.

We land with a shriek (me) and an aggravated grunt of pain (the solid thing I've landed on, which, of course, turns out to be Donovan).

Fuck my life.

He's taken the brunt of our fall and is lying on his back on the concrete. I'm on top of him, our chests pressed together and his hands gripping my hips. It's the perfect position for doing a lot of things, none of which I a) should ever do with Donovan, and b) should be thinking about in front of my boss.

Donovan stares up at me, his eyes wide and shocked. His hair is mussed, and there's a streak of dirt on his cheek. "What. The. Fuck," he manages, his chest heaving as he tries to catch his breath.

An electric shock prickles through me, radiating from every point our bodies touch. Who knows—maybe my nervous system is shorting out. It would be preferable to having to live through the next few mortifying minutes. "I'm sorry," I say, trying to wriggle away from him.

He glares, holding me still. "Don't move," he bites out, and a moment later, I realize why. I can feel him against me, even through the layers of my jeans and his khakis…which, I couldn't help but notice this morning, fit as if they were made for him. They don't leave a lot of room for error, and if our oh-so-sexy encounter against the office door was any indication, room is exactly what Donovan requires.

Shit, shit, shit. "Oh," I squeak out, doing my best imitation of a statue. All I can think of is what he said in the gazebo: *I wanted to pin you to the mirrored wall of that damn elevator and push up that little skirt and ravage the hell out of you. To see you wrecked just for me.*

That prickling electricity heightens, raging through my entire body. Heat follows it, pooling low in my belly and between my legs. I wonder if Donovan can feel it, because his hands grip my hips even tighter. "Not. Helping," he hisses.

Ethan is looming over us now, blocking out the sun. "Are you two okay?" he says, sounding like he's suppressing a chuckle.

"I'm fine. Donovan, um, broke my fall." I gesture down at him, in case Ethan hasn't noticed that I'm straddling his data engineer like a bar's mechanical bull on Tequila Tuesday.

Donovan shifts uncomfortably beneath me, which *really* doesn't help. My muscles clench in response, and his grip tightens so much, I'm pretty sure it's going to leave bruises. If we weren't in public, sweet purple ponies only knows what would happen next.

Two things are certain: This man and I have combustible chemistry. And we should never, ever be alone with each other. Not even on a public sidewalk.

Let go of me, I telegraph to him with my eyes. His communicate an equally clear message: *This is your fault. Also, bite me.*

"That was quite the heroic move, Frost," Ethan says, sounding cheerier than ever. "Didn't know you had it in you. Anything broken?"

"I'm not a hero," Donovan snaps, shifting me off him at last. "I was just *walking*, for Christ's sake. She cannoned into me." He spits the last words like a malediction.

"It was an accident," I protest, getting gingerly to my feet and looking anywhere but at him. The last thing I want is to get an eyeful of Mr. Happy, concealed by his khakis or otherwise.

Donovan snorts. "Please. You're a living, breathing agent of chaos."

The last time he called me 'chaos,' it was an endearment. Now, it's clear he means anything but. It stings, and I glare at him. Or at least I try to. I end up gaping, instead.

Mr. I-Probably-Iron-My-Underwear Frost is a disaster zone. His white button-down has come halfway untucked (probably a good thing, given the circumstances), and his khakis are ripped. Add the tousled hair and the streak of dirt, and he looks like he's taken a ride on the Hot Mess Express, paying special treatment at every station along the way.

A giggle escapes my lips, and he glowers at me, eyes narrowing to slits of blue murder. "What?" he growls.

A shiver ripples through me again, this one unrelated to the incendiary sexual tension that flares between the two of us anytime we're in the same vicinity. It's easy to forget how *big* Donovan is, given that he's usually ensconced in his ergonomic desk chair, muttering at his multiple monitors. But right now, disheveled and furious and at his full height, a foot away, he looks downright terrifying.

Cooper said Donovan was innocent. That he had nothing to do with the world of witches or magic. Certainly, he didn't recognize the scroll-and-dagger symbol when I showed it to him. But I have no reason to believe anything Cooper says. Was I wrong to eliminate Donovan from the list of suspects that might somehow be connected to my parents' death? Sure, he would've been too young then, but that doesn't mean his *family* wasn't responsible.

What if he and Cooper weren't enemies? What if they're somehow in cahoots?

No. That makes no sense; why would the Blood Witches want to kill one of their own? Donovan is a victim here. Or a potential victim, anyway. My job is to keep him safe from me, not implicate him in the worst event of my life. Never mind that since the day I met him, my life has gone completely off the rails.

He's just pissed off that my clumsiness resulted in humiliating both of us. And I don't blame him. I want desperately to put his shirt to rights, to wipe the streak of dirt from his face, to stand on my tiptoes and whisper that I'll make it up to him later. But 100 percent of that is a terrible idea.

"Why are you looking at me like that?" His brows have lowered now, thunderclouds descending over blue skies.

I do my best to pull myself together. "I'm not looking at you any way," I tell him, just as Ethan says, "Can you blame her, Frost? I don't think I've ever seen you with a damn hair out of place before, man. You took quite a beating in the name of chivalry. I mean, look at Rune, here." He gestures at me. "Not so much as a wrinkle in that lovely silk shirt of hers. Maybe you should take up a career as a bodyguard."

"Or an acrobat," I offer. I don't mean to say it, I swear. It just slips out.

What can I say? I babble when I'm anxious.

Donovan glares between the two of us, mutters something in which only the words, "Let's get this over with" are audible, and storms off in the direction of the historical society, putting his clothes to rights as he goes.

Thirty-Four

THE MEETING at the historical society is most notable for Donovan's grudging attempts at civility, Ethan's irrepressible enthusiasm for Sapphire Springs' genealogy, and my struggle not to shoot meaningful glances in Mrs. Fontaine's direction.

I'd forgotten she sits on their board, which wouldn't normally be a big deal; Sapphire Springs' old families are all intertwined in one way or another. Early on in my career, when I was still a hungry freelancer, I designed a ton of programs and marketing collateral for local fundraisers. After a while, I couldn't help but notice the names that appeared again and again, both as board members and as sponsors. Mrs. Fontaine, Mrs. Grant, and Mrs. Hernandez were freaking *everywhere.* Back then, I thought it was just because they were committed to *doing their civic duty,* as Charlotte's mother would put it. But now, I wonder if it's because they wanted to keep their fingers on the pulse of what was happening at the highest level of Sapphire Springs, where the folks with old money spent their time. Is that what a coven's supposed to do? What *do* they do, anyway? I have so many questions.

Ethan briefs the society's board on our project, which is essentially 23andMe for our local area, with some bells and whistles, and the society's board members have some interesting suggestions about graphic user interfaces that have worked well for similar endeavors. I try to do my best impression of an attentive listener, but honestly, I couldn't care less. All I can think about is pulling Mrs. Fontaine aside and asking if she's had any luck connecting with this High Priestess, Marilyn Whoever-She-Is. As one minute fades into the next, it takes every bit of my self-control not to leap up and run from the room, screaming.

At long last, the meeting comes to an end. Donovan stands without looking at me and stalks out, Ethan stays to glad-hand with some of the board members, and I escape to the bathroom, motioning for Mrs. Fontaine to follow.

As soon as the door closes behind us, I lean back against the marble sink and get right into what's on my mind. We don't have much time, after all; someone might come in at any minute. "What happened when you tried to contact the High Priestess? Did you learn anything?"

Mrs. Fontaine adjusts the trademark black cat's-eye glasses she's worn as long as I've known her, her lips pursed in disapproval. "Shhhh. We can't talk about this now, Rune. It's not safe."

"There's no one in here! Look." I make a show out of ducking my head to peer under each stall. "I have to go out of town soon. At least give me something."

Her eyes narrow behind her glasses. "Out of town? When? And why?"

"For work, some kind of stupid corporate retreat. Ethan just told us about it; I don't have the exact dates yet. But"—I lower my voice—"I bet I can use it to find out something. If Ella's right about someone at Smashbox being behind my family's death, then maybe whoever it is will be at the retreat, too. I could snoop around, turn up some evidence."

Mrs. Fontaine's hands fall to her hips. She's wearing a very proper tunic from Talbot's, cinched with a belt, but the expression on her face is feral. "You most certainly will not! You can't put yourself in jeopardy that way, Rune." If someone could whisper-yell, that's what she's doing. "I've asked the—the *higher authority* what she thinks of all this. She wants to come to Sapphire Springs. To meet you. And to do that, you need to be here. Not off on a fool's errand with the very people who might have killed David and Lorelai!" She claps a hand over her mouth, shooting a glance toward the door, like she thinks there might be someone out there with their ear pressed to the other side.

"It's not a fool's errand," I say stubbornly. "And I have to go. I need this job."

"A fat lot of good it'll do you if you're dead!" She raises a hand, counting off her points one by one. "The brand on your palm. The spikes in the ley lines' power. Andrew Cooper's presence here, to investigate them. Ella's premonition. Whatever's going on with your own powers, which you can't even speak to me about. All of it adds up to something highly suspicious, Rune. And you're at the center of it. The goddess only knows what danger you'll be in if you hare off this way!"

Maybe it's the fact that the monster, the man I feared for so many years, is dead. Maybe it's that I'm sick of being at the mercy of premonitions I can't control. Or maybe it's that some secret, stupid part of me relishes the idea of going on a retreat with Donovan Frost. Either way, I dig in my heels. "Where was this *higher authority* of yours when I was being shuttled from one crappy foster home to another?" I demand. "I've waited my whole life to meet her. If she wants to talk to me so badly, she can wait a few days more."

Mrs. Fontaine tucks her silvered hair behind her ears, forehead creased with alarm. "I understand that you're upset, Rune, and I don't blame you. But the High Priestess doesn't wait for anyone. If she wants to see you, you obey her summons."

Seriously? "I don't know what to tell you, but I'm going on this retreat. You've got my cell number. If you find out anything while I'm gone, please call me."

"But—"

"I have to go," I tell her. "Ethan will be wondering where I am."

With that, I brush past her and push open the bathroom door. Her face scrunches into a knot of concern, and she toys with the strap of her mammoth purse, as if she's considering swinging it at my head to knock me out cold. But she doesn't attempt to stop me.

Ethan intercepts me halfway toward the conference room. "There you are!" he says. "Frost took off, probably to catalogue the damage. You really did a number on him."

My cheeks burn. "I just tripped. I didn't mean to knock him down."

"Ah, it was good for him. He's a helluva data engineer, but a little uptight, you know?" He winks at me. "Anyway, I think this little get-together went well. The historical society's a fantastic resource. Don't hesitate to consult them if you think they can help. In the meantime, Ellen will be sending you an itinerary for the retreat. It starts tomorrow at 10:00 a.m., up at the center in Granville Falls. You're familiar with it, right?"

My phone buzzes, but I ignore it, fixated on the words that have just come out of his mouth. One word, in particular. "Tomorrow?"

He's busy staring down at his smartwatch, swiping through what looks like a thousand emails. "Yes," he says, sounding absentminded. "Sorry about the short notice. We've been planning it for a while, of course, but I didn't think to include you, since you normally work from home, and Frost—well, he'd sooner spend his free time tethered to a keyboard than hanging out with actual human beings. But I can tell the two of you could use some assistance navigating your working relationship, and the timing's perfect."

I want to ask him what gave it away, but I don't trust my voice. "How long is this retreat, anyway?" I ask instead.

"Oh, just two nights." He's poking away at his watch now, his index finger stabbing at a shiny icon. "I've got to go. Lots to organize, you know? But we'll have a great time in Granville. Watch for that email." And then he's gone, striding out the historic society's double wooden doors, heedless of the cluster fuck he's left in his wake.

I can't go on a retreat with Donovan *tomorrow*. We're not even speaking to each other, by which I mean *he's* barely speaking to *me*. Sure, he fed me that line about needing to interact for professional purposes, but what does that even mean? If we had to participate in a trust fall exercise, I bet he'd accidentally-on-purpose let me hit the floor. And if our roles were reversed, he'd probably think I'd let him crash and burn on purpose…that I planned to humiliate him and then go running right back to Cooper with the news.

My head roiling, I dig my phone out of my purse to see who texted me. It's Charlotte, who's been checking in on me ever since I ran out of her house during the blackout.

> Let me know when you want to get together and talk about the parent thing some more

Oh, God. With everything that's happened, I haven't even thought about what to tell Charlotte. Last thing she knew, I was desperate to discover my parents' identities. Now I know who they are and how they died…but there's no way I can explain that to my best friend. What the hell am I going to do?

When in doubt, delay.

> thanks, I will. just found out I have to go out of town for work tho

Her response is instant.

Omg. with grumpy sex spreadsheet guy? 

This is going from bad to worse.

Yes unfortunately. I'll keep you posted. Would you mind feeding Valentine while I'm gone? I'll owe you one

When she agrees, thank goodness—the girls are obsessed with my cat, and she thinks this will "teach them responsibility"—I shove my phone back into my purse and walk outside, half-hoping, half-fearing that Donovan will be waiting for me, so we can have a much-needed conversation about how to handle the next two days. But no such luck. Because the moment I step onto the historical society's wide front porch, there, in full uniform, arms folded across his chest and jaw clenched so tight he could give Donovan a run for his money, is Andrew Cooper.

"Goddamn it, Rune. What the hell did you do to my brother?" he growls.

I GAPE AT HIM, bewildered. "Where did you come from?"

"I live here." He folds his arms across his chest, lounging back against one of the white brick columns that lines the porch. "Surely you gathered that much from our little chat."

"You live *here*? Like, on the porch of the historical society?" I'm not being sarcastic—who the hell knows what witches do?—but under the light-brown prickle of his five-o'-clock stubble, his jaw clenches even further. The local dentists must've sent up celebratory flares when he and Donovan moved to town.

"Yes, Rune," he says from between gritted teeth. "My residence is underneath that rocking chair." He stabs a finger at the handcrafted object in question. "I piss in the corner whenever the need arises. You know, to mark my territory."

Okay, so this isn't going well. "There's no need to be such a dick."

His brows rise. "I beg to differ. And I'm here because *you're* here. I told you, I'm drawn to power. About an hour and a half ago, I felt a surge. When I trace it to its source, what do I find? You and Donovan, inside this building. And when he comes storming out, his pants are ripped, his shirt is wrinkled, and he's even more of an uptight asshole than usual. So, I repeat"—he pushes off the

column, glaring down at me with those unnerving blue eyes—
"what did you do?"

I'm getting damn tired of being glared at by the two of them. "I tripped."

Cooper blinks at me, like a large, incredulous owl. "You what?"

"I *tripped*, okay? And when I fell, I knocked him over. That's how he got all…ripped and wrinkled. I didn't have my wicked way with him on the table of the historical society's board room. Satisfied?"

Cooper's face goes through a bizarre series of metamorphoses: annoyance, comprehension and, finally, amusement. "That's quite an image," he drawls, leaning back against the column again. "Also, oddly specific."

"It's the truth! You can ask any of the fifty people who were probably spying on us through their windows. I'm surprised it hasn't hit the Sapphire Springs Facebook page yet."

"Let's look, shall we?" He cocks a brow, pulling his phone from his pocket. "Ah yes, there it is. You, on top of my brother, looking like you're about to violate twenty public decency statutes. Let's see… Oh, how charming. #donorune #ronovan #steamyinthesprings."

His delivery is so deadpan, I can't tell if he's joking. I wrench his phone from his hand, earning an outraged growl, and stare down at the screen. And…yeah, he's not lying. There we are: Donovan staring up at me, his hands fisted on my hips. Me, straddling him, my hair spilling down everywhere. And Ethan, in the background, looking bemused.

"Oh, no," I mumble, more to myself than to Cooper. "Who posted this? I want to wring their neck. And then maybe sauté their liver with some fava beans."

"Please do." Cooper snatches his phone back, scowling down at it. "Nothing would give me more pleasure than arresting you again and sticking you in a cell where I can keep an eye on you. I told you to stay away from my brother. Not tackle him and give him a lap dance."

Hot blood surges into my cheeks. "It was an accident! And I *have* stayed away from him."

"I beg to differ." He waves the phone at me. "Exhibit A. Also" —he jerks his head at the building behind me—"Exhibit B."

"I *fell*, Cooper. And we work together! I have no choice about that. Not if I want to keep my job." First Mrs. Fontaine, then him. What is so hard to understand about this? "I don't have a family to back me up. I don't have a safety net. Every single good thing in my life exists because I worked my ass off for it. I need this job to keep a roof over my head and pineapple pizza in my mouth. Unfortunately, Donovan comes with it. But the project we're collaborating on is finite, and then I'll go back to working at home, from my little cave. Okay?"

Cooper's mouth twitches. "Pineapple pizza is disgusting. I knew I couldn't trust you."

Oh. My. God. This entire discussion is a waste of time. Unless I plan to quiz Cooper about his presence here—and I'm not entirely sure if I should, until I talk to this mysterious High Priestess— then the less I have to do with him, the better.

"If one of us shouldn't trust the other, I think you've got the shoe on the wrong foot," I tell him, hoisting my purse strap higher on my shoulder. "I have to go."

His brows lower, as if he can't make sense of what I'm saying. "You don't trust me?"

He looks so affronted by the very idea, it forces a laugh from my throat. "Why should I? The first time I meet you, you arrest me. Then you sideswipe Donovan's car. The next time I see you, you interrupt my conversation, explain you've got secret super- powers, and refuse to answer any of my questions. Your own brother can't stand you. Now here you are, ambushing me like a stalker and criticizing my pizza preferences. Tell me, what's to trust?"

Cooper's jaw drops open. A breeze sweeps through the porch,

ruffling his hair, and he completes its dishevelment by shoving his hand through it. "I'm not a stalker, Rune. I'm the guy who arrests the stalkers. And you tackled me before I slapped the cuffs on you. Something you seem to make a habit of." He shakes the phone, with its incontrovertible evidence. "As for the car wreck, that's on you, not me. If you weren't leaking power all over the place like a goddamn sieve, I wouldn't have lost control that way." He bites out 'lost control' like a curse. "Donovan and I have…history. It has nothing to do with you. And I told you why I couldn't answer your questions. You should trust me more for honoring the protocols I'm sworn to, not less."

I eye him, my desire to punch him in the face only tempered by the knowledge that it would surely end with me in a cell. I have no desire to reinvigorate my arrest record, potentially losing my job and my best opportunity to track down my parents' killers in one fell swoop. "I was saving your life. And don't pin your inability to control yourself on me. That sounds a hell of a lot like blaming the victim, *Cooper*. Surely they teach you better than that in cop school. Now, either give me useful information or get out of my way. I have to pack."

An expression I can't quite decipher ripples across his face—disbelief, maybe, with a chaser of respect. His tongue darts out, tracing a path across his lower lip, but not in a lascivious way. It looks…like he's tasting something. Namely, me. "What *are* you?" he whispers hoarsely.

"I'm in a rush, is what I am," I tell him. "So, if you don't mind…"

I gesture beyond him, at the steps of the historical society that lead down to the sidewalk. But he doesn't budge. "I do, actually. Come here." He takes hold of my sleeve before I can protest and tugs me around the corner of the wraparound porch, out of view of the street and anyone who might come through the double doors.

"What are you do—"

"Be quiet for a minute. If that's possible." Dropping my sleeve, he backs away from me. "I talked to…certain people about you. You shouldn't exist, Rune."

Well, this is a new low. "Excuse me?" My voice emerges in a squeak.

"That came out wrong. But you know what I mean. You should be dead. Why aren't you?" He peers down at me like my existence is a personal affront.

"Wow, you really know how to flatter a girl." I roll my eyes at him. "You probably know more about me than I do, Cooper. And if you talked to that High Priestess of yours, you can just say so. You don't have to hide behind all this ridiculous subterfuge, like some kind of magical 007." First Mrs. Fontaine with her *higher authority*, like she's talking about Hebrew National hot dogs rather than some wacko mystical politician. Then, this.

"Don't say her name!" His blue eyes widen in alarm. "You're messing with things that are way over your head, Rune. And your power…" He shakes his head. "When you…fell…on top of Donovan that way, I felt the surge five blocks over. I don't think the spikes in the ley line are just about you. I think they have something to do with the two of you, together."

A shiver wracks me, followed by the memory of the strange electricity that rippled through me when Donovan's body pressed against mine. "That's ridiculous," I say feebly.

"Is it? Weren't the two of you together, the first time it happened?"

"Well, yes. But not the second time."

"The damage was already done." Cooper swallows hard, his Adam's apple shifting above the collar of his uniform shirt. "Ley lines are the source of all the magical power in the world, Rune. If they malfunction, so will our gifts. Imagine powerful magicians all over the country, unable to control themselves."

Now it's my turn to swallow. "You mean…"

He nods grimly. "Natural disasters. Ghosts rising from the dead. A hundred other things I don't have the time to explain to you. It'll make hitting you with my car look like a picnic." He leans toward me, as if desperate to make me understand. "My… other boss…is trying to get to the bottom of this. I know about the vision you had, Rune. About what happened to your parents, and the symbol you saw. And about who's responsible. We need to drive them out of the shadows. Then you'll get justice. But in the meantime, I reiterate—stay the hell away from my brother, before you bring us all down."

The hell with the ley lines. A week ago, I didn't even know they existed. And I'm sick and tired of getting ordered around. "No can do. I'm going on an overnight retreat for Smashbox tomorrow. And so is Donovan."

Cooper jerks back, as if I've slapped him. "That can't happen."

"Well, it *is* happening," I say irritably. "And I think it could be a good thing. You know that justice you mentioned? I'm not just going to sit by and let other people get it for me. I'm the one who lost my parents. This is my past and my future."

"It's all our futures! Don't you understand that?" He snatches up the hand bearing the faded brand, his eyes fixed on my palm. "This isn't normal, Rune. It means…they…are rising. We need to put a stop to all of this, and we can't do that if you go galivanting off. And you especially can't go galivanting off with my damn brother, who you're destined to *kill!*"

"Don't tell me what to do. And let go of me," I snarl, trying to yank my hand away.

His grip is iron. "Not until you tell me you understand."

"I *understand* I barely know you, and what I know, I don't like. And if you don't let go of me right this moment, I'm going to scream bloody murder, cop or no cop."

Cooper's eyes narrow. I glare right back at him. But he doesn't let go.

And so that's what Donovan sees, when he comes around the corner: Cooper holding my hand, the two of us inches apart, locked in an intense stare-down.

Freaking fantastic.

THE SCOWL DONOVAN levels me with when he sees me with Cooper could freeze hell over. But by the time I manage to yank my hand out of his asshole brother's, he's long gone.

I resolve to explain—somehow—when we're at the retreat together. The whole time I pack, following the instructions on Ethan's assistant's comprehensive list, I try to figure out how. It's probably for the best: the more pissed off Donovan is at me, the less our combustible chemistry will matter to him, even if we're stuck atop a mountain together. I just don't want him to be angry at me over a lie.

The good news is, all night long, no one shows up on my doorstep to yell at me or deliver disturbing revelations about my life. No one posts more photos of me and Donovan in a compromising position, and despite Charlotte's gleeful texts, I ignore the comments on the #ronovan Facebook post. (Thanks a lot, D'Andre.) No premonitions ambush me all night or on the drive up to Granville Falls, where I blast *Born This Way* in defiance of my fate.

The retreat center is gorgeous, located atop a mountain with stunning views in every direction, rustic log cabins, and sprawling meadows edged by woods. In my room, I tuck my jeans into the dresser and stow my toiletries. Then, at ten on the dot, I walk into the main lodge.

The first thing I see is Donovan, standing in front of the wall of windows that overlooks the mountain backdrop, backlit and looking unfairly handsome. He's wearing a forest-green Henley, which clings to his chest in ways that ought to be illegal, and his jaw is clenched, Heathcliff-on-the-moors-style.

Swallowing hard, I force myself to take in the rest of my surroundings. There are twelve of us total—ten employees, plus Ethan and the facilitator. I only know two of them: Georgia, of sex-spreadsheet fame, and Jill, who once called Donovan *sexy as sin but cold as ice.* He lives up to his name, stubbornly refusing to so much as look in my direction.

I need to apologize to him. But this isn't the time. Instead, I give myself strict instructions: 1) Observe all attendees closely for suspicious behavior, 2) Explain to Donovan about Cooper but do not kiss him, no matter what, 3) Try not to humiliate myself in spectacular fashion.

And then, because God hates me, the first team-building exercise I have to do on the retreat is the human knot…with Georgia, Jill, Dean from IT, and the Ice Man himself.

"Here's the deal," Rosa, the chirpy retreat leader, says from the front of the room. She looks like she's lifted straight from a Disney movie, her blonde hair scraped back into a perfect ponytail and her brown eyes bigger and shinier than eyes have any right to be. I half-expect little birds to start buzzing around her head. "Each of you grabs the left hand of someone across the circle from you, using your own left hand. Then you do the same thing with your right. After you've done that, your goal is to use verbal communication to disentangle yourselves, so that you wind up in your original circle. There's only one rule: you can't let go."

I gape at her, dismayed, but it's Donovan who speaks. "You want us to *what?*" he says, each syllable a gravelly scrape of horror.

"I'll demonstrate." Rosa bounces in our direction like an

overly caffeinated, Sephora'ed kangaroo. "What's your name?" she says, coming to a stop next to him.

Donovan looks even more horrified than before. "Donovan Frost," he mutters, so low she has to ask him to repeat himself.

When I first met Donovan, I would've thought he was just being an ass. But now, I know he's shy. A day of icebreakers and forced teambuilding is basically his worst nightmare. Add in my presence, and he's entered the ninth circle of Hell.

I feel awful for him. And I feel even worse that I can't show it.

"Okay, Donovan!" Rosa chirps. "This is how it works. You— what's your name?" And then, of course, she points right at me.

"Rune," I say, a familiar, encroaching sense of doom creeping over me.

"Super groovy," Rosa says, beaming with delight. "Okay, Donovan! Raise your left hand, reach across the circle, and take Rune's."

Donovan closes his eyes, as if he's commending his soul to God. "Is that really necessary?"

"I understand you're uncomfortable," Rosa says, patting his shoulder. "That's normal. But if you just let go and surrender to the process, it'll transform you. You'll see."

"I'm not *uncomfortable*. I just think this is…" For once, his expression is completely transparent to me. I can see him sort through and discard *total bullshit, a waste of time, the worst moment of my professional life* before he settles on, "…not for me. No offense. I'll just sit this one out and—"

"Not happening, Frost," Ethan calls from across the room, his grin matching Rosa's. "This is exactly why you need to be here. Now come on. Go with the flow."

Maybe Ethan's the one I ought to be investigating. No one should be that happy all the time. And God knows you'd have to be low-key Satanic to organize one of these retreats. But what kind of criminal mastermind spends his days running a tech company in a tiny town, talking like a surfer boy and collecting Marvel bobbleheads?

Looking like he'd rather be getting a root canal, Donovan braces himself, reaches across the circle, and takes my hand in his. His skin is warm against mine, his thumb sliding against my palm and his fingers skating across my knuckles, as if they belong there.

I will myself not to feel anything. To have his hand in mine be nothing more than the touch of skin on skin. The instant our fingers touch, though, I know I'm kidding myself.

The electric sensation that prickled through me when I landed on top of him is back, but this time it's much more intense. My whole body hums, as if I've plugged myself into an electrical socket. Goosebumps erupt on my bare arms. Desire coils in my belly, slipping eager and hungry through my veins.

I steal a glance at Donovan and suck in a startled breath. His lips are parted, his eyes hot. Gone is the Ice Man who wouldn't so much as look in my direction. His hand tightens on mine, his grip convulsive, like he's resisting the urge to pull me toward him. And God help me, even knowing what I do, I would let him.

The rest of the human knot activity is honest-to-God torture. I've never been so grateful for Donovan's superior analytic skills, which piss me off on a regular basis but at least allow our group to untangle ourselves in record speed, beating the other group by a country mile. The moment we're free of each other, I excuse myself and dash for the restroom, where I splash cold water on my crimson cheeks and stare in dismay at my dilated pupils. I look like a woman who's just had the best sex of her life, not an employee who was just forced to engage in a cliched team-building exercise. And if I can see it, so can everyone else—including Donovan.

We break for lunch, which I eat with Georgia and Jill, trying my best not to glance in Donovan's direction. Instead, I focus on trying to assess whether either of them could possibly have played a role in what happened to my family. But they're just so... ordinary. It doesn't seem possible. Georgia's ten years older than me, with two kids and a husband who doesn't pick up his dirty socks. Jill's unabashedly single and spends her weekends singing karaoke. Neither one of them screams "notorious Blood Witch, destroyer of worlds."

Maybe I was crazy, thinking I could figure this out. Maybe Ella's premonition was wrong. Maybe…a thousand things.

Maybe our next activity is Profile Bingo.

"Okay, everyone!" Rosa hands each of us a neon Post-it, then claps her hands. "I want you to write down something about yourself that not a lot of people know. Then hand it to me. I'll type it up on a Bingo-style grid, give each of you a copy, and you'll walk around the room and talk to everyone, matching them with their little secret. When you're done, you'll hand your sheets in to me. Sound good?"

I've changed my mind. Rosa is the villain I've been searching for, in perky, shiny disguise. Because somehow, I find myself scribbling "likes pineapple pizza" on a piece of paper and handing it to her, along with eleven other poor souls who have fallen under her spell. She collects all of our little slips, humming and chuckling to herself as she reads them, then types them up, prints them out, and sets us free.

Jill, I discover, is obsessed with Red Vines and the Shrek franchise. Jack, who works in HR, orders Mallomars in bulk from Amazon. Catelyn, a redhead in the sales department, designs her own board games. Gia, who's been with the company from the very beginning, was once kissed by John Travolta. Ellen, Ethan's assistant, has visited forty-seven countries. Thatcher, who works in R&D, can say "hold my beer" in six languages.

None of these people seem like uber-villains, or even remotely nefarious. Some of them even make me laugh. But the whole time I'm talking with them, I can't help but be aware of the six-foot-two data engineer who's leaning against the wall, glowering at the room at large, ignoring the rules of Profile Bingo. He waits for people to come to him, and when they do, they always wander off looking rattled. After one such encounter, Georgia leans into me and whispers, "I can't decide if he's hot, or just…terrifying."

I consider avoiding Donovan altogether. But Rosa's patrolling the room like a prison guard searching for infractions and contraband, and finally I have no choice. "Here," I say, thrusting my sheet toward him. "X out your thing."

He looks down at the only free box left. In bold, black Times New Roman 14-point font, it reads, "I don't like liars." Which, clearly, is a message meant for me.

"You know," I say, shoving a pen into his hand, "if you were actually speaking to me, you could have conveyed this aloud, rather than scaring everyone here. And then I would have told you that I haven't lied about anything."

Donovan Xes through his Profile Bingo box with so much force, he tears through the paper. "Right. Like your mystical curse. And your relationship with my brother, who I saw you *holding hands* with. Is that what you want me to talk about, Rune?"

Tears sting my eyes. "I—"

"Or maybe you want to talk about what happened on the sidewalk. Or when that sadistic cheerleader made us touch, before. You want to talk about that? Because I sure as shit don't." He pushes the paper back into my hands, his jaw a hard line.

The tears overflow, spilling down my cheeks. "Donovan, please."

He shakes his head, his gaze ice-cold. "I don't know what your game is, but whatever it is, I don't want to play. Go back to Cooper and tell him that, why don't you? Tell him he wins. I'm out. And for the rest of the time we're here…stay away from me."

He stalks off before I can say a word, his Profile Bingo page crumpled in his hand.

Thirty-Seven

I STAND AGAINST THE WALL, watching him walk away. My heart aches. My eyes blur. And then the worst happens, as it so often does when my emotions run high.

The red haze rises, clouding my vision. The door cracks open. And the undertow comes, pulling me onward.

Not now, I beg, though I have no idea to whom. *Please, not now.*

I can't have a premonition here, in front of my boss and the people I work with. I can't look odd or pass out or mumble about the inexplicable. I have to do something. But what?

Help, I think again. And then I hear it: Cooper's voice, clear and calm in my head.

Breathe, Rune, he says. *Like before, remember? Take a deep breath in…count to four…hold it…then out for eight…*

I have no idea if he's real or an invention of my desperate subconscious. And at this moment, I don't care. All I know is that he helped me once before. He can help me again.

I do as he says, obeying as he stops counting and simply breathes, letting me listen to him, guiding me. Until, the same way it happened before, the haze retreats. The door closes. And somehow, miraculously, the premonition is…gone.

Holy shit.

Thank you, I think in Cooper's direction, but there's no response. He's vanished, if he was ever there at all.

Trembling, I straighten and assess the room. No one's staring at me. They're standing around in small groups, chatting—all except Donovan, who's peering down at his phone, probably wishing it would open up like a portal to another world and spirit him away. Rosa is busy recycling Profile Bingo pages. From what I can tell, less than a minute has passed.

I press a hand to my chest, feeling my racing heart slow. I don't know what just happened, whether it was wishful thinking or coincidence or a figment of my imagination. Or something else entirely—if Cooper somehow found a way inside my mind. If that's the case, he and I will have to have some serious words. In this very moment, though, I'm grateful.

Premonition or not, I don't want to stay here. All I want is to run out of the lodge. To pack my stuff, jump in my car, and drive home. Either that, or to throw my arms around Donovan and beg him to believe me. But none of those are viable options, so I wipe the tears from my face before anyone can see, pour myself a cup of bad coffee from the carafe at the back of the room, and take a seat next to Georgia at one of the round tables.

She eyes me suspiciously, then hands me a napkin. "Have you been *crying*, Rune? Are you okay?"

"I'm fine," I say, willing it to be true. The weakness that usually accompanies one of my premonitions is nowhere to be found. Aside from my Donovan-induced misery, I feel…normal. And there's nothing to do about my broken heart but deal with it.

"Sure you are." She wraps an arm around my shoulders. "I watched you talking to Donovan, right before he marched off. And I saw those Facebook posts, you know."

Oh, no. "Which Facebook posts, exactly?"

Georgia squeezes me tighter. "All of them, honey."

I. Want. To. Die.

"What did he say to you?" she asks, brows lowering. "Do I need to have a word?"

At the thought of short, plump Georgia confronting a glowering Donovan Frost, I almost giggle. But then reality sets in. "Oh, no. Please, don't say anything. It's just a misunderstanding." Of epic proportions. Never to be resolved.

"If you say so," Georgia says doubtfully, squeezing me one last time and then letting me go. She shoots Donovan an exceedingly dirty look, which he doesn't see because he's still staring down at his phone.

Georgia can't be a terrible human being, affiliated with murderous Blood Witches. Can she? She's always been so kind to me. But the more of this world I see, the more I realize that nothing is what it seems.

At the front of the room, Rosa clears her throat. "If I can have everyone's attention, please!"

It takes a couple tries to get the room to quiet down, but Rosa doesn't seem to mind. Maybe she's happy that Profile Bingo generated such camaraderie. Or maybe she's just impervious to irritation. I should take lessons from her.

"Our next activity will be an escape room!" she announces, rubbing her hands together. "We're going to divide you randomly into pairs, and you'll have to solve a series of puzzles in order to find your way out."

Georgia lets out a happy *eep*. She and her family adore escape rooms. For years, she's been telling me about how everywhere they travel, they try a different one. Next to me, she bounces in her chair.

"This is such a *meaningful* activity," Rosa goes on. "It forces you to work together one on one rather than in the larger groups we've been putting you in this morning. You'll have to really trust each other to succeed, which is what this retreat is all about, right? After you all escape, we'll have a special surprise for you in the main lodge."

I've never done an escape room. But how hard can it be? All I have to do is get through the next couple of hours or however long it takes, and then I'll be free to snoop around as much as I want. Sure, the people I've just met seem nice enough now, with their *hold my beer* and their John Travolta kisses, but it's not like they're going to expose their dark sides during team-building exercises. At night, though, especially with a few drinks in them, who knows what they might let slip?

"We've got everyone's names on pieces of paper in here." Ethan holds up a mason jar. "Rosa will pull them out two at a time. She and I will be participating, too. Remember," he looks between us, grinning, "you get what you get, and you don't get upset!"

Ugh. Why do I have the distinct feeling that that comment might be meant for me and a certain infuriated data engineer?

Before our most recent argument, I wouldn't have been that unnerved about being paired with Donovan. Sure, it would've been challenging to negotiate, but I wanted time alone with him anyhow, to clear the air about what happened with Cooper. And since he's been avoiding me like the plague, having him as a captive audience would've been the perfect time for us to talk. But now, when he's made it clear that nothing I say will make any difference to him—when he's so enraged that he's taken to communicating with me through Profile Bingo—the thought of being trapped with him in a scenario where we need to collaborate to escape makes my stomach roil.

Well, there are twelve people here, Rosa and Ethan included. Math isn't my strong suit, but even I can tell the odds are against me being paired with Donovan. *That won't happen,* I tell myself. *Maybe I'll even get lucky, and be matched up with the mysterious Dr. Evil.* That would certainly take the guesswork out of things.

I've talked myself halfway into believing this will happen when Rosa pulls the first slip from the jar. "Georgia," she announces happily, then pulls out another one. "And Ellen. Fantastic! The two of you, go stand by each other, please." She gestures to the wall of windows.

Looking elated, Georgia bounces across the room, Ellen following in her wake, as Rosa pulls two more slips out of the jar. "Ethan and Doug! Excellent, excellent."

Two pairs down. Four to go.

"Who's next?" Rosa rummages in the jar, her shiny, pink nails glinting through the glass. She grasps a piece of paper, pulls it out, and holds it up to the light. "Jill! Great, great. Now, let's see…"

She delves into the jar again, and I hold my breath, hoping the slip she pulls out next will have my name scrawled on it. Jill doesn't seem like a super-villain, true, but you never know. Maybe beneath her addiction to Red Vines and Shrek lurks the heart of a murderer. I don't know what it says about me that I'd rather be stuck in an escape room with a killer—or even, someone killer-adjacent—than with the man whose bones I'd like to jump, but there you have it.

But no. "Rosa!" our fearless leader announces gleefully. "That's me. Of course I can't go stand by the windows, since I've got a job to do here, but Jill, I'll be with you just as soon as I finish up. I'm so excited!"

Dutifully, Jill trots over to stand next to the other chosen ones. That leaves six of us standing, Hunger Games-style, waiting for our fate to be pronounced.

Rosa unfolds the next piece of paper. "Catelyn," she says. "And Jack!"

Crap, crap, and double crap. I watch Ms. I Design My Own Board Games happily cross to the windows, joined by Mr. My Guilty Pleasure Is Mallomars, and feel my heart sink into my toes. Because there's just four of us left, and the odds are definitely not in my favor.

I bite my lip as she pulls another slip from the jar. "Gia. Very nice. And…let's see…"

Please say Donovan, I chant to myself. *Please, please, please say Donovan.* I steal a glimpse at his face, but it's stony, expressionless.

Rosa sticks her hand back into the jar, digging around on the bottom. With just three slips of paper left, they keep skating away from her fingers. My heart pounds as she finally snags one and pulls it free. *Donovan Donovan Donovan* echoes like a drumbeat in my head as she unfolds it and holds it up to the light.

"And…Thatcher!" she says.

I am so screwed.

Thirty-Eight

DONOVAN and I follow Rosa's bouncing blonde ponytail down a set of stone steps carved into the mountainside. They're steep, and I pray I won't lose my balance and go hurtling to my death before I have the chance to investigate possible suspects tonight.

Oh God, what if that's what the Blood Witches have in mind? What if this is a trap, and they intend to kill us both down here?

But no. My premonition showed me that Donovan would die at our wedding. If he's going to live long enough for us to tie the knot, then neither of us can meet a terrible fate today.

But…what if I've somehow changed the future by making him hate me? If that's the case, then all bets are off. Maybe inside the so-called escape room, hooded killers are lying in wait. Maybe we're just marching to our deaths—or his, anyway—like complacent little piggies.

The sun is at its zenith, beating down on us, hotter than it has any right to be for September. I break out in a sweat as worries compete for my attention, popping up and down like lottery balls. The whole way down the stairs, an oblivious Rosa chatters about how this is the most awesome escape room at the retreat center, how we're about to have an experience we'll never forget.

"That's what I'm afraid of," Donovan mutters, and I resist the urge to kick him in the shin. I'd do it, if I wasn't petrified of falling and breaking my neck.

"Rosa," I say, trying not to sound overly suspicious, "why are there escape rooms here? That's not a thing retreats normally have, is it?"

"Well no," Rosa admits, somehow managing to look over her shoulder at me while navigating a particularly tricky step. "But Granville Falls isn't a typical retreat center. We specialize in adventures and next-level experiences. You should see our ropes course. You never know what you might discover up there!"

"Yeah, like how much I hate heights," comes from the grumpy data engineer behind me.

Rosa ignores him. "And here we are!" she announces, as we arrive in front of a tiny door cut into the rock face. Digging a key out of her Lululemon belt bag, she unlocks it. The door swings open, sending a welcome breath of cool air wafting outward.

If I'm going to be murdered, I'd rather take my last breath inside an air-conditioned room than here, in Hell's antechamber. I trail Rosa inside, followed by Donovan, who practically has to fold himself in half to fit.

And then I blink. And blink some more.

The three of us are standing in a huge chamber so elaborate, it would be right at home in Disney World. The central area is neutral: gray slate floor; high, white ceiling; ivory-and-navy-blue chairs clustered around a coffee table. But when I look to the left and the right, it's a different story. One side of the massive space is dominated by vibrant hues of red, orange, and yellow, with flickering flames that dance in contained fire pits. Their crackle fills the air, along with the aroma of burning wood. On the other side, closer to the door where we entered, is the source of the cool breeze: a full-on reproduction of a winter wonderland. Snowflakes drift from the ceiling, falling on lush evergreens from which icicles drip. The walls are covered in frost, and the floor is a smooth sheet of ice. Beneath the surface, multicolored fish dart.

"Well?" Rosa asks, rubbing her hands together with glee.

I'm scrambling for a reply when Donovan beats me to it. "What," he mumbles, "the actual, ever-loving fuck."

"Isn't it amazing?" Rosa chirps. "We call it Fire and Ice, for obvious reasons. Also known as, Opposites Attract."

The ice creaks ominously, and Donovan gives an equally ominous rumble. "You did this on purpose," he accuses Rosa. "That drawing was rigged."

Her microbladed eyebrows draw down in puzzlement. "I don't know what you mean."

"I mean," he says, emphasizing the word, "that it's no coincidence that Rune and I were paired up. It's all part of Ethan's ridiculous plan to make us get along. Well, we don't have to get along. We just have to work together. This is total bullshit and a waste of time."

Oh, for the love of God. "You're being an asshole," I tell him. "Don't take your issues out on Rosa. She just works here."

His only response is an inarticulate growl.

"It's okay, Rune," Rosa says, hands on her leggings-clad hips. "The drawing was random, but I did confer with Ethan before assigning each group and he suggested this would be the best match for the two of you. And after spending a little time with you," she says, her gaze lingering on Donovan, "I think he's absolutely right. This is our most challenging room, and by the time you're done with it, the two of you will be an unstoppable team. Just wait and see."

Donovan snorts, folding his arms across his chest.

"Now," Rosa goes on, "as the Game Mistress, let me give you your ground rules. First, all activities can only be completed with each other's support, so no cheating and going off on your own." She wags a finger at Donovan. "You'll have to decide together which side of the room to start on. Once you do, you'll need to solve each puzzle before you can move on to the next one. After you complete the final puzzle, you'll be free to go. Any questions?"

Yes, I want to say. *So many.* But none of them are ones she can answer, so I shake my head. After a long, painful second, Donovan does the same.

Rosa gives us a cheery wave. "Off to my own escape room, then! Mine is pirate-themed. Can't wait. See you soon!" She skips away, through the door where we came in. The lock snicks shut behind her, leaving me and Donovan alone together.

The two of us stand there in silence, broken only by the crackle of the fires and the creak of ice. At last, I can't take it anymore. "Look, I can't help that we're stuck here. But if you would just let me explain about Cooper, then maybe this would be a little less—"

He straightens, his lips pressing into a grim line. "Christ, Rune. What about 'I don't want to talk about that' do you not understand? Everything that comes out of your mouth is a lie, which makes conversation between us pointless. Let's just get through this and get out of here."

I know he has no real reason to trust me. But after a lifetime of not being believed, hearing Donovan call me a liar cuts deep. "Fine," I snap. "Where do you want to start?"

"I don't care. You pick."

"This side, then," I say, stalking in the direction of the fire pits. The ground here is uneven dirt, littered with tiny rocks and pebbles. Heat from the flames curls around me, like a reassuring hug. Maybe it'll thaw Donovan enough to make this experience bearable.

"Fine." He prowls across the room, muscles coiled, jaw locked, blue eyes cold and hard. I want desperately to see him soften for me, the way he did that night in the office, his defenses falling away. I want to stand on my tiptoes and press my lips to his, to taste him again. But if I tried, he'd probably bite me. An ache rises in my chest, and I rub at it, trying to make it leave.

"Of course this is what you chose," he says, coming to a halt two feet away.

"I like this side of the room." I do my best to sound as if the gulf between us, stretching wider every second, isn't tearing me apart. And as if I'm telling the truth.

A minute ago, this looked like a cozy option—like puzzle-solving by a campfire. Now, though, the warmth of the fire pits is no longer inviting—it's stultifying. The logs pop, sending a shower of sparks upward, and smoke fills the air, scorching my throat. The rising flames cast shadows on the stone walls, whose cracks and crevices seem to go on forever. I peer closer, trying to make sure nothing's crawling out of them to eat us, but I can't see much. This side of the room is dim, lit only by the leaping flames.

I take it back. This isn't Disney World. It's the foyer of Mordor.

Next to me, Donovan pushes up the sleeves of his Henley and swipes sweat from his forehead. "What's not to like?" His voice is husky from the smoke, which has the unfortunate effect of making him sound even more sexy than usual. "Why enjoy a cool, refreshing experience when you can roast yourself alive?"

Sweat beads on my forehead, trickling down my back, but I'll be damned if I'll let him see how uncomfortable I am. "We can't all have a heart of ice."

Donovan scoffs. "One of us has a heart of ice, all right. But it's not me."

Really? "Look," I say, taking a step toward him. "If we're going to get out of here, then we'll have to find a way to—"

Mid-stride, the toe of my Docs collides with a pebble. It sails through the air, hitting the stone wall and vanishing into one of the crevices. There's a groaning sound, as if the earth itself is shifting. Then the wall cracks open and the ground beneath us spins. I fall forward, onto my hands and knees, so close to the flames that sparks land on my shirt and I have to beat them out. My stomach churns as the room blurs past me: fire, ridged gray stone, Donovan's shocked face, fire again. For a horrible moment, I'm afraid I'm going to throw up. I shut my eyes, dig my nails into the dirt-packed ground, and cling for dear life.

And then, just as suddenly as it began spinning, the room

stills. Next to me, Donovan is swearing a blue streak. I open my eyes, push myself up to my knees—and gasp.

I'm encircled by a hundred Donovans, getting to their feet and dusting off their jeans and glaring. They're all around me, their dark hair tousled and their eyes arctic and their mouths spitting expletives. And staring at him in disbelief are a hundred versions of me—big dark eyes, pale face, tangled mane of hair, holes pinpricking my scorched shirt. We're backlit by the red glow of a thousand flames.

For a moment, I think I'm having a premonition. But no. There's no sense of the undertow I always feel, no double vision that always comes with having a foot in two realities. But then how the—

I turn in a circle, ignoring Donovan's increasingly creative litany of curses, forcing my breathing to slow. As my pulse falls to a post-adrenaline-rush rate, I focus, taking in our new surroundings.

The fire pits are still here, scattered throughout the room. But the stone walls have disappeared. In their place is pane after pane of reflective glass, stretching from the dirt floor to the twelve-foot-high ceiling. Donovan scowls from each one of them, looking unfairly gorgeous and undeniably furious.

Fantastic. I'm trapped with a man who can't stand the sight of me. A guy I can barely look at without wanting to punch or ravage, romance-novel-style.

Inside a hall of mirrors.

I KNOW it's not possible, since they're all the same image, but every version of Donovan looks more pissed off than the next. "What did you do?" he growls.

"Me?" I'm half-tempted to shatter one of these mirrors and impale him with a shard. "If you recall, I was trying to find a way for us to cooperate. Which is more than I can say for some—"

"Shhh!" He holds a finger to his lips.

"Did you just shush me?" Now, each of the hundred Runes looks as enraged as he does, my eyes wide with fury and my arms folded across my chest. "Who do you think you—"

"Shhh!" he says again, and this time he points.

It's a struggle to keep my eyes on Actual Donovan, rather than his myriad of reflections, but I manage it, following his finger to its inevitable conclusion: a stone that's popped up from the floor, containing a small speaker, as well as a tiny pad and pencil. A quiet stream of static issues from the speaker, interrupted by a series of beeps. It pauses, then starts up all over again.

"Um," I say, "what the hell is that supposed to be?"

Donovan doesn't answer me. Instead, he edges closer, peering down at the speaker as it starts its little ditty all over again. His eyebrows are knitted, like it's the most fascinating thing in the world. "No way," he breathes, and damn if he isn't smiling…not a lot, but still. The corners of his mouth quirk up the tiniest bit, the way they do when he's amused but trying not to show it. "I think it's Morse Code. I learned it in Scouts."

My mouth falls open, and around us, a hundred Runes' mouths do the same. "You're kidding me."

"No. Listen!" He gestures at the speaker. "It's not random. There's a rhythm to it. I've been listening to it over and over, and I think…" He kneels, grabbing for the pad and pencil. His dark head bends as he scribbles furiously, tilting his head as the beeps do their thing. Then he shoves the pad at me with a triumphant smile.

I glance down at it, hoping for answers. Instead, I see this:

.-- . .-.. -.-. --- -- . / - --- / - .... . / .... .- .-.. .-.. / --- ..-. / -- .. .-. .-. ---
.-. ... .-.-.-

Donovan's looking at me expectantly, his sapphire eyes alight with excitement. I never thought I'd see him look at me that way again: with true happiness, like there's no place he'd rather be. My gut twists, and I have to clear my throat twice before I can speak.

"What does it say?"

He takes the pad back from me and translates: "Welcome to the Hall of Mirrors."

The speaker starts up again, emitting a different set of rhythmic beeps and pauses. Donovan sinks to the stones, braces the pad on his leg, and scribbles some more. I sit down next to him, peering over his shoulder, but it's pointless: all I can make out is a series of meaningless dashes, dots, and slashes as his hand flies over the paper with lightning speed.

There's something alluring about the purity of his concentration, the way everything in the world disappears for him except what he's focused on. It's almost…gravitational, as if being around him holds the scattered pieces of myself together. I glance away, but that's no help: everywhere I look, there he is, a hundred Donovans with his dark hair falling over his face and his mouth quirking up as he scribbles and his attention hyper-focused on the page.

This is a freaking nightmare.

All I want is to reach for him, to brush his hair out of his eyes and tell him how sorry I am. To explain everything, even though I know he won't believe me. Instead, I wrap my arms around my knees and grip my wrists tight. *Don't do it,* I tell myself. *He doesn't want you anymore, and that's a good thing. Just get through this, and do what you came here to do.*

I bite my lip and close my eyes. Behind my lids, the echo of the flames from the fire pits flickers. The air fills with the crackle of burning wood, that interminable beeping, and Donovan's running commentary. "I think…" he mutters. "Maybe…" He huffs with frustration, and I picture him running his hand through his hair, the way I've seen him do so many times. But then his breathing evens out. "Okay!" he says, sounding triumphant. "Got it."

Blinking my eyes open, I find him smiling at me, a disarming grin that cracks me wide open. "Here," he says, shoving the pad back at me. I take it and read aloud:

"I am a test of communication, a challenge of reflection. Two must stand and face each other's direction. They must follow the path, or face fire's wrath. Their eyes must not waver, their focus must be true. For if they break contact, they'll begin anew."

Oh, fabulous. "A riddle?" I say, frowning down at it.

Donovan shrugs, the light of discovery fading from his eyes. "I guess. The sooner we solve it, the sooner we're out of here."

"Right," I say, trying to sound as businesslike as possible. I scramble to my feet, and he follows, standing opposite me. *Two must stand and face each other's direction,* after all.

He's just inches away, his vanilla-and-cedar scent filling the space between us. But he's also everywhere. He's all I can see. My voice is breathy when I say, "But what path?"

As if my words have summoned them, some of the stones beyond the speaker begin to glow, as if lit from within. The glowing stones are set in an irregular pattern—two to the right, then nothing, then three to the left. I watch, brows drawing down in puzzlement, as the stones between the glowing ones fall away, replaced by honest-to-God streams of bubbling lava.

"There's your answer," Donovan says, one dark brow rising. "Man, I hope Smashbox has solid liability insurance. Because if that shit is real, and I burn so much as my pinky toe, I plan to sue the bejesus out of them."

I shake my head, my hair flying. I came here to avenge my parents' murder, not get barbecued. "This is crazy. I can't...I don't..."

"Rune." His voice is calm, steady. "I'm just joking. It's some kind of illusion."

"Sure," I say dubiously. It doesn't look like an illusion to me.

"Ethan thinks we can't get along, right? That we don't have what it takes to finish that damn project of his. What did that thing say? *A test of communication*, right? So let's fucking communicate, and prove him wrong."

"We *can't* get along," I point out, trembling as I look down into the lava. What will happen if we lose our balance and fall in? Worse still, what will happen if I've misjudged Donovan and he pushes me? What if this is all a trick, to take my life? Or his?

"Sure we can. At least, long enough to get out of here. Now, look at me."

With considerable effort, I drag my gaze from the fiery depths and meet his gaze. "Good," he says. "*Their eyes must not waver,* remember? Don't look away."

And so I don't. I stare into those deep blue pools as the mirrors shiver, their surfaces rippling to reflect distorted, funhouse versions of ourselves. "Step to the right," all the Donovans say— the one right in front of me and all of the warped versions of him. "With me. Here."

His hands rise, gripping mine. The moment we touch, the floor beneath us shudders. That electrical shock is back, flowing between us, sparking over our skin.

"Do you feel that?" Donovan's voice is a hoarse whisper.

I nod, my mouth dry. "Donovan—"

He shakes his head. "Just…step to the right, would you? Onto the stones."

The air between us wavers, and I can't help but think about what Cooper said—about how our proximity is what's causing the ley lines to spike. About how it could unravel the world. But I can't make myself let go of Donovan's hands. I don't want to.

"I can't see the stones," I whisper. "Not if I'm looking at you."

His throat works as he swallows. "I…I could pick you up, so we're at eye level. And then you could look, for both of us. From your angle, you'd be able to keep eye contact with me in the mirror, and see the reflection of the stones, too. And I'd look at your reflection, so we wouldn't break the rules."

"Pick me up?" The words emerge as a squeak.

"If you'll let me."

I should say no. God, I know I should. But instead, I manage another nod, and then I'm in Donovan's arms. He scoops me up, like I'm a bride he's carrying over the threshold. I can feel his heart thrashing against me, but his voice is calm when he says, "How far to the right should I go?"

I peer at his reflection, the up-close scent of him intoxicating me. My head swims with it. In my peripheral vision, I make out the glowing stones, somehow shining clearly despite the funhouse warp of the mirrors. "E-eighteen inches," I stammer.

"Very precise." I swear I can hear the smile in his voice.

This is, so, so wrong. I ought to insist that he put me down. But I don't. I let him cradle me as he steps eighteen inches to the right. Then another five, at my direction. Then two. And then at last, onto the first of the glowing stones.

"Holy fuck." He clutches me tighter as the heat from the lava streams rises, washing over both of us.

I don't dare take my gaze off the Donovan in the mirror. "Now what?"

"Now," he says, slowly and deliberately, "we have to figure out how to make it to those three stones to the left."

I try to glance at them out of the corner of my eye, but the angle's all wrong. I can't see a thing, not unless I look away from him.

"How?" I say, my voice trembling.

"Do you trust me?"

His eyes hold mine in the mirror, their expression grave. And despite what's passed between us, despite everything, there's only one answer I have to give. "I do."

"That's all I needed to hear," he says. And then he *jumps*, with me in his arms.

We're airborne for a moment, the lava flowing below us and our eyes fixed on each other's reflection. Tiny flames lick their way across Donovan's irises, and for an instant I worry that I've made a terrible mistake. But then we land on the stones with a thud that sends him to his knees, eyes still locked on mine in the mirrors, which ripple once more, their distortion vanishing.

I want to make some crack about his Clark Kent alter-ego. About the superhero hiding inside his data engineer shell. But I'm too busy forcing my heart to resume a normal rhythm. All I can do is cling to him and stare into his gorgeous eyes and try to remember how to breathe.

Donovan kneels on the stones, arms still wrapped around my body, like he's afraid of what will happen if he lets go. His chest heaves against me. "Rune," he says, sounding breathless. "Rune, I—"

But before he can finish whatever he was about to say, there's a horrible cracking sound, and the floor falls away, hurtling us into the darkness beyond.

Forty

I SHRIEK as we fall through the air. Donovan's grip on me is so tight, I'm pretty sure it's going to leave bruises. But I cling to him just as tightly. If we're going to die, we might as well do it together. And I can think of worse ways to leave this world than in his arms.

The red haze teases at the edge of my vision, a premonition threatening to break through. *Our day will come* echoes in my ears as we plunge downward, the heat of the Hall of Mirrors dispelled by a blast of cold wind that plasters my torn shirt to my body and sends a shiver racing through me. I squeeze my eyes shut, press my face against Donovan's chest, and brace.

We tumble through the air for another long moment. Two. And then we hit, with an impact that steals the air from my lungs and forces a sharp grunt from Donovan. But this time, I take the brunt of our fall, and what I crash into is…soft. Also, freezing.

Donovan is swearing again, struggling to catch his breath between some of the most creative expletives I've ever heard. He's also on top of me, every inch of his solid body pressed against mine. My fingers are knotted in the back of his Henley, his arms cradling me. It's ridiculous, I know, but part of me doesn't want to find out where we are or figure out what to do next. I want to stay here with him, just like this, premonition be damned, and pretend we're in the bedroom of my cottage or against his office door or in a different reality entirely.

Donovan's litany of curses trails off. "Rune?" he says instead. And oh God, the sound of my name in his raspy voice. It *does* something to me. I want to curl up inside it. I want to record it, so I can listen to it again and again.

And so I don't move. Maybe it's cheating, but I don't care. I want to keep him close to me. I want to hear him say my name again, when it's not followed by an accusation, but filled with possibility. And sure enough, he does.

"Rune? Are you okay?" He strokes my hair, his touch tentative and feather-light. And there's that electricity again, lighting every one of my nerve endings on fire.

I couldn't pretend to be unconscious any longer if I tried. "I'm here," I say, and open my eyes.

We're in some kind of...snowbank. That's the best I can do, except snow isn't soft, not when it's packed together like this. Whatever this is made of feels like a feather bed, if feather beds were icy cold. But I don't take in much more than that, because Donovan's staring down at me, his face inches from mine. When my eyes meet his, he jerks back, like I've surprised him. This is a tactical error on his part, though, because the snow shifts beneath us and his hips settle between my legs. And sweet purple ponies, is he happy to be there. Apparently near-death experiences turn him on.

But I'm not one to judge. Because at the feel of him, right up against the place I've wanted—*needed*—him to be ever since what we started in his office that night, a rush of warmth prickles over my entire body. My empty core clenches, craving more. The sensation forces a breathy moan from me—the smallest sound, but Donovan hears it.

His gaze falls to my lips. His eyes darken.

Around us, I hear the splinter of cracking ice, as if the very world is disintegrating. Which is fitting, because it's how I feel inside—like I'm shattering. Like the heat of his mouth on mine, the possessive grip of his arms around me, is the only thing that will put me back together again. I arch into his warmth, away from the cold beneath me, and feel his heavy exhale, ruffling my hair, gusting down the sensitive skin of my throat. His eyes are fixed on mine, emotions passing across them like clouds: fury, frustration, desire, and something else I'm afraid to name. My lips part in anticipation, my tongue darting out to moisten them, and a low groan rumbles from his chest. The sound ripples through him and into me, like we're already one.

He lowers his head, as if to kiss me. Even though there's still a sliver of space between us, I swear I can *feel* the velvet brush of his lips, the hot slide of his tongue.

That sound of cracking ice reverberates again, louder this time, breaking the spell. Donovan's eyes widen, a horrified expression sweeping his face. And then he wrenches himself away and pushes himself up. He literally *leaps* off the snowbank or whatever the hell we're lying in to get away from me.

What the actual fuck.

I lie there in the not-snow, my heart pounding so hard, I can taste it. My core pulses in time with it, an ache settling deep in my belly. Without Donovan's warmth, the cold beneath me seeps into every pore, but the idea of navigating the rest of this place with Sexual Tension Spreadsheet Guy after he just fled like I was dipped in poison feels like a nightmare.

Except you might as well be dipped in poison, I remind myself. *You can't go around kissing him, Rune. You ought to have been the one to push him away.*

But...but maybe if his death is connected to the person who killed my parents, and I figure out who they are...maybe I can change the future. Maybe I can put a stop to their plan and change things so Donovan will live. So that a kiss between us doesn't equal a curse.

Maybe, maybe, maybe. None of this changes the fact that I have to go after him, to figure out whatever challenge lies in store for us next and conquer it. Because if I don't, I'm giving up my best shot at getting to the bottom of this mystery and avenging my parents' deaths.

I push myself to my feet, my sneakers slipping in the fake snow, and immediately lose my balance. Instead of gracefully jumping off the snowbank, I fall on my butt and slide all the way down, skidding across the stone floor and fetching up at Donovan's feet.

Because of course I do.

I can't even look at him. Instead, I scramble up and examine our surroundings. Anything would be better than meeting his eyes.

We're standing in a less pleasant version of the winter wonderland we encountered when we first walked into the escape room. The walls are solid ice, and flakes of snow drift from the ceiling, buffeted by a breeze that emanates from an unknown source. Behind us is the snowbank we landed in. And in front of us is a narrow corridor filled with ice blocks, arranged at odd angles to each other. The blocks are taller than Donovan, at least eight feet if I had to guess, and stretch for as far as I can see. I edge forward to get a better look and realize what it is: a maze, standing between us and freedom.

Frigid air hisses between my teeth as I suck in a breath. I don't have a lot of fears, but being stuck in small spaces is one of them. The monster used to lock me in a closet for his entertainment and sit against the door, listing all of the things he wanted to do to me when he finally let me out. I designed my cottage during those awful hours, imagining every wall color, piece of furniture, and painting I'd choose when I grew up and got free of him. It's one reason I love my little house so much, why the idea of losing this job and failing to be able to pay the mortgage devastates me to the core: it represents the fulfillment of a dream, how far I've come since I was a girl huddled beneath winter coats, the monster's bowling shoes digging into my butt and the stale smell of his Newports mingling with the musty scent of long-unworn clothes.

I've washed myself clean of every piece of him, but try as I might, I can't shake my hatred of enclosed spaces. Even at home, where I know I'm safe, I open all the windows rather than turn on the A/C. And now I have to find my way through an underground, narrow maze.

Oh God, what if we get stuck in there? Those cracking noises… What if something's *in* there, waiting for us? What if the ice or the snow falls on us somehow and we have to dig our way out? How far beneath the surface are we, anyway?

"Well? Are you coming or not?"

Donovan's impatient voice penetrates the haze of panic that's descended over me. I force myself to focus on him, using the skills that the stupid court-mandated therapist gave me way back when I entered juvie: *Use all your senses, Rune. What do you feel? Taste? Smell, hear, see?*

Easy enough. I feel scared as shit and ice fucking cold. I'm dressed for early fall in Sapphire Springs, not winter in Narnia. I can't taste a damn thing, because my mouth's gone so dry with terror, my tongue's sticking to the roof of it. Aside from Donovan's irritated jab, I hear the small creaks of the maze's icy walls settling, like the foundation of an old house. I smell the clean nothingness of a world made of snow and frozen water, a scent that reminds me of open spaces and freedom, not the hot, sticky confines of the closet. And in front of the entrance, I see my nemesis himself, his jeans damp from the not-snow, the sharp line of his jaw set in annoyance as he turns toward me, the sleeves of his Henley pushed up so far I see a glimpse of…is that ink? Does Mr.-Taking-Chances-Is-For-Suckers have a *tattoo*?

It's a tiny thing, but the sight of that black curlicue somehow peels back a layer of the dread that's threatening to consume me. Amusement takes its place, with curiosity nipping at its heels. When, not *if*, we get out of here, I'm going to find out what Donovan values so much, he'd inscribe it on his body. Focus on that little discovery instead of the frozen hellscape that awaits, and maybe I'll make it through this without having a total meltdown.

"What are you grinning at?" he says suspiciously, dark brows lowering.

"Nothing," I lie, striding forward with a bravado I don't feel. If there's one thing a lifetime of covering for my premonitions has taught me, it's how to bluff like a champ.

In front of me, the maze looms, its translucent walls shimmering in the eerie blue light that reflects from within. I draw one more breath of the frosty air, then square my shoulders.

"Come on," I tell Donovan. "Let's do this."

And then I step inside.

CHAPTER

Forty-One

THE FIRST THING I notice when I enter the glittering labyrinth is how beautiful it is.

It's dim in here, deep wells of shadows pooling in the spaces between the towering walls. The blue-tinged slabs of ice and the dark path that winds between them fit together perfectly, like one of M.C. Escher's tessellations. But up close, the ice isn't a single, solid surface. The light shining from far above reflects off it, creating a mesmerizing display of fractured colors and patterns. Pale blues and greens compete with deep purples and pinks, all etched in lines, swirls, and geometric shapes so intricate, the artist in me itches to get my hands on a paintbrush. If Rosa hadn't insisted we leave our phones behind when we entered the escape room—*so you have an authentic experience!*—I would try to capture the image in a photograph, so I could recreate it later. But honestly, I don't think my cell phone's crappy camera could do it justice.

The second thing I notice is that the further in I go, the more the walls close in.

Initially, I think it's my imagination. My good friend claustrophobia, rearing her oh-so-persistent head. I try to ignore it, taking another step, then one more. But with the third step comes an ominous creaking sound, the noise that a layer of ice atop a frozen lake makes before it gives way. And when I take an involuntary step backward, I bump into the uneven surface of the wall behind me.

I *know* it wasn't that close before.

Like a virgin in a horror movie who's realized the call is coming from inside the house, I turn my head, a feeling of doom penetrating every inch of my body. Sure enough, the corridor between the icy walls is even narrower than it was when I stepped into it. I don't even have enough room to extend my arms fully on either side. What happens if the walls just keep closing in? What's to stop them from crushing us?

The red haze starts to descend, but I can't tell if it's a signal that I'm about to have a premonition or the side effect of my blood pounding in every vein, artery, and capillary. I struggle to drag air into my lungs, but it's a losing battle. Dimly, I'm aware of Donovan saying my name, asking if I'm okay, but I don't have it in me to answer. The hell with bluffing: I can't even try to pretend that I'm all right.

I *hate* looking weak. And now here I am, having a total system shut-down in front of Donovan, of all people. The guy who already thinks I'm a liability. God, please don't let me have a vision here. Please, don't let anything make this worse.

My breath rasps, getting shallower with each passing moment. My head swims.

Oh, no. What if I faint?

I sway, and Donovan's hands descend on my shoulders, steadying me. He turns me to look at him, tilting his head down so he can see my face. "Rune," he says, enunciating each word, "are you claustrophobic?"

I want to make a smartass comment, like *no, it's been my lifelong dream to reenact the Star Wars trash compactor scene. If only I had Leia's bikini, everything would be perfect—minus the frostbite.* But I can't manage to form a word. All I can do is nod.

"Shit." He peers down at me, then over my head, at the maze

beyond. Whatever he sees makes him stiffen. "Shut your eyes. Don't look at the walls. Don't look at anything, okay? I'll get us out of here."

Now I *really* can't breathe, but for a whole other reason. Five minutes ago, he leapt off a snowbank to get away from me. Now, he's made himself into a human shield to protect me. A sexy, sexy human shield. I ought to step back, to tell him I can take care of myself, but with him holding onto me like this, I feel…safe. Like nothing can get to me.

Donovan presses my face against his chest, one hand cradling the back of my head. His other hand twines in mine, squeezing tight. And the moment it does, the ice creaks again.

Terror whips through me, and my teeth start to chatter. But Donovan stills. "Hold on," he says. "I wonder if…"

His hand still gripping mine, he presses our palms to the closest block of ice. I can't see anything but the waffle-knit of his shirt, but I can feel the jagged texture of the frigid wall under my fingers, not to mention the pins-and-needles sensation of cold that shoots through me. The creaking sound comes again, louder than before, followed by a sinister *drip-drip-drip*.

I jump, trying to recoil, but Donovan won't let me. "Look, Rune," he says.

I'm pretty sure there's nothing I want to see other than a way out of here. But he sounds so convinced, I lift my head. And then I gape.

Rivulets of water run down the surface of the wall, pooling on the ground at our feet. The longer Donovan presses our hands against the wall, the faster the little streams flow.

Our touch is melting the freaking ice.

"That…that shouldn't be possible," I mumble.

He gives a rough laugh. "I mean, neither should falling through a goddamn trapdoor and landing in a snowbank without breaking half our bones. It's an escape room, right? Man-made. There's no reason to expect this to act like real ice. Who knows what it's actually made of, or what it's programmed to respond to."

Or what magic is behind it, I think but don't say. I'm too relieved to have discovered a way out of this maze to question the reason behind it.

The *drip-drip-drip* intensifies, the wall liquifying and sliding aside enough to reveal the dim gap between the next two blocks. Still holding hands, we squeeze through. Behind us, the wall solidifies again, blocking the way back.

"This is crazy," Donovan mutters. His voice echoes, reverberating in the small space. "How the hell are we supposed to know which way to go? We could end up wandering in fucking circles for hours. What the hell was Ethan thinking?"

"He was thinking that he wanted us to work together. Which we're kind of doing." I look pointedly down at our intertwined hands.

Donovan snorts, his gaze following mine. "Oh yeah. The next time you and I are paired up on an Arctic expedition, we'll have the perfect game plan."

He looks like he wants to say something else, but his mouth snaps shut when the walls shift toward us, forcing us to the left. "This way?" he says, glancing at me. "Or the other?"

"Hold on." I pull my hand out of his and grab the hem of my shirt, tearing at the material. Or trying to, anyway. They always make it look so easy in action movies, when people need makeshift bandages...or in romance novels, when lust-crazed lovers tear each other's clothes to bits. But no matter how hard I try, even hooking my fingers through one of the holes that the sparks burnt in my shirt and tugging as hard as I can, nothing happens. Of course, maybe that has something to do with the fact that I'm freezing, and my hands are all but numb.

Donovan's eyebrows rise in shock. "What the hell are you doing?"

Now that we've figured out how to melt our way out of here,

my dread has retreated, replaced by adrenalized euphoria. The walls have stabilized for the moment—they seem to be triggered by movement—and I can't help but seize the opportunity to tease him. "What does it look like? I'm stripping, of course. It's my dream to have sex in Santa's workshop, and this seems like the anteroom, don't you think? A little gloomy, but beggars can't be choosers."

His jaw drops. "You—you want to—"

"Oh, come on," I say, still fruitlessly tugging. "You've never been propositioned in an ice maze before?"

Donovan scrubs a hand through his hair, his expression appalled. "You're kidding, right? Please say you're kidding."

"I have a Saint Nick fetish," I say, moving on to another hole. "So sue me."

"What are you really doing, Rune?" His voice is a growl. "Because I swear, I can't tell if you're serious or not, and if you—"

I take pity on him. "I want to leave something behind, okay? So we'll know if we're retracing our steps. I figured scraps of material from my shirt would do, since it's already ruined. But apparently every romance novel ever is a big fat liar. I'll be sure to let the Sinsters know."

He blinks, as if I've suddenly begun speaking a foreign language. "Romance novels?"

"You know." I turn my attention to a jagged hole near the hem. "Where people are so desperate to have each other, they just can't wait, so they rip each other's clothes off. I'm sure that's why they call them 'bodice rippers.' Well, maybe bodices were a lot easier to tear, because my shirt sure as hell isn't cooperating."

The marked silence that falls lasts long enough that I glance up. Donovan's standing stock-still, his gaze raking over me, heating as it goes. And then he moves, batting my hands out of the way. "At this rate, we'll be here all night," he says, his voice hoarse. "Allow me."

"I—" I squeak out. The sound is swallowed by the shift of the ice again, triggered by his approach. Or maybe I just can't hear my own voice over the pounding of my heart.

"It's a good idea." He clears his throat. "Press your palms to the wall, would you, so we don't get crushed before we have a chance to carry it out?"

My mouth is dry again, but this time not from fear. Speechless, I obey, and he drops to his knees in front of me, in the sliver of space between my body and the block of ice. He fists the material of my shirt in both hands so tightly the muscles in his forearms flex, the apex of that curlicue of ink sliding into view. And then, God help me, he yanks.

CHAPTER
Forty~Two

MY POOR SHIRT doesn't stand a chance. It tears nearly in half. Cold air rushes over my skin as Donovan lifts his head and looks up at me. His lips part as he takes me in. His breath hitches.

Seeing him on his knees like this breaks something inside me. Possibly, my ability to form coherent thoughts. "I stand correct-ed," I babble. "You, um, could teach garment-rending to authors of bodice rippers everywhere. I'll be sure to alert the Sinsters, in case they want to invite you to do a demo at their next book club." Or coven meeting. Whatever. Jesus, what is happening here?

I don't think Donovan has heard a word I've said. His eyes are fixed on the expanse of skin that my torn shirt has revealed. And then, as if drawn by a magnetic force, he edges closer and presses his lips to my belly. He does it again and again, his dark hair brushing over my skin and sending shivers through me.

"Donovan—" I try, but he shakes his head.

"Let me have this," he mutters against my skin. "Just this. Unless you don't want—"

But I do. I *do* want, so much my body aches with it. He's right—things never have to go further than this, right here, do they? What happens in the ice maze can stay in the ice maze. And so I knot my fingers in his silky hair, urging him on.

His breath stutters, his big hands moving to grip my hips, his lips tracing their way upward, to the valley between my breasts. I'm lost in him, in his heated praise—*so beautiful, goddamn perfect*—and the groans that rumble from his chest. Desire slides through my veins, and I whimper, wanting him to touch me like this everywhere, wanting *more.* I'm not cold anymore; I'm burning up, his kisses leaving a trail of fire in their wake. Only when the wet heat of his mouth ghosts over the blue lace of my bra and my fingers tighten in his hair do I realize one very important, terrible thing: I've let go of the wall.

But nothing's closing in on us. Nothing's crushing us. Because…holy shit.

All around us, the ice walls are melting, the maze crumbling to nothingness. The heat I feel isn't just because of him…it's real.

"Donovan," I whisper, tugging at the strands of his hair.

"Hmmm?" He flicks his tongue against my nipple through the flimsy barrier of the lace, then nips at me with his teeth, and I buck against him. I can't help it, and from his vise grip on my hips, he likes it…a lot. But oh God, we have to stop.

I tug again, harder, and his head comes up. His eyes are glassy, the pupils blown wide, color burning high on his cheekbones. "What is it?" he manages.

He looks *destroyed,* and I'm sure I do, too. How can this be such a terrible thing, when it feels so right?

But that's a problem for another time. Because—

"Look," I say, raising a shaking hand.

He turns his head, and I hear his shocked intake of breath. Together, we watch the last of the walls disintegrate. And beyond them, for just an instant, we see a door—the way out.

But then it disappears, obscured by plumes of red and gold that spring from the floor, flickering and crackling and *burning* with so much heat, it singes me where I stand.

We're trapped in a ring of flame.

Donovan gets up, turning in a slow circle. I turn with him, watching as the water from the ice walls flows downhill, disappearing into a grate in the floor. It swirls around our feet, a welcome contrast to the conflagration.

I don't understand. How in the world did my touch melt an entire ice maze? That couldn't have been the point of the exercise, could it? We were supposed to complete the maze, not thaw the entire thing before we barely got started. Did it malfunction somehow? Did I accidentally press some kind of recessed button? Or did Donovan kneel on something—

I can't think about Donovan kneeling, not now. I focus instead on our surroundings. With the maze evaporated, we're standing alone in a high-ceilinged room, no more than a hundred feet from freedom. The door is right behind that wall of fire, but there's absolutely nothing we can do to reach it. There are no additional instructions, no mysterious codes. Just us and Mission Freaking Impossible. We're screwed…and not in the good way.

"Fuck, fuck, fuck," Donovan mutters, looking anywhere but at me. The heat between us seems to have evaporated in direct proportion to the appearance of those damn flames. And even though I know I shouldn't, I would do anything to get it back again.

Instead, I make a joke—my go-to when I have no idea what else to do. "Is this a good time for my Johnny Cash impersonation?" I say, my voice shaky. It's the best I can manage, given that I can still feel the scrape of his stubble and the insistent pressure of his mouth against my skin. God, what were we doing? What did we almost do?

Donovan glares at me, his dark hair mussed from my hands, his eyes impassive, his jaw set in that familiar stubborn line. When I met him, I thought that expression meant he didn't feel strong emotions. That he was indifferent to everything and everyone around him. But now, I'm beginning to think he feels way too much and spends most of his time trying to hide it.

"Excuse me?" he says, folding his arms across his chest.

"You know. Because of the burning ring of fire." I gesture at the circle of flames.

Something moves beneath the surface of his impenetrable expression—amusement, maybe. And then it cracks, dissolving completely. His eyes blaze down at me, and too late, I remember the rest of the lyrics to that song—about how two people fell for each other, right into that damn burning ring, and their desire consumed them. "Donovan, I didn't mean—"

But he doesn't let me finish. "Ah, fuck it," he bites out. And then he cups my face in one hand, tangles the other in my hair, and lowers his lips to mine.

If I thought our kiss against the office door was passionate, it has nothing on this one. Donovan *devours* me, licking at the seam of my lips until I let him in and then, when I do, slipping his tongue inside to duel with mine. It's a battle, like everything else between us, and I give as good as I get, nipping at his lower lip as he pulls back to skate his teeth over my throat. His mouth closes on my collarbone, licking and sucking as he pushes what remains of my shirt off my shoulders. It falls to the floor, but I hardly notice. I'm too busy digging my nails into his back as he lowers me to the floor, levering himself over me. My breasts swell beneath the lace confines of my bra, hungry for his touch, and I moan in response, shimmying against him.

The flames roar around us, growing higher by the moment as he growls into my mouth, sliding a hand beneath me, moving me how he wants me. "This is fucking torture," he rasps. "You're killing me, and I just—I can't—"

Beneath us, the floor trembles, as if preparing to eject us through another trapdoor. Maybe that's how we're meant to escape the flames. Well, if that's the case, I'm happy to go just like this. Besides, maybe it's my imagination, since Donovan doesn't say a word about it. He just hisses through his teeth as my fingers push up his shirt, desperate to feel him against me skin-to-skin. To see the rest of that tantalizing swirl of ink. To know every bit of him, even—especially—the parts he keeps hidden from the world.

"You can't what?" I gasp, slipping the top button free.

He pulls back, enough to see my face. And then, never breaking eye contact, he presses into me, circling his hips in a way that has me spiraling higher and higher, the ache inside me building. Beneath me, the ground shakes. Above me, Donovan does the same. The expression on his face, in those deep blue eyes…it's pleasure, so acute it's almost pain. Other than my shirt, we're fully clothed—but then why do I feel like I'm naked before him?

"No matter what I do," he says, tracing my face, my throat, my breasts, "I can't stop wanting you. Christ, what have you done to me?"

His last words echo, an accusation that shudders through my bones. Reality comes crashing over me, like a bucket of icy water from the melted walls.

I can't stop wanting him, either. But I have to. Because if he's as addicted to me as I am to him, if he craves my touch the same way, then there's no way what happens now will end here. If we do this—if I let him inside me in every way—then there will be no turning back.

Wanting me like this will kill him.

I draw a deep breath, bracing myself to say the inevitable. Hating myself, because finding ourselves in this position again is my fault, just as much as his.

It's not what I've done, I want to tell him. *It's what I'm doing. What I'm fated to do.*

But I never get a chance to, because, like it's been waiting for this perfectly imperfect moment, a premonition hits.

Forty-Three

THIS TIME, when the red haze descends over my vision, there's no fighting it. I try breathing deeply, like Cooper showed me, but it doesn't help. The door in my mind creaks open, revealing the red-tinged room beyond, and the undertow tugs at my feet, pulling me forward. *Come,* it coaxes. *See.*

I don't want to go. I want to stay right here with Donovan, even if he doesn't believe a word I say. But here comes the double vision, the world of my premonition layering over this one. I see Donovan stroking my hair, hear him saying my name. But I also see myself walking closer and closer to the open door, then stepping through into—

I expect to find myself in the small white room, the way I usually do. Or worse, in my childhood home, in the moments before my parents were taken from me forever. But instead, I'm standing in that damned garden, the one that smells of honeysuckle. The melodic notes of Pachelbel's Canon fill my ears, and when I look down at myself with a dawning sense of horror, I'm wearing the same gorgeous, delicate wedding dress. My bare toes peek from beneath the hem, the nails painted a gleaming champagne hue to match.

I open my mouth to scream. I try to run. But no sound comes

out, and just like before, I find myself floating over the rose-petal-strewn grass toward the groom beneath the arched, white-flowered arbor. Toward Donovan.

He looks so handsome. So happy to see me. But he's not alone. Because from among the crowd seated on the folding chairs rises one hooded figure after another. Blood Witches, concealed among my friends and the residents of Sapphire Springs. They stalk down the aisle, toward the place where Donovan stands.

"Donovan, run!" I shriek. This time, my voice rises loud and clear, drowning out the musicians. But Donovan doesn't obey. He just stands there, looking perplexed, watching his death barrel toward him.

I want to save him. To stop this. But the world of the premonition shimmers, the undertow pulling me back through the doorway, into the world I've left behind.

I expect to land back in my body, to feel Donovan's touch. Instead, my consciousness floats upward, hovering somewhere near the vaulted ceiling. From my vantage point far above, I see Donovan shaking me. My head lolls back, my eyes open but glazed, my body limp. He runs his hands over me, then shoves them through his hair in desperation. The cords in his neck stand out as he shouts for help. But no one comes.

He must think I'm dying. Or having some kind of seizure. My heart wrenches as I watch his agony, unable to tell him otherwise.

Donovan might act like he wants nothing to do with me other than to bury himself inside my body, but seeing this, I know better. For whatever reason, against all odds, he cares about me. Rejecting him, the confusion over Cooper…I've *hurt* him, and he's been protecting himself the only way he knows how: by pretending he doesn't give a crap.

Him. Me. Cooper. All of us are trying to keep him safe. But looking at him right now through the strange double vision of my premonition, I know we've failed. Because we can save his life, sure. But that doesn't do fuck-all to cure a broken heart.

The undertow tugs at me again, sucking me back through the

doorway, into the desecrated garden. In the seconds I've been gone, the hooded figures have formed a circle around Donovan. Just like the day my parents died, one of them pulls a knife from their robe. I recognize the raw arrogance in the gesture, the undiluted sense of triumph.

It's my father's murderer. Still alive and kicking, after all these years.

"Our day has finally come. *Non sine sanguine gloria*," he bellows. And the other figures echo, "No glory without blood."

Like the doomed band on the Titanic, the musicians are still playing. The cellist drags her bow across the strings, the instrument voicing a raw, guttural note as the leader bares his forearm and slices it with the blade. Blood wells up, and beneath it, half-obscured by crimson, the scroll-and-dagger symbol appears on his skin. It glows the same way the stones did in the Hall of Mirrors, as if lit from within. Looking almost like a—

No. It can't be.

Donovan's arm. The curlicue of ink. The tattoo he never bares in its entirety.

I don't have time to follow my train of thought to its horrifying conclusion before the rest of the hooded figures follow suit, slicing their forearms. One by one, the symbol materializes on their skin. One by one, they dip their fingers in their own blood. And just like it did in my memory of my parents' deaths, the scroll-and-dagger emblazons itself in the air.

It burns there, its edges ragged, as the rest of the wedding guests scramble to their feet. I don't know if they can see the symbol, but they sure as hell can see *something*. They shove past each other, leaving purses and suit jackets behind. Even the musicians have dropped their instruments and taken flight. Alone among the crowd, Mrs. Grant, Mrs. Fontaine, Mrs. Hernandez, and Ella Campbell stand their ground. Their hands curve through the air, tracing intricate shapes, and their lips move, chanting the same words again and again: *Cavea ad tenebras continendas.*

I don't know what it means. But I can see what it does.

Sparks fly from the coven members' fingers. They flicker, then merge and elongate into chains of fire that stretch toward the Blood Witches, seeking to contain them. To bind them.

Hope ignites within me. The first time I stood in the garden, this didn't happen. The blood tide rose, and Donovan drowned. No one intervened. Did I change the future by meeting with the coven? Even though I couldn't tell them the truth about my premonitions, have they come to defend me somehow? To save Donovan and change the course of history?

More than anything, I want to see if they succeed. But as the chains of fire weave through the air, I'm sucked back into the real world once more.

Inside the ring of flames, Donovan kneels on the stones, with me in his arms. As I watch, he lowers his head and presses his mouth to mine, as if his kiss can wake me.

The moment his lips touch mine, the floor beneath us buckles. Cracks spiderweb outward, with us at the epicenter. Bursting through every fracture and crevice, blue light gleams. It's every color at once: sapphire and navy and cobalt and aquamarine. Haunting and tempting and somehow impossibly familiar, it *calls* to me. *Mine*, it whispers.

And I only have one answer. *Yours.*

Donovan's jaw drops, clutching me tighter, his face gone pale. And I realize what the blue light reminds me of, with its shifting shades and undeniable allure: his eyes. It's like a piece of the light is inside him, revealing itself the only way it can.

What in the—

Inside my head, Cooper speaks, his voice heavy with resignation. *Like calls to like*, he murmurs. *What is done cannot be undone.*

The undertow grabs hold of me again, sucking me back into the world of the premonition, leaving the light behind. I land with a thud, my eyes fixed on the circle of hooded witches. An impossible amount of blood drips from their arms onto the ground, flowing toward me, rising like the tide. The chains of fire haven't bound them. Instead, it's as if the witches are encased in an invisible bubble. The chains climb it like ivy, searching for a way in, but they can't penetrate.

But maybe I can.

Donovan's talking now, gesticulating, demanding to know what's going on. No one answers him. And I know we're out of time.

I run for him, the blood tide swirling around my ankles, the coppery scent filling my lungs and the train of my dress dragging behind me. Screaming *no* and *wait* and *don't*.

I have the unmistakable sense that the leader is staring at me, though I can't see his face. I can feel his gaze on me, cold and calculating, as he gestures to the Blood Witch next to him. "You," he says. "Now."

Their face obscured by their hood, their eyes sunk in shadow, the witch lunges for Donovan, knife held high. And I leap for them, straight through the invisible bubble, knocking their blade out of their hand as we tumble into the sea of blood.

For an interminable, awful moment, my head goes under. Then I'm up, gasping for air, grappling with the witch. Their robes weigh them down, and I scramble on top of them, my hands around their neck, dragging them beneath the surface. I haven't felt rage like this since I lit the monster on fire. It electrifies every part of me, imbuing my muscles with more strength than I ought to have.

I don't care what I think I saw on Donovan's arm. They're not going to kill him before I have answers.

The witch fights, twisting beneath me, slippery with blood. Their hood slips back, baring their face. And then I gasp, shock and fury reverberating through my limbs in equal measure.

The man beneath me—the Blood Witch who was about to take Donovan's life—is no stranger. I'd know his blue eyes and the sardonic twist of his mouth anywhere.

Cooper.

CHAPTER

Forty~Four

OH MY GOD. I worried that he was in league with them, but this is so much worse.

He's one of them.

"You traitor," I spit at him. "How could you do this? You lied to me!"

But the blood-soaked garden is already retreating, Cooper slipping through my hands. I'm sucked back down the aisle as the tide creeps higher and higher. Just like last time, the chairs are adrift in it. Just like last time, Donovan sinks beneath the surface, gasping for air, reaching out to me as he drowns.

Back through the door I go, and this time, it slams shut behind me. I sink into my body, sitting up in Donovan's arms with a gasp that shakes both of us.

"Rune?" His voice cracks. "What the hell just happened? I thought—I thought you—"

I look up into those depthless blue eyes. Unlike before, they're anything but opaque. They're dark with an emotion he isn't even bothering to hide. Fear—for me.

Aside from Charlotte, no one's ever been afraid for me like this before. No one's ever cared enough to bother.

But does that even matter, if he's working with the Blood

Witches? If he bears their mark, a mark he was only pretending not to recognize in the gazebo?

Cooper said Donovan was innocent. That he didn't have magical gifts of any kind. But then, why are his eyes a perfect match for the light that's pouring through the fractured stones? The light that calls to me, even as I struggle to focus my eyes on Donovan's worried face?

I could swear his concern is sincere. But people can be two things at once, can't they? Like the monster, who coached Little League and went to church every Sunday and was someone else entirely behind closed doors.

"Show me your arm," I say, taking hold of his shirt.

"What?" He jerks out of my grip, his brows knitted in puzzlement. "Are you delirious?"

"Not in the least." I slide out of his lap, onto the stones, but that doesn't help. Because oh God, I swear I can feel some kind of power seeping through them and into me, as if whatever's emanating from those crevices is using them as a conduit.

Could it be that the fractures in the stones are...*ley lines*? And if that's the case, was Cooper right about what Donovan and I have the power to do, even if he was lying about everything else?

My body buzzes, like I've been plugged into a supernatural generator. It takes everything I can muster to concentrate on what Donovan's saying, to remember what I need to know.

"You passed out, Rune. I couldn't wake you up. And then there was some kind of earthquake—did you even see?" He gestures around us, at the broken stones and the blue light. "I yelled for help, but no one showed up. This has to be some kind of worker's comp suit in the making. It's total bullshit, and I swear the moment I get out of here, I'm going to—"

He keeps babbling, but I ignore it. "Your arm," I say again, grabbing at his shirt, and this time, he's not fast enough to get away.

I push his sleeve up as far as it will go, bracing myself. Sure, the scroll-and-dagger symbols only appeared on the witches' arms once they'd drawn blood, but what if Cooper *was* telling the truth about Donovan not being gifted? What if he has the symbol tattooed on his arm permanently, since he doesn't have what it takes to make it materialize through magical means?

I'm so certain of what I'll see that, when the entirety of Donovan's tattoo comes into view, I think I'm hallucinating. That I didn't want it to be a scroll-and-dagger so badly that I've conjured something, anything else in its stead.

Because inked on his upper arm in ornate, looping print is a date, and beneath it, four familiar words.

Cavea ad tenebras continendas.

"Why do you have this?" I blurt, just as Donovan says, "What the hell are you doing?" He pulls away from me, rolling his sleeve down, but the damage is done.

"Your tattoo," I say, breathless with relief and confusion. "What does it mean?"

"Seriously?" He gapes at me. "I thought you were *dying.* The world fucking *broke.* I thought this whole place was going to go to pieces. And you want to know about my *tattoo?*"

"Yes," I say, struggling to steady myself against the power that thrums through me. "Tell me. Please."

His teeth sink into his lower lip. "It's personal."

I just eye him. Because…really?

We glare at each other, deep blue eyes into light gray. Once again, I can see the tiny reflection of the flames dancing in his irises. The power emanating from the cracks in the floor bubbles inside me, like my body is a well and that blue light is filling it up, up, up.

Donovan breaks first. "It means 'a cage to contain the darkness,' okay? The date is…when my father died. I…he took his own life, all right?"

Oh, God. "I'm so sorry, Donovan. I didn't mean—"

"No, Rune. You started this. I'll finish it." He swallows hard, the shadows from the flames flickering across the column of his throat. "If you want to know, I'll tell you."

I'm not sure I do want to know, anymore. Not when it seems pretty clear that this is a mere coincidence. And now I'm dragging Donovan back to what has to be one of the worst times of his life, making him talk about something he didn't want to share with me, to satisfy what amounts to my own morbid curiosity. "It's not what I thought," I manage. "You don't have to say anything else."

He keeps going, as if I haven't spoken. "I've always been afraid that the darkness inside him lives inside me, too. And so I…got that tattoo. To remind me that even when the darkness comes, I don't have to let it devour every part of me. I can cage it, and go on." His eyes meet mine, and now the flames don't dance in them anymore. Now, his irises are pure blue fire. "Because I own it, not the other way around."

The words echo between us, lingering in the air. I open my mouth to say again that I'm sorry for making him talk about such painful things. To apologize for doubting him, even though he doesn't even know what for, and wouldn't believe me if I told him. To insist that we have to find a way to escape this place, because if those are really ley lines, breaking through dirt and stone right in front of us, there's no telling what will happen next. But all I get out is, "Donovan, I truly am so sor—" before a roar fills the air and the door behind the ring of fire slams open, so hard it hits the wall.

The flames flare brighter for an instant, towering above us. Then they dwindle, sucked back into the earth. Framed in the doorway beyond where they used to be stands Cooper, his chest heaving and his eyes wild. He takes in our surroundings—the fractured stones, the glowing blue light, my tattered shirt on the ground—and loses his absolute shit.

"What the fuck have you done?" he hisses. "I warned you to stay away from my brother. I told you what would happen! And where do I find you? Missing half your clothes in the middle of a preternatural goddamn disaster!"

"Cooper," Donovan starts, but he might as well be spitting into the wind.

"She's no good for you, Donovan, don't you understand?" He tugs at his hair, looking crazed. "There's only one place this ends, and it's with you dead!"

"What the hell are you talking about?" Donovan yells right back at him. "Why are you even here? How did you find us?"

"It's my job to find you!"

"Oh, *that's* your job?" The power bubbling inside me crests. I can't back it down. I can't turn it off. And right now, I don't want to. "Because in case you forgot, I can see the future. This time, I saw a little more of it. And you want to guess who held the knife in my vision this time, *Coop*? You wanna guess who's to blame for *everything*, because he doesn't have the spine to stand up for his own brother?"

Cooper's eyes narrow, the blue gone so dark, it's almost black. "Shut up about what you don't understand, why don't you?" He curls his lip, flashing his teeth at me, looking almost feral. "You've never had a family, Rune Whitlock. So you don't know the first goddamn thing about standing up for your kin. All you know is how to burn your life and everyone else's to the ground."

For a moment I'm frozen, unable to believe what just left his mouth. Then the power roars through me, obliterating my ability to do anything but seek revenge.

"You absolute bastard," I snarl at him.

And then I lunge for his throat.

DONOVAN GRABS me before I can reach Cooper. He wraps his arms around me from behind and pulls me back, his muscles flexing as I twist and fight to get away from him.

"What is *wrong* with the two of you?" he growls. "Cooper, I'm going to ask you one more time. What the fuck are you doing here?"

"What am I *doing* here?" Above the collar of his shirt, Cooper's pulse throbs. "I'm here to *help* you, you stupid asshole. Not that you'll ever believe me."

Despite everything, I have to stifle a laugh. Apparently Cooper and I have something in common. Except in this case, I don't believe him, either.

"Your definition of help is extraordinarily fucked up," I snap at him.

Cooper glares right back at me. "You have no idea what you're talking about. And this…this…" He points beyond me, at the blue light bubbling up between the cracks. "You've done something that can't be undone, Rune. Now we're all going to pay."

The words send a shiver through me. Earlier, I'd heard his voice echoing in my head: *Like calls to like. What is done can't be undone.* I thought I'd imagined it, along with the sensation that he'd calmed me when I was sliding into a premonition, but now...

"Did you...were you..." I'm not sure how to articulate what I want to know. It's one thing for him to help me head off a premonition when we're in person, when I have the ability to back off or say no. But for him to invade my privacy, to get inside my mind and talk to me without my consent...it's a terrible violation.

"Projecting inside your head? Unfortunately." He sneers at me, baring his teeth again. "Not that it did any good. You're the most stubborn person I've ever met. Might as well try to stop the tide... if you know what I mean."

Oh my God. How much does he know? How much has he seen? And, given the revelation in my latest premonition, how does he plan to use it against me? "How dare you!" I say, making a renewed attempt to put an end to him. But Donovan holds me fast.

"I have no idea what the two of you are talking about," he says, "but I would really like to get the fuck out of here. Maybe we could continue this discussion elsewhere. Or—" He lets go of me, then spins me to face him. "Maybe you just want to discuss things with Cooper. Maybe I'm not the one you want to be talking with at all."

You've got to be kidding me. "Seriously?" My voice rises to a squeak. "You still think I might be into him, Donovan? That this is —what, some kind of elaborate prank? Sure, that's it. I arranged for your brother to show up in town. Then I conspired with Ethan to have you and me work together, and I funded this shitshow of a corporate retreat. Next, I applied my design skills to create an escape room scenario that almost killed us both, because that sounded like fun. I broke the earth all by myself and made blue crap spill out of it, because I'm *just that powerful.* And for the capper, I decided it would be an awesome idea for Officer Asshat here to show up and rescue me, because it was a great way for him to see me with my shirt off and humiliate you at the same time. Two birds with one stone, am I right?"

By the time I'm finished, my voice is so high that probably only dogs can hear it, my throat hurts from screaming, and Donovan's regarding me like I'm a feral beast that might sink my teeth into him at any moment. Gingerly, he removes his hands from my shoulders.

"Well, when you put it that way…" he says.

"I don't want anything to do with him!" I stamp my foot. "And neither should you." Bending to scoop up the tattered remains of my shirt, I slide it back on. It doesn't cover much of me, but it's better than nothing.

"I already didn't want anything to do with him." Donovan looks over my shoulder at Cooper, who's still lingering in the doorway, arms folded across his broad chest. "But none of this explains why he's here, why he's so determined to keep us apart, or what the hell that"—he points at the sapphire-lit crevices—"is."

Together, the three of us stare at the bubbling blue light. I want to roll around in it. To luxuriate in it. To—

Hold on just one freaking moment. "You told me you were drawn to power," I say to Cooper. "And that's what those are, aren't they? Pure power."

"Those are *ley lines*," Cooper says, confirming my suspicion. "Like I fucking warned you."

"Jesus H. Christ on a goddamn bicycle." Donovan's gaze is ping-ponging between the two of us, like we've both lost our minds. "Ley lines? Power? What are the two of you babbling about? Is this another one of Rosa's damn riddles? Because I swear—"

Cooper heaves a massive sigh. He runs a hand through his hair again, then squares his shoulders. "You're a null, Donovan. We shouldn't even be talking about this in front of you."

"What did you just call me?" Donovan snaps, as I say, "So what's the deal, *Coop*? Did you trail me here? Are you going to arrest me again? Or are you here in an…unofficial capacity?"

Cooper is staring at the ley lines. With what looks like considerable effort, he drags his gaze away from them to glare at me. "I did follow you," he says. "But not like you think."

"How many ways to stalk someone can there be? I *told* you I had to come up here. And I told you why. I'm here for work, damn it."

"You told him?" Donovan says, eyebrows lowering. "So you two are in touch?"

"I ran into him outside the historical society meeting. Where he'd showed up to badger me into staying away from you. Something I don't need reminding about."

"Apparently you *do*," Cooper said. "I mean, look at you." He points at me—specifically, at my ruined shirt—and I can feel myself blushing.

"Look at her like that some more," Donovan says evenly, "and it'll be the last thing you ever do." He steps in front of me, blocking me from view, and my heart lurches. Even angry and suspicious, his first instinct is to protect me.

"Are you threatening me? Now that's a joke." Cooper unfolds his arms and strides forward, until he's standing right in front of Donovan. "What are you going to do? Data-entry me to death?"

I edge out from behind Donovan, not wanting to be in the middle of things if their altercation comes to blows. The two of them are about the same height—Donovan is maybe an inch taller —but Cooper is broader. And he's a cop, for God's sake. Just because I can't see a gun right now doesn't mean he's not carrying one.

I should stop this before it gets out of hand. But I can still feel the blue light coursing through my veins, hungry and avid. It *wants* to see them fight. It wants to devour, to consume.

"You think you know Rune?" Cooper hisses. "You don't understand the first thing about her."

"And you do?" They're nose to nose now, Donovan's fists clenching and unclenching.

"I understand a hell of a lot more than you do. Like why she's really here. I told you we would get to the bottom of this for you," he snarls at me over Donovan's shoulder. "That we would get justice. But you wouldn't listen. And that's why I'm here. *She* sent me, to stop you before you kill us all."

"You're such a freaking liar!" The heck with staying out of it. I shove my way between the two of them, pushing them apart. "I saw what you did, Cooper. I know you're really the one who—"

He claps a hand over my mouth before I can finish speaking. I pry at his fingers, trying to loosen them, but it's pointless. "They're coming," he whispers, eyes wide with alarm. "We have to get out of here—we can't let them see—"

His panic bemuses me. It must bemuse Donovan too, because he lets Cooper shove him out of the room and slam the door behind us, without asking a single question. *I* have a lot of questions, though, and the moment the door shuts, I turn on him, ready to ask every single one of them. But before I can get a word out, a craving sweeps me, so intense it takes my breath. I want to go back into that room, where the light is. No, I *need* to. It's calling to me, urging me on—

"Rune!" Cooper snaps. Somehow, though I don't remember moving, my hand is on the doorknob, turning it. He pulls me back, his fingers trembling. "No," he says, his voice hoarse. "It's too dangerous. You—"

"You made it!" It's Ethan's voice, cheery as ever. "A little the worse for wear, I see, but that's what the escape room challenge is all about. Surmounting obstacles together. Cooper, I see you found our final competitors. Nicely done."

So he *does* know Cooper. No matter how much Donovan's brother insists he's on the side of the angels, I know better—and this proves it.

"Cooper here works security for the retreat center," Ethan says as I turn to face him. "A little moonlighting gig. We asked him to make sure you two...well, *escaped* safely."

Donovan suppresses a snort. "No thanks to you," he says, and opens his mouth to deliver a rant about safety, OSHA standards, and workers' compensation. But I stop listening about five words in. Because there's a tear in Ethan's shirtsleeve, as if he's caught it on something. The sleeve itself is speckled with tiny red dots. And through the rent in the fabric, I can see a tattoo, fading even as I stare at it but visible nonetheless.

A scroll and dagger.

Forty-Six

I SWEAR the world stands still.

It's a cliché, I know. Like saying "my life flashed before my eyes" when describing a car accident. But clichés exist for a reason, and the moment I see that tattoo on Ethan's arm, everything else ceases to matter. Donovan's probably still ranting, but I can't hear a word he says. I can't hear anything but my own heartbeat, thumping in triple time.

I've known Ethan for two years. Never in all that time, other than his obsession with punctuality, has he been so much as grumpy. If a surfer dude had a baby with a tech bro, it would grow up to be like him. The man collects Funko Pop dolls, for God's sake.

And yet…

The flecks on his sleeve are blood. When I zero in on them, I can see that well enough. The tattoo is fading even as I watch, but it's definitely there.

Which means he's one of them.

Ethan. My boss. The one whose salary made it possible for me to buy my cottage. The one whose job offer ensured I would stay in Sapphire Springs.

Has he been watching me, this whole time? Did he *keep* me here, for his own ends?

A sick feeling swirls in my stomach as I think about Ethan's insistence that Donovan and I collaborate on this project...a project whose nature he's been oddly secretive about. One whose intricacies I still don't understand. About how, the first time I saw the scroll-and-dagger symbol, Ethan was standing right next to me. About how he demanded Donovan and I attend this retreat.

Something is badly wrong here. And he's at the epicenter of it.

He's probably somewhere in his early fifties. Which means he could've been there when my parents died. Maybe, he even could've been the one who killed my father. The one who gave the command to kill Donovan in my premonition. Surely I would've recognized his voice—but maybe Blood Witches can disguise how they sound.

I know one thing for sure. I have to get away from him. From *them.* And I have to take Donovan with me, before they do something terrible to him.

Forcing my gaze away from Ethan's arm, I paste a smile on my face. "This was a wild experience," I babble. "I'm glad I did it. Really. And I'm relieved Cooper came to find us, because otherwise we might've been stuck in there forever. But as you can see, I need a new shirt. And Donovan and I have a lot to discuss. Issues that came up when we were, um, working through our differences. Excuse us, please."

Ignoring Cooper's protests, I grab hold of Donovan's arm and tow him away, back up the stone steps that we descended to reach the escape room. I half-expect Ethan to chase after us, but he doesn't move. Nor does Cooper, his good little lapdog.

I have no idea why they're letting us leave. But I'm going to make the most of it.

Donovan twists in my grip, trying to get free. "What are you doing? I was right in the middle of—"

"I don't care what you were in the middle of. Trust me, none of it matters."

"Oh, it matters. This was a fucking lawsuit waiting to happen. He needs to understand that." Donovan sounds so indignant, I'd laugh if I wasn't afraid for my life—and his.

The stairs are steep, and by the time we reach the top, I'm breathing hard. Donovan, damn him, is unscathed. "Where are we going?" he says.

I look desperately to the left and right. Where can we go that we won't be overheard? Where will we be safe?

Through the trees, I see a flash of blue. A lake, maybe. Which means there might be a boat.

It's a crazy idea, but it's the best one I have. "This way," I say, and take off through the trees. There's a trail, but it's narrow, and my shoes aren't meant for hiking. Branches slap at my face as I plow through the woods, heading for the slice of blue in the distance.

"Have you lost it?" Donovan says behind me. "There are probably ticks in here!"

Wow. There are Blood Witches on the loose, our boss is probably a homicidal maniac, his brother is hell-bent on killing him, and there's raw power bubbling up out of the ground—power that the two of us triggered, because our attraction to each other is strong enough to destroy the world. But heaven forbid we be bitten by a *tick*. A giggle escapes me, then another. "They don't matter, either," I manage to get out.

"Tell that to the three hundred thousand new cases of Lyme disease that are diagnosed in this country each year," he huffs as we crash through the trees that border the end of the path and spill out onto a small, sandy beach.

I was right—it is a lake. A large one, with a rowboat moored at the foot of an oak tree. I make straight for it, with Donovan behind me. "Help me push this toward the water," I say, shoving the boat out of the grass and onto the sand.

Donovan gives a disbelieving snort, but he doesn't protest. Maybe he's given up. Instead he mutters, "Fine," and grabs hold of the boat. Together, with me pushing and him pulling, we get it to the water's edge. I climb in, and Donovan regards me, eyebrows raised. At last, he gives the boat one final shove, pushing it into the water, and steps in after me.

"Do you know how to row?" I say as the boat drifts away from the shore, guided by the wind.

"It's a little late to ask that. But yeah. I told you, I was a Scout." He peers at me. "I'll make you a deal. I'll row, and you talk. Whatever the hell's going on here, you know a lot more about it than you're letting on."

"Okay," I say, glancing back nervously at the trees. No one is following us—yet. But I don't know how much time we have.

Sighing, he grabs the oars and dips them into the water. The boat snags on something—a rock? a branch?—and for a terrifying moment I think we're going to get stuck. But then Donovan digs the oars in harder, his muscles flexing, and with a horrible scraping sound, the rowboat judders free. I grip my seat, the wood hot under my palms, as he pilots us deeper. "Now," he says. "Your turn. How do you really know my brother? And what's the deal between the two of you? This time, I want the truth."

"And I want to give it to you. But I don't think you'll believe me." I take a deep breath. "I wasn't lying when I said I met Cooper for the first time when I tackled him out of the path of that bus. He is a cop, yes. But he's also involved with something else. Something…bad."

A wary look flickers in his beautiful irises. "You mean, something illegal? Like, corruption?"

Inspiration strikes. There's no freaking way Donovan will believe that his brother and our boss are witches. But if I go with something more mundane, maybe I'll have a chance of pulling this off. "Yes. I think he's in it up to his eyeballs with Ethan. Cooper doesn't want me anywhere near you, because he knows I'm onto him, and he thinks if the two of us spend enough time together, I'll tell you what I suspect. The way I'm doing right now."

Donovan's shoulders bunch as he digs the oars into the water again. Droplets fly from them, sparkling in the sunlight, and I watch them scatter, feeling strangely hypnotized. It occurs to me that the further I've gotten from the ley lines, the less crazed I feel, and the better I can think. They *did* something to me, made me lose control of myself, just like Cooper warned me they would. And maybe some of the things he did and said were because he'd lost control of himself, too.

Why would he warn us to get out of the room with the exposed ley lines before Ethan arrived? Why wouldn't he want to show them to Ethan? Now that my mind is actually working again, none of this makes sense to me. What kind of game is Cooper playing?

"What about all that crap about ley lines and power, then?" Donovan says, interrupting my train of thought. "Why would Coop say he warned you about them? And what was he talking about when he said someone sent him to stop you, before you killed us all?"

Oh, crap. "I can give you two answers. One you won't believe. The other you might accept."

He glares at me. "All I want is the truth."

I give "the truth" one last desperate try. "Would you believe that your brother is a witch, that he knows I'm cursed to see the future but have no one take my premonitions seriously, and that he wants me to stay away from you because he knows I foresaw your death? That on our wedding day, you'll die at the altar? That there are ley lines beneath Sapphire Springs, wellsprings of magic, and Cooper thinks if you and I are together, we'll break those wide open and destroy the world?"

Donovan gives me a disgusted look from beneath lowered brows. "Not this again. Christ. You had me row all the way out to the middle of this goddamn lake so no one can hear us, just to feed me some stupid fairytale?"

Exasperation floods me. "What do you think those lines of blue light were, then, Donovan? How about the mini-quake that caused them?"

"I have no damn idea. Bad engineering. Toxic chemicals. Not fucking Tinkerbell!"

The wind gusts, blowing my sweaty hair back from my face. I breathe in the smell of the lake, brine laced with a faint hint of sulfur, and try again. "If you don't like that explanation, then let's go with the idea that your brother's unhinged, and he's in league with our corrupt boss."

"That's a serious accusation, Rune." We've reached the center of the lake, and he stills the oars. "I admit Ethan didn't demonstrate the best judgment today. But it's a far leap from that to an accusation of corruption."

"Look," I say desperately. "What do we actually know about the purpose of the database we're working on, or the client we're working on it for? When's the last time you were given a project with so little information to go on?"

"Well, never, but I'm sure Ethan has a—"

"A what? A good reason? I'm telling you, something's fishy at Smashbox. Why would Ethan need Cooper up here to work security? Security for what? It's a freaking mountain retreat. Besides, who the hell has a retreat with an escape room like the one we just went through? Something isn't adding up."

The sunlight gleams off Donovan's black hair as he tilts his head. "I hear you, Rune. I don't disagree. But what would you like me to do about it?"

I draw a deep breath of the briny air, then go for it. "I want you to hack into Ethan's personal files."

His eyes widen. "Excuse me? That's a serious violation of privacy. Not to mention, illegal. I've told you and told you, I'm not a hacker."

"But you know how to, right? It's a matter of morals, not ability, yes?"

Donovan nods, grudgingly. "Yes, but—"

"Just think about it. It's a matter of doing something illegal this one time, or maybe being party to a whole bunch of illegal acts to set up and market a database whose purpose we don't understand."

"This isn't fair, Rune." He shakes his head, as if to shake me out of it. "You know I w—"

It's possible he was going to say any number of things: *You know I won't. You know I will. You know I want you.* But before he can get any of them out of his mouth, the water beneath us heaves, like we're in the midst of a storm-tossed ocean. Whitecaps shudder across the surface of the lake, and the boat rolls heavily to one side, then the other. Cold water splashes over the side of the hull, dousing me, and I shriek, clinging to my seat for dear life.

"Shit!" Donovan's face pales as he reaches for me. His fingers graze the skin of my arm, their touch sending that familiar electric sensation shooting through my body. And then the wind picks up speed, a rogue wave breaks across the bow, and the boat capsizes, sending us plummeting into the lake.

CHAPTER
Forty-Seven

THE WATER IS FREEZING—FAR icier than it ought to be. The cold penetrates my entire body, sending pain shooting through every limb. I gasp, flailing, but it's no use. Another wave swamps me, and I have a split second to suck in a breath before my head goes under. The current tugs at me as I kick for the surface, unable to tell the difference between up and down. My lungs burn as I fight not to inhale.

Maybe Donovan doesn't die at the altar because of me, but right now, here, in this freaking lake. Maybe the red tide was some kind of metaphor.

Oh, God, Donovan. Where is he?

I force my eyes open, but all I can see is churning water. The cold gnaws at my bones with eager teeth. *Surrender,* it whispers. *You'll be safe here, with me.*

The hell with that. I kick for all I'm worth and, by a miracle, my head breaks the surface. The water is a sea of whitecaps, stirred into a frenzy by the wind. I suck in a blessed gulp of air, searching for Donovan as I struggle to stay afloat.

He's nowhere. I call his name, but a gust swallows it, whipping lake water into my open mouth. It tastes bitter, like defeat and grief and rage.

No. *No.* I am not going to die this way. And I'll be damned if I'll lose him.

But I can't find him, either.

A wave washes over my head, and I kick frantically, desperate not to go back under. When it recedes, I can see a faraway hint of green: the trees. I strike out for shore, forcing my heavy limbs to move. *Swim,* I tell myself. *Keep going, Rune. Don't give up.*

By the time I finally feel the scrape of the sand beneath my feet, I wonder if I'm hallucinating. But no—it's real. I drag myself the last few feet, out of the roiling water, and collapse, choking and sputtering. It feels like I inhaled half the lake.

When I can breathe again, I lift my head, praying Donovan is sprawled on the beach a few feet away. I'm terrified that I'll see Cooper or Ethan instead, blood dripping onto the sand and that damn tattoo gleaming on their arms. But there's no one here except me.

"Donovan!" I scream, my throat raw. "Donovan!"

There's no answer, and my heart plummets. What if I dragged him out here to save him, and killed him instead? What if I led him to the very death I was trying to prevent? What if—

"Rune."

The sound is hoarse, barely audible. But I hear it nonetheless. Propping myself up on my elbows, I turn in the direction it came from and see Donovan crawling out of the water, his dark hair sticking up every which way and his soaked clothes plastered to his body. There's an abrasion on his cheek, his jeans are ripped, and waterweeds are stuck to the shirt that began this morning worthy of a sexy photoshoot. But none of that matters, because he's alive.

And so am I.

Relief cascades through me, followed by joy so overwhelming, it's an adrenaline rush. I forget that Donovan and I aren't supposed to be together. That the last time he held me in his arms, the earth cracked open. Or maybe I just don't care.

I push myself to my feet, ignoring the water pouring off me

and the exhaustion that trembles through my limbs, and run for him. He's just made it onto the sand and is lying flat on his back, chest heaving, when I fling myself on top of him, kissing him so fiercely that the stubble on his jaw scrapes my skin. I don't care about that, either. The pain means we *survived*.

Donovan's arms come up to hold me, banding so tightly around my back, it feels like he never wants to let me go. "Are you all right?" he murmurs into my mouth.

I nod, clutching him. "Are y-you?"

He pulls away a little, enough to look up at me. His jaw is a hard line, but his touch is gentle as he tucks my sopping hair behind my ears. "Nothing some dry clothes and the red pill won't cure."

It takes me a second, given my sodden brain. "Did...did you just make a *Matrix* joke?"

His chest vibrates beneath me as he laughs. Maybe the adrenaline rush of survival has gotten to him, too. "What other explanation for what just happened can there be? And I swear, if you say anything about ley lines, magic, or curses, I won't be responsible for my actions."

Now that I know he's okay, shock is setting in. Or maybe I'm just that damn cold. Either way, my teeth start chattering, so hard it feels like I might bite my tongue right in half. "We're not in the M-matrix, Donovan," I manage.

"Hmmm." He strokes my wet hair over and over. "That's what you'd say if we *were*, though, right? Maybe I'm hallucinating all of this. In what other universe would you be lying on top of me, soaking wet and wearing a scrap of fabric for a shirt?"

His words penetrate the fog that's settled over me, and I scramble off him, trying—and failing—to tug my clothes to rights. Donovan sits up, scrubbing a hand across his face. He shades his eyes from the sun, peering up at me. "I'm not hallucinating, am I? Too bad. Maybe I should nearly drown every day."

"That isn't f-funny." I grab his arm with clammy fingers, trying to pull him upright. "We have to go."

"And leave all this?" He gestures at the lake, which, impossibly, is settling back to its original state. As we watch, the waves slow. The wind dies down, only the slightest breeze stirring the water's surface. Our boat drifts in the middle of the lake, forlorn and abandoned.

I have no idea what just happened. But I don't want to be here when it happens again—or worse. Nor do I want to wait on the shore of a possessed lake for the Blood Witches to find us. A cloud passes across the sun, and I shiver even harder. "I don't care if you believe me about what's really going on or not—you can't deny that this situation is batshit crazy. How many times today have we almost died? I'm telling you, Ethan has something to do with this."

He stands, towering over me. Water drips from his hair, the hem of his shirt, his torn jeans. Goosebumps line his bare forearms. "So maybe we should talk to him. Or someone else. Don't you think our fellow employees would like to know that there's some kind of weird seismic activity going on here? Maybe they'd like to, I don't know, *leave*?"

"Unless they're in on it." In an effort not to freeze to death, I rub my upper arms. It doesn't do much good. Maybe the plan is for both of us to die of pneumonia.

"Okay. Now you're just talking crazy." He shoves both hands through his hair, splattering water everywhere. "Listen to yourself, Rune. You think Jill from accounting is some kind of criminal mastermind? Look at her, for God's sake! The only thing she's masterminding is what bar she's going to sing karaoke at next weekend."

"I have n-no idea what she is or isn't. That's the point," I say, heading back toward the trailhead on trembling legs. "You brought your laptop with you, right?"

Donovan doesn't say yes. He doesn't say no, either. But he quits arguing, and when I step between the trees, he's right behind me.

I half-expect to find Ethan or Cooper waiting for us, to demand to know where we went and drag us off to their lair. But when we emerge from the woods, the retreat center is strangely deserted. Maybe everyone is resting up before dinner. It's the least nefarious explanation I can think of. Either way, it buys us some time.

The cabins are off to the right, in the opposite direction of the main lodge. They're down a long gravel road lined with trees, a steep drop-off on one side. A road I could swear is getting longer with every step we take. I've been moving as fast as I can, in the hopes that no one will see us, and now I'm both shivering and sweating—a lethal combination.

"Which one is yours?" I pant as the cabins finally come into view—rustic log exterior, adorable front porches, isolated location perfect for a murder, and all.

"Number four." He points. "Honestly, Rune, if you could just slow down so we could talk about this—"

Oh, sure. Why don't I stroll to my doom, giving everyone who has it out for us as much time as possible to do us in? But I don't have the breath for a sarcastic retort, so I just come to a skidding halt in front of Donovan's cabin and double over, hands on my knees, while I wait for him to open the door.

He fumbles in the front pocket of his battered jeans for his key, digging around so long that, for an awful heartbeat, I'm afraid it's gone, lost at the bottom of the lake or in the escape room's snowbank. But no—even in the face of mortal injury and death-defying odds, Sex Spreadsheet Guy has hung on to his powers of organization. He slides the key into the lock, turns the knob, and then we step inside.

CHAPTER
Forty-Eight

DONOVAN'S CABIN looks much like mine did, in the cursory inspection I gave it when I dropped off my baggage. The walls are exposed logs, and the living area is one large, open space. To my left is a small galley kitchen, straight ahead is a bathroom, and to the right is a writing desk, a stone fireplace that takes up an entire wall, and a queen-sized bed covered in a homey patchwork quilt. Donovan's navy duffel bag sits patiently beside it, a dog awaiting the return of its master.

He locks the door behind us. Silence falls, broken only by our harsh breathing, the drip of water from our clothes onto the hardwood floor, and the renewed chattering of my teeth.

There are two towels stacked on the desk. Donovan hands one to me, then kneels and pulls some folded clothes from his duffel. "Here," he says, thrusting them in my direction. "Sweats. They're much too big, but at least you'll be warm."

At this point, I wouldn't care if he'd handed me a muumuu. Muttering my thanks, I take the clothes and flee for the bathroom. My last sight is of Donovan pulling off his shirt, which falls to the ground with a *splat*. Even in these dire circumstances, I can't help but notice how toned he is, and the V of muscle that leads to his—

No, Rune. Down, girl. Look away.

I shut the bathroom door behind me with a mingled sense of relief and regret. Then I lean against it, shivering, trying not to think about how the man I shouldn't sleep with under any circumstances is getting naked on the other side. I've never needed stress relief so badly in my life, but this is not the time—and he is not the man. "Not going to happen," I say aloud. "Focus."

"Did you say something?" Donovan calls, too close to the door for comfort. "If the clothes don't work, I could give you a different—"

"The clothes are fine! Don't come in here!" I set the sweats and the towel down on the corner of the sink. With fumbling, half-frozen fingers, I tug my destroyed shirt loose, then start working on the drawstring of my pants. The water has done a number on it, solidifying the knot into a mass that I can't pick apart, no matter how hard I try. I dig at it, trying to pry it loose, and almost peel my nail right off. "Ow!"

"Are you okay in there?" Donovan says, sounding even closer this time.

"Great. I—I just—" In desperation, I search the bathroom for anything that might help—tweezers, maybe, or even scissors. At this point, I'd settle for cutting the damn drawstring in half. I pull open the two small drawers that flank the bathroom sink, then the cabinet beneath it, but no luck.

As I straighten, I catch a glimpse of myself in the mirror: blue lace bra that's seen better days; porcelain-pale skin; hair tangled with seaweed; irises so huge, I look like one of Margaret Keane's big-eyed children. I'd give my kingdom for a shower, but we don't have the time. Instead, I settle for picking greenery out of my hair, gasping in pain when something thorny stabs me in my injured finger.

"Are you sure you're all right?" Donovan sounds worried now. "I heard you slamming things, and then— Just answer me, will you?" When I don't reply, he knocks. "Rune?"

I scoop up the hoodie Donovan gave me. It's soft, forest-green, and smells like him—that enticing hint of cedar and vanilla. More than anything, I want to slip it over my head and disappear inside it, all cozy and warm. But no…the moment it touches my saturated pants, it'll get soaked. Unless I want to put my nasty, shredded shirt back on, I only have one option.

"Rune!" Panic laces his voice. "Will you please—"

I really, really am not looking forward to what I have to do next. But I also don't have the fortitude to track down the villain who killed my parents and figure out what the hell Ethan is up to while wearing soaking-wet, ice-cold pants. Sighing, I jerk the door open.

Donovan is standing on the other side, dressed in a navy t-shirt that brings out his eyes and a fresh pair of jeans. He must've had his shoulder against the door, because when it creaks inward, he nearly topples onto me. He steadies himself, one hand gripping the top of the frame, and takes me in: blue lace bra, tangled hair, and all. His jaw drops.

"I, um, can't get my pants off," I mutter, feeling a blush color my cheeks. "The knot in the drawstring is, um…the water made it impossible to…"

My voice trails off. Donovan is staring at me, his gaze tracking slowly downward—from my mouth to my throat to the lace of my bra, where it lingers. I swear I can feel the heat of it on my skin. It tracks lower still, down my belly to the aforementioned knot, and doesn't budge.

"There are no scissors in the bathroom," I say, fidgeting under the weight of that piercing gaze. The woman I examined in the mirror looked about as alluring as if she'd been dumpster diving. But clearly, Donovan isn't seeing the same thing I did. "That's what I was looking for," I rattle on, unsettled. "I thought you might have some out here, in the, um, kitchen."

At this, his eyes flick upward, meeting mine. Humor lurks in their depths. "Let me get this straight. You're asking me to cut off your pants?"

Sweet Jesus. "I can cut them off myself!"

"Sounds hazardous," he drawls.

I want to tell him that what's hazardous is me standing in front of him, half-naked, ten feet from a bed. What's hazardous is the storm that I can feel brewing between us, the way the space between us is too small and not big enough, all at the same time. But the words freeze in my throat when Donovan lifts the hand that's not gripping the doorframe, so slowly that I have all the time in the world to back away. Which I should absolutely do. But I don't move.

With a single finger, he traces the same line his gaze took a minute ago: over my cheekbone and my throat, between my breasts, down my stomach. His hand closes on my hip, its warmth a welcome contrast to my lake-chilled skin. "Chaos," he says hoarsely, and in those two single syllables I hear both an invitation and a warning.

I don't know if he's labeling the mess we've found ourselves in, or whether he intends it as the nickname he gave me, the one I haven't heard him use since that very first night. One thing I do know, though: I'm a millisecond from telling him he can undo the knot in the drawstring, all right…with his teeth. But as I open my mouth, the ground beneath us shifts, the foundation of the cottage creaking. Behind me, the sink turns on, water splashing into the basin.

"What the fuck?" Donovan says, stumbling back from me. He stares at the stream flowing from the faucet, his face blank with shock.

I seize the opportunity to duck under his arm, heading for the kitchen. There are scissors in the first drawer I open, and I grab them, thinking that if need be, I can use them as a weapon…not against Donovan, but against whatever forces we might find ourselves confronting before we get off this mountain.

Maybe I should leave right now. A smarter person would probably do just that. But I'm not going anywhere until I get some answers.

When I finally make it out of the bathroom, there's a fire blazing in the hearth and Donovan is sitting at the small wooden desk with his laptop open. I pad over to him, swallowed up by his hoodie and sweatpants. I probably look ridiculous, but I don't care. At least I'm dry.

He shoots me an unreadable sidelong glance, then hooks a second chair with his foot and drags it over. "I'd say I like you wearing my clothes, but I have a feeling we'd just wind up somewhere it's not a great idea to go, for a shit-ton of reasons."

"I—"

"Let me finish." He clears his throat. "I believe you about Cooper, okay? And even though I don't understand it, I'm starting to agree that there's something…off. I don't believe in magic or curses, but the car wreck, that first power outage, the mini-earthquake and the weird blue light, the lake, what just happened in the bathroom—they all happened when we were together. Once is a good story. Twice is a coincidence. This many times is a data set worthy of analysis."

Oh, thank God. "So, let's analyze it, then," I say, hugging my knees to my chest. "If you trust me about the rest of it, then please trust me when I tell you that there's something off about Ethan, too."

Donovan scrubs a hand over his face. "I do trust you, Rune. God knows why, but I do. Otherwise I wouldn't put myself on the line for you this way. Because what I've just done is illegal as hell, and if anyone finds out about it, my job will be the least of the things I'll lose."

Those mesmerizing blue eyes of his are fixed on mine, and for once, they're not icy with rage or burning with desire. This time, their expression is open and sincere. Vulnerable, even, the way they were when he told me about what Cooper had done to him, back before everything between us went so horribly wrong.

He doesn't believe magic exists. He doesn't think my premonitions are real. He still thinks there has to be a logical explanation for all this. But he's willing to take this big of a risk—for me.

No one has ever done anything like that for me before.

I swallow hard, my entire body aching with the urge to throw my arms around him. "Thank you," I manage to get out. "Thank you for trusting me."

"Don't thank me yet." He tilts his laptop so both of us can see it, his tone all business. "These are the files on Ethan's hard drive. He had some serious encryption on them, but I was able to break through. From what I can tell, this is the one he accesses most frequently." His fingers fly over the keys, and some kind of record-keeping system flashes up on the screen. "Look at the names, Rune."

I lean closer, peering at line after line of text. "Holy crap. Charlotte's in there, and Mrs. Fontaine, and Cooper, and you, and... Who *isn't* in there?"

Donovan scrolls down the page, his jaw set hard. The list of familiar names goes on and on and on. "These are coded," he says, gesturing at the screen. "And here—a ton of them have 'BBB' in the right-hand column. It's like he's been collecting some kind of information on all of us. But what the hell could he possibly—"

I hold up a hand, cutting him off. "BBB," I say slowly. "Like, 'Books, Bites, and Bedlam'?"

"The library fundraiser? What could that have to do with anything?"

I stare at the list of names, revisiting the day of the festival in my mind, walking myself through it step by step. And then, with a sick rush of heat, the answer comes to me.

Oh, God. Oh, no, no, no.

"The blood drive, Donovan." I jump to my feet. "How could I be so stupid?"

His brow wrinkles in puzzlement. "You mean the mobile van? It was a donation to Sapphire Springs' blood bank, Rune. There's no reason to associate…that…with this. It's protected health information, for one thing."

I shake my head, my still-wet hair cold against my cheeks, as the full impact of my realization sinks in. "We weren't donating to the blood bank. We were donating to *him*."

Ethan is a Blood Witch. For reasons I don't yet understand, he wanted samples from as many residents of Sapphire Springs as he could get his hands on. And the blood drive provided the perfect excuse.

He played us, all of us. And we fed right into his hands.

The codes next to each of our names…they mean something vital. They're at the heart of why he brought me and Donovan together, why my parents died and my curse exists, why Donovan's destined to die at the altar. I feel it in my bones.

This information is the key.

And if it's the last thing I ever do, I'm going to figure out how to turn it in the lock.

Forty-Nine

"WOULD YOU PLEASE SIT DOWN?" Donovan says, swiveling to look at me as I wear a path from the hearth to the windows that overlook the drop-off and back again. "I don't know what you think you've figured out, but you're not going to get any closer to learning what it means if we don't actually sort through this data."

Sitting is the last thing I want to do. My body feels so full of adrenaline and rage, pacing is the only way to burn any of it off. The red haze that signals the onset of one of my premonitions crowds the edge of my vision, and with a groan of frustration, I bury my face in my hands. I can't afford this, not now.

I draw a deep breath, then another. The haze retreats, thank God, but when I lift my head, that damned scroll and dagger is emblazoned everywhere. It's in the air, on the quilt of the bed, branded into the floorboards.

When I spare a glance for Donovan, though, it's clear he hasn't noticed anything out of the ordinary. His eyes are still fixed on me, his expression expectant.

"Rune? Did you hear me?" he says.

I take a careful step toward him, avoiding the red-hot circle on the hardwood. "You don't see that?" I say just to be sure, pointing at it.

Donovan follows the direction of my finger, leaning down to get a better look. "What? The scratch in the wood? I mean, sure, but what does that have to do with anything?" He sounds bewildered—who could blame him?—and I heave a sigh.

"Never mind," I tell him, inspecting the seat of my chair for any indication of a brand before I sink down onto it. The day would not be improved by lighting my butt on fire. "Come on. Let's dig into this, before something else goes wrong."

There are thousands of names in that database.

Some of them I don't recognize, but many of them I do. All of the Sinsters. Charlotte and Jess. Donovan. Cooper. Ethan, and every single Smashbox employee at this retreat. Jenny. D'Andre. Gracie Liu, who owns Brew Box. I scroll further, my eyes widening as I take in name after name: Mrs. Garcia, my third-grade teacher. Dave Cassady, the owner of The Bookaholic, who always saves the new Ilona Andrews books for me. Rosa, for God's sake.

Many of them have 'BBB' listed next to their names. Others don't. But I'd put money on the fact that Ethan and whoever's in league with him got these people's blood samples from somewhere else. Medical records, maybe.

A field next to some of the names is marked with 'WDCC7.' Others are marked with 'BDCC8.' And in some cases, the field is blank. There are other notes, links to family trees that I itch to dig into. Later, maybe, when our lives aren't on the line. When I'm not afraid Ethan's going to charge through the door at any moment, Cooper right behind him.

I make a small sound of distress, and Donovan takes the laptop from me. "What are you looking for, specifically?" he says.

"I'm not sure. Keep scrolling," I tell him. My eyes scan the screen, taking in each new name as it's revealed. And then I gasp.

"Oh my God. Stop," I say, grabbing his wrist. That now-familiar electrical shock ripples through me, but I ignore it, my jaw dropping as I stare.

There on the screen is the monster's name. And beneath it is Julia's.

They don't even live in Sapphire Springs anymore. What the actual fuck?

Why are they in here, with their names so close together? Why is Ethan tracking *them?*

Why can't I get away from the monster, even in death?

Dizziness sweeps me. Spots dance in front of my eyes, and crimson tongues lick at the edges of my vision. My pulse pounds in my ears.

Donovan's arm wraps around my shoulders, pulling me tight against him. "Rune. Hey." He strokes my hair back from my forehead, his voice soft. "What's wrong? What did you see?"

His touch steadies me, but I force myself to sit upright, away from him. *Be strong,* I tell myself, clearing my throat.

"You heard what Cooper said about me not knowing what it's like to have a family. That's because…well…my parents died when I was a baby." There's no way I'm getting into the details of what actually happened to them, not right now. "I got put into foster care. Julia Delgado"—I point a shaking finger at her name—"was my foster sister. The night you were driving by my house, when I passed out…Julia had just left. She was there to tell me something about…him." I gesture at the monster's name, my hand trembling even harder.

Donovan's jaw clenches. "Who was he, Rune?"

"My foster father." It's all I manage to get out, but it must be enough, because Donovan's eyes narrow, becoming slits of blue.

"What did he do to you?" The words emerge in a low, threatening rumble.

"It doesn't matter."

"Yes, it does. *You* matter, Rune, damn it. You matter to me." He takes me by the shoulders, his narrowed eyes boring into mine. "What. Did. He. Do?"

I have to fight not to quail beneath the intensity of his gaze. "Bad things, all right? But I handled it. And it *really* doesn't matter anymore, because that first night we were working together, alone at Smashbox…well…I found out that he's dead."

Donovan's head tilts, the way it does when he's thinking hard. I can practically see his mind whirring as he puts the pieces together. "That phone call." His grip on my shoulders loosens. "Someone told you he died. And then…you kissed me?"

"One spontaneous kiss, to take place between the hours of 6:00 and 10:00 p.m." I swallow hard. "Once again, sorry I didn't schedule it on our shared calendar."

His teeth sink into his lower lip. "And I told you about what Cooper did. But you—you really weren't using me. You were… celebrating. God, I'm such a dick. I'm sorry, Rune."

"Apology accepted," I say, sitting back, away from him. I can't afford to get all emotional, not now. "Anyway, that's who he is. But it doesn't explain why he's in here. And see, there's 'WDCC7' next to Julia's name, but nothing next to his."

"Hang on." Donovan's eyes flick to the screen again. "Maybe there's a pattern to those codes. Let's take a look at the people both of us know."

His fingers fly over the keys again, and then I'm looking at Charlotte's name. Ethan's, Rosa's, and all of Smashbox's employees'. Donovan's and Cooper's. But not mine. Come to think of it, I haven't seen mine at all.

Next to Charlotte's is that familiar 'WDCC7.' The Smashbox employees are a mixed bag: Ethan is coded 'BDCC8,' as is everyone else on the retreat with us, including Rosa. Many of the rest, though, have blank fields next to their names. Cooper is

marked 'WDCC7,' with a note that simply reads 'special circumstances. Half-brother: Donovan Frost,' with a link to their shared
family tree. And next to Donovan's name, most puzzling of all,
are both codes.

"I don't get it," Donovan says. "What do those codes mean?
Why would he be tracking us like this? And what the hell is he
doing with this information, anyway?" His fingers drum the
surface of the desk. "Whatever he's after, we could sue the shit out
of him, provided that we can prove this is linked to protected
medical data. Of course, then I'd have to find a way of getting
access to this that isn't illegal as fuck…"

"Where's my name?" I interrupt him.

Donovan shrugs. "I included you in the search parameters.
You're not in here, Rune."

That makes no sense. Why everyone else, and not me? "I have
to be. Try again."

He does, typing my name in so I can see. Sure enough, the
search yields nothing.

I lift my head, gaze fixed on the scroll-and-dagger that shimmers in the air above the kitchen counter, thinking hard. I must be
missing something. The premonitions came to me. Ethan paired
me with Donovan. The Blood Witches murdered my parents and
stole me from them. Why would I possibly not be in this database,
when everyone else is?

And then it comes to me. "Search for Iris Duval."

"What? Who is that?"

I think of what Mrs. Hernandez told me. *David and Lorelai
Duval died when their house burned to the ground. They had a young
daughter, Iris.* "Me," I say, my voice a whisper. "It's my birth
name."

One of Donovan's hands squeezes mine. With the other, he
does as I asked. And a moment later, there it is. *Iris Duval.
WDCC7.*

"Click on the family tree," I tell Donovan, my mouth impossibly dry.

He does. Up it pops, linked to two other names in the database: David and Lorelai. When Donovan clicks on their records, both of them show the same code: WDCC7.

There are more names on the tree. Grandparents, aunts and uncles, cousins. A whole family, just waiting for me to find them. The whole time, when I was abused and alone, mocked and bullied, all these people were out there, thinking I was dead.

Caught between fury and devastation, I watch as Donovan pulls up one name in my family tree after another. 'WDCC7' appears next to all of them.

"They're genetic markers of some kind," I tell him, wiping away the tears that have flooded my eyes. "They have to be."

"Okay," he says, "but then Cooper and I—"

"You have different fathers. It stands to reason you wouldn't be an exact match."

"But then…" His lips purse, and he types something again, then sits back. "Shit. If you're right, I'm the only one in the database that has both markers, Rune. Out of thousands of people, only me."

It's my turn to bite my lip. "Who was your father, Donovan?"

"Jonathan Frost. He was a mechanical engineer. Why?"

"Look him up," I say, a terrible suspicion taking root inside me.

"He never lived in Sapphire—"

"Look him up anyway."

Brow knitted, Donovan does as I ask. Sure enough, Jonathan's name pops up, linked to Donovan's family tree. And next to it: BDCC8.

Holy shit. If these really are genetic markers… Then what if 'WDCC7' indicates the presence of a marker for regular witches, the ones I'm descended from? And the 'B' in 'BDCC8' stands for 'Blood Witch'?

If that's the case, then Donovan's father was a Blood Witch, and his mother must have been a regular one, like Cooper. Could that be why he's a magical null—because the two markers canceled each other out? But does it also make him something unique, something that, when linked to me, somehow has the potential to wreak havoc on the magical world?

I'm in way over my head here. I need to call the Sinsters. But Rosa took my phone, and Donovan's, too. And there's no landline in this cabin.

I turn to Donovan, who's still staring at his father's name. "I need to call Charlotte," I tell him. I have her number memorized; she can reach out to Mrs. Fontaine, Mrs. Grant, or Mrs. Hernandez for me. "Can you dial out on FaceTime?"

"Sure." He drums on the desk again, faster this time. "She's a lawyer, right? But before you talk to her, we need to think, Rune. Yeah, this looks bad, but we don't know what we've found, not for sure. Plus, the way I got this information is about as far from being on the up-and-up as it gets. And—"

He's still in the middle of his recitation when all of the scroll-and-dagger symbols flare. The overhead lights flicker and die. And then, with a sizzling sound reminiscent of a steak on a grill, Donovan's laptop's screen blinks once, twice, and then goes completely black.

Swearing, he punches the power button again and again. It's no use. His computer is dead.

And with it, our best way of communicating with anyone who isn't on this mountain.

Fifty

"YOU'VE GOT to be kidding me." Donovan glares at his laptop, which is doing its best impersonation of the world's most expensive paperweight. "How—why—"

He inspects the laptop, muttering about the battery and the fan and God knows what else. I watch him, not saying a word. Because I have a sinking suspicion that what just went wrong has nothing to do with technical difficulties and everything to do with the Blood Witches.

Somehow, they've found out that we hacked into the database. That we're on to them. And I'm sure there's going to be hell to pay.

"Grab your stuff," I tell Donovan. "We need to get out of here."

"Yeah? And go where?" He sets the laptop down on the desk. "We need to get our phones back, in case you've forgotten. And no matter what we suspect Ethan might be involved in, we're still on company time."

I throw my hands in the air, narrowly avoiding one of the flaming brands. "Listen to yourself! *On company time*—really? Have you forgotten every single damn thing that's happened since we got here this morning? Or the fact that Ethan's tracking all of us using information that he's probably obtained in a way that's illegal as hell?" Stabbing an accusatory finger at his laptop, I say, "Whatever happened to '*Twice is a coincidence. This many times is a data set worthy of analysis*'? You think it's coincidental that your computer died? Or do you think it's more likely that Ethan knows what we just did?"

Donovan pales. "Fuck, fuck, fuck," he mumbles. "Okay, fine. We'll go back to your cabin and get your stuff. Then we can leave. We'll, I don't know, go to the cops. Or talk to Charlotte. Whatever. We can figure it out when we get back to Sapphire Springs."

"I can't get my stuff," I say. "My keys are in my purse. Which are in the retreat center with my phone." All of which is pretty damn convenient. *Too* convenient. After everything that's happened, how could I be so trusting?

"I have my keys." He stands, grabbing his laptop and stuffing it into his messenger bag. "I agree with you, things here are getting way too fishy for comfort. Why don't I drive you up to the retreat center, and you can run in and get your purse. Then I'll take you back to your cabin, you'll get your car, and we'll get the hell out of Dodge."

It makes me a little anxious to think about spending even that much extra time here. But I hate the idea of leaving my wallet and phone behind. "Okay," I say, giving him a weak smile. "Maybe I'll even change."

Donovan winks at me. "Unnecessary, Chaos," he says. "I like you just like this."

My mouth falls open. But before I can respond, he crosses to the bedside table and snags a few items, sliding them back into his duffel. "Luckily, I didn't actually unpack. Who would believe this fucking bullshit? I'm telling you, whatever explanation there is for this whole mess better be a damn good one, because…"

He's still talking when the premonition hits me in the chest with the force of a punch. I fall to my knees on the hardwood, gasping for breath. It feels like the lake all over again, like drowning. But this time, what fills my lungs isn't water.

It's blood.

There's no door. No undertow. I'm thigh-deep in a crimson ocean, the waves smacking into me with concussive force, threatening to drag me under. *Our day has come* echoes in my head over and over again, ringing in my ears. *Our time is now.*

And oh God, it's Ethan's voice.

"Rune!" Through the red haze that consumes my vision, I can see Donovan kneeling in front of me. He grips my upper arms, holding tight. "What's happening? Are you hurt?"

I suck in air, wanting to tell him not to touch me. Because every time he does, the world breaks a little more. But I can't manage to form a word.

Does that mean Ethan was the one…that he…

Ethan's voice rises, until it's all I can hear. But on its heels comes another one, even louder. *Fight it, Rune,* the second voice pleads. *Fight* him.

Cooper.

Get out of my head, I shriek, as the red tide rises higher. It's up to my chest. My throat. My chin. It's drowning me. I know it isn't real, isn't *here,* but oh God I can't *breathe*—

Donovan shakes me, his fingers biting into my arms. He's talking, his voice frantic, but I can only make out every other word: *scaring* and *what* and *help* and *go.* Ethan is laughing inside my head and Cooper is telling me to fight and all I can do is struggle for breath, pulling in one iron-tasting lungful of air after another.

What the hell does Cooper mean? Fight who? Does he mean Donovan, who's only trying to help me? Or Ethan? But Cooper and Ethan are on the same side. They have to be. Otherwise, why would Cooper be in my premonition? Why would he obey Ethan's command to kill Donovan?

In this moment, though, none of that matters. I'm of little use to anyone if, while Ethan and the Blood Witches plot to take even more from me—another one of the few people I care for—I'm stuck kneeling on the floor, trapped inside my own mind. And so, no matter whose side Cooper is on, I decide to listen to him. To fight.

Before, I'd always accepted that once I was truly in the grip of a premonition, there was nothing I could do but ride it out. But this time, I have the remnants of the ley line's energy bubbling inside me. Even though we've left the escape room's chamber behind, I can still feel a hint of that blue light, calling to whatever makes me able to see the future. It's not enough to make me lose control, the way I did when I confronted Cooper. But it's enough for me to stand against the darkness in my mind.

Inside my premonition, I close my eyes and reach down, down, down into the depths of myself. I picture the blue light as a pool at the very center of my being, a well from which I can draw. And then I imagine reaching into that well and scooping up a handful of light, cupping it in my hands and letting it sink into my skin. Its enticing warmth penetrates my bloodstream, heating me from the inside out. It creeps upward, from my palms to my wrists, and then further, up my arms. Everywhere it goes, it leaves behind an undeniable sensation of heat. Of power. My blood feels like it's bubbling in my veins, fizzing like it's been infused with carbonation.

The power isn't mine, not really. I'm just borrowing it. But it's enough to do what must be done.

The blood tide closes over my head. This time, though, I'm not afraid. I don't kick for the surface or thrash in terror. Instead, gritting my teeth against that strange bubbling sensation, just this side of pain, I plunge my hands deeper into the murk. And I open my eyes.

Everywhere that the warmth of the light penetrates is encased in a blue glow. It emanates from me, spreading out and out, illuminating the crimson depths. Obliterating them.

I can still hear Ethan's voice, but it's growing fainter. And then, with a sucking sound that shakes me to my bones, the tide retreats, pulling back all at once until it dumps me, shaking, onto the shore.

I blink, then blink again. The red tide is gone. I'm kneeling on the hardwood of Donovan's cabin, his hands still on my upper arms, his face inches from mine.

"Rune!" he says again, sounding desperate this time.

"I-I'm here." I clear my throat, then try again. "I'm fine."

"What the fuck *was* that?" His gorgeous eyes, containing all the hues of that incredible blue light, search my face. "You—I could swear you started to—"

I wish I could explain it to him. That I could tell him how amazing it felt to be able to feel that power flood through me, to be able to chase my terrible premonition away. But he wouldn't believe me. The weight of my predicament settles onto my shoulders as the warmth of the light fades, leaving only icy certainty in its wake. "Come on," I say, shrugging his grip off and getting to my feet. "We don't have time to talk about this now. We have to go."

Muttering under his breath, Donovan grabs his duffel and his messenger bag. I shove my wet shoes back on—luckily I didn't have to unknot *their* laces—dump my soaked, ruined clothes in the trash, and follow.

Under normal circumstances, I'd feel embarrassed about being outside, at a work event, wearing Donovan's oversized sweats. But these circumstances are so far from normal, it's laughable. I'm paranoid that people are looking at me, all right, but not because I'm afraid I'm going to become fodder for the gossip mill. Because I'm terrified that Cooper or Ethan or God knows who will come barreling out of the trees and drag me away by the hair.

I spare a glance for Donovan, who is bending down to—

"Holy shit. Did you just lock the door and stick the key under the doormat? Seriously?" I snap at him. "What is wrong with you? Are you afraid you're not going to get your deposit back or something?" I spin on my heel, heading for his Prius, peering left and right to make sure we're not being followed. "Oh, that's right," I toss over my shoulder. "We didn't pay one. Because this is a goddamn corporate retreat where we've almost gotten murdered three times over on our boss's dime! And then we—"

"Shhhh," Donovan hisses, cutting me off.

"Did you just 'shhh' me? I swear to Christ, Donovan Frost—"

He ignores me, slipping past me to open his car door and toss the duffel into the back. The front end damage has been repaired, and even through the fog of my anxiety, I spare a moment to think that he must have a hell of a mechanic. Apparently, not even Sapphire Springs' lone body shop is immune to the Ice Man's obsessive need to restore order.

Giving our surroundings one last glance, I storm around to the passenger side and climb in, slamming my door behind me. I expect Donovan to at least wince, but he just sits there, his brows knitting.

"What is wrong with you *now?*" I tug on the strings of my—okay, his—hoodie in aggravation. "Did you forget to tip the maid?"

Mutely, Donovan shakes his head.

"Then what? Can we please get going, so we can grab my stuff and get out of here?"

"The car won't start."

You've got to be fucking kidding me.

"What do you mean?" I say, staring at his smart key, which he's dropped into the cup holder. "Is your key's battery dead or something?"

"The key is fine. The car is fine. It just had its thirty-thousand-mile tune-up. Look at it!" He gestures around his perfectly maintained vehicle, which doesn't have so much as an abandoned coffee cup or granola bar wrapper. "My Prius is in perfect condition. It just won't start. Watch." Scooping up the smart key, he brings it closer to the Power button, then presses the button again. "If the key's battery was on the fritz, this would help. But see? Jack shit. This makes no logical sense, but it's like whatever fried my computer...also fried my car."

"Or," I say, my heart sinking, "like whoever fried your computer and your car…has no intention of letting us leave."

Fifty-One

DONOVAN and I stare at each other, dumbfounded. *He* looks dumbfounded, anyway, his brows knitted and his eyes narrowed. I'm panicking and doing my best not to show it, so I probably just look…blank.

He jabs the Power button again. "Do you seriously think someone's sabotaging our ability to leave? That they fucked with my car? Maybe it's some sort of seismic activity interfering with—"

"Oh, for God's sake." I bury my head in my hands. "Donovan, I know you think magic is a bunch of bullshit. That you don't believe in curses or premonitions or ley lines. But I'm telling you, your brother really is a witch. And so is Ethan. Whatever he's doing with that database, the samples he got, the codes next to our names—it's connected to his magic. He wants something from both of us. And you…he's trying to *kill* you."

There's a marked silence from the driver's seat. Then a warm hand descends on the back of my neck, its touch assessing. Aggravated, I jerk away, head still buried in my palms. "What are you *doing?*"

"I'm trying to figure out if you have a fever. Because you sure as shit sound delirious. Yeah, Ethan's acting outside the lines here.

Yeah, something fucked up is going on and we need to get to the bottom of it. But all this crap with witches and murder—"

I dig my nails into my scalp, tugging at my hair in frustration. Tears burn my eyes. "I think Ethan killed my parents, Donovan. He wants to do the same to you. And I can't lose you, okay? I've already lost so much, and I can't…"

"Hold up. Did—did you just say Ethan *killed your parents*?" His voice cracks. "If you really believe that, Rune, you should go to the police. You should—"

"Your brother *is* the police!" I shriek. "And I told you, he's in league with Ethan. I was so stupid, coming up here like this. Mrs. Fontaine warned me, but I didn't listen. I was dumb and stubborn and I thought I could handle this myself and now… now…"

A sob tears loose from my throat, followed by another. Huddled in Donovan's too-big hoodie, I draw my knees up to my chest and freaking lose it. "You think I'm crazy," I weep. "You don't believe me. No one ever believes me, and I'm used to that, but now you might d-d-die, and it'll be all my fault, and I can't…I don't…"

I choke on my sobs, my breath coming in shallow pants. The red haze crowds the edge of my vision, and at the thought of battling that crimson tide again, I sob even harder. I am so tired of fighting. Sometimes it feels like my whole life has been a fight. Like I'm banging on a door, and no one can hear me, and the water is rising, and I'm drowning drowning drowning—

"Hey." His arms come around me, holding me close. I resist, but he pulls me against him, tucking my head under his chin. One big hand smooths back my hair. "If you say there's magic, then I believe you, Rune. I can't pretend to understand it, but I believe you, okay?"

"Don't p-patronize me," I hiccup, shaking my head against his chest.

He cups my chin, lifting my tear-stained face. "Rune," he says, slowly and clearly, his eyes fixed on mine, "I. Believe. You."

"You c-c-can't," I stammer. "You only believe in 0s and 1s or bits and bytes or…"

"Don't tell me what I can and can't do." His expression is grave. "When I met you, my life was so predictable, it was ridiculous. I got up every morning, ironed my clothes, drove to the gym, worked out, maybe volunteered at the shelter, rinse, repeat. But then you showed up and you blew that routine all to hell. You made me mad and you made me happy and you made me want you." Those gorgeous eyes of his darken, and he strokes my wet cheek. "You remember that night in my office? You asked me to make you *feel*."

"I remember." My voice is a whisper.

"Well, that's what you make me do, all the time. You make me *feel*, Rune. Sometimes I hate you for it. But mostly…mostly, I just want more. More of the unpredictability and danger and, yeah, chaos that's come into my life since the moment you stepped into the elevator with me. More of *you*."

"So you w-want me," I manage, knuckling away my tears. "But that doesn't mean anything when it comes to—"

He presses his fingers to my lips, silencing me. "I already told you I trusted you. I put my career and my reputation on the line for you. But it seems like *you're* the one who didn't believe *me*. So now I'm telling you—I'll step outside the lines of everything I've ever counted on, everything I thought defined the world, if that's what it takes for you to realize how far I'll go for you. What I'm willing to risk."

We regard each other in silence. My breath comes in harsh gasps. "Why would you do that?" I say finally. "Why would you risk everything for me?"

Donovan's chest rises and falls. He braces his shoulders, as if girding himself. The moment hangs between us, fragile as hand-spun glass. "Because," he says, his jaw setting in a harsh line. "Because, Rune, I—"

I really want to hear what he has to say. Even if it's going to condemn us both to the pits of hell, I want to hear it. But I don't get the chance to, because before he can finish his sentence, someone slips around the car parked next to us and materializes inches from Donovan's door.

I shriek, jerking back from him so hard that I slam into my seat. Bewildered, Donovan turns, following the direction of my horrified gaze, just as Rosa—because that's who it is—knocks on his window.

"Yoo-hoo!" Her voice is as chipper as ever, her blonde hair still in its perfect ponytail, as she motions for Donovan to roll down the window. Which he can't, of course, since the car won't freaking turn on.

"Don't open it!" I hiss at him. "What if she's one of them?"

Donovan swivels to look at me. "What, an evil witch? She looks like an aerobics instructor." His tone is dry. "Besides, what choice do we have? It's not like we can drive away."

Much as I hate to admit it, he's right. Rosa can just wait us out. Worse, if she's on Ethan's side, she could bring him running. Better to feign cooperation. "Fine," I mumble. "Go ahead."

The moment he cracks the door, she starts talking. "Hey there, you two! Here you are. I thought y'all got lost or something."

"Here we are," I agree. "Um, Rosa, Donovan's car won't start. Do you happen to have jumper cables? I'd get them out of my own car, but you still have my purse, and—"

"Oh!" Rosa chirps. "I almost forgot." She bends, scooping something up from the ground. "Here," she says, reaching across Donovan to hand my purse to me.

Donovan shoots me a look that says *see, not an evil witch, after all.* But I'm too busy digging in my purse for my phone and yanking it out.

It's dead. Which makes no sense at all, because I charged it in the car all the way up to the retreat this morning.

"Oh, and Donovan, here's your phone," she says, pulling it out of her belt bag. I catch a glimpse of the lock screen as she drops the phone into his palm, and relief shoots through me. His phone is on, which means maybe mine just died, after all. All we need to do is to get rid of Rosa, and then we can call Charlotte, and—

"That's totally weird about your car," Rosa says. "Good thing you're here overnight anyway. Were you and Rune going somewhere?"

Her tone is cheery, but the words sound foreboding, all the same—like what she really means is, *You thought you were going somewhere, didn't you? Well, too bad…and also, what exactly did you have in mind and how can I put a stop to it? And by* it, *I mean* you.

"I, um, wanted a chai latte." I give her a bright smile. "That escape room was pretty challenging, huh? All that melting ice made me thirsty. And as awesome as this retreat center is, I don't think it has a coffee bar anywhere!"

"No," Rosa agrees. "It doesn't. But you know what it *does* have?"

I run through possible responses, discarding them as I go: *A lake that tried to drown me? A murderous boss? A coven of Blood Witches tracking genetic data that they have no right to access?* I glance at Donovan, but he's no help. One hand is poking at his phone. The other's tight on the wheel, like he expects the car to start up any moment and drive away, *Christine*-style. "Nope," I say at last. "What?"

"A fancy dinner, with live musicians!" Rosa claps her hands, bouncing up and down. "It's a reward for all of you, for being such good sports. Of course"—she spares me a glance, her smile slipping—"you can't go looking like *that*, Rune. What happened to your clothes?"

Oh, Jesus. "I, um—the lake—"

"Did you go swimming?" She gives us a sly glance. "Or did the two of you cooperate so well that you decided to continue your collaboration elsewhere?"

She did *not* just say that. "Excuse me?" I say as Donovan blushes so hard, I can feel it in my own cheeks.

"Those are his clothes. Right?" Her smile cranks up a few notches. "That's okay! You don't have to tell me. It's your business, after all. The point of the escape room was for the two of you to figure out a way to work together, and obviously, you have."

"We almost drowned," Donovan snaps. "Was that part of the point, too?"

For the first time, Rosa's smile falters. "I have no idea what you're talking about."

"Really? Do you have any idea why my phone won't dial out, then?" He brandishes it at her. "Why my laptop's dead? Or why my car won't start?"

Rosa's lower lip trembles. "We're isolated up here at the retreat. Maybe it's an electrical issue. Or a problem with cell service. I promise, after dinner, we'll get jumper cables. If you really need to go anywhere and your car still won't start, I'll drive you there myself."

She looks so bemused and pathetic, I want to believe her. But maybe she's just a really good actor. Could it be that she doesn't know what the Blood Witches are up to? That if we go along with her, she'll really get us out of here?

I've got my keys, after all. Maybe my car will start. Maybe we won't even need her.

"Come on," Rosa wheedles. "Please? We've got everything set up all special. You two are the only ones who're missing. Rune can go get changed, we'll have dinner, and then we'll figure out whatever you need."

Maybe this is a trap. But I can't figure a way out of it, not without tipping off Ethan. "Okay," I say, opening the passenger-side door. "Fine. Donovan, would you come with me?" There's no way I'm leaving him alone with her. For all I know, Ethan plans to snatch him and do terrible things to him the moment my back is turned.

"Sure," he says, eyeing Rosa warily as he gets out and comes around to my side of the car. The two of them trail me to my cabin, Rosa chattering a mile a minute. I was hoping to speak with Donovan privately, but she follows us inside and waits while I change into a clean pair of linen pants and a blue silk tank top. I put on flats, just in case I have to run for my life.

I desperately want to try to start up my car, but there's no chance, not with Rosa on my heels as I lock the cabin and start walking down the hill. She leads us past the main lodge and toward a meadow that I noticed when I drove in earlier. "Almost there!" she says. "Oh, we're going to have so much fun!"

"I seriously doubt that," Donovan mutters, and I let out a snort.

But my laughter dies in my throat the moment we get close enough to hear the music emanating from the meadow. It's a live string quartet, playing the haunting strains of Pachelbel's Canon.

The music from my visions of our wedding.

Fifty-Two

I STOP DEAD, so abruptly that Donovan runs into my back. His body is warm and solid, and that familiar sense of electricity quakes through me. It's more intense this time, like a miniature bolt of lightning.

And lightning, of course, can kill.

"What's the matter?" he whispers, his voice gentle. Caring.

I can't lose him. But, oh God, I'm sure I'm going to.

"We can't go into that meadow, Donovan. Whatever's waiting for us there isn't dinner," I say, thinking of how the musicians played as the blood tide devoured us. "It's something else, something terrible. Please believe me."

I turn, peering up at him, and see the conflicting emotions at war in his eyes. He wants to listen to me, I can tell. But my curse is working on him, pulling him in the opposite direction. Before, when he told me he'd believe in magic if I said it existed,. I wasn't asking him to directly buy into one of my premonitions. But this…this is different. Still, maybe Donovan's trust in me, the fact that he told me he'd step outside the lines of everything he ever counted on for me…

"Please," I whisper, gripping his sleeve. "You promised."

Donovan's mouth twists, as if he's in pain. His muscles bunch, like he's battling an unseen foe. And for a moment, I dare to hope he'll win.

But then his eyes glaze over. "Don't be silly, Rune," he says. "There's music, just like Rosa said. There'll be some decent food—and I'm starving, after everything that happened today." He leans down, lowering his voice so that Rosa, who's stopped a few steps ahead of us, can't hear. "We'll have dinner with Ethan and everyone else, so whoever's involved in his little scheme doesn't get suspicious, okay? And then we'll get some jumper cables from Rosa, see if your car's cool, pack up, and get out of here. No one will ever be the wiser."

"No," I say, clutching his sleeve desperately. "Donovan, you promised to believe me. We can't go to that dinner. We'll hike out of here if we have to. Please don't go. If you do, you'll die." My voice breaks on the last word.

He detaches himself from my grip, the motion automatic, as if an external force is controlling him somehow. As if he's at the mercy of a puppeteer. Which, I realize in horror, is true. My curse is acting on him, driving him toward the meadow even as I beg him not to go.

And I...I have no choice but to follow.

I stand, frozen, wondering what to do. Maybe I should stay here. After all, in my premonition, we were together. If I don't show up, maybe that will be enough to change what happens. Maybe Ethan needs me there to do whatever must be done.

Or...or maybe I'm being ridiculous. Pachelbel's Canon is a common piece of music, after all. Musicians play it at any number of occasions. Maybe this *is* just a dinner, in which case I'm making a huge fuss over nothing. I'll draw attention to myself, and people will notice, and I'll somehow bring about the very fate I'm trying to prevent.

Donovan's caught up to Rosa now, and she turns, looking back at me over her shoulder. "Are you coming, Rune? The food's divine! Sundried tomato pasta salad and olive tapenade and mango salsa with homemade tortilla chips. It's to die for. Wait 'til you see!"

Her expression is open, guileless. Expectant. Next to her, Donovan is practically vibrating with eagerness. "God, I'm so hungry," he says. "Rune, what are you waiting for?"

It's to die for is an expression, I tell myself. *An unfortunate one, but an expression all the same. Get it together, Rune.* "Nothing," I tell Donovan. "Nothing at all." And I stride after him.

With every step I take, the music grows louder and the air seems thicker, harder to move through—as if it's not air at all, but some other substance. The crimson tide of my premonitions, maybe. I swear I can smell the coppery tinge of blood on the breeze. But maybe I'm just losing it, because Donovan and Rosa walk along, happy as you please. Rosa is practically skipping.

"And here we are!" she announces happily as we round the corner. "Take a look!"

I do. And then I gasp, my heart picking up speed until it threatens to choke me.

The meadow spreads out before us, edged by live oaks hung with Spanish moss. Along one side are tables heaped with food. White folding chairs filled with people flank an aisle that leads to a white-flowered arbor. And next to it, on a red-brick patio, is the string quartet.

It's an exact replica of the premonition of our wedding. Except I'm not wearing a dress, and Donovan's not in a tux. But otherwise, the scene is identical, right down to the scent of honeysuckle, drifting atop the unmistakable tang of blood.

Oh, God. What have I allowed to happen? "We have to get out of here," I say to Donovan, stumbling backward—right into Rosa, who steadies me with a hand on my shoulder. "We have to go." Maybe if I phrase it as something other than a premonition, he'll listen to me. "I think I have, um, appendicitis," I babble, grasping desperately at straws. "I need to go to the hospital. Please, Donovan, let's just leave—"

He turns toward me, puzzlement stamped clear on his

features, just as Ethan rises from one of the folding chairs. "Our guests of honor have arrived!" he announces, grinning widely. "Everyone give a big hand to Rune and Donovan!"

As one, the seated guests swivel to look at us and then begin to clap. Their hands move in eerie unison, the synchronized sound echoing through the meadow. It's freakish, and when I peer more closely at them, a shudder ripples through me.

Seated in the white folding chairs, their expressions dazed and their hands clapping in synchrony, are people I know—people who have no business being here. Mrs. Fontaine. Mrs. Grant. Mrs. Hernandez. Ella Campbell. Jenny. Charlotte. D'Andre. Gracie Liu. Mrs. Garcia. Dave Cassady. And about fifty residents of Sapphire Springs I recognize, just from growing up in town.

What are they doing here? And why are they all acting like stunned, complicit robots?

I open my mouth to ask, but Donovan beats me to it. "What do you mean, your guests of honor?" he says, eyeing Ethan. "I thought this was a retreat dinner. Why are all those people here? And why is everyone acting so peculiar? Exactly what the hell is going on?"

"Great questions!" Ethan says, slapping Donovan on the back. "And I intend to give you answers. But for now…friends, can you please escort our guests to the dais?"

The clapping dies away as, from amidst the seated guests, familiar figures rise. Jill. Dean from IT. Georgia. Jack, who's got a thing for Mallomars. Board game-obsessed Catelyn. Gia. Thatcher 'Hold My Beer' Cruz. Ellen, Ethan's assistant. Cooper. They stride toward us with purpose, their faces clear and focused, obeying Ethan's command.

Whatever's going on here, they're not under the influence of it. Which means that they must be willing participants. And it probably also confirms that every single Smashbox employee on the retreat…is also a Blood Witch.

With a sinking feeling, I try to twist out of Rosa's grip, but it's become a vise. "I don't think so, Rune," she says in her cheery voice. "The party's just starting, after all."

"Let me go!" I say, struggling to get away from her. To reach Donovan and flee. But it's too late. Dean, Cooper, and Ethan grab him, pulling him toward the arbor. He fights, but it's no use: there are three of them and one of him, and they have no intention of letting go.

I scream his name as Catelyn and Jill take hold of my arms, their nails digging into my skin. "Get your hands off him. Charlotte! Mrs. Fontaine! Help me!"

But none of them move. None of them so much as look my way.

Rosa shoves me forward, her high giggle ringing in my ears. "They can't hear you, silly. Besides, we put this whole thing together just for you. You and Donovan are so cute together. True, your time is limited, but quality over quantity, that's what I always say!"

I make a concerted effort to dig out her eyeballs with my bare hands. But Catelyn and Jill drag me onward, depositing me in a folding chair in front of the arbor. Out of the corner of my eye, I can see Dean, Cooper, and Ethan doing the same to Donovan, who's thrashing in their grip. "Rune!" he shouts, breaking free of them only to have them grab hold of him again. "Let her go, you bastards. Just let her go, and I won't say a word about what I found. I'll—"

His voice cuts off as Cooper stuffs a gag into his mouth. "That's right, you won't say a word," Ethan says pleasantly, ignoring his muffled screams. "Because that's how I want it. And I'm in charge here. Right, Rune?"

I may not be able to get away. But right now, at least, I can still speak. "You evil, disgusting excuse for a human being," I hiss at him. "I know what you did to my parents. What you did to *me*. And make no mistake, you'll fucking pay."

"I don't think so," Ethan says, smoothing a hand over his beard. "No, today you're the one who will pay, Rune. You and our little sacrificial lamb." He jerks his chin at Donovan. "You'll pay again and again and again, until we have what we want. What we *need*. Just like they will." His gaze travels to all of the residents of Sapphire Springs who are sitting silently, obediently in their chairs, observing what's happening without so much as a peep. Charlotte, who's been my best friend since we were tiny, who's devoted her life to fighting injustice, is just watching me get assaulted and threatened.

"What have you *done* to her?" I snarl at Ethan, pulling against Catelyn and Jill's implacable hold. "To all of them?"

Ethan smiles at me, the same friendly, open smile I've seen a hundred times. "Nothing you need to worry about, Rune...or, should I say, Iris? Now," he says to Georgia, "tie her up."

I've known Georgia ever since I started working at Smashbox. We give each other holiday gifts and remember each other's birthdays. But none of that stops her from stepping forward, rope in hand.

Fifty-Three

THE MUSICIANS' bows bite into the strings, the notes shivering through the floral-scented air. Humming along to the melody, Georgia begins binding me as efficiently as she organizes her marketing campaigns. The rough strands of the rope bite into my skin, and I howl in pain, bucking against them. "Georgia, you *know* me! We're...I thought we were friends," I say, hating how pathetic I sound. "You don't want to do this. Please, please let me go."

"Hold her," Georgia snaps at Jill. "She's going to knock the chair over and bang her head if we're not careful. Stupid cow," she says to me, knotting my hands behind my back. "You have *no* idea how exhausting it's been to be nice to you all these years. '*I can't decide if he's hot or just terrifying,*'" she simpers, dropping back into the sweet, soccer-mom voice she's used as long as I've known her. Straightening, she smirks at Donovan, who's struggling against his bonds, his eyes telegraphing pure fury. "Not so terrifying now, are you, Donovan Frost?"

I gape at her in shock. She sounds like a different person entirely—like she's peeled off her mom-of-two, bring-you-soup-when-you're-sick Georgia-mask to reveal the Blood Witch bitch who lurks beneath. When she turns back to me, that smirk still on her face, I see something sly and avid in her eyes, swimming just below the surface...a shark, eager to devour its prey.

You'd think that after all the years of being shunted from one place to the next, of having to suss out threats on the fly, my judgment would be better. But no—I'd wanted to believe that plump, kind Georgia, with her butterscotch-chocolate-chip-cookie recipe and her epic hugs, was the real thing. Some part of me had thought of her almost like a big sister. And all along, she'd *hated* me. She'd been in on this. Pain stabs my stomach, and I clench my jaw, vowing revenge.

"Stop looking at me like that," she snarls, stepping back. "It's not my fault you're a gullible fool. Ethan, can we get on with it?"

"My pleasure." Ethan slices his hand through the air, and the musicians lift their bows from the strings. "Donovan, you must be wondering why you're here. Why you're one of our guests of honor. My guess is that Rune has tried to tell you, but you haven't believed a word she said. That pesky little curse can be so problematic, can't it?"

I suck in my breath. "Did...did you do this to me?"

"All in good time, little Rune. I know that's not your real name, but it *is* the one I gave you. Indulge me, won't you, as I use it?"

Ethan named me? What the—

"I know you saw the tattoo on my arm, Rune. That wasn't my intention." He sighs, glancing sideways at Cooper, who is looming over Donovan. "When you exposed those ley lines, you...well, let's just say you interrupted a little ritual. But that's not a big deal. We just had to speed up our timeline. Honestly, it's a good thing. The two of you are more powerful than I'd dared to hope. I'm impressed."

Donovan is making furious noises behind his gag. I don't know why Ethan hasn't muzzled me, but I plan to make the most of it. "What do you mean, you named me? And what did you do to my parents? You're the one who killed them, aren't you?"

"Of course I am." He paces back and forth between me and

Donovan, and the seated crowd's gaze follows him, their heads turning left and right in that eerie unison. "Taking your father's life was the most delicious meal I've had in decades. His blood sacrifice fueled me. Enlivened me, you could say."

He gestures at his unlined face, and a sick revelation breaks over me. Killing my father was some kind of freaking fountain of youth for him. The thought makes my stomach churn.

Ethan ignores my disgusted expression. "Yes, I'm responsible for your parents' deaths. And not a moment too soon," he says. "They were going to rise up against us. To lead an insurrection and put us down once and for all. Their words, not mine. Like we're a bunch of curs, instead of the world's most powerful magic users." He spits on the grass at my feet.

"I don't understand. How…how could they…"

"Your father was a firewitch, Rune, and an animator. But your mother, may her spirit never rest, was something rare. A persuasio." He scoffs, coming to a stop in front of me. "Years ago, they killed persuasios on sight. But your mother was allowed to live. To thrive. To exercise her filthy powers. She could convince anyone of anything, if she so chose. And one of our seers foretold that she would bring us down."

He gestures at an elderly woman seated among the crowd. "Mina, come forward, won't you?"

The woman stands, making her slow, halting way toward us. Her back is crooked, her gait uneven, her cheeks wrinkled. As she reaches us, I can see that her rheumy eyes are filled with tears.

"Meet Mina," Ethan says cheerfully. "She's the reason your parents died. Also, the reason you're alive. Think of her as your fairy godmother."

"Are you completely insane?" I strain at my bonds, but it's no use.

"What a silly question." He pats me on the head, as if I'm an errant puppy. His touch sends a frisson of horror through me, like I've been stroked by a snake's tongue. I shrink from it, and Ethan laughs. "Rune, Mina. Mina, Rune. How rare it is for two powerful seers to meet. Am I right, Cooper?"

I crane my head back, trying to meet Cooper's eyes, but he won't look at me. "It is an unusual gift," he says in his deep voice. "Not that Rune's been able to make the most of hers."

"True," Ethan says, dipping his head in concession. "Mina, why don't you tell Rune all you've done for her?"

Mutely, Mina shakes her head. Tears slip down her cheeks, staining her shirt.

"No? Ah, well." Ethan sighs. "As I said, Mina here foretold that your parents would be the ones to destroy us, Rune. We would have killed you, too—so much more convenient!—but her vision had an unfortunate caveat. Our powers have been waning, you see. Embarrassing, but true. Mina saw that you and Donovan were destined for each other. Through your blood union, your gifts would be united. He would die, of course. And then we would gain the power we needed to overthrow the International Coven. Then, our powers would be strengthened beyond our wildest dreams. And we would rule, the way we've always been meant to do."

"You're *sick*," I spit at him.

"Oh, no. Just enterprising." He gestures at Mina. "She had to curse you, of course. To invert your gift. It was very creative of her, really. Otherwise, who knows what you would have done?"

My breath catches as I look at Mina, who's wringing her hands, her tears flowing more freely now. "What do you mean, 'invert my gift'? You mean, make it so no one would believe me?"

"All in good time," Ethan says, tsking at me like I'm a naughty child.

The desire to tear him limb from limb trembles through me anew. "So you killed my parents, stole me from them, and had me cursed." I curl my lip at him. "And then you threw me out like the trash. After all that effort, I wasn't good enough to keep?"

Ethan chuckles, a condescending sound that makes me want to rip his head off. "Don't be ridiculous, Rune. We couldn't have you connected with us, or have anyone know you'd lived. In the wrong hands, you'd be far too powerful. So we hid you in plain sight, where the Coven would never find you."

Fury makes my voice shake. *"What did you do with me?"*

He smiles, looking happier than ever. "I took you to the fire station. Put you in that box they have for abandoned infants. Pinned a note to your shirt. *Please take care of my Rune,"* he says in a high-pitched voice, batting his lashes. *"She's the most precious thing in the world to me."*

At his words, my heart breaks a little more. I can feel it splinter, right along the fracture line that losing my parents etched deep inside me. "You impersonated my dead mother?" My feet aren't bound, and I scrabble for purchase in the grass, fighting to get to him. "What kind of sick bastard does that?"

Georgia and Rosa's hands come down on my shoulders, restraining me, as Ethan rolls his eyes. "You should be grateful to me, Rune. I saved you, after all."

"For your own purposes! Do you have any idea what kind of people wound up taking me in? What kind of *life* I've had?" Tears burn my eyes, and beside me, Donovan gives a growl of frustration. I can hear him struggling for breath behind the gag, and panic spikes in my chest. What if he suffocates before these murderous lunatics have the chance to do him in?

"I admit, it's been regrettable at times," Ethan says, rubbing a thoughtful hand over his beard again. "Especially with that pathetic prick you lit on fire. Too bad you didn't kill him. But don't worry—we finished the job." He winks at me.

Oh my God. He's talking about the monster. "You…you had him murdered?"

"Of course." Ethan folds his arms across his chest. "If he got out, he was going to kill you. I couldn't have that. I needed you."

My head swims. "But—but how—"

He turns his gaze skyward, as if he can't believe my naivete. "We have people everywhere. It was simple enough to get a guard to do what had to be done, and make it look like he'd taken his own life. Really, you should be thanking me, Rune. That's two you owe me."

Jesus Christ. Ethan has been watching me all this time. He knew everything that went on behind the doors of that ramshackle house. At any point, he could've saved me. But he let me suffer. He let that monster live, until it wasn't…what word did he use? *Convenient.*

Rage bubbles up my throat, eating away like acid. "You stole the life that should've been mine," I spit at him. "You murdered my family. I'm going to get loose. And when I do, you're the one who's going to pay."

Fifty~Four

A FOND, indulgent grin lifts Ethan's lips. I want to smack it right off his face.

"Oh, I don't think so, Rune." He snaps his fingers, and Ellen comes forward, a blade across her palms. Engraved in the metal hilt is the all-too-familiar scroll-and-dagger.

I know this blade. I've seen it, right before Cooper used it to cut Donovan's throat.

Terror sweeps me, and a crimson wave obscures my vision. When it clears, Ethan has claimed the blade and is tracing the tip along the inside of his forearm. A bead of blood wells up, and I watch in horror as the scroll-and-dagger tattoo blooms beneath it.

It's happening. Donovan is going to die right in front of me and I won't be able to stop it. And then what? Will they kill everyone in the crowd? My neighbors? My friends?

Will they kill me too? Or leave me alive after they force me to witness the slaughter of everyone I care about? Will they use me for their own purposes, again and again?

My breath rasps, harsh and panicked. I have to think of something. To get us out of this. But how? A cursed woman and a magic-less man raised for slaughter, against an army of manipulated people and a coven of Blood Witches…what do I think I can do? And where is that damn High Priestess who's supposed to be so all-powerful?

Ethan passes the blade to Jack. To Jill. To Georgia. To Dean and the rest. One by one, they cut their arms with it, muttering the incantation. And one by one, that tattoo seeps to the surface of their skin. Just like in my premonitions, they dip their fingers in their own blood, then flick them outward. The scroll-and-dagger symbol emblazons itself in the air of the meadow. It hangs above the crowd, who tilts their heads back to regard it, mouths dropping open in awe.

Ethan's acolytes stand in a semicircle, bleeding and smiling. Waiting. All except Cooper, who grips Donovan's shoulder, and Rosa, who is guarding me.

There are no robes. No hoods. No wedding dress or rose petals scattered in the grass. But my nightmare is gnawing at the edges of reality, just the same.

"I know you and Donovan hacked into my files. Tsk, tsk," Ethan says, wagging a finger at both of us. "So you've probably surmised that the blood drive we held at that cutesy little fair was an excuse to discover who in Sapphire Springs might have magical blood."

"That information wasn't yours to access!"

"Po-tay-to, po-tah-to," Ethan says. "It'll all be ours eventually, anyhow."

The red haze bites at my vision, inevitability barreling down on me. Desperate, I press him for answers. This is his master plan. Surely he'll glory in explaining himself, and that can buy us some time. "What did you need it for, anyway? What have you done to them?"

Ethan's gaze drifts to the mute, enraptured crowd, following the argument between us as if they're watching an intriguing play. "I told you our powers are weakening, Rune. Humiliating, really. But that's what happens when you force an ancient, powerful magical line to live in the shadows. Our bloodlines become diluted." He heaves a put-upon sigh. "You can think of them as batteries, charging us until we take back what's rightfully ours."

I stare at Charlotte's blank face, horrified. At the Sinsters' glazed eyes and parted lips. "Out of all the people who submitted to that drive," I say, revelation breaking over me, "these are the ones who had magical blood, Coven and Blood Witch alike. You brought them here somehow. And now you're…what, siphoning them?"

"Very good, Rune." He throws back his head and laughs. "To activate our gifts when we sacrifice loverboy here"—he nudges Donovan with a sneakered foot—"we need a stronger power base than the two of you can provide. No offense," he says with a jovial grin.

"Oh, none taken." My tone is as sarcastic as it gets, and Rosa narrows her eyes, yanking on the rope that binds my hands behind me. Pain shoots through my wrists, and she gives me a self-satisfied smile. *Bitch.* When I get free, I'm going to kick her ass.

"Sapphire Springs has always drawn those with power." Ethan runs his finger over his tattoo. "The ley lines called our families here long ago, Blood Witches and Coven members alike. I knew there had to be those with latent gifts among us. Harvesting their blood samples was easy enough. But figuring out the right spell to use…well, that took work. We discovered it just in time." He gives the crowd a paternal smile. "You see what we can do with a tiny bit of their blood. Once we overthrow the Coven, we'll collect samples nationwide to fuel our reign. Not that we'll need nearly as much borrowed power, thanks to you and Frost here."

From behind his gag, Donovan makes an ominous sound. He's saying something, but it's too garbled to make out. In frustration, he twists his head left and right, chewing at the cloth, but it's no use. Pained, I look away from him, at Jenny, who's devoted her life to saving animals. Mrs. Grant, whose milkshakes have seen me through many a heartbreak. Mrs. Fontaine, who was there for me in my darkest days. Charlotte, my best friend. All of them, made into zombies to serve this asshole's insane cause.

Keep him talking, I remind myself. When he's talking, he isn't killing. "So the project Donovan and I were working on—was that just an excuse to bring the two of us together?"

Ethan shrugs. "Mina told us you needed to have genuine feelings for each other for the sacrifice to be effective. That you couldn't help but fall in love as soon as you met. So we dangled a great job offer for Donovan, something he couldn't resist. When the time was right, we invited you to collaborate with him."

"You manipulated him into moving to Sapphire Springs?" I say as Donovan growls from behind his gag. "You tricked him?"

"We offered him a great job!" Ethan says, sounding almost offended. "And sure, the project was an excuse for you to meet. But it had a purpose, too. As we broaden our reach, we'll need a better system to analyze the data we collect. Alas, Donovan never got to perfect his database, but techies like him are a dime a dozen."

Fucker. "Not to me!"

"Of course not." Ethan claps delightedly. "That's what makes this so perfect. And we're almost ready."

Donovan yells something indecipherable. His chair rocks back and forth as he tries to free himself, but Cooper holds him still, one hand on his shoulder and the other gripping the blade. "Don't fight, bro," he says. "This will happen no matter what. You're making it worse."

Ethan is a lost cause. But maybe Cooper will still listen to me. "You pretended to be a member of the Coven," I say, desperation making my voice hoarse. "To be looking out for him. And all along, you were planning to kill him—your own brother! What the hell is wrong with you? How…how are you possibly going to face your mother after this?"

For a moment, I think I see a flicker of indecision in his eyes. But then Cooper bares his teeth at me. "I told you, Rune. Don't talk about things you don't understand."

Damn it. "Oh, I understand, all right. You're a liar and a soul-less worm, just like Ethan." I glare up at my former boss, his lower lip protruding in an honest-to-God pout.

"You're hurting my feelings, Rune. But no matter. Time waits for no witch." He takes the blade from Cooper, lifting Donovan's chin with the tip. Donovan's muscles go rigid, his gaze stony. But he doesn't move, and thank God. If he did, he'd probably cut his own throat and spare the Blood Witches the trouble.

"It's true, Cooper and Frost's mother is a well-regarded member of the Coven. But Frost's father was a Blood Witch," Ethan says, his tone conversational. "He is…shall we say…the fruit of a forbidden union."

Behind his gag, Donovan makes a muffled sound of protest, but he stays stock-still. His gaze slides to me, though, and I clear my throat. "That's why he had both codes next to his name in the database." *I knew it.* "But what do you mean, forbidden?"

"Coven Witches and Blood Witches are prohibited from marrying each other, since our gifts cancel each other out. They produce nulls, like Frost here. Such a waste of magical blood." Ethan purses his lips, regarding Donovan like he's a streak of mud on a newly washed floor. "When Cooper here learned of his mother's betrayal, he was so disgusted with her, he decided to join forces with us. He's been a valuable man to have on the inside. After the Coven sent him here to investigate the spike in the ley lines, we knew our time had come."

My eyes flick to Cooper, whose gaze is expressionless, then back to Ethan. I should be grateful that, for whatever reason, he's toying with Donovan rather than slitting his throat. This is Ethan's moment, and he wants to savor it. But God, the pleasure he's taking in this is repulsive.

He twitches the blade again, then bends, speaking directly to Donovan for the first time. "Null or not, your blood has more latent power than anyone I've ever seen. That's what will make you such a formidable sacrifice, when harnessed to Rune's gifts. The combination of her blood and yours will set us free."

"Mmmmph!" Donovan says from behind the gag. But he doesn't move. He can't.

It's hard to keep my voice from shaking, but I manage it. "Are you going to kill me?"

"Don't be ridiculous." Ethan frowns. "We're going to use you, Rune, thanks to Cooper's ability to sense the extent of your power—hobbled though it is. After Frost here kicks the bucket, you'll be an inexhaustible source of blood, if we just take a little at a time."

He digs the tip of the blade in a little harder, grinning when it pierces the flesh beneath Donovan's chin. Blood wells up, but Donovan doesn't make a sound.

"Here's a little secret for you, Frost." Ethan bends closer still, until his face and Donovan's are only inches apart. "Your father didn't do himself in. After he betrayed us with your pathetic witch of a mother, we had him killed." Drawing back the knife, he runs his fingers over the blood that slicks it, then straightens and licks them clean. A sinister smile lifts his lips. "Just like we're about to kill you."

Fifty~Five

OH MY GOD.

Donovan's tattoo, *cavea ad tenebras continendas*… All along, he thought he was caging the darkness that led his father to kill himself. He believed it so deeply, he inked it on his skin. But no. Donovan's father was murdered, just like mine. And that darkness? It's what comes from living a lie. From having two kinds of magical blood inside him, warring with each other for dominance until they canceled each other out.

I didn't think it was possible for me to hate Ethan more. But he just keeps on proving me wrong.

Donovan chokes and coughs behind the gag as he fights to escape his bonds, nearly toppling his chair. He has to know it's pointless, but he struggles anyway, the blood flowing more freely from the wound beneath his chin. When Cooper grips his shoulders, grimly holding him in place, Donovan glares, fury sparking in his eyes…and beneath it, a deep, abiding hurt. His mute accusation is clear: *Did you know about my father? Have you been keeping it from me, all this time?*

Cooper stares back at him, silent and impassive, and I decide it's a tossup between who I despise more: him or Ethan. When I get loose—and I will—I will put an end to both of them.

And then an agonized shriek shatters the air of the meadow. It's the cry of a wounded animal, soul-deep and raw.

Mina.

The elderly Blood Witch falls to her knees in the grass, wailing. The tears slipping down her face have become a torrent, falling hard and fast. "You...you..." she sobs, pointing at Ethan.

"Don't be dramatic, Mina." Ethan's lip curls in contempt. "It doesn't become you."

She takes a huge gulp of air. "You're a murderer," she howls. "And you've made me into one, too. You...you killed my..."

Her *what?* What the hell is going on here?

"Watch your mouth," Ethan warns, gripping the hilt of the blade.

Mina gives a bitter chuckle. "What are you going to do to me? You've already taken everything I love. It was bad enough when Jonathan was shunned. I thought that was why he took his own life...because we'd turned our backs on him. But he didn't. He didn't!" She pounds the ground with her fists. "He wanted to live. To have a chance to raise his child. And you killed him and lied to me about it! All these years, you let me believe I failed him. And the whole time, it was *you*." She's shaking all over, sobs ripping from her throat.

I don't understand. Why does she care so much? Who was Jonathan Frost to her?

"He betrayed us, Mina." Ethan's tone is condescending, like he's explaining the facts of life to a small child. "What kind of example would it set if we let him live? It's not my fault you were naïve enough to believe I would tolerate such disrespect. Consorting with a Coven Witch...siring a null..." He spits in the grass again. "He was a blood traitor."

Mina rises from her knees. Tiny and wrinkled though she is, the sheer rage emanating from her small body is formidable. Her hair lifts, the strands buoyed by an invisible breeze, and when her voice comes it is ice cold, each syllable a dagger. "He. Was. My. Son."

Holy shit. Mina—the woman whose prophecy led to my parents' deaths, who foretold the connection between me and Donovan and engineered his sacrifice, who *cursed* me—is Donovan's freaking grandmother.

My heart aches for Donovan, whose gaze is fixed on Mina. She's staring back at him with undisguised longing, as if she's waited his whole life to be reunited with him. Which would be sweet, except he's bloody, gagged, and about to be killed. And it's her fault.

Everything…this whole fucked-up situation…can be laid at her feet.

"How could you do this?" I demand, my voice so choked, I hardly recognize it. "You didn't have to share your premonition about my parents with Ethan. You didn't have to destroy my life! And now…now you're going to be responsible for the death of your own grandson."

Mina knots her hands together, crying harder. "You must understand. I owed Ethan allegiance," she says, shifting her teary gaze to me. "When you were born, when I foretold your destiny… Yes, I saw you marrying Donovan, but I didn't know who he was. I had no idea Jonathan had gone outside the fold. That he had sired a child with a Coven Witch." Her eyes are huge and wet and pleading. "You know as well as I do how unpredictable our powers can be."

I strain against the ropes that bind me to the chair. "I don't know *anything*, because you *cursed* me. You're right, you're a murderer. Because of you, my parents are gone. Because of you, I've been a pariah my whole life. And now, because of you, Donovan is going to die!"

The old woman's lips set in a thin line. "No," she says. "He isn't." She turns to Ethan, her shoulders set. "You took my son from me. I won't let you take my grandson, too."

A thin thread of hope winds its way through the anger and fear that threaten to consume me. If she cursed me, then maybe she can undo the curse. And if she does, then maybe I can access the ley lines, not just the pool of blue light inside me. Maybe I can somehow use their power to free the Sinsters, and they can help me save Donovan and defeat the Blood Witches. Sure, the ley lines also apparently drive people power-mad, but beggars can't be choosers.

"Please help—" I begin, but Ethan cuts me off.

"Just how do you plan to stop me, Mina? Rune's right—we owe all of this to you. But you've outlived your usefulness. I think I'll keep you alive just long enough to see the fruit of your labors."

He turns to me, a too-bright grin splitting his lips, still stained with Donovan's blood. "She had to curse you, Rune. You see, you're very powerful. The child of a gifted firewitch and a persuasio…well, one never does know quite how magical blood will mix, does one? It's one of life's great surprises. But you…" He brings his fingers to his lips in a chef's kiss. "Too bad you'll never know what it's like to harness that power. At least you'll have the satisfaction of knowing that your gift gave rise to a dynasty."

"That's never going to happen," I hiss at him, but he just steps forward, blade in hand.

"Receptacle, please," he says to Ellen.

Efficient as always, Ellen reaches beneath one of the tables that holds the food, coming out with a small silver bowl. "Here," she says, handing it to him as reverently as if it's a religious chalice.

"What is that for?" Panic bubbles beneath my breastbone.

Ethan doesn't answer me. Instead, he closes his eyes. *"Non sine sanguine gloria,"* he intones. And the other Blood Witches echo him: "No glory without blood."

Ethan's eyes flash open, their brown irises gleaming. "Hold her," he snaps at Rosa.

I try to twist away from him. To sink my teeth into any part of Rosa I can reach. But she and Georgia grip me tight, holding me still. And so there's nothing I can do but watch as Ellen kneels, silver bowl cupped in both hands, and Ethan lowers the blade.

With my arms bound behind my back, the tender skin of my inner forearms is exposed, and that's where he slices me open.

The pain is immediate and agonizing, and I bite my lip to stifle a scream as hot blood trickles over my skin. A moment later, I hear the *plink-plink-plink* as it drips into the bowl. Its rust-rich scent rises, filling the air.

"Good girl," Ethan croons. "You see, there's no point in fighting. It will just hurt more if you do. Come, now… Just a little more…"

The greed in his voice is unmistakable, and my stomach churns. Chin held high, I fix my eyes on Mina. She is their weak link. If anyone can save us now, it's her.

She watches me bleed, her chin trembling, tears still coursing down her cheeks. "Help us!" I shriek at her, but she doesn't move. And then the premonition comes.

One second, I'm holding the crimson tide at bay. The next, it sucks at me, washing over my field of vision. I can feel the grass tickling my feet and the bite of the rope into my wrists. But I can also feel the hot rivulets of blood licking at my toes as the premonition shifts to accommodate my new reality: the Blood Witches in street clothes, Donovan not in a tux waiting for me beneath the arbor but in jeans and a t-shirt, bound to a chair, his eyes darting back and forth and his muscles straining, rock-hard, beneath Cooper's grip.

I need to stop this. To be *here,* in the present moment, if I have any shot at saving us all. I refuse to be helpless, trapped between realities, as Donovan dies.

And so I do the only thing I can think of: I reach deep inside me for that blue light. *Help me,* I think, as if it's a living entity that can hear my plea. *Please, help me stop them.*

For an instant, nothing happens. And then I feel it: a spark igniting in my chest, kindling and spreading outward. Giving me strength.

The premonition retreats, driven back. I'm here again, back in the meadow, bound and bleeding, but fully in my body. I can hear the voices of the crowd in my head now: Mrs. Grant, telling me to fight. Mrs. Hernandez, begging me to hold on. Mrs. Fontaine, insisting I have the strength to defeat the Blood Witches. Their faces are blank, their eyes giving nothing away. But they're still in there, I know it. If I free them, then they can help me.

But how?

Dizziness makes the world tilt sideways as Ethan stands back and crosses to Donovan, Ellen trailing in his wake, knife in his hand. It's not Cooper holding the blade, like in my vision. But so much has changed; why wouldn't this change too?

They're going to kill Donovan. Oh God, it's happening happening happening—

He turns his head to look at me, and in his eyes, those beautiful reflections of the ley lines, I see such sorrow. I see the life we could have had together. I see his helplessness and his rage. "Let him go," I plead, even though I know it's a useless effort. "You don't have to do this. There has to be another way."

"There is no other way," Ethan says, his tone almost pitying.

And then the blade comes down.

"NO!" I scream, pulling desperately on the ropes that bind me. "Please, please, please don't. I'll do anything. Please—"

Ethan ignores me. All I can do is hold Donovan's gaze as the blade descends, giving him what small comfort I can. Dreading the moment when Ethan stabs him.

But instead of plunging the blade into Donovan's throat, Ethan draws the tip of it across his arm, the same way he did to me. A thin line of blood wells up, but it's nothing like the vicious assault I expected. I draw a sharp, relieved breath, and Ethan chuckles.

"You should see your face, Rune! I'm not doing Frost in quite yet. We need your combined blood first to cast a circle. Something to keep us safe when the ritual kicks in. I anticipate it'll be quite… dramatic."

Ellen kneels beside Donovan, catching the droplets of blood in her bowl. As it mingles with mine, the earth beneath us shudders, the way it did before the ley lines burst to the surface. My chair threatens to tip, and Rosa grabs the back of it, holding me upright.

Ethan licks his lips again. "Our day has finally come. *Non sine sanguine gloria*, yes? My friends, it has begun."

I watch, horrified, as Rosa steps away, joining the other Blood Witches who have lined up to dip their fingers in our shared blood. One by one, they take their place in a circle around me and Donovan—all except for Cooper, who still stands by Donovan's side, and Ethan, who's walking the perimeter of the circle, bowl in hand, sprinkling our blood on the ground as he goes.

Faster than I imagined she could move, Mina charges toward him. But the other Blood Witches close ranks, forming a solid wall she can't penetrate. She scrabbles at their backs, howling, but they won't let her through.

"*Centrum caeli,*" Ethan chants above the melee. "*Centrum terrae.*"

Circle of heaven, Mrs. Grant supplies, inside my head. *Circle of earth. He's calling on the elements to protect him. To form an impenetrable barrier.*

"Stop!" Mina shrieks. "Donovan's innocent. You can't do this!"

But Ethan's words have invoked an invisible shield. Through the slivers of space between the Blood Witches, I see Mina hit it and fly backward. She falls into the grass, sobbing.

Please, I beg Mrs. Grant, watching Ethan walk the circle. *Tell me how to stop him.*

The sun will set soon. As it sinks beneath the horizon, the power to summon the ley lines will be at its strongest. Whoever holds the lines' gifts in their hands will...will...

Static rises, obscuring her voice like a radio station whose signal is fading. She's still talking, but it's impossible to make out the words.

Will what? Mrs. Grant, I can't hear you. What happens when the sun sets?

Too late... Her voice trails off, taking the static with it. I'm alone in my own head again as Ethan closes the circle and comes to stand by Cooper's side. "Brother against brother," he says, holding out the knife. "Blood against blood. The sacrifice is yours to make."

The light of the sinking sun glints off the blade, nearly blinding me. "Don't take it," I plead. "You still have a choice."

Cooper looks down at Donovan, and for an instant I think I see indecision on his face. But then he shakes his head. "No," he says, taking the knife. "I don't. I'm sorry."

"You're sorry, all right." Bile floods my mouth as I watch Donovan pull uselessly against his restraints. "If you do this, I'll make sure you spend the rest of your life paying for it."

"You said that before," Ethan muses. "And yet again, I must tell you how wrong you are. It's pathetic, really, how you've fallen for this magicless null. Unworthy of your blood. Ah well, at least he'll cease to be an issue soon. Cooper, if you would?"

The Blood Witches raise their hands to the fiery sky, chanting an invocation. The sun sinks lower, the outline of the scroll-and-dagger brand visible against it. And Cooper turns, his fingers white-knuckled on the knife, and buries it deep in Ethan's throat.

Holy freaking shit.

I blink, hardly able to believe it. Thinking that maybe I wanted this to happen so badly, I'm imagining it—that Donovan is the one who's choking on the blood that pours from his slit throat. But no. He's still bound to his chair, alive and whole. His eyes widen as Cooper yanks the blade free, and from behind the gag, he lets out what sounds like a stream of expletives.

I've never been so happy to hear someone curse in my life.

Ethan coughs again, spraying blood. Then his knees buckle, and he crumples to the grass. A collective gasp of rage emanates from the circle of Blood Witches, and they charge at Cooper. I expect them to grab him, to wrest the knife away from him and stab him, or to down him with some kind of spell. But they can't get near him. Every time they approach, they're driven back, just like Mina was when she tried to breach Ethan's circle.

I swivel my head to look at Cooper—and stare. Every inch of his body emanates the eerie blue glow of the subterranean ley lines. He stands there, feet spread apart, Ethan's blood dripping from the knife onto the ground, and stares the Blood Witches down.

What the hell is happening?

"Help…me…" Ethan chokes out, his eyes darting from Georgia to Rosa to Dean and Jill and back again. "Stop… them…"

His voice trails off into a gurgle as Mina pushes her way past the Blood Witches, their circle broken. "Yes!" she cries, triumphant. "You will die just like my Jonathan. In pain, frightened, and betrayed by those you trusted. *Maledicta tua super te decuplo reddantur!*"

Inside my head, Mrs. Hernandez echoes, *Let your curses be returned on you tenfold, Ethan of the Blood Witches. We will rise, and you will be no more.*

"*Debiliteas et comburas,*" Cooper shouts, the blue light that surrounds him glowing brighter with every word. And one by one, the Blood Witches fall—alive, but struggling to move. Ethan collapses face-down, hands pressed to his neck, trying to stanch the flow of blood.

"Ethan!" Georgia howls. She crawls toward him, one hand extended, trembling. Cooper ignores her, stepping over Ethan's prone body, toward his brother. He raises the knife again, and for a terrifying moment I think he's going to kill Donovan, after all. But instead he severs Donovan's bonds and yanks the gag out of his mouth, freeing him.

Oh, thank God. But then—

Donovan sucks in a deep, ragged breath. "What the hell is going on here?" he says, leaping to his feet, his arm still oozing blood. "Who are you people? Cooper, why the fuck are you… glowing? And are you just going to let Ethan bleed out in the goddamn grass?"

"He was going to kill you," Cooper points out dryly, crossing to me. "As for what I'm doing, I'm saving your ass. Yours and Rune's both. You should say thank you." He cuts me free, slicing through the ropes with quick, efficient strokes. Red marks mar my wrists, and my hands tingle as the blood rushes back into them. My forearm stings, the gash jagged and ugly.

"*Thank you*? You just stabbed someone! Rune and I were just tied up and sliced open. You're part of a creepy cult, aren't you? All of you are—"

"Cooper is on our side," I interrupt, leveling Officer Asshat with a glare as I get to my feet. "Aren't you?" It's the only explanation that makes sense.

He nods, turning to look at the crowd, which has begun to fidget and stir. Their expressions are still blank, but a hint of personality has found its way back into their eyes. "I'm a loyal member of the Coven. And you're my goddamn brother," he says, glancing back at Donovan. "Much as I've wanted to kill you sometimes, I wasn't about to actually *do* it."

Relief floods through me. This whole time, Cooper was playing the role of double agent. He may be an obnoxious bastard, but he's not a traitor and a killer.

Skirting Ethan's body, I cross to Donovan and throw my arms around him. The power of the ley lines shudders through me, and I can swear I feel it ripple into him, then back to me again, a perfect circuit. "Thank God you're alive," I say, holding him tight.

Donovan's chest heaves, his eyes wide with shock. Together, we regard Ethan, face-down and twitching. Mina, arms lifted to the sky, as if to welcome the setting sun. Georgia, Jill, and the rest, fighting to crawl toward us, marked with our blood. Beneath our feet, the earth trembles.

"Everything you told me was true." Donovan's voice sounds distant, disbelieving. "There really are witches, then? And my father—"

"We don't have time for this," Cooper snaps. "The power's cresting. I can feel it."

The sun sinks lower still. And he's right: deep within me, the power of the ley lines sparks, then courses through my veins. My body heats from the inside out, like I've swallowed a small sun. I don't know how to harness the power, or what to do with it. But it pulses through me nonetheless, lighting every nerve ending aflame.

Goosebumps spring up on Cooper's bare arms. "Ethan's death

will free everyone he bespelled," he says, the words coming with difficulty, like he's fighting for each one. "But spilling his blood this way, combined with the raw energy of the ley lines, will also give his Witches great power, and they'll want vengeance. Even in the hands of those with good intentions, raw ley line power is a dangerous weapon. In the hands of the Blood Witches..." He shakes his head. "We have to put an end to them."

"What do you mean, 'put an end to them'?" Donovan's voice cracks. "You mean, kill them?"

Before Cooper can reply, Ethan's body twitches one final time, then stills. In the time it takes me to swallow hard, his hold on the crowd breaks. They glance at each other in confusion, then catch sight of the carnage and begin to shriek.

The Sinsters don't shriek. They stand in the aisle, shoulder to shoulder—Mrs. Grant, Mrs. Fontaine, Mrs. Hernandez, even Ella Campbell—their faces grimly determined. Over the crowd's wails of horror, they begin to chant: *"Cavea ad tenebras continendas."* A *cage to contain the darkness.* The words from my premonition. From Donovan's tattoo.

The Blood Witches rise, their gaze fixed on me, Donovan, and Cooper, as sparks fly from the Sinsters' fingers. They merge into chains of fire, snaking down the aisle to ensnare the Blood Witches. But the Witches are raising their hands, too, half of them facing the Sinsters and half facing us, their expressions pure fury.

"Debiliteas et comburas!" Cooper bellows again, but it has no effect this time. The Witches keep coming, teeth bared. And holy crap, I'm going to die here, murdered by Jill from accounting. I'm going to die and leave Valentine all alone and—

Mina steps in front of us, her frail shoulders squared. "Enough Frost blood has been spilled," she says, voice hoarse but firm. "No more will feed the earth today."

Jill snarls at her, fists clenched. "Step away from them, Mina."

Donovan's grandmother shakes her head. "Not this time." She turns, her gaze lingering on Donovan. Then her eyes meet mine. In them, I see so much: regret, yes, but also a fierce resolve. "Iris

Duval, daughter of David and Lorelai, once I cursed you and set your destiny in motion," she says, each word hitting me like a blow. "Now, in the name of the son I loved more than my own life, I revoke that curse and set your destiny on another path."

"No!" Georgia screams, and lunges for her.

But it's too late. The ground cracks open, the ley lines spider-webbing to the surface. Their power floods through me, consuming every thought, swallowing every breath. I fall to my knees, then forward, onto my hands. My head pounds. My heart struggles to beat.

And then there is nothing but the light.

THE WORLD behind my eyes is bathed in blue light, so intense it's all I can see. My head throbs in sync with the beat of my heart.

And then a face emerges from the iridescent glow, familiar but much younger: Mina, without her wrinkles and the bitter sadness that pervades every facet of her being.

"Iris," she whispers, leaning close to me. "So small to have suffered so much. To be so important to so many."

My hand rises, trying to bat her away. It's small and chubby, the knuckles dimpled. The hand of an infant, not an adult woman.

This is a memory, I realize, like the one Mrs. Grant was able to evoke. Except this time, I'm inside the body of the baby I was back then. Somehow, Mina's efforts to lift the curse have brought me back to where it all began.

The blue light flares around Mina's face as she leans forward to stroke my cheek. Her fingers are rough, leaving an uncomfortable burn behind when she pulls away. "You're all alone in the world," she cooes. "But not for long. We'll find you a good home, don't you worry. First, though…"

She pricks my tiny finger. It hurts, and a wail erupts from my throat. Murmuring assurances, she draws an X on my forehead with my blood. "Iris Duval," she says, voice solemn, "your mother and father have passed beyond the veil, but their blood lives on in you. It must not be allowed to speak. *Ab incunabulis*, I bind your magic. When once it rose, so will it fall."

Pain bursts from my epicenter, stealing my breath. I scream again, louder this time, and she hushes me, a finger pressed to my lips. "With these words, I lay a curse upon you. You will see, but none will believe. You will speak, but none will listen." She takes her hands away, guiding them through the air. Again and again, she makes the same shape: a helix, winding tighter and tighter. *"Maledicto tibi,"* she says, and the shape flickers into being, branded into the air just like the scroll and dagger. "I hold your magic in my hands, Iris Duval. I strip you of your name and bind your gift to my will. Thus I twist your fate, and set your destiny on another path."

The pain I felt before was nothing. This is agony, as if someone has taken a giant melon-baller to my center and is scooping out my very essence, ripping my soul free of its tendrils. I'm suffocating, strangling. My body is fire, it is ice, it is shattering and burning all at once and I am screaming, my tiny fists pummeling the air. I'm fighting but I'm so small and there's no stopping this, not when Mina is chanting and my gift is winding back into itself like one of those old-fashioned cassette tapes, back and back and upside down and inside out and I'm wrong now, everything is wrong, I can't breathe and the world is broken or maybe I am and my shrieks are ripping from my throat with such force, my mouth tastes like iron, like old blood—

And then it stops. Everything stops. The chanting, the screaming, the pain. Mina is hovering over me, the helix fading from the air, and inside I am empty, a cold white room, the room I will see again and again in my premonitions for years to come.

"You are ruined," Mina whispers, her lips against my ear. "You are Rune."

I want to howl for all I have lost. To punish her for what she's done to me. But the blue light is flaring brighter now, consuming her. Her face retreats down the tunnel of it, her voice fading as other sounds take its place: Georgia and Jill yelling. The Sinsters chanting. Cooper and Donovan competing to be heard over the melee. Charlotte, shrieking my name. And a cacophony of other voices, filled with horror and desperation. The voices of the residents of Sapphire Springs, all of whom have magic lurking in their veins.

I land back in my body with a thud that jars me to my bones, and find myself in the midst of chaos. The ground is splintered, bubbling with blue light. I struggle to raise my head and see, to my horror, that the members of the crowd have turned on each other. Jenny is shrieking at Mrs. Fontaine, who's making a concerted effort to get her hands around Charlotte's throat. Gracie Liu and D'Andre are wrestling in the grass, folding chairs scattered around them. Mrs. Garcia and Ella Campbell lunge at each other just as the ground between them heaves and cracks, glowing blue light erupting from the crevice. They snarl at each other from opposite sides of the divide, and then Mrs. Garcia leaps it, knocking Ella into the grass.

Cooper told me this would happen—that the release of the ley lines' power would drive people mad. I try to think, to figure out what to do. But I can't. Pressing my hands to my chest, I struggle to breathe. Something is broken inside of me. It feels like I'm cracking open, the same way the ground is. As if the pool of blue light inside me has caught fire, and my heart is a vacuum, sucking in that fiery light, setting me aflame.

Donovan. Is he still alive? *Where is he?*

It's not easy to turn my head, but I manage it—and realize I'm lying at the epicenter of the ley lines' explosion. The Blood Witches are on one side. On the other is the frenzied crowd.

The devastation on the Blood Witches' side is far worse—maybe because of the magic they channel. They're scattered across the grass by the arbor, some of them standing, others lying on the uneven, shattered ground. The light that emanates from the cracks is near-blinding, but I can make out Mina on her hands and knees yards away from the others, blood pouring down her face in sheets. Cooper lies next to her, unconscious but breathing. But Donovan—

"Rune!"

It's his voice, thick but unmistakable. Propping myself on my forearms, I catch sight of him crawling toward me, yelling my name. Behind him comes Jill, her expression pure hatred.

I want to tell him I'm all right. But when I try to speak, my throat feels like it's been scraped raw by the blue fire bubbling inside me. My mouth opens and closes soundlessly, and terror etches its way across Donovan's features—not for himself, but for me.

Through the blood that coats her face, I see Mina's eyes lock on mine a moment before she pushes herself to her feet. "*Incantatio fracta*!" she screams, her voice tight, pained. "I set you free!" And then she crumples, falling face-forward, and doesn't move.

Inside me, the blue light roils, the sucking sensation intensifying. The earth heaves again, and a roar fills my ears: the sound of the ocean, of the rush of my own blood, of a thousand screams. And then it all goes still.

My body feels heavier than it should be, weighted and impossibly full. But *right*, as if for the first time in as long as I can remember, I'm not off-balance. As if a piece I've always been missing has fallen into place.

I raise my head, that strange sense of peace pervading me. The residents of Sapphire Springs are still brawling. Mina lies dead on the ground. But Jill…in one hand she holds the knife that Cooper used to kill Ethan. Her other hand blazes with blue light. And as I watch, she fits it gently, neatly, around Donovan's throat.

The other Blood Witches bellow in triumph as she squeezes. Donovan fights, struggling against her, but her strength is superhuman, driven by the ley line magic that floods through her. A maniacal grin spreads across her face, widening as he tries to peel her fingers off and fails. I scream Cooper's name, but it's no use; he's still out. The other Blood Witches are closing in, surrounding Donovan and Jill, their bodies haloed with blue light. Begging the

Sinsters for help does no good—the chains of light they'd tried to capture the Blood Witches with have run amok and are now sparking through the crowd of Sapphire Springs residents like downed power lines, igniting rage everywhere they land.

I do the only thing I can think of, useless though it is. "Stop!" I scream, as loud as I can—over the thump of Dave Cassady battering the owner of Sapphire Springs' sole tattoo shop with a folding chair, the cackles of the Blood Witches, the groaning of the earth as yet another seam of light breaches the surface. "Don't you touch him!"

I don't know what I expect to happen. Maybe Jill to give me a mocking smile before she chokes the life out of Donovan once and for all. Maybe nothing at all.

But instead, she lets go.

Donovan staggers back, coughing but otherwise unharmed, his hands going to his throat in disbelief. "Rune?" he says. *Says,* not yells.

Because around us, everything has fallen silent. No one is screaming or fighting or even *moving*. Other than Donovan, every single person has become a statue.

Stop, I said. And they did.

It's the opposite of my curse. Instead of no one believing me, they're all doing exactly as I said.

Except him.

Fifty~Eight

"HOLY SHIT, RUNE," Donovan says into the silence. "Are you okay?"

I'm about five thousand things right now—terrified, stunned, confused, relieved. *Okay* doesn't begin to make the list. "Wh-what —" I gaze around me, trying to make sense of what's happened. "Are *you* okay? She was ch-choking you…"

"You saved me." He smiles, a huge, beautiful grin that lights his eyes. "I have no clue what's going on here, except that you were telling the truth all along. You can see the future, Rune. You tried to warn me. And I'm so sorry I didn't listen."

"You *believe* me?" My voice shakes. It makes sense, though, right? Mina lifted the curse. But how did I freeze all of these people? How did my curse invert like this?

Donovan looks stricken. "I should have believed you from the start. I don't understand why I wouldn't listen. When I try to think of it, it's all foggy…" He runs a hand through his hair. "I'll apologize more later, I promise. When we're not in the middle of the goddamn apocalypse. Mina—my *grandmother*—" His gaze roves over her prone body, then over the Blood Witches and the paralyzed crowd. "What the hell happened? And why are all of them…like that…and I'm fine?"

"I-I'm not sure. She reversed my curse. And I-I just wanted them to stop hurting you…" I wrap my arms around my body, trying to hold myself together. Around me, the exposed ley lines bubble and surge. Their pull echoes inside me, a magnetic draw that has me edging closer to them, away from my sanctuary at the epicenter of the quake.

Donovan's eyes narrow. "Where are you going?"

"I just want to touch them." My voice is low, filled with yearning. The lines call to me, their energy a crooning, alluring siren song. If I could dip my hands into them, let that energy flow through me, everything would be all right.

I'm meant for them, and they are meant for me. We are a perfect circuit. If I could only—

"I don't think you should do that. Whatever the hell is in these ley lines, they made everyone lose their shit, until you stopped them. Look."

I tear my gaze away from the shifting blue light, taking in the Blood Witches and the residents of Sapphire Springs. All of them, including Charlotte, are still frozen. Only their eyes shift back and forth, glazed with panic. They may be unable to move, but they're still in there. Trapped.

"I need to save Charlotte and the Sinsters," I say, edging closer still to the ley lines that surround me. "To set them free, without doing the same to the Blood Witches. If I let the power of the lines run through me, I know I can do it. The lines will show me, Donovan. They'll teach me. You'll see."

He shakes his head, taking one tentative step toward me, then another. Through the glowing light, I can see him setting his jaw, squaring his shoulders. No matter what the ley lines might do to him, he's determined to reach me. And if he does, he'll stop me from knowing what it's like to bathe in that blue energy. From becoming what I'm meant to be.

"Your brother," I blurt. "You need to check on him."

"Shit, *Cooper*." Donovan spins, catching sight of Cooper, who's as frozen as the rest of them, eyes wide open, staring up at the sky.

It's ablaze with red and orange, the sun still above the horizon but sinking fast. "Don't do anything reckless, Rune, okay? Just wait. I'll be right back."

He picks his way over the buckled ground, through the Blood Witches' immobilized bodies—some on their feet, some on hands and knees, some on the ground—careful to step over the exposed ley lines as he goes. And I seize my chance.

Leaning forward, I plunge my hands into that glowing blue light. My fingers sink beneath the surface of the earth, into a well-spring of pure power. It shoots through me, traveling up my arms, heating me as it goes, until finally it connects with the pool of light that lives within me—filling it, overspilling it, flooding me with energy the likes of which I've never felt before.

My head goes back and I let out a roar that shakes my entire body. I can't contain this power. It's too much. I'm glowing, just like Cooper was—that blue light spilling forth from every single pore. I've become the light, nothing but a vessel for its power. And I understand what Cooper meant when he said it could drive people mad. The energy inside me is too big for my skin. It seeks an outlet. It wants to be used.

My head snaps left, as if controlled by a force outside of my body. *Your mother was a persuasio*, I hear Ethan whispering. And then I know.

I am a seer, yes, just as Cooper said I was. But I am so much more. I hold my mother's persuasive power within me, and it is that power Mina bound when she cursed me years ago. When she lifted the curse, it didn't just mean that people would finally believe me when I foretold the future. It meant that I could claim my legacy. The one that, with a word, has the power to bring the Blood Witches down.

This is why my mother's murderers muzzled her, why they wouldn't let her speak. This is why my parents were killed.

I know this power is dangerous, that in the wrong hands it could do terrible damage. But with the blue light of the ley lines throbbing through every vein and artery, demanding to be used, reason eludes me. Dimly, as if from a great distance, I hear Donovan screaming my name. With my hands plunged deep into the closest ley line, I can feel his footsteps shake the ground as he abandons Cooper and runs for me. But none of that is enough to make me stop.

"People of Sapphire Springs!" I howl, wrenching my hands free and rising to my feet. The earth cracks beneath me, the grass tearing loose in chunks beneath the orange light of the setting sun. Every blade glows blue, every root illuminated with that uncanny light. Above the crowd, the sigil of the Blood Witches crackles and spits, blazing sapphire, then red, then sapphire again.

"Claim your power!" I scream, the words ripping free from my throat, amplified so loudly, they ring in my ears. "Rise, and stand against the Blood Witches once and for all!"

It's not my voice, but the voice of the ley lines themselves. The voice of the power that's fed the witches of Sapphire Springs for centuries—that runs deeper and wider, branching out to supply the entire country. *We've been buried for so long,* the lines whisper. *Set us free, Rune. Use us, as we were meant to be used. As only you can do.*

For an instant, nothing happens. And then I see it: the blue power of the lines shooting like lightning across the grass, following an unerring path toward the crowd. I watch, caught between wonder and horror, as that blue light finds Charlotte and winds around her ankles, crackling upward until it encircles her entire body. It does the same to DeAndre, to Mrs. Garcia and Mrs. Hernandez, Mrs. Grant and Ella Campbell, Jenny and Gracie. And then, as one, they charge across the space that separates them from the Blood Witches, trampling heedless over clods of earth and glowing crevices. Except—

I'd forgotten the fact that many of the residents of Sapphire Springs have Blood Witch heritage. And my command—it hadn't been specific. Mad with the power of the ley lines, those who possess Coven heritage are attacking those with latent Blood Witch power. And the Blood Witches themselves—well, they live in Sapphire Springs, too. They've unfrozen and are flinging spells at each other left and right, cutting themselves with jagged rocks to channel the power of their blood, encased in the same blue light as everyone else. The air reeks of blood and fire.

"Rune!" Donovan screams over the melee, trying desperately to hold Cooper back from gouging out Georgia's eyes. "You have to stop this!"

Why aren't they attacking him? His father was a Blood Witch. Is it because he's a null?

The power of the lines surges up my throat, making it hard to speak. "I c-can't," I manage. "The lines are hungry. They're so, so hungry. All they want…is to feed…and I…"

The words end in a shriek as the blue light wraps around my throat, throttling me. Whereas before, the power felt good, flooding me with life and strength and energy, now it's gnawing at me. It's like I'm a wick, and the power of the external ley lines and the pool of blue light that glows within me are consuming me from both ends. Soon, there will be nothing left. I'll burn myself out, a victim of their endless, inexhaustible hunger, and everyone in this meadow will go on destroying each other. Everyone but Donovan, who's somehow immune. When they all lie dead, the ley lines' power will move outward, seeking more people with magical gifts to control. Cooper was right—I've been a fool.

I fall to my knees, fighting for air. My eyes drift shut, the blue light illuminating the darkened world behind my lids. Premonitions flicker past like images on a movie screen: a tiny girl with brown curly hair and Donovan's eyes, a meadow strewn with bodies, Charlotte's daughters sitting with Jess around a table with an empty chair. Tears stream down my cheeks.

I can't let this happen. "S-stop," I try to say, but the invisible hand around my throat tightens and all that escapes is a puff of air. My body sparks, a column of blue fire.

I'm going to die. Right here, like this. And all of this will be my fault.

And then I see Donovan, striding through the chaos, backlit by the blue glow that emanates from the struggling bodies and bubbles up from the ground. Coming straight for me.

I want to tell him to stop. To stay away. But I can't get out a single word.

He steps right over the crackling ley lines. The energy doesn't reach for him, doesn't touch him as he falls at my side.

"Rune." His voice is inches from my ear. "I'm here. You're safe. Now stop this."

"I-I—"

He wraps his arms around me, and I wait for the fire to take him too. To devour him and leave him a husk at my feet. But instead I feel myself start to steady, feel the grip of the ley lines begin to loosen just a little bit.

Sweet purple ponies. He is grounding me.

That electricity that has coursed between us since the moment we met—it's been our energies, trying to equalize. Now, with the curse lifted—

He's not a null, not really. His gift is to render mine neutral. To keep me safe.

We were always meant to be.

"Stop this," he whispers again, holding me close. "I know you can do it."

I grip his arm for dear life, dig deep inside me for strength, and raise my voice, fighting the loosening chokehold of the light. "Stop fighting!"

All around me, at my command, people step away and let each other go. And in that moment, I feel it: Donovan's energy moving through me, calm and cool as still water. It slips along the ley lines, moving toward the Blood Witches, seeking them out. With Donovan wrapped around me like this, I see the Witches' energy in the network of the lines, red pinpricks in the web of blue light. And I feel it, too, when Donovan's gift reaches them and neutralizes their power.

One by one, the red pinpricks wink out as the lines absorb the Blood Witches' magic, gathering it back into its source. One by one, the Witches howl in agony, crumbling to the ground. And one by one, the ley lines settle under the influence of Donovan's energy, the blue light sinking back into the earth and the crevices knitting themselves together.

We sit at the epicenter of the destruction, clutching each other, as darkness falls on the meadow at last.

Fifty-Nine

WE'RE ALIVE, I think, watching Charlotte tug her clothes to rights and look around bemusedly. *Somehow, we're all alive.* I want to hug my best friend, to hold her close. And I will, as soon as I can find the strength to move. For now, I let Donovan hold me, reveling in the knowledge that my curse has been lifted. That the awful vision of him drowning in the blood tide, of his death on what should've been one of the happiest days of our lives, didn't come true.

We stopped it, together. When I was out of control, when the power of the ley lines threatened to destroy me and everyone around me, he saved me from myself. It was his gift that sapped the Blood Witches of their power. His ability that stabilized the ley lines.

Together, he and I can accomplish anything.

The knowledge that I'm no longer alone—that this beautiful, stubborn, impossible man risked everything for me—courses through my body like sweet, drugging wine. I twine my fingers through his, never wanting to let him go, and he holds on just as tightly.

"Rune." Mrs. Fontaine emerges from the crowd and rushes to

my side, her gaze flicking over every inch of me. "*Iris.* Sweet girl. I was so afraid we were going to lose you."

"I'm fine," I tell her, even though shivers run through me from head to foot. The after-effects of shock, I guess. A girl doesn't channel the power of countless greedy ley lines, have her curse revoked, discover mysterious secrets about the man she's fated to marry, watch her boss die right in front of her, and learn she has the power to make the world bend to her bidding every day. I think I've earned the right to shake a little.

She eyes me doubtfully, the way she always used to when I told her I knew *exactly* where that misplaced library book was, cross my heart and hope to die. One of her silver brows arches in an unmistakable gesture of skepticism.

"And you," she says to Donovan. "Clearly there is more to you than meets the eye."

"I—" Donovan starts, but he's interrupted by Mrs. Hernandez.

"Louise!" she snaps. "We could use a little help here!"

Mrs. Fontaine looks over her shoulder at her fellow Sinsters, who are standing in front of the assembled Blood Witches, faces fixed in identical expressions of disgust. Cooper strides toward them, a trickle of blood running down his cheek. He catches Donovan's eye, then gives him one of those guy-nods. Even though I don't speak fluent Officer Asshat, I can interpret it just fine. *We have a lot to talk about,* that nod says. *But I'm here for it if you are.*

He's obnoxious, yes. But I don't hate him anymore. I can't. When it counted, he came through. He saved Donovan's life. If he hadn't played the role of double agent so well, if he hadn't acted when he did, Donovan wouldn't be holding me right now. He'd be dead, and I'd be a prisoner of whatever these monsters wanted to do with me next.

A sob escapes me as Mrs. Fontaine walks away, and Donovan strokes my face, his fingertips rough but his touch gentle. "Hey. It's over," he whispers against my hair. "We're alive. We're going to be okay."

Cradled in his arms, sniffing back tears, I watch Cooper confront the Blood Witches. Next to him stand the Sinsters, their expressions grim. "*Cavea ad tenebras continendas,*" they chant in unison as soon as Mrs. Fontaine joins them, and those fiery chains emanate from their fingertips once more. The chains bind the Blood Witches where they stand, keeping them from fleeing.

"All of you colluded in dragging Rune and Donovan to this retreat under false pretenses," Cooper accuses, pacing in front of them. "You tricked the entire magical population of Sapphire Springs into coming up here, even those who didn't know they possessed magical blood, and then stole their free will. And you tested their blood without their knowledge, obtaining access to privileged medical information and using it for your own gain. Make no mistake, High Priestess Marilyn will try you for your crimes."

Georgia snarls at him, fighting the fiery chains that bind her. "You killed Ethan. The murder of a Blood Witch scion is no small thing. When the Scion on High finds out about this, there will be no place on earth you can hide from her vengeance."

"*You* would have killed my brother." Cooper's lip curls, and Donovan's arms tighten around me. "And how, exactly, do you think your precious Scion will find out? Certainly, you're not going to be the one to tell her."

"What do you mean? I'll tell her every last—"

Mrs. Grant steps forward, away from her fellow Sinsters. "Jenny," she says, turning toward the crowd. "Come here, please."

I watch, perplexed, as Jenny breaks away from the milling residents. "You want to alter their memories, I assume," she says, coming to a halt at Mrs. Grant's side.

My jaw drops. Sweet, kind Jenny, who'd always stood up for me, who runs the animal shelter, who I've known since I was a little kid—she's a witch? I saw in the database she had Coven blood, but this is different. All along, she's known who she was, that she had power?

Mrs. Grant nods, the gesture matter-of-fact. "There are a lot of them, but together, we can do it. I'll call their memories of tonight to the surface; you alter them. We'll do it for this scum first"—she jerks her head at the Blood Witches—"then for the rest of them. It'll be a mercy."

"What the hell?" Donovan sounds as shocked as I feel. "They can do that?"

"I guess they can," I say, watching as Jenny sets her shoulders in determination. "This is almost as new to me as it is to you. Until I saved Cooper from that damned bus, I thought I was the only one who was…different. Every day since then has been a revelation."

He holds me tighter still. "Yes," he murmurs, his voice a low, delicious rumble. "It certainly has."

"Cooper," Mrs. Hernandez says, without dropping her hands. Those fiery cords still emanate from them, holding the Blood Witches in place. "Donovan. We'll need you to move these bodies. Once everyone's memories have been altered, seeing a couple of corpses will prove more than distracting. It'll be traumatic, and we'll have to start all over again."

"God forbid something traumatic should happen," Donovan mumbles, getting to his feet and pulling me up with him. "Just another day, right? Analyze some data, move some dead bodies… You'll be okay here?"

"Yeah," I tell him, realizing it's the truth. "I will."

I watch as Donovan makes his way through the dusk, navigating by the light of the fiery bonds that hold the Blood Witches. He kneels by Mina's body first, then touches her face, closing her eyes. She was his grandmother, after all, and in the end she sacrificed herself to save us all. If she hadn't lifted my curse and I hadn't been able to channel the power of the lines, we'd be facing a very different scenario right now. I close my own eyes, giving a moment of gratitude for her sacrifice, no matter what she did to me.

When I blink them open again, Cooper is kneeling next to Donovan, one hand on his shoulder. A low conversation passes between them before they lift Mina's frail body, carrying her in the direction of the lodge.

"Let us begin. We look to the east," Mrs. Grant says, just as she did the night she brought the memories of my parents back. "To the place where the sun rises, giving birth to each day."

"To the east," Jenny, Mrs. Hernandez, and Mrs. Fontaine echo. Hot Yoga Grandma has come to stand by their side—I guess they've made up, in light of recent events?—and when Mrs. Grant continues, "We look to the north," she joins in the chorus.

If the Sinsters are going to erase Charlotte's memories, I want to see for myself first that she's all right. My legs still tremble as I wind my way through the crowd, but I don't start crying in earnest until Charlotte sees me and bursts into tears, too.

"Oh, Rune," she says, throwing her arms around me. "What happened? I was home...I got a letter about some kind of surprise award dinner here at the retreat, and so I came...but when I g-got here... I don't know what happened. I don't remember anything after getting in the car. I just woke up here, and there were dead bodies, and you were all glowy and b-blue..."

"Don't worry, Char," I say, squeezing her so tightly, she lets out a gasp. "It was all a misunderstanding. A mistake. It'll be better soon." The Sinsters are right—it's better not to remember this. How would I ever explain?

She pulls back, her wide, tear-filled eyes fixed on mine. "What time is it? I was supposed to check on Valentine with the girls while you were away, give her dinner—"

It's so Charlotte, to be worried about pet-sitting in the middle of a magical apocalypse. At the thought of my sweet, adorable cat, snuggled up on her cushion in the cottage I worked so hard to buy, I cry harder. Do I even have a job now? Where will I work? How will I live?

These are problems for later, I tell myself firmly. Behind me, I can hear Jenny saying, "You all went for a drive to contemplate the errors of your ways. You realized that you're terrible, terrible people. Mina died of natural causes. Ethan decided to move to Antarctica, where he can do a minimum of harm."

Antarctica? Really? I picture Funko-Pop, murder-obsessed Ethan toddling amongst the penguins, and snort with laughter as I wipe away my tears. Through my blurred vision, I see Donovan and Cooper come back, bend to pick up Ethan's body, and carry it away.

"You discussed it and you want to turn yourselves in for illegally collecting personal medical information with the intention to use it against others, as well as conspiracy in the attempted murder of Donovan Frost—or whatever the technical terms might be. How should I know, I run an animal shelter!" Jenny goes on. "You decided to sit down together and agree on a story. First, you'll confess to the High Priestess. After that, you'll find Cooper and ask him to meet you at the police station. Whatever the charges, you'll plead guilty. You want to go to prison. You look forward to it. This discussion will be your only memory of tonight. Correct?"

She pauses, waiting for the Blood Witches' response. One by one, they reply, "Yes." "Absolutely." "Fantastic idea." They sit down on the grass in a circle, and Jenny folds her arms across her chest. "Never gets old," she mutters. "God, they deserved so much worse."

The Sinsters drop their arms, the fiery chains evaporating. "Rune," Mrs. Hernandez calls. "Come away from Charlotte. It's time."

"What is she talking about?" Charlotte's brow furrows. "Time for what?"

I hate lying to my closest friend, especially after a lifetime of not being believed even when I was telling the truth. The only thing that makes it bearable is knowing this is what's best for her. "Let me go find out," I say, disengaging myself from her.

I feel her eyes on my back as I make my way through the buzzing crowd. Some of them are righting the downed chairs, some attempting to patch torn clothes, some blotting scratches.

"All right," Mrs. Grant says when I reach the Sinsters. "Here's what we're going to do. I'll stand to the east, Louise to the west, Dru to the south, Jenny to the north, to magnify the force of our spell. Then, Rune, you will tell them to stand still and pay attention. And we will begin."

"What—" I say. And then I understand.

I'm one of them, now. They want me to use my gift, not of seeing the future but of persuasion.

"You'll need to be specific," Mrs. Hernandez says. In the growing darkness, her gaze holds mine. "Don't be afraid."

The Sinsters take their places and begin to chant. The fiery chains encircle the crowd. And this time, when I speak, I make my words precise. I watch in awe as the crowd stills in response, as they listen when Mrs. Grant tells them to think of the most beautiful memory they've ever had. As Jenny tells them that they've just experienced something even better, something they'll remember for the rest of their lives. And then I speak one more time, persuading them and the Blood Witches to go home.

Watching as they turn to leave, feeling my gift settle into place inside me, I feel complete. I'm not *Rune Whitlock, the liar* or *Rune Whitlock, the weirdo* or *Rune Whitlock, the orphan who has no idea where she came from.* I'm Rune Whitlock, born Iris Duval, daughter of David and Lorelai, seer and persuasio. I am among my people.

For the first time I can remember, I belong.

CHAPTER
Sixty

"SO," Donovan says. "Do you want me to go?"

It's three in the morning, and we're standing on the front porch of my cottage. After hours of cleanup and a whole bunch of spellwork by the Sinsters—not to mention High Priestess Marilyn, who showed up at the eleventh hour and was Big Mad at me for taking matters into my own hands—we're back in Sapphire Springs. Both of our cars started right up, surprising me not one bit. Somehow, the Blood Witches must have channeled the ley line energy to mess with their electrical systems. Donovan's laptop is okay, too. But even though I told him I was fine, he insisted on following me all the way home, just to make sure I got there safely.

I argued with him, but honestly? Not too hard. Because having him a few car lengths behind me was still too far away.

"No," I tell him, staring up into those eyes of his, the ones that will never cease to mesmerize me. "I don't want you to go anywhere. Unless you're tired?"

A slow smile lifts his lips. "I could sleep here, maybe."

"I have a feeling," I say, turning to fit my key into the lock, "that if you stay here, we won't do much sleeping."

"Aw." He presses a kiss to the crook of my neck, and a

delectable shudder ripples through me. "I've had a tough day, Chaos. It started with some idiotic ice breakers, included some freaky revelations, and almost ended in the Red Wedding. Maybe I need a nap."

His lips trail down my collarbone, leaving a trail of heat in their wake, and I squirm against him, struggling to insert the key. "First a Matrix joke. Now a Game of Thrones reference," I manage. "Aren't you just Mr. Pop Culture?"

"Turns out," he says, sliding my shirt off my shoulder, "that a guy has a hell of a lot of free time on his hands when all he does is design databases for a homicidal maniac. But you know what I'd rather have in my hands?"

"Don't say it." I shove the key into the lock and turn in the circle of his arms, intending to press my fingers to his lips. But he's just *right there*, his eyes playful and his hands braced against the door on either side of my head, grinning down at me.

"I'd rather—" he begins, and I stop his mouth with my own. He tastes like cinnamon, and he smells like vanilla and cedar, and now that I've started kissing him, I don't ever want to stop. We're outside; anyone could see. But for once, I can't bring myself to give a crap. If the Sinsters have enough energy after tonight to post this on the Facebook page, then we'll damn well give Sapphire Springs a show.

Before, I was always holding part of myself back, afraid of what might happen if I gave myself to him completely. Before, there was only one way I saw this ending. But now, when he groans and licks along the seam of my lips until I open for him, when he sucks on my tongue and tugs on my hair, angling me how he wants me, I kiss him back the same way. My fingers slip under his shirt, ghosting over the hard planes of his stomach, and he draws a sharp breath.

"You're driving me insane, Rune. Do you know that? Since I met you, I haven't been able to think about anything but being inside you. And now—tonight—"

"Survivor's lust," I pant as he lifts me, pinning me against the door the way he did in his office. My head falls back, and he skates his teeth along the delicate skin of my throat.

"I don't care what you call it," he says, sounding breathless. "And I understand if you don't feel the same way. But if that's the case, then tell me now. Because if you don't want me like that—or if you're not ready—I should probably go home and take a cold, cold shower."

Even as the words leave his mouth, he's rocking forward, into me, as if he can't help himself. My legs tighten around his hips, feeling him just where I need him most. Where I crave him. "Donovan," I say, digging my nails into his shoulders.

Those brilliant irises of his fix on mine. In his gaze, I see so much—hope, doubt, fear, desire. "Yes?"

"I want what you want," I tell him. "So open this damn door and take me inside. And then, take me to bed."

Donovan's eyes widen, like I've surprised him. But all he says is, "Yes ma'am."

I'm giggling as he shoves the door open so hard it bounces off the wall, then yanks out my keys and tosses them on the floor. He almost trips headlong over Valentine, who's winding between his legs and meowing up a storm, which brings on a fresh spate of laughter. But when he lays me down on my bed and props himself up over me, when he brushes the hair back from my face with such tenderness it brings tears to my eyes, suddenly I'm not laughing anymore.

"I don't know where you came from," he whispers. "Or how I came to feel so much for you, so soon. I'd be lying if I didn't say it scared the shit out of me. But I want you, Rune, and not just for now. I want to wake up with you every morning and have your face be the last one I see before I go to sleep at night. I want you to challenge me and push me so far out of my comfort zone, it pisses me off. I want you by my side when we figure out what the next steps are after the crazy crap that went down today, when we finally lay my dad to rest. I *want* you."

His eyes scan my face, desperation clear in their depths—like he thinks I'll tell him he's alone in this. Like I'll say he's lost his mind.

I reach up, tracing the pads of my fingers across his cheekbone. "I want you too. I always have, even when you were being an ass. I just…being together would've killed you, Donovan. I was trying to save your life. But we were always meant for each other. I saw our future, remember?"

He smiles, bending to brush his lips across mine. "And what do you see now?"

"I see you." I tug at the hem of his shirt, urging him to take it off. "And I'd like to see a whole lot more of you, if you don't mind."

He kisses me again, slow and deep. And then, without another word, he pulls his shirt over his head, baring the full inscription of his tattoo. I outline it with my fingers, marveling at the connection to his heritage that he felt compelled to ink on his skin, even when he didn't know why he was doing it. At the hundreds of threads that brought us together, the impossibility of our connection. At how so much grief and loss has culminated in this: a moment I'll remember for the rest of my life.

As his hands rove over my body, as item after item of our clothing falls to the floor beside the bed, as I learn the places that make him moan and he does the same for me, our future unfurls behind my eyes. I see us starting our own company, with Donovan doing the programming and me doing the graphic design. I see the Blood Witches getting their comeuppance from both the High Priestess and the justice system. In my mind's eye, I see us sitting down for dinner with Charlotte, Jess, Emma, and Sophie, Donovan laughing as Charlotte tells the story of *text spreadsheets nigh.* I see myself starting a support service for those, like me, who were forced to lose or hide their gifts due to the Blood Witches' schemes. I see Julia, sitting across from me in Brew Box, telling me she's a witch, and her actual job is to work with women and children all over the world who have been the victims of magical crimes. That she's been looking out for me, ever since she graduated, trying to keep me safe. I see me joining the Coven, learning how to use my abilities, and Donovan putting up with #donorune #ronovan #steamyinthesprings posts even though they drive him around the bend. And that's just the start.

There's so much waiting for us. So much for us to look forward to.

But first, there's this. And I don't want to wait anymore.

"Donovan," I beg, knotting my fingers in his dark hair. "I want you inside me. Now."

He rears up, over me, then bites his lip. "I don't have—"

"Don't worry. We're both clean. And it doesn't happen this time," I say, arching against him. "What happens is that we absolutely fucking sizzle together. Like, off-the-charts chemistry. You should probably come up with an algorithm just to analyze it, because holy hell is it hot."

"Oh, yeah?" He slides one hand beneath me, angling my hips. "I don't think I needed to see the future to know that."

I revel in the feeling of being believed. Of the caress of his breath on my skin and the way his free hand tightens on the sheet as he pushes that first hot, velvet inch inside me. "What if," I say, breathless, "I told you we elope to a tiny island somewhere and get married? You tend bar on the beach and I spend every morning doing goat yoga and our six kids surf from dawn to dusk."

That crooked grin lifts his lips as he fills me, as I gasp and set my nails into his back and he begins to move. "If you told me all that," he whispers against my neck, "I'd say I've got a lot of work to do. Because the only drink I know how to make is a martini."

I'm losing track of my ability to form a coherent thought. But I started this, and so I have to finish it. "Is…is that all you'd say?"

He does something with his hips that he should probably patent. "Nope. I don't really know how to surf either, so if all six of our kids are gonna be doing it, I should probably learn."

I'm panting now as he drives me higher and higher, the world a kaleidoscope of color behind my eyes. "Is…is that it?"

"No. But I'm done talking." Slipping a talented hand between us, he pushes me over the edge. And then he shows me just how right my premonitions were.

After, when we're curled up together, with Valentine at our feet and the sun beginning to creep over the horizon, he whispers against my skin, "I'm more of a mountain guy than a beach guy, and goats kinda freak me out. But I'd go just about anywhere for you. So if you told me all that, I'd have a little meltdown. And then I'd say… Okay, Chaos."

THE END

Fans of *Divergent* and *Fourth Wing* will be captivated by this dark, seductive tale of power, betrayal, and the ultimate forbidden love.

"An absolutely mind-blowing, spine-tingling, action-packed extravaganza."—*Emerald Book Reviews*

"An absolutely wild ride... I couldn't stop reading."
—*The Word Traveler*

"Much of the fun here is watching Colin build her world... The book should prove a hit with fans of *The Hunger Games*."
—*Wilmington Star News*

"A rollicking ride through forbidden love and deadly adventure... I haven't ached for love like this to conquer all since Tris and Four."
—Leigh Statham, author of the *Daughter Trilogy*

"A romantic dystopian with a fantastic—and unexpected—twist... SEVEN SINS is powerful, sexy, hopeful, and unsettling."
—Heidi Ayarbe, award-winning author of *Freeze Frame*

"Sizzling hot and exploding with tension."
—Lisa Amowitz, author of *Breaking Glass*

"This book has kept me glued to my chair— turning the pages and biting my nails... It's insane and I am loving it."
—@booktalesanddonuts

"I devoured it in 48 hours."—@lilareads

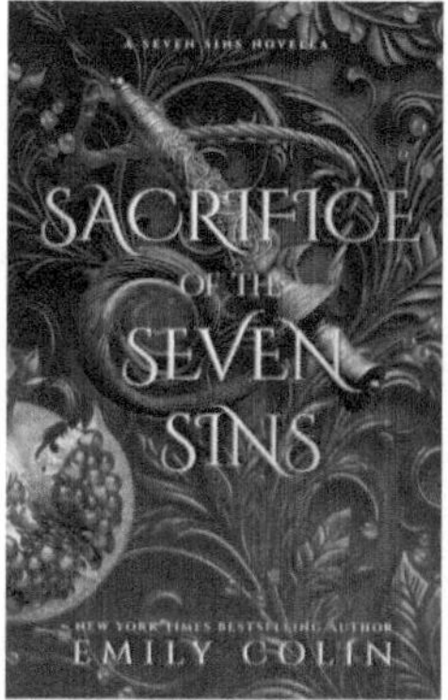

CHAPTER
Sixty-One

Acknowledgments

As usual, this book would never have seen the light of day without the assistance of an ensemble cast. Credit goes first and foremost to Ángela "The Book Bruja" Álvarez Vélez, whose brilliant seed of an idea grew into this wackadoodle story. Without her, there would be no Rune or Donovan!

Thanks, too, to Christy "The Story Jedi" Swift, for coming up with the mobile blood bank—you saved me!—and to Lisa "The Plot Fairy" Amowitz, for talking me through sticky issues & lending me her incomparable design skills. Donovan can be your shared book boyfriend anytime! What happens in Sapphire Springs stays in Sapphire Springs…

I bow down to Shelf-Care Queen Empress Amanda Curry, Goddess of Hype Kara French, and my indefatigable PA, Nancy Mendoza Smith. I don't know what I did to deserve all of you, but I couldn't have a better team in my corner. Every day, I pinch myself in disbelief that I found you (it's starting to hurt, tbh). 😆 One day I'll understand Discord, Kara, I promise!

I also owe a massive debt of thanks to my reader group, The Shelf-Care Queens, and my street team, which cracks me up, keeps me sane, and fills me with gratitude on a regular basis. You are the best readers ever!

And to Sex Spreadsheet Guy and Rune "Chaos Is My Middle Name" Whitlock, who never fail to make me laugh. Sorry about that whole "almost-murdered-at-the-altar" thing. I hope the drunken goat yoga on the beach makes up for it!

About the Author

Emily Colin wrote her first romance novel in the fourth grade and never looked back. Today, she is the New York Times and USA Today bestselling author of books with kissing, ghosts, magic, sword-play, and lots of banter. If it's got romance in it, she writes it! When she doesn't have her nose in a book, you can find her making comfort food, chasing her badly behaved puppy, or drinking mochas by the sea.

For more books and updates
www.emilycolin.com

instagram.com/emilycolinbooks
facebook.com/emilycolinbooks
tiktok.com/emilycolinbooks